In the Shadows

L.B. August

INK OF FATE PUBLISHING

In The Shadows

Editor: Tali Ijack
Cover: Getcovers.com
Map: Melissa Nash
Interior Design: Painted Wings Publishing
Publication Date: February 27, 2024
Paperback ISBN: 979-8-9896191-0-8
Publisher: Ink of Fate Publishing

To my fellow neurodiverse folks—I see you behind those masks. May you find a safe space to let them fall and be your true self. You're perfect just the way you are. Be proud of your unique self and don't let anyone tell you that you're too much.

To my little end bringer—Never let anyone stomp out your flame. Always be the light through the darkness. Mold the world to fit you, and not you to the world. If you want to burn it all down and start anew, mommy will be beside you, lighting the match. I love you sweet pea.

LUX
TERRA
N
W
E
S

UMBRA
OMNIA
TI

CONTENT/TRIGGER WARNINGS

In The Shadows is an adult dark fantasy romance containing content not suitable or appropriate for all readers. Please read responsibly.

This book contains general content warnings for strong language, violence, graphic descriptions, and trauma.

The list below provides more specific content warnings with corresponding chapters. This does not guarantee you will not read or experience any of these potential triggers. However, this may act as a reference guide. Your well-being is important, so please use caution while reading potential triggers.

Murder	**Torture**	**Detailed Sex Scenes**
Chapter 1	Chapter 2 (flashback)	Chapter 4
Chapter 8 (flashback)	Chapter 15	Chapter 13
Chapter 10 (off page)	Chapter 26	Chapter 23
Chapter 12	Chapter 31	Chapter 30
Chapter 15	**Attempted Sexual Assault**	Chapter 31
Chapter 17	Chapter 3	Chapter 35
Chapter 26 (flashback)	Chapter 17	Chapter 36
Chapter 31	Chapter 26 (flashback)	Chapter 38
Chapter 36 (death)		**BDSM**
Chapter 37		Chapter 38

PROLOGUE

THE THREADS OF AMARI—A CHILDREN'S STORY

Long ago, before life walked the land,
Four gods created a realm they could command.
The all-seeing fates wove threads of golden light,
To bind the mortals' hearts; their destinies to unite.

Simple beings the gods had chosen,
Blessed them with powers that made them emboldened.
Threads of fate bound hearts together.
Souls linked as one, entwined forever.

A gentle pull, a hum low and sweet,
Awakened hearts to a love so deep.
Two new souls, tightly tethered,
Only in death could the bonds be severed.

But the gods asked for the fates to decree,
For the threads to bind an Amari of three.
Cords pulling one to heart, one to soul,
But the gods hid their deceitful goal.

To create a union of greatest power
And bring on the darkest hour.
Destroying the realm to start anew,
Only for the chosen few.

The fates, betrayed as lovers scorned,
Severed from the gods, forever torn.
In the gods, the fates could no longer trust:
The gods' games and schemes so cruel and unjust.

So, wary of gods with motives sly,
The fates kept track, always nearby.
Controlling the threads of the gods' creations,
Weaving tales of love through all generations.

CHAPTER 1

THEO

10 YEARS AGO

The harsh sunlight beams down, illuminating her pale skin. She looks like a beacon from the gods calling me to worship. The threads of fate wrapped tightly around my heart hum at her close proximity, seeming to rejoice.

Sweet jade-green eyes lock with mine, and my racing heart freezes. Lily looks away quickly and fidgets with a strand of her long, curly red hair.

"Theo, are you even listening to me?" Juniper's teasing voice calls from beside Lily on their shared boulder.

I rub the back of my neck, trying to recall her question but failing. Junie glares at me with a knowing smirk. Her bright-blue eyes are even more striking with her stark-blonde hair twisted back.

"Um, what was your question again?" I reply, sheepishly.

"I asked if there were any girls you had a crush on?" She asks with an arched eyebrow. Her eyes flick between Lily and me.

Lily. She's the only one who has ever made my heart sing—the only person who makes me feel happy and whole. For years, I've longed to tell her how I feel, but the fear of rejection stops me.

For a moment, the only sound between us is the water lapping against the rocky shore of the river. I swallow hard as my cheeks heat with embarrassment. I open my mouth to speak, but nothing comes out.

Junie leans into Lily, whispering into her ear. Lily shifts uncomfortably on the rock as her cheeks turn a soft shade of pink.

Boots click on stones behind me, and I turn to see Breton taking long strides toward us. I let out a huff of irritation as I cross my arms on my chest.

"Princess Juniper and Theodore, your fathers have summoned you both to the throne quarters for monthly court. They will start shortly, so we need to be on our way," the captain of Lux announces.

Junie simply nods. She takes her role and duty as princess of Lux with the grace of a stoic future queen. She pulls Lily into a tight hug before bringing their hands together on her lap.

"I'm sorry I can't spend your birthday with you, Lil. I tried talking to my father about not going this one time, but you know how he is. After dinner, we'll eat dessert under the stars; just the three of us, like we always do for our birthdays." Junie brushes her thumb lightly over the back of Lily's hand.

"Your birthday will be different this year, though. Won't it, Juju? Your sixteenth is going to be a huge celebration. I doubt King Leopold will let you spend time with us." Lily's voice is soft, as if she's holding something back.

She's right. Divinus, or the god-blessed, descend into their powers on the day of their sixteenth birthday. King Leopold has waited patiently for his only heir to show a glimmer of our goddess Astra's lightning power. He likely won't let Junie out of his sight until she shows that she wields his same power.

"It will be, but afterward, everything will go back to how it is now," Junie assures gently.

"Except you will throw lightning bolts out of your hands whenever you feel like it," I reply sarcastically.

"Maybe then I'll get you to listen to me, Theodore," Junie replies playfully.

I laugh, shaking my head.

Junie's smile falters as she releases Lily's hands. "I'm ready for it. I can feel my power pulsating within me, but it feels locked behind a door, waiting to be released."

A look of uncertainty flashes on Lily's face, and a knot forms in my stomach, but I can't place why. Divinus powers are just part of being a royal in Omnia.

Junie rises to stand. Her elegant dress is a stark contrast to the green forest, deep-blue water, and gray stones around us. She strides toward me, patting my arm as she passes.

She joins Breton, ready to head into the Lux castle, Brightwick. I can feel Breton's eyes burning into the back of my head.

"Tell him I'm not in the guard so he can't summon me, Breton." My words are harsh, but the tone is directed at my father not the messenger.

As general of the guard, my father has been pushing me to enlist for as long as I can remember. Claiming I need to "follow in his footsteps," when what I wish to be is a scholar. I dream of days filled with learning and teaching, not combat and training.

Breton lets out an exhausted sigh, and I turn to look at him. His long black hair is pulled into a tight bun, allowing the streaks of white to show distinctly. His indigo, blue, and silver formal uniform complements Junie's dress perfectly.

"I told him that would be your answer, but he ordered me to ask. He should know by now you're too smart for his antics—being a future scholar and all." Breton gives me a wink before extending an arm for Junie. I smile as the two of them head back up the gravel hill to the castle.

As I turn back around, a dark shadow skirts the ground between Lily and me. Above, an all-black bird circles us. I squint, trying to get a better look. As if catching my gaze, the bird quickly darts toward the forest on the other side of the riverbank, out of view.

"What kind of bird was that?" Lily asks, obviously as confused as I am.

"I'm not sure, but it's not a bird of Lux. I'll see what I can find out about it in the library tomorrow." I try to sound reassuring, but the perplexing knot in my stomach grows.

My gaze falls to Lily—like it always seems to do. I often catch myself staring helplessly at her beautiful face, wishing she would see me as more than a friend. I wonder if she has ever thought we could be Amari, like in the stories our mothers told us as children. Two souls bound together through this lifetime and, if I'm lucky, all that comes after.

Her eyes meet mine and my breath hitches. My gaze trails down to her soft, pink lips, desperately wishing she would be my first and only kiss.

"Theo." Lily's voice is breathy, and I close my eyes at the way my name sounds on her lips. It makes my heart flutter in ways I've never felt before.

"Hmmm," is the only response I can muster. When I open my eyes, a smile curls one side of her lips, and I swear it's the most perfect one in all the realm.

"You never answered Junie's question." Her voice is low as she chews on the inside of her cheek, her eyes cast down again, staring at the ground. She looks as nervous as I feel.

Does her heart reach for mine, too? A wave of hope rushes through me at the thought. I step toward her, taking a deep breath to ease my anxiety.

"I might like someone."

I take another step closer as the stones click under my boots.

"Do you?" I ask, unable to disguise the hope in my voice.

Her breaths are rapid as I close the distance between us. My heart nearly bursts from my chest. Her eyes slowly rise from the ground as I stand before her. When her gaze finally reaches mine, it feels as if the realm around us falls away, leaving only us in this moment.

"You," is all she says.

One word and I'm falling to my knees, kneeling in front of where she still sits on the boulder. The smooth stones on the ground dig into my skin. I cup her face and pull her into me. When our mouths finally meet, I find that her lips are softer than I had dreamed they would be. She melts in my hands as a sigh escapes from deep in her chest.

Releasing her lips, I press my forehead to hers. Our breaths are short and ragged. Her delicate hands wrap around my wrists. As I lean back, Lily's eyebrows pinch together as she searches my face for any uncertainty.

"Lily, I've wanted you to be my girl for as long as I can remember. It has always been you and me, and for me, it will always be you," I say, hoping she feels the same.

Her lips curl into a smile. *Gods, I would do anything to see that smile all day, every day.* She gives me a slow nod of reassurance. I kiss her again, cherishing the feeling of her soft mouth.

Before my growing desire overtakes the moment, I pull out of the kiss and stand.

"Are you ready to go swimming?" Taking a step back, I pull my shirt over my head and step out of my trousers. Lily's eyes roam over me as she bites her bottom lip.

"Enjoying the view?" I say, mustering every bit of confidence I have.

Her eyes freeze and pink colors her cheeks. I walk to her and offer a hand to help her rise from the boulder. She slides her smooth hand into mine. Tingles erupt across my palm as our skin touches.

She pulls her dress over her head, dropping it on the boulder. I stare, transfixed by her beauty. Her delicate frame matches the soft flower her mother named her after. *My flower.*

Taking both her hands in mine, I walk backward into the river, pulling her along with me. The chilly water nips at my ankles as we enter. Since it flows down from the snow-capped mountain range that skirts the edge of the Lux kingdom, it's always chilly regardless of the time of year.

Passing the small rock blockage near the shoreline, I wade into the deep-blue water until I can barely touch the bottom. I release Lily's hand and duck under the crisp water, allowing it to cool my heated skin.

As I break the surface, Lily drops under to do the same. I watch as the black bird from earlier drops from the sharp cliff face high above where Brightwick sits. It flaps silently through the air, circling above us before darting into the thick forest on the other side of the river without ever making a sound.

Lily treads water beside me and I can't help but smile. Her long, red hair is slicked back and cascades down her shoulders. The freckles along her cheeks and nose accent her sweet face.

She notices me watching and turns toward me. Her lips pinch into a thin line.

"Do you think we're Amari?" She asks hesitantly, watching for my reaction.

My soulmate.

"Yes," I answer as the cords that link our hearts vibrate, confirming the deep bond we share.

Growing up, our mothers would tell us stories about Amari and the threads that bind two destined mortals, always leading them to one another, no matter the distance.

"And since we're Amari, I get to kiss you as much as I want for the rest of our lives." I swim to her and bring my lips to hers again, but she doesn't kiss me back this time.

As I draw back, I notice Lily's furrowed brow and that knot in my stomach twists. "What is it?" I ask, hoping she can't hear the disappointment in my voice.

"I don't know. Something feels off. Maybe we should head back to shore," she answers, her breathing becoming rapid.

I rub a hand along her back. Her body trembles under my touch. Lily's mother, Eleanor, says the gods will warn you of danger and to follow their intuition when they give it to you. Whatever has Lily's instincts flaring can't be good. We need to get moving.

I grab her hands in mine and start leading her back to shore.

"Theo, what's that?" Lily's voice quivers as her eyes lock on something in the distance.

Following her line of sight, my heart stops when I see glowing white pupil-less eyes staring at us from just above the waterline.

"What is a nobu doing in Lux?" I ask, more of the gods than of her.

The scaly, gray skin on the nobu's massive head barely crests the surface of the water. Only its long snout; large, high-set eyes; and small, rounded ears are visible.

The nobu are monsters of Umbra, a dark shadow kingdom filled with cruel and evil beings. I've only ever read about their beasts in books. I never expected to see one with my own eyes. The nobu hide in the rivers of Umbra and eat unsuspecting fools who dare to step foot on their land.

Why in the realm is it here?

"We need to go. Now," I say quietly, but forcefully, as I cautiously retreat toward the safety of the shore, avoiding any sudden movements.

I walk backward, dragging Lily with me, while ensuring I don't break eye contact with the nobu.

As if sensing its meal getting away, the nobu charges. It glides effortlessly as it rushes toward us, barely disturbing the water.

"Run!" I shout, turning forward and quickening our pace.

Using the rocky bottom as leverage, I push us hard to the shore. Lily frantically kicks her legs under the water behind her. My heart hammers in my chest as I gasp for air.

Small ripples churn in the water, seeming to vibrate around us. Lily squeezes her face into a pained expression.

"Theo," her voice wobbles with uncertainty.

I don't stop. I need to get us to shore as fast as possible. When I glance back, the empty glowing eyes of the nobu are still on us.

We finally make it where Lily can touch bottom, and we both use it to thrust further away, trying to gain as much distance as possible. The monster is only a few feet away now.

My eyes find Lily's for a moment, and my realm slows as her panic filled eyes slash through me. *I know what I must do.*

The water splashes at my hips as we race toward the shore, and I debate if I have enough leverage to get her out of harm's way.

Taking one more glance over my shoulder, I see the nobu is quickly gaining on us. It's now or never. If I hesitate any longer, I may not be able to save her.

Looking down, I take in Lily's beautiful face one last time, trying to memorize everything about her: those freckles that look like stars, the jade-green eyes that cause my heart to flutter every time they land on me, and her curly, red hair the color of leaves in autumn.

"I love you, Lily," I scream into the air for all to hear.

Her mouth opens to speak, but I'm too fast. I grip her sides and throw her with all my might as far as she'll go. She lands near the shore with a loud *thump*.

I steady myself and spin to face the nobu. I continue to walk backward into shallower water as it splashes along my thighs. The monster slows its pursuit as it nears. Its round, scaly body takes powerful steps toward me. Its mouth opens wide, revealing its sharp teeth, ready to shred me to pieces.

I drag a foot on the bottom, looking for a large rock or anything I can use to defend myself, but come up empty. Dropping into a fighting stance, I prepare to take on the nobu with my fists. I won't survive, but I won't make this easy on the beast. It will give Lily time to get away.

The nobu snaps its jaw closed with a *crack*. It stalks toward me, slow and menacing. Its iridescent scales glow brightly in the sunlight. The monstrous beast towers over me. Its gray snout wiggles as if tracking me by my scent. I suck in a breath, preparing myself for impact, as the nobu crouches into a charging position.

"No!" Lily's scream pierces the air right before darkness descends.

A swirling black mass encircles me, blocking the nobu. My chest tightens as my skin tingles. I find myself staring at a wall of shadows.

Thalos? Why would Thalos shield me from certain death? The dark god of Umbra has no reason to be watching over a mortal in Lux.

"Theo!" Lily's pained and broken voice halts my spiraling thoughts. I spin, frantic to find her.

"Lily!" My voice strains in the shadowed space.

Water splashes, and I chase after the sound, desperate to get to her. Choked sobs grow louder as a shadowed form runs toward me. I reach out and grab it.

Lily.

I slam her into my chest. She gasps before wrapping her arms around me, crying on my shoulder. I hold her tight, never wanting there to be any distance between us again.

"Are you ok?" I ask as I softly kiss her wet hair.

She trembles in my arms as the shadows continue to dance around us in agitated motions.

"I thought I lost you," she answers through tears.

Leaning back, I place my hands on her cheeks and pull her in for a hard kiss. I need to feel her. Make sure she's ok. That we're both alive. She kisses back with the same intensity.

I break our kiss and place my forehead on hers, noticing how cold her skin feels against mine. I pull back to look at her and see her skin is ashen.

She weakly lifts her arm, pointing at the dark mass surrounding us. "What is all of this?"

"I don't know," I answer, staring at the shadows. "The gods, maybe? These are Thalos' shadows."

I reach out tentatively and place a gentle hand on the darkness, expecting it to hurt, but it's warm and sends sparks like lightning along my skin.

Lily flinches in my arms. "I felt that," she whispers.

"What do you mean?" I ask hesitantly, the knot in my stomach twisting again.

She points at the blackness enveloping us. "I felt your touch when you brushed the shadows."

As she speaks, I reach out and run a hand down the wall again. Lily's entire body shivers in my arms as her paler-than-normal cheeks turn pink. She swallows hard.

"Please stop, Theo. I can feel you everywhere on and in my body," she says, her eyes not leaving my chest.

My mouth falls open in silent realization of what this means.

"Well, it looks like Thalos has chosen his new divinus line," I say, looking at her in pure wonder.

My Amari is a divinus. How could this be? Could the god of shadow and light have finally picked someone who's good, kind, and worthy?

The gods are free to choose a family line to receive their blessing at any time. From the beginning, the divinus have become the royals of each kingdom and ruled over the people with their power. The current divinus line of Umbra consists of only King Oren Griffin. He is a power-hungry, bloodthirsty man out to destroy anyone who crosses his path—no different than all the Umbra kings before him. But it seems that he has lost Thalos' favor because instead of waiting for him to sire an heir, Thalos bestowed the shadow powers to Lily. A simple servant's daughter.

Lily's nails dig into my skin. I look down to see that her eyes have filled with renewed terror.

"No. Thalos and his divinus are pure evil. They're death and malice. I … I can't be one of them." Her shaky voice pleads.

The air grows tense as the shadows deepen the dark abyss around us.

I hook a finger under Lily's chin and force her to hold my gazed. Her eyes are wet with unshed tears. The fear of this new power seems to be overwhelming her.

"Listen to me, Lily. You may share the same god-given power as those monsters, but you're not them. You're sweet and caring. No matter how much darkness you carry within, you'll never be like them. I know your soul. It's pure and brilliant. Thalos' gift doesn't change that." I stroke my thumb along her jawline, and she relaxes into my arms.

The shadows lighten as tension leaves her body. They slowly spiral through the air, dancing along Lily's skin and fading away. I watch in amazement at the sight of the darkness receding into my beautiful, delicate flower.

With the black wall gone, we can see what happened to the nobu. Its dead body floats in the water, bobbing in the small waves. Its eyes now resemble chunks of coal, black and empty.

Lily gasps and buries her face in my chest. I pull her in close before turning us toward shore. I can't wait to get us out of the river. She takes one step and collapses in my arms. All the color in her face is gone.

"I'm not sure I can make it back, Theo. I'm so tired." She can barely get the words out as she clings weakly to me.

Reaching down, I lift and cradle her limp body in my arms. "Being a shadow goddess must take a lot out of you. Let me get you back to your mother. She'll know what to do."

Lily's nod of agreement is almost imperceptible.

I trudge through the water and back onto shore. Before my feet even crunch on the gravel walkway back to Brightwick, Lily is asleep in my arms. I hold her tight as I climb the steep path, up the cliff, back home.

My feet pad softly on the gray stone floor of Brightwick. A chorus of voices from the throne room float through the halls. I turn the last corner, and the door to Lily's chambers comes into view. The faint etching along the trim sets her door apart from the others.

I place a gentle kiss on Lily's forehead. "My flower, we're back at your chambers. It's time to wake up."

She stirs in my arms, and I smile as she yawns loudly and opens her eyes. I lower her feet to the ground, keeping one arm around her waist for support.

We walk inside, and I help her sit in one of the worn chairs around a small table. I pull a blanket off the back of the chair and wrap it around her.

"Nata, is that you?" Eleanor's soft voice calls for her daughter from their small bathing chamber. She enters the common space with the same beauty and grace as Lily. Her long, auburn hair hangs in light waves along her shoulders.

Eleanor's smile falls when she sees Lily's soaked and fragile state. Her face pales as she rushes toward us and bends to cup Lily's face in her hands.

"Nata, are you ok? Tell me what happened. Now, Theo!" Her voice is harsh and demanding.

I've never heard her use that tone before, and it has me fumbling for words.

"There was an incident at the river," I reply quickly.

Eleanor's deep-green eyes flash to me. They're the same shade as the evergreens in the forest near the mountains. They burn into me, and I swallow hard and rub my neck, trying to figure out a way to explain what happened.

"Theo and I went swimming in the river where a nobu tried to attack us. But shadows poured out of me and protected us. We think Thalos has chosen me as his new divinus," Lily spits out the whole ordeal. She straightens in the chair, looking to her mother for answers.

Eleanor's face drains of all its color as she rapidly shakes her head. "No." she whispers as her hands fall from Lily's face to rest on the chair.

Suddenly, Eleanor's eyes widen, and her breathing quickens.

"Lily, where's your necklace? Did you have it on during the attack?" Panic laces her voice as she scans Lily's body.

"No, I left it on the shore so it wouldn't get ruined. But I don't need it anymore. My divinus power will protect me now," Lily replies reassuringly.

Eleanor grabs Lily's arms, hard, causing Lily's face to twist in pain. I step closer, wanting to protect her like she did me.

"You must never use your power ever again. Do you understand me, Lily?" Eleanor's voice is harsh.

Lily doesn't respond, and she shakes in her mother's grasp.

"You must never let them out again, Lilith. Tuck them deep into the darkest hole inside of you and never let them see the light of day. Do you understand?" Eleanor's words echo in the sparsely decorated space.

Lily's palpable panic causes my own heart rate to increase in response.

"Yes, I understand. But I don't know how I use or control them. They just came out of me," Lily replies weakly.

Eleanor finally releases her, and I place a hand on Lily's shoulder, trying to comfort her. Eleanor leans back on her feet and looks up at me. Those dark-green eyes look directly at my soul.

"You were protecting Theo, weren't you?" Eleanor asks both of us.

Lily and I glance at each other before she nods.

She was protecting me and I her.

Eleanor nods in understanding before her eyes fall to the floor for a moment, as if deep in thought.

"Divinus powers protect those connected to them—their Amari—and even the ones they hold dear. Your power felt your fear and protected both of you. Your heart, body, and soul control your power. The shadows are yours to wield and control, but they can also act on your will if needed," Eleanor imparts this knowledge as if reading from a book.

I look down at Lily as she fidgets with her damp hair. *My flower. My goddess.* I'm helplessly in love with her and my heart hums at the sight. I'm hers, utterly and completely.

Lily's hands fall from her hair as she stares at her mother.

"Where do you think the power came from? Could it have been from my father?" Lily asks innocently.

Eleanor stiffens at the question, jaw clenching tight.

"No," she answers as her eyes turn cold as stone, and she speaks through clenched teeth.

Just as quickly, Eleanor's eyes soften again, and a small smile curls her lips as she leans forward, picking up a strand of Lily's hair.

"No, I think the legends of red hair being the gods' favorite are true, and the shadow god has blessed you. I always knew you were special, and it seems the gods agree," Eleanor preens.

She drops the strand of hair as her eyes study Lily.

"But we know how angry the kings can get if someone new shows any sign of being a divinus. King Leopold would be upset to learn a servant's daughter descended into her god-given power before his own daughter. He can't find out," Eleanor says gently.

Both Lily and I nod our heads, letting her know we understand the dangers of anyone outside these chambers finding out about Lily's power. I make a silent vow to never speak of it unless we're truly alone.

Eleanor stands abruptly, dusting off her legs. "I need to go run an errand," she says, walking to her quarters.

Lily and I glance at each other with furrowed brows. A drawer clicks closed on the other side of the doorway, then Eleanor steps back into the common space. She shoves a crystal into the pocket of her dress as she walks back toward us. A glimmer of purple catches the light before it's put away.

"I will be back before dinner tonight to celebrate your birthday, Lily. You're going to be hungry, so grab a few things out of the cabinet to tide you over until we eat this evening." She instructs.

We nod our heads but remain silent, still confused by her abrupt departure.

Eleanor gives Lily a kiss on the forehead, and me a pat on my arm before walking out the door. The latch clicks shut and neither of us move.

"Where do you think she is going?" I ask, turning to Lily, who's still staring at the door.

"I don't know. How did she know I was hungry?" She looks up at me questioningly.

"You need to eat something, and we both need to change out of these damp clothes," I say, offering her a hand to rise, and she accepts it. She's much more stable, having gained some of her strength back.

I lean forward and give her a soft kiss. "I'll be right back," I say and take in her sweet smile one more time before leaving to race to my own chambers to change into dry clothes.

When I return, she's sitting at the table in a simple light-blue dress eating a handful of crackers. The lack of crunch tells me they are likely stale.

"Has your mother returned?" I ask, scanning the quarters.

Lily shakes her head and takes a sip of water from her mug. I kiss her on the cheek before taking a seat in the chair beside her.

"If you're feeling up for it, I thought we could go pick some flowers from the meadow. A fresh bouquet would look beautiful on your table for our celebration tonight," I say to Lily, hoping she has the strength to go. I want nothing more but to bring back the lightness and joy we felt for a brief moment when we finally revealed our feelings for one another.

Her face lights up with the idea, and I'm happy to see she is feeling like herself again.

"We also need to stop at the shore to get our things. Mainly, we need to get my necklace before my mother returns. And never let me take it off again, Theo," she demands.

I smile and give her a simple nod. "It's a date. Shall we?" I say, standing and offering my arm to her.

Lily rises to join me. We interlace our fingers and then head out the door.

We wind through Brightwick, making our way to the other side of the castle where the meadow sits along the hillside. We follow the gray stone wall along the pathway leading up the hill to the meadow.

Flowers of all colors stretch out before us, their strong fragrances almost overwhelming our senses. Lily runs her fingertips along the velvet-soft petals as we enter the meadow.

Thunder booms loudly overhead, and we both look up at the ominous sky.

"Astra is angry." Lily's voice is low.

Gray clouds hang thick above us as large streaks of lightning flash in vibrant blue. Our goddess often expresses her frustration with mortals through violent storms across the realm. By the look of the clouds, Astra's furious, and I say a silent prayer, hoping it isn't because of us.

Warm tingles along my wrist force me to look down. Faint wisps of black shadows wind around our joined hands, and I smile as they appear to knit us together, locking us in their black cords.

"Oh, no," Lily whispers beside me.

I bring my gaze to her to see her eyebrows raised in panic as she stares at her shadows dancing along our arms.

I grab the back of her neck and pull her to me, so her forehead presses into mine.

"Take a deep breath for me," I command.

I watch her eyes close, and her chest rise.

"That's it. One more," I say again, and I watch as her shadows slowly coil back into her skin as if they were never there.

"That's my powerful goddess," I say, filled with admiration and adoration. This beautiful, kind, and strong woman is all mine. I'll thank the gods and the fates every day for this honor. *My flower.* I'll cherish every moment we share for the rest of our lives.

We set to picking beautiful, vibrant-yellow sunflowers, deep-red roses, and light-pink primroses to make a lovely bouquet.

"I feel like it's missing something," Lily says. She is standing with her hands on her hips, scanning the meadow. I continue to pick purple pansies as I watch her.

"Daisies! It's missing daisies. I'm going to head over there and pick some while you finish up," Lily says with glee while pointing across the meadow.

Far in the distance there's a grouping of delicate little flowers with white petals and a stunning yellow center.

"Ok, I'll be over in a moment," I reply hesitantly, not wanting her to leave my side.

She bends down and gives me a kiss that nearly knocks me to the ground. Lily makes quick work of the distance, switching between frolicking and jogging.

The clouds darken and a boom of thunder echoes in the distance. The hairs on my arms rise as the charge in the air increases with the storm.

A loud croaking sound comes from above, and I stand to see what animal could have made it.

"Theo!" Lily's panicked scream comes from across the meadow.

I turn my head to see a black-haired man walking out of a red-rimmed mist. Dark tendrils of shadows swirl around him. He strides toward her as she backs away from him. A malicious smile curls his lips as he stalks Lily.

I can't move. I'm frozen, rooted to the ground like the flowers. All I can do is watch as the man pulls a dagger from his hip and buries it to the hilt in Lily's chest. She claws at him at first but stops moving as he pushes the blade into her body.

I hear screaming, only to realize it's me. I scramble and sprint toward the shocking scene unfolding before me.

"Lily!" My voice cracks as I yell for her, hoping she knows I'm coming.

I watch as her blue dress stains crimson.

The man yanks the dagger from Lily's chest. The light-purple blade glints in a flash of lightning. Then he plunges it deep into her stomach.

And again.

And again.

And again.

He's killing her. I couldn't protect her. I just need to get to her. If I get to her, I can save her.

The man finally steps back from Lily. He turns and walks back through the mist he appeared from before it vanishes entirely, taking him with it.

Lily collapses to the ground. I push myself harder to get to her, my muscles burning, my eyes fixated on her lifeless body, surrounded by wildflowers.

It feels like an eternity before I finally reach her. I slam to the ground beside her, pulling her limp body into me.

Blood.

There is too much blood. Red dots splatter the once pristine white daisies scattered around Lily. Thin wisps of black shadows seep from the holes in her chest.

Tears stream down our faces. *This can't be happening*. I need to get her back to the castle. They'll know what to do.

Suddenly, she moves in my arms, raising a shaky hand to feel the shadows leaving her.

She's alive.

"Theo," Lily tries to speak. Blood splatters from her wounds, soaking my shirt.

"Shh. It's ok, Lily. I'll get help," I say, my voice trembling.

"I love you, Theo. It's always been you and will always be you," Lily whispers as if she's saying goodbye.

I brush the blood-coated hair from her face and rub my thumb along her cheek. "I'm sorry, my flower. If I were faster or stronger, I could have stopped him. I love you. Please don't leave me. Please." I beg through sobs.

Lily's breathing becomes ragged, and her body goes limp in my arms. Her shadows disappear. My heart shatters into tiny pieces. A tug on the threads of fate makes it feel like a sliver of my heart is being carried off to the Underrealm along with my Amari. All my hopes and dreams for us drown with my screams as Astra's storm finally breaks.

CHAPTER 2

THE QUEEN

PRESENT

I watch him from the shadows. Sweat drips down his well-defined chest like morning dew on a leaf, tracing every ridge. His physique is the result of years of extensive training with the royal guards.

The sun shines high in the cloudless sky over Lux—the thick heat forcing the men to remove their shirts to cool themselves. We all must be in Astra's good graces, for now.

The clashing of swords and grunts of the men below drown out the birds chirping in the woods. Body odor and pine mix heavily in the air.

I've watched them going through various stances and positions all morning. My shaded forest overlooks the open training ring, hiding me from sight. The hillside provides the perfect vantage point for me to keep a close eye on him. I must be leaving soon, but I can't seem to pull myself away. His sun-kissed skin beckons me to stay a little longer. The muscles of his back flex as his sword collides with another from one of his guards. He looks like a god preparing for battle. It's a delicious image I will dream about for years to come.

I marvel at how different we are. His body hardened through dedication and skill. His role as captain requires him to be sharp mentally and physically. The years have been far less kind to me. My once smooth, pale skin is now marred with scars, too deep to be healed by any elixir. A constant reminder of how my training was never a choice, but something forced upon me regardless of how much I fought back.

Pushing off the ground, I kneel and pick up my canteen from beside me. The water I gathered this morning from the brook is still crisp and provides a brief relief from the increasing heat. I wipe a bead of sweat from my warm brow before standing and dusting dirt from my trousers.

I allow myself a few more moments of watching him, needing to soak up every minute I can. Scanning his perfectly chiseled body, I commit every line to memory. The way his brown hair shimmers with streaks of gold when the sun hits it at a certain angle. The way the corner of his mouth curls up slowly as he taunts his guards into another round of sparring.

My heart and skin hum as I stare at him. It did the same when I found him two years ago. The threads wrapped tightly around my heart, pulling me toward him. Ten years of being trapped in the dark and bound to the shadow king only made me want to seek him out more.

Memories claw at my mind, yanking me back into the dark.

"You stupid girl. They don't even know who you are," Leopold said with a haughty smile. *"You made a deal for people who barely remember you even existed."*

Ash fills my mouth as I gasp for air. My nails bite into my palms as I tighten my fists.

I am alive. I am safe. I am not in that damned cell.

I swallow hard and take several deep breaths. Relaxing my hands, I shake off the last of the memory. I'm not that young, weak girl anymore. King Oren made sure of that. He methodically removed all of my softness with each slice of his dagger, every crack of his whip, and all the victims left in my wake.

"Goodbye, my Amari," I say into the wind.

This will be my last time checking in on him. I can't keep coming here and torturing myself as just a spectator of what he's doing … whom he's doing. I have to believe Leopold will hold up his end of the deal and keep him safe within his kingdom. My soul was a small price to pay for his life. I may be bound eternally to a monster, but at least he'll live.

I turn and slip into the thick coverage of trees I've been using to hide. Generations-old evergreens and aspens fill the forest along the foothills. Their woodsy and fresh aroma fills the air. The chirping birds grow louder as I move further into the thick of the woods, and their song combines with the trickling of a babbling brook as I wind my way down the hillside.

In the distance, the rough, gray stone of the snow-capped mountains that trail the outskirts of Lux peek through the various shades of green. Powerful, icy rivers dance along the rocky edge of the kingdom before appearing to fall off. The rest of the range remains below in Fati. The two halves were ripped apart by angry gods millennia ago.

As I step through the shaded tree line into the grassy meadow, I shield my eyes from the harsh sunlight. Delicate and soft-blue poppies dot the field, and I step lightly around them to leave no trace of my path.

I roll my shoulders, trying to ease the stiffness that's settled from crouching too long on the ground. Pausing at the edge of the meadow, I briefly stretch my aching muscles, groaning as I bend.

Standing tall, I set off in a jog, which quickly turns into a full-on sprint, back toward the village. My body protests at the exertion, but my mind sharpens.

The gravel path clicks under my boots as I run beside the towering boundary wall surrounding the Lux kingdom. The massive gray stone structure looms above, seeming to kiss the clouds. Rounding the last bend before the entry gate that leads into the village, I slow to a stop. I steady my breath and check my appearance. Under the disguise of a Fati viator who wanders the realm, I must look fragile and submissive. While those traits were beaten out of me, I have mastered the art of deception. It's an easy trick when you barely know your true self anymore. A mask simply slipped on and used to become whoever you need to be.

I tuck a loose curl back into the cream cloth wrapped around my head. Red hair is a rarity in Omnia, and it is easier to conceal all of mine to prevent questions or unwanted touching.

I draw my attention across the realm to the dark shadows of Umbra. My kingdom. My home. Thick tendrils of shadows twist and twirl along the stone column tethering Umbra to the land below. The black mist weaves into the white clouds skirting the sky-bound land. The thick tendrils swirl in response to my attention.

Satisfied with my unassuming look, I continue along the walkway, eyes trained on the gravel. The path narrows as it nears the entry gate, and I look up to find a predatory stare locked on me. The gate guard licks his bottom lip as his eyes roam all over my body, and I suppress a gag.

I give him a polite smile before dropping my gaze back to the ground and walking through the gate. His large hand grabs my wrist, pulling me to a stop. The darkness inside me swirls in agitation, itching to be released. I take a deep breath, ash settling on my tongue.

"When are you going to do what's good for you and let me take you out? You know I can offer you more than the measly scraps you're used to," he says in a stern tone, demanding my compliance.

His other hand reaches to lift my chin, but I jerk my head back and out of his reach. His fingers tighten around my wrist as a warning. I'm nothing but a meek viator woman he can manipulate to get what he wants. I'm not a person but an object for him to use. He believes that just because I'm among the lowest class mortals in the realm, I should appreciate the attention he has given me over the past week. Sadly, there are many others who think the same way in Omnia.

I swallow the bile creeping up my throat and plaster a sickly-sweet smile on my face.

"I told you, I'm here to work. You know where to find me if you want to see me," I say with as much seduction as I can muster and force myself to flutter my eyelashes at him.

"You know, I may have to take you up on that tonight. Maybe I can convince a few of the guards to come out. We could have a lot of fun with a pretty thing like you," he says, giving my arm a slight pull toward him.

I dig my heels into the ground, preventing my body from moving. His lip twitches with my defiance, revealing a hint of teeth.

"The more the merrier," I say, giving him a wink and tugging my wrist free from his grip.

I saunter away and feel his eyes stalking me as I go. My heart twinges in pain, thinking about how I wish it were a different guard asking to take me out tonight or promising to come see me at work. But that's not how our story is written. I'm bound to the shadows while he must remain in the light.

Once through the gate, the gravel path winds through a small grouping of wattle and daub homes. The little gardens provide the residents with their own small food source into winter. Firewood smoke burns in the air. Children chase each other, their laughter warming the space. I smile at their joy and freedom.

The crack of a whip pierces the air, causing me to halt.

Tears stream down my face as agony overwhelms me. The sharp, burning pain spreads through my body like a lightning bolt as the leather whip slices my back. Another crack and another scream from me.

I grit my teeth, forcing the memory to fade from my mind. The whinny of a horse grounds me to the present, and I exhale. I focus on the path forward and not the past that threatens to drag me into the darkness again.

The gravel turns to cobblestone as I turn the corner, heading back to Amelia's home. Closely set stone buildings line the streets, colorful wood accenting their doors and windows. Everything blends perfectly with the landscape as if sprung up from the mountains and forests.

Voices from the market reverberate off the walls, making the path feel as if it's crowded with people. I crisscross through the streets, drawing as little attention as possible.

Soon, the deep-crimson door of Amelia's home pops into view. Its color, reminiscent of the deep-crimson of the Umbra crest, stands out from the homes surrounding it. Amelia painted it this color after meeting a soothsayer viator woman a few years before who shared stories of angry gods and destruction coming to Omnia. The seer warned the villagers to paint their doors red to show their devotion to the gods or else they would suffer their wrath. No one listened but Amelia. Her belief in the gods is the strongest I've ever seen. She believes their intent is always for the best. I don't share the same view of our benevolent deities.

Inside the quaint home, it is cool despite the sweltering heat of the day. There are small knickknacks throughout, with only the essential pieces of furniture filling the space. The common-room holds the hearth, which we've used on many cool nights during my visits over the past two years. I smile thinking about the stories we've shared around its glowing fire, laughing all our cares away. A small pallet bed is set in the corner, out of the way, as to not impede on the limited space. While I love my stays with Amelia, I long for my big, comfortable bed in Umbra.

I kick my boots off by the door before making my way to the bathing chamber tucked in the far back corner of the home. The small chamber is more than most others have in the village. Only the lords and royals of Lux enjoy the luxury of spacious bathing chambers with all the amenities. A well-kept secret of my kingdom, Umbra, is that everyone has access to running water and enjoys comfortable bathing chambers. I long for my deep tub and shower as well.

After pouring some water from a pitcher into the water basin, I strip before scrubbing the dirt from my body and washing until my skin no longer feels sticky with sweat.

Feeling as refreshed as I can, I dry and slip into the basic uniform of a barmaid: a light-beige dress that comes to my knees and a crisp-white apron to wrap around my middle. A simple job to help maintain my cover while outside of my kingdom. The tavern owners, Harvey and Tillie, provided me with these clothes for the week I'd be working for them—a kind gesture I know many wouldn't extend to a poor viator.

I untie the cream cloth from my hair and let my long, red curls cascade down my shoulders. Snagging a cord off the small counter, I gather my hair and tie it atop my head. I find a fresh white cloth and wrap it tightly around my topknot, hiding its color from sight.

I open the door to the bathing chamber at the same time that Amelia opens the door to her sleeping quarters. She must have finished her daily tasks early. What she does? I have never asked. Nor did she ask what I did when I wasn't with her.

We respect each other's privacy and never ask the other to share more than she's comfortable with.

Her blonde hair, the color of wheat ready for harvest, floats in the light breeze that blows through the common-space. Her sky-blue eyes meet mine, and I can't help but smile, remembering the first time we met two years ago. It was as if the fates yanked us toward one another.

It was the first time I laid eyes on my guard. While staring at him with intense adoration, I completely missed Amelia walking toward me, slamming right into her, resulting in the vine-ripened tomatoes she was carrying exploding all over us. When she started laughing instead of screaming, I knew I liked her. Most people would have alerted the guard while chastising a viator for being where they weren't wanted, but Amelia showed me kindness, resulting in an instant friendship.

"Take a seat, Vivienne. I have some bread and soup for us to eat before you leave for your shift," Amelia says while gesturing at my seat at the table on the other side of the common room. My stomach growls in response, earning a giggle from Amelia.

Plopping down in my seat, I watch as she gets to work slicing the freshly baked bread and pouring soup into bowls for us. A beautiful bouquet of bright yellow and orange sunflowers with purple and pink pansies sits in the center of the table. Their floral scent is almost overwhelming but still inviting. I run a finger along their delicate petals, remembering warm honey eyes and soft kisses.

Amelia sets down two bowls of hearty soup, a plate of sliced bread, and two mugs of water. She takes a seat across from me as we both dig in.

"This soup is delicious, Amelia," I say, taking another bite.

It's a thick, savory mixture of roasted root vegetables, lentils, and beef. It's just the type of meal that will keep me going while slinging mugs of ale for the patrons tonight.

She gives me a soft smile while tearing off a piece from the bread. The crispy crust and soft inside of the bread are the perfect complement to the soup.

I chew the inside of my cheek as I debate how to ask Amelia the question that's been eating away at me since I heard a bit of gossip in my village in Umbra. Just some whispers shared among my people while I hid in plain sight as a viator, no one knowing my real name or title. Would they have spoken so freely if they knew their queen walked among them? Or that the captain they spoke of was her Amari?

That gossip was a big reason I came to Lux. But so far, I haven't been able to find any answers. I steady my breath to sound as casual as possible.

"While in the village, I heard some good news. It sounds like your captain of the guard will be marrying the princess soon. May Astra bless their union," I say, not looking up from my empty bowl.

"Oh, I don't know how true that is. I think it's just a rumor —villagers hoping the handsome captain will marry the beautiful princess. Like they are characters from a children's storybook," she replies.

I open my mouth to say something, but her brows pinch together.

"Unless they don't have a choice," her voice trails off as she seems to consider her own statement.

"Why would King Leopold force them to wed? You don't think he would want his daughter to find her Amari and fall in love?" I ask, even though I know he doesn't care.

He's the one who offered mine to Oren, after all.

"I think our king would do what it takes to keep the divinus powers strong. We all fear what's happening in Terra could happen here," she says with concern.

The fear is not completely unwarranted. The divinus of Terra have been losing the strength of their powers with each generation. What used to be a power strong enough to move whole pieces of the ground to create castles and homes is now only a sliver. King Royce Winfielde might be able to manipulate large boulders on a good day. But he can only move them short distances, hardly enough to make a real impact. The two princes can't move anything larger than a carriage, and Princess Violet wields no power. No one knows what caused their god to neglect them.

"Or what happened to Fati after their god left them," she says with a shiver.

I snicker. "Their god didn't leave them. They died. That's what happens when power-hungry men fight for control."

She stands and clears the table, taking everything to the sink to wash before speaking again. "I refuse to believe their god died. I think they left for a reason and when they can, they will return. Restoring their power and their glory in the realm. Maybe then Fati viators won't be treated so poorly," she says with such confidence, I want to believe it.

But Fati's god disappeared, and nobody has seen them for generations. When they vanished, they took their power, along with the respect of the other kingdoms, with them. With no divinus to lead and protect, the people of Fati fell into poverty until desperation forced them to travel throughout the realm looking for work. As viators, they float through the realm with no proper home, struggling to survive.

Not knowing how to respond, I join her at the sink and help clean the dishes, falling into a comfortable silence.

When the dishes are washed and dried, I take a seat on my pallet bed and slip my boots on, tucking in a sleeved knife. Amelia leans on the counter on the opposite side of the common-room.

"Are you coming to the tavern tonight? Harvey got a new shipment of the Fati wine you love so much," I say as I finish gathering my things to leave.

The delectable fruity taste of the Fati wine is smoother than the cobblestone roads. The vineyards sit directly beneath Lux and branch out from its shadow.

Amelia is a big fan of their seasonal wines and could drink an entire bottle, if I let her. And I don't, because the last time she did, she brought some ogre of a man home and had loud, unfulfilling sex with him while I tried to sleep in the common-space. The next morning, I told her never again, and she embarrassingly agreed.

"Oh, I think I might have to then," she replies, giving me a wide grin. "Plus, it is your last night working here. It would only be right of me to come for a visit before you leave us."

While there's a hint of sadness to her tone, her smile doesn't falter.

I will miss my routine visits to see Amelia, but I can't come back here. While I have loved watching my guard, knowing that we can never be together is torture. He's so close, but I can't touch him or speak to him.

In the two years of hiding in the shadows, watching him to make sure Leopold would uphold his end of our deal even after Oren died, it has been hard to resist approaching him. But I know he wouldn't know me, anyway. The kings erased all traces of me from his mind. His memories of me are trapped beneath a hazy veil, preventing him from knowing who I am. They forced those closest to me to forget, knowing no one else would remember a poor servant's daughter who never left the castle grounds.

I give Amelia a big hug before heading out the door. The sky overhead is turning shades of vibrant orange and red. The sun sets behind the mountains, allowing the air to cool slightly. The heat has been unrelenting for this time of year, but in a few short months, summer will fade into autumn.

Hurrying along the main path toward the center of the village, I quickly reach Harvey's tavern. The typical gray stone façade and dark wood door blend in with the surrounding shops. A wooden sign hangs above the door reading "The Blue Stag" in handwritten indigo script. Several windows line the wall to help with airflow and lighting.

Uneven rows of wood line the floors of the Stag and metal candelabras with cooled candle wax collecting along the rim hang from the rafters. The bar countertop stands on one side with a handful of stools set along the lip. Shelves filled with clean mugs line the back of the bar, ready for a busy evening. Tables of assorted sizes and heights are arranged on the opposite side, chairs already placed around them.

It's a warm and inviting space, which is why it has been so successful over the years. And since Harvey recently acquired a trove item, which allows him to keep drinks and food at a cooler temperature, business has been booming. Legends say the gods blessed the rare and highly sought-after trove items during the creation of Omnia. Most of the trove items were destroyed when the gods warred. The salvaged items are now mostly owned by the royal families. How Harvey found and purchased this chilled box? I have no clue. But the timing couldn't have been more perfect for me as the tavern was desperate to hire a new barmaid when I arrived in town.

As I enter the Stag, I spy Harvey, already busy at work inspecting all the mugs and prepping small food items for the patrons expected tonight. I was hesitant when Amelia said she found me a job for the week at her friend's tavern. Turns out I had no reason to worry.

Harvey is a sweet gentleman, married to an even sweeter woman, Tillie. Their love is something out of the fairy tales we tell children. The love that is true and all-consuming. A fate-blessed type of love—one I glimpsed once, or I think I did, and will never experience again in this lifetime.

"Good evening, Vivienne. I'm finishing up with the food. Can you get the candles lit before it gets too dark in here?" Harvey asks without looking up from his task.

"Of course, my liege," I reply, bowing at the waist dramatically. Harvey lets out a small, deep chuckle in response. I put my bag down in the back room and start lighting all the candles.

CHAPTER 3

THE QUEEN

We are finishing up the last of our opening tasks as the first patrons waltz through the door—a couple of regulars who have been here every night this week.

I plaster a cheery smile across my face while delivering mugs of cooled ale to the men. They attempt to sneak a feel as I walk by, believing they have a right to grab at me. But I'm quick on my feet and can dodge most of them.

The evening progresses with nothing out of the ordinary. Patrons come and go. Harvey and I deliver ale, wine, and snacks upon request. We wash mugs and sweep the floors as needed, trying to keep on top of tasks. The sour smell of drinks and sweat-soaked bodies grows thicker with each passing hour.

Harvey and I have developed a rhythm and routine over the past week. We flow together and anticipate what the other needs without exchanging words. We continue our dance as the sun fades from the sky and the starry night hangs above.

The tavern door slams open as I'm cleaning up a mug of spilled ale from the bar. I look up to see Creepy Gate Guard stumbling in.

Three other guards follow him, and I recognize them all from the training yard. They all walk unsteadily as they enter.

Unfortunately, Creepy catches my attention and flashes me a wicked smile. I groan and get back to cleaning the counter but catch him moving toward me out of the corner of my eye.

He plops down on the stool in front of me, and I tilt my head slightly to look at him. He smells strongly of sour ale and sweat. It makes my eyes burn. I turn around to wring out the cloth soaked with the spilled ale, and I feel his eyes trace over every inch of my body.

My skin hums with the need to show this man what I am capable of. Suppressing the rage building inside me, I turn around, wiping my hands on my apron. His tongue slides over his bottom lip as he stares at me.

I work hard to suppress a scowl and exchange it for the welcoming smile of a simple barmaid.

"What will it be? A mug of ale? Or some Fati wine? We have one of their summer bottles which tastes like sunshine. I don't know how they do it, but it's magical," I say, stepping up to the counter and placing my hands wide atop it.

He continues to stare at my body before landing on my breasts.

"I'll take a piece of you," he says, slowly bringing his eyes to mine.

I clench my jaw so hard I think I may break a tooth.

"Sorry, I'm not on the menu. What else can I get you?" I bring my hands together in front of me on the counter, interlacing my fingers.

Creepy grabs both of my wrists so hard that I'm sure I will bruise. I am shocked by the audacity of this man to put his hands on a woman he doesn't know. I could be a ruthless killer for all he knows. And I am, so he should probably make better life choices.

Through clenched teeth, I spit out, "Let go of me."

The darkness writhes inside of me, wanting a piece of this man. I lock eyes with him, and a look I'm all too familiar with dances across his face. He thinks I'm just another weak woman. I'm just an object for him to play with. This man wants to hurt me, and the thought of doing so excites him.

Oh, how wrong he is. I've taken down bigger pieces of shit than this guy.

"The lady doesn't want your hands on her, Jonathan. It would be wise to remove them immediately," a rich, deep voice echoes through the small space.

The bustling tavern seems to halt in silence, all eyes focus on the situation at the bar. The newcomer moves behind Creepy, whose name is Jonathan apparently, and places a large hand on his shoulder.

Leaning down so his head is even with Jonathan's ear, he grits out forcefully, "Let go of her. Now. That is an order, guard."

Jonathan's face twists as if he is having an internal battle about whether to listen or defy the order. He listens and lets go of my wrists. I pull them back to my chest and rub at them, relishing the fact that he is no longer touching me. The scars around my wrists sting from the tight grasp.

I look up to meet warm, golden honey eyes staring at me with an apologetic hint to them.

He is here. This can't be real.

I freeze, fighting the urge to faint, staring at his handsome face. He pats Jonathan on the shoulder, a silent gesture to move. Jonathan glowers at me with a look that tells me this isn't over yet and slides off the stool to join the other guards at their table in the back of the tavern.

My guard moves into the vacated spot but doesn't sit down.

"I'm sorry about that. Are you ok?" he eyes my wrists where I had been rubbing them.

My mouth must have fallen open because it's dry, and I try to swallow and come up with some kind of response.

"Yes," I blurt out with an unrequired sense of urgency. My rage and my king forgotten.

His cedar scent hits me, and I take a deep breath, inhaling it.

"I'm fine. Not the first time a man has put his hands on me without asking, and I'm sure it won't be the last," I say before realizing that it's probably not the right response.

What am I doing? Gods, this is not going how I dreamed it would.

The look of concern deepens on his handsome tanned face, and the muscles in his jaw flex as he clenches it.

"Well, if anyone else tries to touch you while in Lux, please let me know. I'll inform them that such behavior is not welcome here."

This man looks like a god standing before me. He's gorgeous from a distance, but up close, he's devastatingly handsome. While the years have changed him physically, I'm glad to see his caring heart is still the same and not turned cold by the evil that lies in this kingdom.

"Thank you for that, Captain Kincaid. What can I get for you?" I ask.

"Theo, please call me Theo," he says, smiling warmly at me.

"Ok then, Theo, what will it be?" I reply as a slight blush paints my cheeks.

"Your name, for starters," he replies with a hint of flirtation.

My blush turns from pink to red and I look down to stop it from deepening further.

When I drag my gaze back up, I find captivating pools of honey eyeing me, waiting patiently for an answer. I open my mouth to speak but catch myself before I accidentally spit out my real name. Oh, the disaster that would be.

"Vivienne," I reply, feeling the large foolish smile on my face.

He doesn't seem put off because his smile matches mine.

For long moments, we're lost in each other's eyes, as if searching for the spark that has set us on fire. A man clearing his throat breaks our trance. Harvey stands at the end of the bar with a handful of dirty mugs ready for washing. We both notice him staring at us.

"I'll take a mug of the highly talked about chilled ale, please," Theo says, confirming whatever moment we were sharing is gone.

"Coming right up. Do you want some for your friends as well?" I look over his shoulder at the table of guards who are pretending not to watch us.

"Yes, but not for Jonathan. He can get his own," he says, eyeing them back.

I laugh harder than I should.

"I can definitely do that. Go take a seat, and I will bring them out to you shortly."

He nods at me before turning and taking a seat at their table.

I'm walking toward the back to retrieve the ale from the trove chilled box when Amelia walks through the door.

"Have a seat at the bar. I'll grab you some wine," I say as I push open the door to the back room.

"You are the best, V!" She smiles brightly at me and takes the seat closest to the door.

I grab a tray, load it up with four mugs of ale and one of wine, then walk back to the bar. I stop and give Amelia her wine, which she takes gleefully and drinks immediately. She moans as the sweet fruit wine of Fati hits her tongue. I giggle at her overdramatic response and head to Theo's table.

Theo placed himself at the end of the table along the walkway with his back to the wall. His eyes keep watch over the entire space. Always the guard, even when not on duty.

He catches me approaching, and his face lights up. If I didn't know better, I would say this man finds me attractive. *What I wouldn't give to act on that.*

I stop at the end of the table and squeeze my thighs together as filthy thoughts flood my mind. I hand the ale over to the men, ensuring Theo is last.

"Thank you, Vivienne," he says with a smirk.

I need to move before this man makes me melt from the way he is looking at me.

"Not a problem at all, Theo. Let me know when you need another round," I say with a little too much sexual undertone, but I am sure no one will notice.

"Oh, I will be sure to do that," he says with a hungry look in his eyes that causes me to squirm.

I hurry away to keep myself from drooling on him and make it back to the bar to busy myself with tasks, trying to calm my nerves.

"Sooo, the captain?" Amelia says in a teasing tone.

"What about him?" I reply flatly, trying to hide my sexual frustration.

"If I had a man that gorgeous looking at me with half the fire there's in his eyes, I would be a pile of ashes on the floor," my friend says while cutting a look over her shoulder at the table.

"I don't know what you're talking about," I reply unconvincingly.

A giggle escapes from Amelia as she looks back at me.

"Yeah, keep telling yourself that. I guess I won't need to leave a candle lit for you tonight," she says with a wink as she finishes her mug of wine.

I have no clever retort, so I choose to turn away and work on tidying up.

As the evening wears on, we have a steady flow of people in and out, with a few who seem to linger, socializing the night away.

Harvey and I perform our silent bar dances, ensuring we have satisfied patrons. Amelia sits at the bar until I cut her off after three mugs of wine. She leaves, cursing at me under her breath, all the while telling me she will see me in the morning. I love her and her drunk antics.

I stay close to Theo all night. When dropping off another round of ale, I stand beside him, close enough to feel the warmth of his body. I feel his eyes follow me as I serve other patrons. Heat skirts my skin wherever his eyes trail. The darkness inside me hums happily at the sensation, causing me to shiver.

He watches me as I clean a nearby table. I lean forward, giving him a better view of my breasts. I fight back a smile as he squirms in his seat.

Theo sips on his second mug of ale as Harvey announces last call. I head over to Theo to see if he needs another round before closing.

Jonathan is standing at a high table with a few other patrons, and he watches me as I pass. I've lost track of how much he's had to drink. I tried cutting him off earlier but soon realized his friends were handing him the mugs they ordered. He is visibly drunk and sways as he holds onto the table for support.

At Theo's table, I try to stand as far away from Jonathan and as close to Theo as possible without making either look intentional. Theo smiles up at me, and I notice his eyes are glossier now than before. He must not drink much if he's feeling the effects of two mugs of ale.

"Would you like another round before we close up for the evening?" I ask, making eye contact.

"I think we are all good but thank you for checking," he answers.

"Great. If you could pass me your empties, I'll get those out of your way," I say, reaching over Theo to grab one of the empty mugs.

His hand brushes my thigh as I lean forward, and I flinch as a spark shoots through my body. I nearly combust at the feeling and swallow hard to stop the blazing fire within me. I tell myself his touch was an accident and collect the remaining mugs before heading back to the bar to wash them. Harvey slips into the back to check on a few things as patrons leave. I wish them a good night as I clean the mugs at the basin behind the counter.

I hear shuffled footsteps and assume another patron is leaving. I smell him before I see him. The overwhelming scent of sour ale and musky body odor gags my senses before I can register what is happening.

Slimy hands grab me by the waist and cage me against an equally slimy chest, causing my breath to lodge in my throat. Claws scratch the walls of the sealed well at my center. The darkness lurking within it begging to be freed—to protect.

Jonathan. Fucking asshole.

He squeezes me tightly to his chest.

"How about you stop playing hard to get and let me fuck you on this bar right now in front of everyone?" his words are a slur as he bends his head down to kiss me.

The shock wanes, and I fight to get out of his grasp. I try pushing off his chest, but he is squeezing me against his body so tight I can't get any leverage to move.

You've made a big mistake, Creepy.

I raise my knee to drive it into his balls, but Jonathan's head is yanked back with such force I think his neck may have snapped. His hold on me disappears abruptly and I fall backward, slamming into the bar before landing on the ground.

I look up to see that Theo has a fistful of Jonathan's hair gripped tightly in his hand as he pulls the man backward and spins him, so they are face-to-face. Theo grasps Jonathan's shirt in one hand and with the other, punches him so hard blood shoots from Jonathan's mouth, spraying droplets on the back wall.

Theo's hand comes to Jonathan's throat and squeezes as he lifts the man off his feet. Jonathan struggles to breathe. Suspended in the air and kicking his feet, he tries to wiggle out of Theo's grasp.

Jonathan is not a tiny man, none of the guards are, but Theo makes him look like he is as light as a feather.

The rage flaring through Theo's eyes is primal. Something I have never seen before and never expected to see on his face.

"I told you not to put your hands on her! I'll punish you for defying a direct order from your captain," he declares angrily, his voice demanding.

He looks terrifying.

The act of pure animalistic rage should horrify me. I don't need Theo to protect me, but I can't fight the ache growing between my thighs as my pulse increases from watching him come to my rescue. There is something so arousing about Theo pummeling Jonathan to oblivion.

Something is seriously wrong with me.

Theo drops Jonathan, causing Jonathan's knees to slam into the floor, leaving him gasping for air.

"Leave now before your punishment is any worse," Theo says sternly as Jonathan promptly crawls away to his friends who are waiting at the door.

Scurry away, little man.

Theo watches Jonathan leave before turning and bending to me on the floor. His hands slide along my body, checking for injuries. His touch leaves sparks on my skin as he goes.

"I'm fine, Theo. My body may have a few bruises and so may my ego, but otherwise I'm well," I say, trying to be reassuring.

His still-blazing eyes meet mine and his hands halt on my upper thighs. It takes all my self-control not to open my legs wide for him.

"I'm sorry, Vivienne. He had no right to grab you like that, and I am sorry I didn't make it to you faster. And—"

I place both my hands on his face, cupping his cheeks, forcing him to stop his unnecessary apology.

"You protected me twice tonight and even punched a man for me. You have nothing to be sorry for. You're not responsible for the failures of other men. You're a good man, Theo. Thank you for being my knight in shining armor tonight."

His eyes finally soften, and the anger seems to ebb.

Harvey steps through the back door, finding us on the floor behind the bar.

"V, what happened? Are you ok?" He asks while rushing toward me.

Theo doesn't budge from in front of me, blocking Harvey's way.

"I'm fine, Harvey. That creepy guard, Jonathan, thought it was a good idea to put his hands on me. Theo showed him how bad of an idea it was." I smile at Theo, my hands still on his cheeks.

"There's blood on the wall. I would say that was a hard lesson," Harvey says, sounding impressed. "Thanks for keeping her safe for me, Captain," Harvey pats Theo's shoulder.

"Not a problem at all. It's an honor to protect such a beautiful maiden." Theo doesn't take his eyes off me, they seem to spark.

The pit of my stomach twists and I'm blushing again. Only this man can make me blush so much.

"It's getting late. We should finish up and get out of here," Harvey says softly above us.

I nod and drop my hands from Theo's face. He stands and offers his hand to me. I place my hand in his large, calloused one, causing tingles to shoot across my skin where we touch. The thread around my heart vibrates and goosebumps erupt on my arms. Theo stares at our hands and tilts his head to the side in question.

He feels it too.

Theo helps me to my feet, and I brush off dirt from my clothes.

"I'm walking you home tonight," he says with finality.

"That is very kind of you, but it is already late, and I still have a lot to do before leaving. Plus, you have done more than enough tonight," I reply, tilting my head up at him.

He is much taller than me now.

His eyes trace the line of my neck and his lips part.

"That wasn't a question," he says before turning to Harvey.

"What needs to be done?" Theo asks.

Harvey looks up from scrubbing the blood off the wall. His eyes flick from Theo to me, unsure of what to say.

"The chairs need to be picked up and placed on the table for sweeping," Harvey replies hesitantly.

Theo sets off to do as directed. I let out an exasperated breath and follow him. Harvey chuckles softly as I walk by.

I dash in front of Theo and place my hands up for him to halt. He steps right into them, pressing his hard chest into my palms. I slowly drop my hands as a smirk curls one side of his lips.

"This is all truly kind of you, Theo, but shouldn't you be getting back to the castle? Won't your fiancée be missing you?" I ask, hoping he will confirm Amelia's opinion from our earlier conversation.

He locks on my lips for a breath too long before he steps closer to me.

"You shouldn't believe every rumor you hear in this village."

His gaze rakes over me, stopping on my apron. He reaches out and trails his palm along my waist. I suck in a breath at the deliberate touch.

Theo's hand doesn't move as he steps beside me, pressing his chest into my shoulder.

"I don't have a girlfriend, but I do have my eyes on a gorgeous maiden."

His palm slides across my hip as he passes me to return to picking up chairs. I gasp as I try to calm my racing heart and keep from collapsing on the floor.

CHAPTER 4

THE QUEEN

We silently finish picking up the chairs and sweeping the floor. Once we clean and dry the mugs, we place them back on the shelves behind the bar. With effort, Harvey is able to get the blood off the wall, and he tosses out the cloth to rid us of the memory.

Theo can't seem to keep his hands from reaching for me as we clean. A light touch on my back as he squeezes past me to pick up another chair with ease. A brush of his arm against mine as he reaches to put a mug he was drying on the shelf. Little touches that light me on fire and send it coursing through my veins. I'm not sure if I'm going to survive, especially since he isn't leaving my side until he knows I'm safe at home.

Harvey steps out of the back room, eyeing the tavern.

"V, I'm going to head home to Tillie. She must be worried sick since I'm late. Don't want her storming down here. I have the alley door locked, so once you leave, everything should be closed tight."

He's leaving me alone with Theo.

Oh, gods.

Beads of sweat dampen my forehead, and I swear I hear myself gulp.

"Thank you for everything, Harvey. Tell Tillie I'll miss her the most."

His smile is sad and so is mine, but we both knew this was going to end after a week. No matter how much we enjoyed our time together, it's now over.

"We will miss you too, Vivienne. Write as soon as you get settled, and you are welcome back anytime." He gives me a brief nod before heading out the back-alley door and into the night.

I barely hear the door lock over the sound of my racing heart pounding in my ears. Theo places his hand gently in the middle of my back and runs it down until it settles right above my ass.

"I take it this is your last night in Lux," Theo says into my ear.

The hair on the back of my neck rises as his breath prickles my skin.

"Yes, I start my new job at the Fati vineyards in a few days. I'm leaving in the morning," I reply slowly.

"Well, then we should celebrate. Come, let's get going," Theo says with a sinful smirk. He looks like he will devour me whole, and I'll let him.

"Ok, but let me get the last of the candles, then we can go," I say, hurrying to place a candle by the alley door before putting out all the candelabras in the bar.

Theo patiently waits at the back door like I told him. In all honesty, I'm stalling. I know what will happen next, but do I really want that? To finally have him, only for him not to know who I truly am and then never see him again?

My body says yes, but my heart is already breaking at the thought. I can never come back. His life depends on me staying true to my deal with Leopold. I need to be smart, but the sight of his exquisite body leaning against the door frame makes me want to do something reckless.

Unable to delay any longer, I join Theo in the back room. He holds the door open, and the faint glow of the candle by the alley illuminates the room so we can easily find our way.

I walk past Theo, brushing up against him as I go. His hand finds its spot on my back again. He follows me out the back, but I stop abruptly when I remember I brought a bag with me. Theo slams into my back and wraps his arms around me to keep us both upright.

I can feel every delicious inch of his front pressing into my ass, and I fight back a whimper.

"If you wanted me to touch you, Vivienne, you could have asked. I would happily do so," his voice is low and rough as he whispers into my ear. I bite my bottom lip to keep the moan from escaping my mouth. I swallow hard before gesturing behind us.

"My bag, I forgot my bag," I say breathlessly

His arms fall from my waist, and he turns to fetch my bag.

Chills run over my body when he returns to me. He hands me the bag with a cocked eyebrow. I'm going to need to put myself in that chilled box to help control my body temperature. I briefly debate doing so.

I open the door before blowing out the candle by the exit. I hold the door open for Theo to pass through, then close it, and give it a pull to ensure it's locked tight.

The alley is silent this time of night since The Blue Stag is the last shop to close. The glow of the street lanterns barely illuminates the walkway enough to see where we are going. Boxes and pallets are stacked high along the walls, narrowing the pathway in and out. There are no windows facing the alley, as it is mainly a walkway for shop owners to access the back of their establishments.

Theo extends his arm and asks, "Shall we?"

I smile at him as I place my hand in his, and we both look at our joined hands as a spark shoots through them. He squeezes my hand and starts to walk backward out of the alley, but my feet refuse to move.

My heart pounds. *I swear he can hear it.* My body hums in anticipation. It's been a while since a man has touched me like this. With a king focused on inflicting pain on anyone who threatens our kingdom, pleasure is a rarity.

I try to control my breathing.

"No one is waiting in your bed tonight, right? You don't have anyone expecting you to come warm them up?" I ask, needing to be certain before I risk everything.

As he stares down at me, his eyes sparkle with mischief, and his smile reveals his dirty thoughts.

"My bed has been cold and lonely for a long time now. Why? Do you want to change that and warm it up with me? I could make it worth your time." His deep voice washes over me, snapping my last piece of control.

"Theo, kiss me," I ask, practically panting.

He freezes. His eyes lock on my mouth.

"Please," I beg, tightening my grip on his hand.

In a blink, his lips are on mine and my back collides with the stone wall of the alley. He devours my mouth, and I taste the ale I'd been serving him all night. His lips are soft, but he kisses with a hunger I've never experienced.

His hands dig into my waist as he pushes his body into mine. I trail my hands up his arms, feeling flexed muscles as I go. My hands slide into his hair.

One of his hands slides up my body to fondle a breast. His large hand almost covers it entirely. He pushes his groin into mine and I feel his hard cock straining in his trousers. I moan into his mouth at the friction. The sound makes him push harder into me, causing the stone to bite into my back.

His lips leave mine as he moves down my neck. I push my head against the wall and rest my hands on his shoulders, my nails digging into his skin.

The darkness within me vibrates at the feel of his body on mine, but this moment isn't for my shadows. I push them deep down to prevent them from trying to intervene. I won't let them ruin this for me. It will be the only chance I ever have to be with him like this, and now that I've made up my mind, I won't let some damn god power mess this up.

His hand slides away from my breast, down my chest. His other hand trails along my side. Both palms skim my hip bones, moving toward my ass. Theo grips onto it firmly, making me feel tiny in his hands.

He licks, sucks, and kisses my neck, stealing my breath. He pulls back abruptly, and I open my eyes to look at him in a daze. His eyes meet mine and they are scalding. The fire blazing in them causes me to whimper.

His hands move back to my hips but continue a path lower. Still trying to melt me with that stare, Theo lowers himself without breaking eye contact. I watch him until he is kneeling in front of me, perfectly positioned between my thighs.

He looks away long enough to find the bottom of my dress at my knees and his hands start their way back up, this time underneath the fabric, touching my bare skin. His eyes come back to mine as his hands find my undergarments. My breath hitches as his thumb rubs my clit with the slightest pressure through the fabric. I'm spun tighter than a rope from the close proximity to him all night, and I am sure he can feel the moisture that has gathered between my legs.

His thumb circles my clit a few times, then his hands are on the band of my undergarments, pulling them to my boots. Theo drags his hands down one of my legs, lifting it to pull my undergarment off. He moves his attention to my other leg and does the same, but this time he does not place my foot back on the cobblestone.

Trailing kisses on the inside of my leg, he gathers my dress as he works his way back up my body. He kisses the inside of my thigh and places my leg over his shoulder. Theo continues kissing until he's back at my clit, but this time with his mouth.

I gather my dress behind me and secure it with my back so I can watch him. His eyes flash up to mine as his tongue swirls over my clit. I shudder, my knee threatening to collapse, but Theo has me pinned against the wall, supporting half my body weight on his shoulder.

Theo's tongue circles my clit in taunting spins. He moves in every direction, building the pleasure in a slow, steady rhythm. My head falls back to the wall as I moan into the night air. His tongue licks up every inch of my skin as he goes.

His hands move from their perch on my thighs. His fingers glide through the wetness, then he slides one into me, slowly. The light pressure on my walls is a tease of what's coming. I hum at the feeling, and he rewards me with another finger, moving in and out of me while his tongue continues its dance with my clit.

I dig my hands into his hair as a tingling sensation runs from my pussy to my head. He is far too good at this. It's not like I haven't been pleasured before, but this is so much more than all my experiences combined.

Theo must be a god, and this is his power. He knows exactly when to slow down and speed up. He seems to know how to keep me teetering on the edge of oblivion.

He curls his fingers inside of me. I can't take it anymore. I need him inside me. Now.

"Theo," I plead as he continues to drive my orgasm closer and closer.

"That's it, cum for me," he says between licks.

"Theo," I say again, but he doesn't seem to understand and is enjoying the way his name sounds coming from my lips. I grab his hair and jerk his head back. His fingers go still inside me. A look of confusion and shock streaks across his face.

"Fuck me. Now," I say with a growl. His face turns animalistic and in one smooth motion, he's standing, untying his trousers, releasing his cock from its fabric prison.

He grips the back of my thighs, raising me off the ground, and I wrap my legs around his waist. My arms find their spot on his shoulders as he drives me into the stone wall again, using it as leverage to position me right where he needs me.

One of his arms wraps around my waist while his free hand fists his cock. He runs his length through my wetness and then positions himself at my entrance. He pushes in slightly, and I gasp at the feeling.

Sliding in and out of me, he goes deeper with each stroke until he is fully seated. He pauses and rests his head in the crook of my neck. Both of us are breathing fast.

Bringing his free hand to my cheek, he pulls me in for a kiss. He releases my lips, and his hands find the grooves of my hips.

"Hold on, Vivienne."

With a wicked smile on his beautiful face, Theo unleashes the animal he was holding back. He drives into me hard, using my hips to lift me up and down. The sweet tender Theo is gone, and the hard warrior has replaced him. I feel the wall scratch at my back but ignore it as I moan from the pleasure rocketing through my body.

His hand slides between us until Theo's thumb is on my clit, driving me to the edge. I moan his name louder than I mean to, and he groans in response. The sensation of lightning shoots through my body as he pushes me closer to the edge. His cock twitches faintly inside me and I know he is close, too.

"Wait. Not yet," he says as he plunges deep inside me while playing with my clit.

"Theo, I am about to …" he pulls out abruptly, and my feet hit the cobblestone.

I gasp at the sudden withdrawal.

He grabs the back of my neck and turns me to the stack of boxes and pallets. He steps behind me and pushes my head down while running his other hand down my back. My hands find support on the pile as he tosses the skirt of my dress over my hips. He steps between my legs, tapping my boots, wordlessly asking for me to spread wider for him. I comply, eagerly anticipating and bracing myself for the new position.

Then he is driving back into me, and I yelp as he buries himself as deep as possible. At this angle, he is almost too much, but gods, does he feel so damn good. I moan again as he starts back his punishing pace in and out of my pussy.

His fingers find my clit again, and I almost pass out from the intensity. I say his name again, and I feel his grip tighten on my hip.

"That's it, cum for me. No more holding back," he orders.

He applies more pressure to my clit and plunges into me hard and fast. The combination of thrusts and circles mixed with his words sends me flying over the edge. My orgasm blasts through me roughly, and I feel myself gasping for air as I scream his name into the night. I hear him groan behind me as his release finds him as well.

CHAPTER 5

THE QUEEN

We both compose ourselves. Only the sound of our heavy breathing can be heard in the alley. Theo is still inside me, and his head is resting on my back as mine hangs limp between my braced arms on the pallets.

It takes a moment for us to slow our breaths, and when we do, Theo withdraws from me, tucking himself back into his trousers and tying them closed. I stand and let my dress fall from my hips.

I feel a little light-headed from the realm-shattering orgasm that tore apart my body and soul, making me wobble on my feet. Theo grabs my elbow to steady me and motions for me to take a seat where I had been leaning.

"Please sit," he asks gently.

He bends and finds my undergarment on the ground beside us. He slides it back on as I stand up and adjust myself to be more presentable.

His hands cup my face as he looks sweetly into my eyes. He kisses me tenderly and our tongues dance. It's a brief kiss, but the emotion behind it is jarring. My heart swells at the feelings

57

bubbling to the surface, only to be shattered as I remember this is as far as it can go. Whether I want to or not, I have to let him go. This life of secrecy is not for him, and I can't drag him into the darkness with me. It wouldn't be fair. Nor is it fair to me to keep wishing the fates had a different plan for us. He is destined to be more, and I am destined to never exist.

He takes my hands and places soft kisses on each.

"Let's get you home so I can enjoy you some more," he says.

Heat sinks low in my stomach at the thought of having him again. But I know we can't, and I know he is going to insist on staying together tonight.

"While I would love to take you home with me, my friend's place is small, and my bed is far too tiny to hold you," I say, motioning at his gigantic body.

He grins in understanding.

"Then my place it is," he replies.

Holding my hand, he turns and starts down the path toward the main walkway. He scoops my bag up off the ground as we pass where it had fallen.

I let him pull me along as panic hits me. I can't stay in his castle. If we're discovered, King Leopold will know I've broken the deal and try to kill me, or worse, he might kill Theo to punish me. Oren made it clear that the deal I made with the kings means that I must remain in the shadows to keep Theo and my people safe.

Since Oren's death, the power dynamics have shifted. I'm stronger than I was, and I now have King Asher at my side. But I can't risk an unplanned fight where innocent people will get hurt, especially when the ones I love would be Leopold's prime targets. I wouldn't put it past him to kill Theo, and even his own daughter, to get back at me.

"You live in the castle?" I ask, even though I already know the answer.

Theo continues down the alley without looking back at me.

"Yes, I have lived in Brightwick my entire life. I stay in the captain's quarters now. I think you'll really like it," he replies.

I know that I most definitely won't like it and rack my brain trying to come up with a believable excuse. I don't think 'Sorry, Theo, but your king will try to murder me if I step foot into his castle' will be the best answer.

We finally make it back to the main cobblestone path, and I pause as Theo turns in the castle's direction.

"I don't think the royal family will like a Fati viator girl in their palace," I say, allowing the panic to be clear in my voice.

He turns to look at me, tilting his head to the side, considering my words.

"You will be safe. You're with me. No one will bother you inside its walls," he says reassuringly.

If only he knew how wrong he is.

"I know you will keep me safe, but I'm not comfortable with it. I have been to the castles of the divinus before. They are not a welcoming place for someone like me," I say, trying to drive the point home.

He squares his body to mine, not speaking a word. He appears to be accepting my statement but also not wanting to give up on his attempts for us to stay together tonight.

"What about the inn? I know the keeper and can get us a room for the evening," I blurt out an alternative despite my better sense.

Knowing the keeper of the inn is a bit of a stretch. I have stayed there a handful of times in the past two years.

Theo nods at me, seeming to agree with my plan, and digs into his pockets.

"Ok, at least let me pay for the room," he says.

My sweet, thoughtful Theo wants to make sure his poor lady doesn't waste the money she needs on him.

"I'll pay for it. We don't need the village starting rumors about how the captain spends his time with lowly viator women," I reply.

He grimaces as the words come out with more bite than I intend.

"Viv—" he starts, but I interrupt him, already knowing what he's going to say.

"You have a reputation to protect. I don't. If there is anything I can do to keep you safe, this is it. You don't need the villagers thinking differently of you just because of me," I say sternly.

His face contorts into a scowl. He may not like what I am saying, but he knows it's true. Fati people, especially those who travel for work, are the lowest class mortals in Omnia. People have forced viators to live on the outskirts of society and are always looking down on them for it. The villagers of Lux and Terra do their best to avoid them as much as possible. They only interact with viators when it is required for trade and services.

Anger and frustration flare within me as I think about how poorly they treat viators. Over the years, many people have become so desperate for a better life, they have even risked death in the haunted forest to find refuge in Umbra. These viators have made lives in my kingdom. My people are the misfits of Omnia who have come together to grow Umbra in secret. Beneath Thalos' shadow veil, we have made a place we all are proud to call our home.

Before Theo can object to my decision, I kiss him.

"Wait here. I'll come find you once I have the room purchased," I say, grabbing my bag from his hand and heading toward the inn.

The Aurora Inn sits across the street and a few shops down from The Blue Stag. It's tucked near the bakery, which allows convenient access for anyone who stays there. The inn is nothing unique; it's like all basic inns in any other kingdom. The only difference is the gray stone and wood trimmed outside, the standard façade in Lux.

After getting the key to our room from the elderly innkeeper, I head back to the walk and wave at Theo to come along. He does so silently and unseen in the vacant street.

He takes my hand, and we walk together to our private room, retreating inside. The room is like the rest of the inn: basic. A bed barely big enough for the both of us, given Theo's size, a few candles light the space, and a small table with a pitcher and mugs set atop are all there is to it. It's not luxurious by any means, but it's a place where we can spend the night together that isn't Brightwick. My heart wars with my head about this decision.

I set my bag next to the table as Theo takes a seat on the bed, testing its comfort.

"I'm going to get us some water. I'm parched," I say, picking up the pitcher and heading out the door.

I return a minute later with a filled pitcher, and Theo steps out of the small bathing chamber as I enter the quarters. He comes over to me as I pour us some water. I offer him the mug and he accepts it, kissing me on the cheek. I smile at the sweet gesture.

I down my entire mug in one breath. I pull it from my mouth and wipe the droplets of water with the back of my forearm. Theo stares at me, seemingly shocked by what I've done.

"I said I was thirsty," I say with no expression.

"Obviously," he replies, smiling and drinking his water.

Finishing his mug, he takes the one from my hand and places both on the table. He wraps his arms around my waist and pulls me flush to his chest. He looks down at me, studying my features.

"Have I told you how absolutely stunning you are?" Theo asks, those honey eyes boring into my heart.

I smile brightly up at him. No one makes me feel like butterflies are erupting in my stomach like he does. Even after all this time. His words of praise and affection warm me to the depths of the soul I thought was long buried. His presence awakens a part of me I believed the darkness destroyed.

He leans down and kisses me with a passion that steals my breath. His lips part and I open mine to allow our tongues to taste each other. I slide my hands around his waist, drawing him close and eliminating any space between us.

Theo's hand grips the back of my neck and tilts my head back, and I smile as his lips trace kisses down my throat and along my jawline.

I soak in the feel of him, dreaming of a different realm where this could be our life. Our nights would be spent worshiping each other's bodies, memorizing every inch.

Hope blooms in my chest with a thought, all-consuming and risky. In the two years and nearly a dozen visits I've made to Lux to watch Theo, he has never seen me or spoken with me. Why is this time different? He was brought to me and given a chance to save me. Why?

Could this finally be the opportunity I've been waiting for? Could this be a sign from the fates that our time has come?

My heart races as I struggle with what to do next. If I tell him, he'd have to come back to Umbra with me so we could find an antidote for the elixir Oren and Leopold gave him all those years ago. After the veil is lifted from his mind, I'll figure out a way to explain Asher to him. I know our love is strong enough for him to understand our complicated marriage.

I tilt my chin down, stopping Theo's kisses along my neck. Leaning back, I stare at him again, trying to talk myself out of telling him the truth. He looks at me and the smile on his face laces with uncertainty.

"What is it?" He asks, scanning my face.

My heart flutters as I take him in. In all my dreams, I never imagined I would be here with Theo and believing we still have time left together in this lifetime. I draw in a breath, trying to calm myself before I take the biggest gamble of my life.

"Theo," I start cautiously, "It's me. It's Lily," I say hesitantly, not wanting to scare him.

His eyebrows pinch together.

"How do you know that name?" He asks, taking a step back.

I drop my arms from his waist, letting him have space.

"I know it doesn't make any sense, but I can explain. The day in the meadow, Oren stabbed me with a trove blade. It only made it appear as though I was dead," I say, as Theo's face twists in confusion.

He backs away from me until his legs bump into the end of the bed.

"No. That's not possible. How do you know any of that?" His voice trembles.

I reach up and unwind the cloth from my hair. The curls bounce as I release them from the fabric, and he squints. His furrow deepens as he blinks several times.

Gods, please let this be a sign that his memory is trying to break free.

He shakes his head, refocuses his eyes, and tries to step back abruptly, stumbling and falling into the bed.

"Theo, it's really me. It's Lily. Your flower, remember?" I whisper as I slowly walk toward him.

He shakes his head aggressively before dropping his head into his hands. Taking a seat next to him on the bed, I reach out to comfort him. He flinches as my hand touches his arm, and he jerks away from me.

"You can't be her. You can't be my Lily. I'd recognize my flower. You're not her. She's dead," his voice grows adamant.

His eyes are wet with unshed tears and his whole body is shaking. I scoot away from him and notice he's rubbing his temples. Something's not right. The elixir shouldn't cause a physical reaction to memories trying to be unveiled. Over the years, I have learned what I can about potions, elixirs, and tonics. I had hoped my research would lead me to the antidote on my own, but whatever they used was different.

I've only come up with one ingredient I believe is in the mix. A rowanberry elixir is a colorless, flavorless liquid that can cloud a person's memory if there are things they need to forget. But it only works on short term memories, and I've never seen it cause anyone pain. The remaining unknown ingredients must have a tight hold on his mind to cause this type of reaction.

Theo groans as he holds his head.

"Are you ok, Theo? What's wrong?" I ask, fighting the urge to reach out and comfort him.

"My head. It feels like someone's trying to rip it open," he answers through gritted teeth.

His back muscles flex under his shirt as his entire body seems to tense in pain.

"Let me get you some water. Maybe that will help," I say, not knowing how to fix the agony I've caused him.

My stomach rolls as I stand from the bed to grab his mug.

Why did I have to be so selfish and tell him the truth? I should have known the fates wouldn't make this easy for me.

I pour a mug of water for Theo but pause when my eyes find my bag. I always bring various potions and elixirs with me to get me out of any trouble that might find me on my travels. Reaching into my bag, I pull out a small vial of rowanberry. My heart grows heavy as I uncork the top and swirl a few drops of the clear elixir into the mug. Theo groans loudly, and I know I have no choice. It's the right thing to do, but my heart may never recover from all of this. Forgetting tonight is the only way to ease his pain.

I thought this was my chance to finally have my Amari and be happy. But I should have known. In the end, there will only be darkness and pain for me.

Turning around, I take a seat beside Theo again and offer him the mug of water. He's in too much pain to protest and takes the mug with shaky hands. I sit quietly by his side as he drains the mug of every drop. The effects are almost instant. Theo's eyes become heavy, and his blinking slows.

"Wh ... what's going on?" He asks in mild confusion as the memories start to fade.

"Shhhh," I offer in a comforting tone, "you had too much ale at the tavern. Come lie down and rest your head on my lap. You need to sleep it off."

I take a seat against the headboard. Theo turns and crawls up the bed, accepting my explanation. He curls up next to me and places his head in my lap. I thread my fingers into his hair, playing with it. The silky soft strands caress my skin as I massage his head. He releases a sigh from deep in his chest as his body relaxes into mine.

"My mother used to do this when I needed comfort," Theo says softly.

"Hmmm," I answer, my heart beginning to crack. *I know.* "Did she sing to you too?" I ask, hoping to fill his mind with pleasant memories of his mother as he drifts off in my arms for the last time.

"I don't remember her singing," he says with a yawn.

My instincts flare. What happened to his memories of her songs? She was always singing. If anyone could recall them, it would be Theo. Her sweet voice used to carry down the hall, filling the castle with its lovely sound.

Another loud yawn comes from Theo. I gently lift his head and help him lie on the pillow. I brush his hair back and trace a finger down to his jaw.

"Sleep, my knight. In the morning, you'll have more princesses to save," I say quietly as he fights to keep his eyes open.

His light snores confirm that the rowanberry has fully set in, and he'll be out until the late morning. When he wakes, he will feel as if he drank too much ale but otherwise unharmed. His memories of our night will be a blur, and he won't be able to recall any details about me. I'll be long gone before then, leaving no trace of myself behind.

Sitting up on the edge of the bed, I remove my boots, setting them on the floor. I walk over and remove Theo's as well, placing them by the door as if he had taken them off when he came into the room.

I climb back into bed with him and pull the rough blanket up around us.

"Goodbye, Theo. May the fates decide I'm worthy of you and bring you back to me. It has always been you and will always be you," I say as the first tears slide down my cheeks.

The words cut deep as I say them out loud, and I allow myself to cry softly in the dark where no one can see. I was a fool to think the fates would bless me with a happy ending when all I've known for ten years is pain and destruction.

I fall asleep to the soft sound of Theo's breathing and the feel of his body touching mine.

I wake in the morning as the sun is cresting the landscape, painting the sky in light blues and purples. Theo is still sleeping soundly beside me. Rising from the bed, I take a seat in a chair and put on my boots, tucking my knife inside.

Walking over to Theo, I brush his hair off his forehead, and he smiles in his sleep as if enjoying a delicious dream. The smell of cedar fills the air around him. I study his face, trying to memorize every inch. I place a light kiss on his cheek as more tears streak mine.

"Always. Until my last breath, I am yours, and I will keep you safe. Look for me in the shadows," I say, wishing a part of him could hear me and remember who I am.

I step quietly out of the room and take a deep breath of the fresh morning air, trying to stop the sobs from escaping. It's what is best for him. He deserves a good woman to share his light, not a monster of the dark.

Knowing that I'm right doesn't lessen the pain of my shattered heart. I knew this would hurt, but it feels like a knife ripping apart my soul. I want to run away—to drive my body fast and far before it collapses. Maybe then the ache will fade.

I take another deep breath and start to make my way back to Amelia's to gather my things. The village is still quiet, with a few of the shop owners starting to make their way to work. There is the smell of bread from the bakery wafting on a breeze and the clicking of shoes on the cobblestones. The air is still cool from the evening, causing me to shiver.

I walk through the door of Amelia's home several minutes later, in better control of my emotions. I gather some clothes and head to the bathing chamber to change. A pitcher of water is already by the basin, and a clean cloth is set beside it. I'm going to miss

Amelia's thoughtfulness. I don't have many genuine friends, but I consider her to be one of them.

Freshening up quickly, I dress in my travel clothes: a pair of black trousers, a black short-sleeved blouse, and a black corset vest. It feels good to be partially back in my usual attire. I left the rest of my blades and gear in Fati, along with my horse Midnight, under the care of a farmer and his family, who were more than happy to take the extra coin.

I walk out of the bathing chamber to find Amelia sitting at the table waiting on me. There is a smile on her face, but tears in her eyes. I go to her with my arms outstretched and pull her into a tight embrace. Amelia sobs into my shoulder, and I struggle to hold back my own tears.

While we can write letters as we always have, the thought of never seeing her again hurts. I hope one day I can come back. But until then, I'll deeply miss my friend.

"I wish you didn't have to go, V," Amelia says into my shoulder.

"Me too. But we both know I can't pass up an opportunity to make good money at the vineyard," I say into her hair.

We pull apart and hold hands in the space between us.

"I know, but it doesn't make it feel any less like I'm losing you forever," she says in a broken voice.

I close my eyes and nod, unable to offer words that will lessen this heartache.

"Plus, I won't get to see if anything comes of you and Captain Kincaid," she says, and I can hear the smile on her face without even seeing it.

I open my eyes to see her smiling mischievously.

"It was one night of fun," I say, shoving her shoulder playfully.

"Whatever you want to tell yourself," she replies with a giggle.

Our tears dry up and the moment feels lighter.

"Are you at least going to tell me how amazing he was?" She asks, raising her eyebrows.

I won't be sharing that with anyone, even if it is absolutely true.

"A lady doesn't kiss and tell, Amelia!" I reply with fake outrage.

"You would have to be a lady for that to be true, and we both know we are far from lady quality," she says jokingly.

We both start laughing and the tension in the air dissipates.

"I better head out now before the portal gets too busy with the morning transports," I say, giving her hands a squeeze.

"I've packed you a few things for your trip," she says, releasing my hands and heading to the counter where a bag is sitting.

Accepting the bag, I open and inspect its contents. She has packed me a variety of fruit, dried meats, nuts, and bread, as well as a canister of water. Again with her thoughtfulness. A prick jabs at my heart.

"Thank you for this, Amelia. Thank you for everything," I say, bringing my gaze back to hers, feeling tears forming in them anew.

Her eyes reflect mine as we both try to hold back. She gives me a little nod, and we take deep breaths to push the emotions down.

Checking the common-space for any missed items, I put my boots back on and head to the door. Giving Amelia one last hug, I squeeze her as tight as I can, and she returns the gesture.

"I will write as soon as I get settled, I promise," I say before releasing her.

"I know you will. Or I will come to hunt you down in Fati," she says with a wink.

A part of me doesn't doubt she would do just that. We both smile at the sentiment, and I leave Amelia's for the last time.

I walk the cobblestone path out of the village, winding my way back past the small homes just inside the boundary wall. The air is warming with the rising sun, and I can tell it is going to be another hot summer day in Omnia. I'm ready for autumn and its refreshing cool days. The smell of wood burning is fresh in the air as the villagers wake and start to make their meals.

I spy the guards at the gate, and I'm thankful Jonathan is not among them. Two guards I have not seen before are there, and I breathe a sigh of relief as I walk by.

The portal of Lux is a short walk down a gravel path away from the wall. After each god claimed their own kingdom, they gifted the land with portals to allow their people to travel. Each portal is different and correlates with the land it is tied to. There are two portals for each kingdom, one above and one below in Fati. The portals always look identical and appear as mirror images.

For Lux, both portals are made of gray stone, like the rest of the kingdom that matches the mountains. The stones are stacked atop one another, forming a full circle. All a traveler must do is pay the toll and step through to go between the lands of Fati and the kingdom above.

The guards managing the portals today are in foul moods—rushing people in and out without concern for their safety. It is a chaotic scene, everyone pushing and shoving to comply with the demanding guards. I shuffle through the crowd when I spot an elderly woman losing her footing, falling to the gravel below. She hits the ground hard, and I see her face twist in pain.

I rush to help her, but I'm blocked by one of the angry guards.

"Get up, you stupid woman! You're blocking the way!" He shouts at her but doesn't help.

She struggles to get her feet under her on the loose gravel. Blood from scratches trickles down her arms and legs.

"Are you going to help her up or stand there and be useless?" I say to the guard, matching his tone.

Anger flares through me at the lack of moral decency. The darkness within me circles the enclosed well at my core, wanting to teach this pathetic man a lesson.

He turns to look for the mortal who dares to speak to him that way as I come up behind him. I recognize him as one of the two other guards from last night. One I never got the name of, but also wouldn't remember if I had. He flinches at the sight of me and looks around as if Theo is with me.

"Well, which is it?" I spit the words at the incompetent guard who just stares at me, trying to look intimidating, but he must be too worried his captain is going to hurt him as he did Jonathan.

I clench my fists at my side, fighting the urge to punch him.

Instead, I shove past him and help the poor woman to her feet. She's unsteady as we walk away, and I help her toward the portal. All the while, the guard stares at me with rage contorting his face.

They don't like viators in Lux, but they know they're the ones doing the work their villagers deem beneath them. They need viators, otherwise their kingdom would crumble. Each piece of the pattern must fit perfectly, or it all comes crashing down. Viators are one of those pieces, whether or not the other kingdoms like it.

The woman thanks me graciously for coming to her rescue. It's nice to be the hero for once. My nature has always been to help others, but that has been suppressed for so long that I have grown accustomed to the darkness. I know who I've become and whom I'm tethered to. My soul forever tarnished by the horrors I've been forced to inflict.

I pay the hefty crossing fee and step through the portal to emerge on the other side in Fati. I look up at Lux hovering in the sky above my head. My eyes trace the columns of stone tethering

Lux to Fati. Umbra and Terra each have similar columns tying them to the land below.

Goodbye, Theo.

I can only hope that, with distance, the heartache will ease slightly and maybe by the time I am back in Umbra, it will be a dull ache versus the sharp one I feel now.

I follow the crowd of viators down the gravel path and further into Fati. This forgotten land is so different from the other kingdoms. The harsh terrain has massive plateaus that jut up toward the sky, large enough to be new kingdoms of their own. The land was left to waste after their god died and took their power with them.

Small family farms scatter the land near the portal, with vineyards spreading out beneath Lux. Far in the distance, the tall, green stalks of corn with their golden yellow tassels sway in the breeze.

I make it to the farm that holds my horse and supplies. The same gentleman I met when I arrived, the owner, greets me with a nod. He offers no pleasantries, and his face is all business.

As I get a closer look at him, it looks as if he has aged a few years over the past week. I am hoping Midnight isn't responsible for this man's worn out look. But I know Midnight has, put lightly, a unique temperament.

"Is your horse a beast of the Underrealm or was he created by Thalos himself?" The man says with annoyance and frustration.

"Both, maybe? I'm not entirely sure where he came from," I reply with a shrug.

The man huffs at my response and turns toward the stable without another word. I silently follow, fearing he will double his asking price after dealing with my horse for a week. I'm already paying him double the normal rate, but I needed to secure his silence. I don't need anyone to find out I am here. Specifically, a very nosy, uptight Umbra general.

Before we even reach the stable, I can hear Midnight squealing and roaring through the doors. His large hooves stomp the ground inside, causing the entire structure to vibrate. I push past the man and swing open the stable doors to find Midnight looking livid. There are no people in the stable, and it appears the family has moved their horses down several stalls to avoid interaction with my wild stallion.

Midnight's jet-black eyes meet mine as I step through the doors. He huffs at me and continues to pace his stall, scraping his hooves on the ground. Dirt flies in the air, creating a fine mist to be visible in the sunlight coming through the doors.

"What's wrong, Midnight?" I ask, reaching to stroke his snout.

He snorts and pulls his face out of reach.

If I were anyone else, I, too, would be terrified of this feral horse. He's night incarnate. With a black, velvety coat and a long, onyx mane, he looks like a walking shadow. He is a massively powerful horse, standing over six and a half feet tall at the withers. Warlanders in Umbra are bred for speed, power, and agility. And Midnight has those in droves.

Even as a foal, Midnight gave the trainers a run for their money. He never listened to anyone but me. The first time our eyes met, I swear I felt a thread pull tight inside me. I think he did too because his eyes softened. Oren hated that Midnight would only listen to me, which only made me love the horse more. We were unified in our defiance against Oren.

By the way he is pacing, I know he is mad at me for not taking him on my quest into Lux this time. He always goes with me when I travel to the other kingdoms, but this time there wasn't a place I could keep him for so long. Hence, why he's making such a giant commotion and has been terrorizing this poor family.

I stretch out my palm again to nuzzle his snout, but he snorts again, as if disgusted by the gesture.

"You know I would have taken you if I could. This was the only option this time, Midnight," I say to him as he stomps the ground, kicking more dust into the air.

"Fine, be mad at me. Guess I won't be sharing my snacks with you then," I say teasingly.

He freezes at the word *snacks* and relaxes his rigid body.

"Are you ready to go home?" I ask, opening his stall door.

Midnight lets out a loud sigh.

"Yeah, me too, buddy. Let's go so we can sleep in our own beds tonight," I say as I grab his reins and saddle from the side wall.

He allows me to put both on him, and I lead him out of the stable without issue.

When we step out, the gentleman stares at me slack jawed, and I'm reminded how big of an ass my horse has been over the week. Thankfully, we won't be needing accommodations again soon because this man will never let him come back.

Without exchanging words, I give the man the final payment and gather the rest of my supplies. I strap my blades to my legs and into the hidden slots in my vest.

I palm my favorite dagger, happy to have it back on my body. The silver hilt catches the first rays of the sun, causing the red marquise gemstones on the cross-guard and pommel to sparkle. I run a careful finger along the edges of the large red gemstone in the middle of the hilt. The black blade is still sharp, ready to slice through any trouble that comes our way. The etching down the fuller gleams with the sunlight.

As I examine my dagger, my heart aches for the man who gave it to me. Tobias Davey was the kind-eyed general in Oren's army and was more of a father to me than my own. Tobias did everything he could to keep me alive through Oren's torture. We lost him three years ago while he and Oren were on a secret quest in Fati. Oren made it back to Umbra before dying from his injuries, but we never could find Tobias' body to give him a proper burial. Our best guess is that whatever attacked them took Tobias with it.

Tobias gifted me the beautiful, rare dagger on the summer equinox. Afterward, he would hide it for me, so Oren wouldn't take it away. Now, I'm never without it unless I have to be, and I have missed it this past week. I slide it into its rightful place on my right thigh and then swing my sword across my back.

Pulling myself atop Midnight, I turn to see the man standing with a young girl. I give them both as warm of a smile as I can muster. The little girl grins up at me.

"You look like a warrior queen," she says with glee, like she has never seen a queen ready for battle.

I look down at her, "That's because I am."

I give her a wink and set off on the journey back home. Back to Umbra. Back to my kingdom and my king.

CHAPTER 6

THEO

I wake up to pounding on the door and in my head.

Gods, where am I, and why do I feel like a carriage has run me over?

I press my palms into my eyes to counteract the pain shooting through my skull. Nope, that doesn't help.

The knocking at the door continues.

"Open up!" A man's voice yells from the other side. I finally glance around the room and realize I am at the Aurora Inn.

How in the realm did I get here?

I storm over to the door, begging for the hammering to stop. My limbs feel as though they are being weighed down with stones. Every part of my body hurts.

How much did I have to drink last night?

I swing open the door to find an old man with his fist raised, ready to knock on the door again.

"What do you want?" I shout, the sound sears my ears, causing them to ring.

The abrupt light from opening the door burns my eyes, causing a wave of nausea to roll through my stomach.

The man, the inn keeper, I assume, stares at me, his mouth falling open.

"Umm … ah … Captain Kincaid. I didn't know you were in here. I thought … never mind. I will let you be, but checkout is soon," he stammers.

He seems genuinely shocked by my presence, so I must not have been the one to check in here last night.

"What time is it?" I ask gruffly.

I need to find a physician or healer to help with this pain pulsating behind my eyes.

"It's after eight in the morning, sir," he says timidly.

Shit.

Morning training starts soon and if I'm late, I'll be subjected to more disappointed lectures from my father.

Too preoccupied with my predicament, I close the door on the inn keeper without another word.

What happened to me last night and why does my head feel so fuzzy? I rack my mind, trying to figure out my last memory, but everything feels as if it's hidden within a fog and muffled. I can only recall a ghost-like figure standing before me with no distinguishing elements.

I push my palms into my eyes again and run my hands through my hair. A sharp sting on the back of my hand causes me to wince and look down to see it covered in cuts and bruises. Did I punch someone or something last night?

Gods, I really need to get my head on straight.

I go to the table and down the last of the water straight from the pitcher. There are two mugs that look like they have been drunk out of, which means someone else was here with me. I examine both sides of the bed. It is evident that someone had slept beside me. Leaning down to smell the pillow, I get a whiff of ale and maybe a hint of flowers, but it is hard to tell.

Please, gods, don't tell me I brought a woman here last night.

I shake my head at the thought because it is ridiculous. I have been in a dry spell for months. Or has it been a year?

Shit, it has been way too long.

Dragging my hands across my face, I head to the door, take a seat in a chair, and slip on my boots. I double-check the room to ensure I have everything and head out the door to return the key.

After stopping by the office, I make my way to the apothecary. I hurry down the cobblestone path and people part as they see me approaching. The upside of being the captain is most villagers either respect or fear you enough to get out of your way.

Entering the apothecary, I find a woman not much older than me at the counter. The smell of the shop is a potent mix of herbs, plants, and perfumes. Bile creeps up my throat and I fight to swallow it down.

The woman looks up, and her light-hazel eyes go wide at the sight of me in her shop. I really need to get out more if every person who sees me has the same reaction.

I step up to the counter so she can hear me clearly.

"I'm looking for something to help with a horrible headache. Can you help?" I say before her jaw hits the floor.

She blinks rapidly before responding.

"Umm ... possibly. Can you describe the pain to me? When did it start, and do you recall anything that may have caused it? Were you hit on the head, or did you fall?" She spits out rapid-fire questions, grabbing an ink pen and paper to take notes.

"It's a throbbing, sharp pain in the front of my head, behind my eyes. I don't think I fell, but I remember little from yesterday. I had a few drinks, but I don't believe I had enough to warrant this kind of pain. Everything is very hazy," I say, rubbing my temples.

She eyes me and worry etches her face.

She scribbles a few things down, but I can't read through the blur setting into my vision. If she can't help me, I'll have to go to the physician in the castle for aid. If I can even make it back to the castle, that is. My head feels as though a sword has cleaved my skull wide open and embedded itself into my mind.

"I think I know just the thing to help you, Captain Kincaid. I'll be right back," she says while heading to the back counter to mix ingredients together.

A few minutes later, she turns to me with a bright smile on her face. She sets down a bottle of an oddly green-colored solution swirling with black and yellow flakes.

"Here you go!" She exclaims excitedly.

I eye the vial suspiciously.

"I promise it is a mixture of herbs and plants. Nothing that will harm you, Captain," she says quickly after noticing my hesitancy.

"It has black bitterweed, mountain blood, and honeypalm. All ground together and diluted in water. The flavor may be bitter, but it should quickly reduce your symptoms," she says reassuringly.

I take the vial from the counter, uncork it, and throw back the liquid. She is right, it's very bitter and burns as it goes down.

"Thanks. I really appreciate it. How much do I owe you?" I ask, looking down to pull a few coins from my satchel, which doesn't feel much lighter than when I headed out yesterday.

Did I let a woman pay for a room at the inn?

I really need to get my shit together and figure last night out.

When I bring my attention back up to the woman, she holds her hands up in protest.

"Your money's no good here, Captain. Please take it as a gift from a simple shop owner, thankful to help you in your time of need," she says warmly, looking truly appreciative of my presence in her shop.

"Well then, thanks again for helping me today. I'll tell others of your shop if they need your services," I reply, giving her a small nod.

She beams at me as if I've given her all the coins in the kingdom.

I turn and leave the apothecary to head back to my chambers and get ready for training. I need to hurry if I want to grab food as well. I quicken my pace and people rush out of my way as I jog through the village.

By the time I step into Brightwick, I'm feeling better. The throbbing in my head has reduced to a dull ache behind my eyes and my stomach grumbles. As I step through the doors, I spy one servant and stop her with a wave of my hand.

"Excuse me, would you be able to take some fresh water for bathing and some breakfast to my quarters for me? Quickly, though, I'm due at training shortly, but I'm starving," I request.

She looks a little taken aback to see me at the castle's entrance this early, and I don't blame her. I generally stay in my quarters unless on duty with the royal guard. She nods and hurries away.

I head down the stone halls toward the east-wing where my chambers are located. The castle is still cool. A slight breeze carries the smell of breakfast through the corridor: bacon, fresh bread, and a hint of sweetness, which, I assume, is a dessert being started for the day. My stomach rumbles again.

As I turn the corner that leads to my chambers, knocks echo off the gray stone walls, and I find my father at my doors.

Great, just what I need this morning.

I continue forward, trying and failing to come up with some excuse as to why I am not in my quarters at this hour.

"General," I shout from a few paces away. He stops mid-knock. Looking from side to side, he checks to see if there is someone else with me.

"Why are you not in your chambers?" He asks with narrowed eyes. I clench my jaw at his rough tone.

Why does it matter? I'm an adult and may come and go as I please.

But I know my father well enough to know that isn't the correct answer.

"I had a few errands to handle before training this morning," I reply, already wanting this conversation to be over.

His eyes are still narrow, telling me he doesn't believe my excuse.

"What do you want, father? I need to get around," I ask, stepping to my chamber doors to unlock them, forcing him to the side.

"I wanted to check in on how the new recruits were coming along," he replies while scratching his palm.

What are you really here for?

I learned at an early age how to determine if my father is being deceitful, and scratching his palm is his unmistakable tell.

"They are coming along fine, General. Same as all the recruits before them under my watch. They are being well trained, and all weaknesses corrected," I say, blocking my doorway to prevent him from entering.

His expression doesn't change. In the years I have been the captain, our guard has increased in talent and skill. I have made it my mission to have the best royal guard in all of Omnia, and I won't fail.

Before my father can respond, the servant girl and another arrive with my requests. He eyes them questioningly. I step aside, allowing them into my chambers, and thank them as they go. The girls hurry away as soon as their task is complete.

My father's face is a scowl when I look back at him, and I'm pretty sure it stays that way permanently, or at least when he's in my presence.

"If that will be all, General, I must be going now," I say curtly.

I wait until I'm given the approval to leave, and he gives it with a nod, then walks away.

Finally, alone, I sit down at my oak desk with my breakfast to get some bearings on this day. I grab a pen and paper to make a few notes while last night's memories, even though hazy, still linger in my mind.

I dig into the delicious breakfast of eggs, porridge with nuts, bacon, and bread. This is exactly what I need to help clear my head and restart this confusing day.

As I eat, I jot down everything I can remember. I recall having an ale with the men before Jonathan convinced us to go to The Blue Stag for a mug of their rumored chilled ale. Jonathan talked about a beautiful woman who would be working at the tavern. He described the disgusting things he was going to do to her, and I had to tell him to knock it off several times.

I know nothing beyond that. The entire evening is a mix of gray mist and shapeless dark shadows. I rub my temples, my headache returning from the concentration.

I head to my bathing chambers and strip off my filthy clothes before stepping into the filled tub. I make quick work of scrubbing clean with soap. The smell of cedar fills the air and makes me feel like myself again.

After drying off, I slip into the standard training uniform of undergarments, dark trousers, and a white shirt. Taking a seat on the bed, I pull on my boots, brush my fingers through my hair, still damp from my bath, and head out the door toward the training yard.

The grunts of my men filter toward me before I even open the yard doors, and my heart rate kicks up a beat. The thrill of training, of movement, causes my whole body to hum. As a child, I never expected to love being on the guard as much as I do. I hated it for a long time as it reminded me of my father, and I never wanted to be like him: cold and distant. But that is who he is. It wasn't a result of his duty.

In the training yard, there are several new recruits paired with our more seasoned guards. They are sparring and going through various maneuvers as instructed over the past several weeks. I assess the yard, ensuring everyone is practicing as they should be.

"There you are," Nathaniel's deep-toned voice calls from my left.

I pivot and watch him walk toward me.

"I was worrying about you," he says with a knowing smile on his face.

I wonder if he could tell me what happened last night, but I'm unsure of how to ask without letting him know I have no memory. I never know which side of Nathaniel I'll be interacting with. He can go from my loyal lieutenant to a man I don't recognize at any given moment. And it's hard to know what will set him off.

"I'm fine. Just overslept. Thanks for getting everything started for the day," I say as he steps to me.

As my lieutenant, it is his duty to act in my absence, and it's good to see he did so without hesitation.

"Not a problem, Captain. I wasn't sure you would make it to training this morning. I figured you would be recovering from a wild night with your new lady friend," he says with a wink.

Well, that confirms it then. I took a woman to the inn last night.

Why didn't I bring her to Brightwick? I finally get laid, and I can't remember it.

I hope I didn't embarrass myself. I really don't need word getting around that I'm terrible in bed. Not like my sex life could get much worse. Hard to have one when you've been pining over a dead girl for a decade.

I furrow my brows, and Nathaniel cocks his head to the side.

"I saw her leaving through the portal at dawn, you know? She caused quite the scene. She's a feisty one. I hope her mouth was as hot as it is nasty," he says, smirking.

I flinch at the statement.

"What do you mean?" I ask, and he looks at me pensively, unsure if he should tell me what happened.

"There was an issue with one viator. A woman was on the ground blocking the path and was taking too long to get up. I was telling her to move when your lady friend started yelling at me," he recounts.

She was yelling at a royal guard? What kind of woman would do that?

Nathaniel strokes his chin, as if thinking hard, "What did she call me again? Useless. She called me useless," he says with a huff of annoyance.

I can't hide my shock to learn of her brazenness, and I'm not sure how to feel. Her apparent lack of respect for authority disgusts a part of me, but another part of me wants to learn more about a woman brave enough to stand up for others.

Honestly, I would have paid good money to see someone call my lieutenant useless. I try to stifle a laugh, but it doesn't work. Nathaniel fakes an offended pout.

"I'm kind of shocked you ended up with her last night. She didn't seem like your type. She was fierier than your usual pick," he says.

I don't disagree, but since I can't remember her, it's hard for me to know for sure. Her sharp tongue is not usually my type, but then again, I haven't dated enough to know what my type is exactly.

I scratch at my jaw, unsure how to ask the next question, noticing the stubble I'll need to shave off later.

"I actually remember little of last night, or yesterday," I say.

Nathaniel looks taken aback by my admission.

"Gods, Theo, how much did you have to drink?" He seems concerned.

I'm not sure. Two ales could have affected me, considering I'm not a big drinker.

"I don't know that either. Everything from yesterday is fuzzy, especially after we left for the tavern with Jonathan," I say, rubbing the back of my neck.

Nathaniel looks as if he is about to fall over.

"So, you don't remember punching Jonathan in the face?" He says skeptically.

I did what now? He probably deserved it.

I shake my head.

Nathaniel lets out a small laugh.

"You know? That kind of makes sense. You were exceptionally smooth last night while talking to the barmaid. She was putty in your hands all evening. And even as a viator, she was way out of your league. It had to have been liquid courage," he says.

I have never been called smooth in my life. I've been too hung up on the loss of my flower ten years ago to ever learn how to flirt with women.

"Could you tell me what happened? Everything is fuzzy. I woke up with a horrible headache and needed to get a potion from the apothecary to ease it," I ask, hoping Nathaniel continues his agreeable mood.

Luckily, Nathaniel feels talkative and tells me about the events from last night, ending with him hauling Jonathan out of The Blue Stag before I could kill him for his actions. I was right, though. He deserved to be punched. Sadly, it's not surprising that he put his hands on a woman who didn't consent to it. I'm thankful I was there to step in before he did anything worse.

Entertaining as it is, the story doesn't jog my memory, and now I have to come up with a punishment for Jonathan. This is shaping up to be a disaster of a day.

"Thanks for filling in the blanks. Now I need to figure out what happened after you left me alone with the barmaid," I say, getting frustrated by this situation.

Nathaniel wiggles his eyebrows at me.

"We both know what happened after I left, memory or not," he says, shoving me playfully.

I smile weakly. While I hope we ended the night tangled in each other's bodies, I don't want to assume something happened if it didn't.

"Come on. Let's get to training. Maybe the movement will help clear my head and my memories will come back," I say, motioning for Nathaniel to follow so we can get the day started.

Nathaniel and I head to an open sparring ring. I allow myself one more thought about the barmaid before getting lost in my role as captain of the guard for the rest of the day.

CHAPTER 7

Midnight and I race across Fati, quickly putting distance between us and the Lux Kingdom. The wind stings my face as Midnight pushes hard to get us home in record breaking time.

We ride through the forests along the foothills of the fractured mountain range. The smell of pine and aspen washes over me as we go. Stopping briefly when the sun is at its peak, we rest near the once-mighty river that bends with the rolling landscape.

As I sip cool, crisp water, I take in the scenery around us, trying to imagine what the realm would look like if the gods had never fought and cleaved the land apart. Gods so overcome by their own desires for power that they couldn't see the damage they were doing until it was too late.

The gods and mortals are not so different at their core: both willing to destroy anything that stands between them and the power they believe is rightfully theirs. As much as it hurts, I'm glad I was able to make Theo forget. Leopold can never know of my slip-up.

In a moment of weakness, I risked everything I've been trying to avoid for years. I put Theo in harm's way. But the chance to finally be with him was too hard to pass up. I should have just been content watching from the shadows and ensuring that Leopold was still holding up our deal.

You want to make a deal, Oren? Fine, I will make one under these conditions: as long as there is life in my body and air in my lungs, you will not harm Theo or anyone else I love. Never again. And Leopold? That includes Juniper. You will protect them at all costs, as if it were me watching over them. Only then do we have a deal.

I tighten my grip on Midnight's reins as the memory invades my mind, and I fight to shove it deep down. The darkness swirls at my core with the reminder of the night it was unleashed. Thalos' black, vacant eyes slicing into my soul as his voice echoed in my mind. The darkness invading every part of my being. Ripping into my muscle and bone—tearing it apart and knitting it back together with its own essence woven between each fiber.

A chill up my spine causes me to shiver. I focus my attention on the land stretched out before us. The sun sets through the tree line ahead, painting the sky in striking shades of pink and orange. The black shadows of Umbra become clearer as we rush toward the portal.

Breaking out of the forest, I finally lay eyes on my kingdom after a week away, and my heart warms at the sight. It looms high above, beneath thick swirling shadows.

The lore in Omnia is that when Thalos pulled Umbra into the sky, he veiled it in his darkness to hide its beauty. It is said he did so to protect his people from the other gods, fearing their hunger for power would destroy his land. In the end, he wasn't wrong, it just didn't happen in our kingdom.

Through the years, Umbra's divinus helped to cultivate the legends of the land and heighten the dangers of the shadow kingdom, ensuring no one dared to visit. The monsters in the forests and beasts in our water add to the fear factor.

One long black tendril spirals around the column of stone as I near, as if welcoming me home. I smile at the thought. It hasn't always been my home, but it is now. It's mine and Asher's to protect. I'm the judge, while Asher acts as executioner.

Waterfalls plummet from the edge of the land above and collide with the river below. The portals to Umbra are undulating vortexes of water that look like they will swallow you whole in their overwhelming current. Believing you are about to be drowned by stepping through the portals prevents many from trying to cross.

There is one guard standing watch at the portal, which is mainly to provide my people with a sense of ease. Only the villagers of Umbra, or those with nothing to lose, use our portal—brave souls daring to risk it all in the land of beasts and monsters.

The guard spots me and stands at full attention.

"Good evening, Marcus," I say, looking down at my guard.

Midnight stops in front of him, and Marcus drops into a deep bow.

With an arm over his chest, Marcus says, "My queen. Welcome home."

Home indeed.

Midnight huffs as we push toward the portal entrance. I have to force him into it, and he calms as we step through the other side. The captain of my guard, Hiram, is waiting for me. He smiles at me from atop his own tan Warlander. Hiram's brown eyes are a warm and familiar sight.

As he bows at the waist with an arm across his chest, Hiram says, "We're so happy you have returned to us safely, my queen."

I roll my eyes at his statement but smile back at him. We both know I can handle myself.

"I'm happy to see you too, Hiram," I say as he returns to an upright position.

"How was your quest?" Hiram asks, and I take a moment to contemplate how to respond.

I can't say outright what I did or whom I saw. That would cause too many questions.

"It went well. Only time will tell if the information I gathered is worthwhile."

Not exactly a lie, but a clear sign I don't want to speak further on the subject. Hiram takes the hint.

"Let's head back to The Keep. I had Pyke save you a plate, and it's keeping warm near the hearth," Hiram says.

My stomach rumbles at the prospect of a meal from my cook.

"I knew you were my favorite captain, Hiram," I say as I tap Midnight with my heels to get him moving.

We walk past Hiram and his horse.

"I'm your only captain, my queen," he says, and we both laugh as we head off toward The Keep.

The haunted forest separates the entrance to Umbra from the rest of the kingdom. It's a menacing, dark, thick grove of massive trees. The wide branches of the bloodwood trees overlap, preventing light from piercing the canopy to the ground below.

A heavy, knee-high layer of fog ripples across the forest floor. The trees ooze sap the color of rich, fresh blood. The trees alone cause trepidation, and many who have made it this far turn around running when they see them. But the real horror of the forest are the Cypres who have claimed it as their home. These shadow creatures have no known origin and kill intruders by flooding their minds with nightmares horrendous enough to cause death. Only those who prove themselves worthy to the Cypres can exit the forest and live another day.

The sounds of hooves on the gravel path ricochet off the forest, mixing with the noises of breaking branches and rustling leaves. A cold breeze cuts into me, and the hair on the back of my neck stands.

Large, black shadows skirt the edges of our periphery as we near the center of the forest. They circle around us, just out of sight, seeming to stalk their prey. The ominous feeling slowly closing in would cause most people's hearts to skip a few beats. But my heart thunders with excitement to see my creatures again.

We slow as the four shadows, partly hidden by the trees, stop in front of us. Climbing off Midnight, I hand the reins to Hiram and step into the small clearing at the center of the forest. The speckles of light peeking through the canopy allow the beasts to get a better look at who's traveling in their territory. At the sight of me, the four shadows shift into their physical forms, something they only do for me.

The first to sprint toward me is the black three-headed dog. She is taller than me, with paws that are larger than my head. Three long snouts with glowing yellow eyes, sharp elongated canines, and pointed ears atop muscular necks that merge into one powerful body make for an intimidating creature who turns into a puppy at my feet.

Each head greets me with a wet, sloppy lick across my cheeks, which I wipe away with my sleeve. I rub each head affectionately, being sure to scratch each neck like she loves.

"I missed you, too."

Next to approach is the serpent. Iridescent scales trail her body, creating a distractingly beautiful creature. She's at least twenty feet long in this form and has a girth wider than a tree trunk. If her size doesn't send a wave of terror straight through you, her multi-spiked morningstar tail will finish you.

She coils around my legs and up my body, putting the slightest hint of pressure on my skin. Her head comes to mine, and we touch our foreheads together. I place my hands on each side of her gigantic head, and I feel her deepen the embrace around my body. A tight hug letting me know she's happy I'm finally home. I pull back to look into her yellow eyes.

"I'm happy to see you as well."

The serpent rejoins the circle, and the hare is up next. Her round body, with gray and black fur, hops over to me. The top of her head reaches my chin, but her antlers extend three feet above her head, with prongs jutting out in all directions. She looks up at me with her yellow eyes, then leans into my chest to nuzzle softly while carefully avoiding taking out my eyes with her antlers.

I stroke her head tenderly and whisper to her, "I'm sorry I was gone so long."

Instinctively, I know she's missed me the most. My connection with her is stronger than with the others, causing my quests to affect her the hardest.

She hops away to rejoin her siblings, and I expect the final one to come to me. But she doesn't. She stares at me with the same glowing yellow eyes as her siblings. They're the distinct eyes of the Cypres. She has always been the most standoffish of the four beasts, but from the flicking of her curved scorpion tail, she, too, is happy to see me.

"Stop pretending you didn't miss me and get over here," I say.

She hesitates for a moment, wanting to continue the charade. She's always overdramatic. She strolls over to me, circling my body while rubbing her head along the way. She's the same height as the hare, and her black fur tickles my chin as she brushes against me.

I wrap my arms around her neck, pulling her close into a hug.

"You don't always have to play hard to get," I say playfully.

She leans into me, and my chest vibrates with her purr for a fleeting moment.

I release her and she saunters back to the other three. I smile at my creatures and give them a nod to show they are free to return to their shadow forms. They bow to me, and in the blink of an eye, they're nothing but black shadows.

Returning to Hiram and the horses, I climb back atop Midnight and take the reins. We return to our journey with the wind no longer chilling us. The Cypres remain on the edges of our vision until we are out of the forest.

On the other side is the spectacular sight of Umbra's realm-renowned waterfalls. The horseshoe falls form a semicircle in the onyx stone. A black stone bridge spans the width of the vast pool. Clear, blue water glistens in the moonlight as it descends from the brink high above.

The stars shine bright on this cloudless night, their twinkling reflected in the pools below. The smell of fresh water and rich earth permeates the air, warming my heart and calming my soul.

We approach the pool from which silvery-white, pupil-less eyes stare back at us, just above the surface. The nobu act as security to The Keep, safeguarding it from any would-be intruders.

Their large, scaly heads barely crest the water to peer at us. I walk to the edge, noticing the small ripples from the creatures vibrating with anticipation of a snack. I allow the shadows to seep from my hand as I place my palm on the surface, not breaking the tension. My dark power stretches out along the water, allowing the nobu to know I have returned. Through the black tendrils, I can feel their rough hide, abrasive and cool.

With a distinct *plop*, their beady eyes disappear under the water. Recalling my shadows, I watch as they disappear into my skin.

"I'm sure the long day of travel has exhausted you. Same with Midnight," Hiram says. Midnight lets out a loud whinny and moves his head in agreement. I smile and nod my head as well.

"I'll take Midnight back to the stable so you can head in to eat and get some sleep," Hiram says.

Climbing off Midnight, I pet his snout before handing the reins over to Hiram. Before taking them, he reaches an open palm out to me, revealing a simple dark metal ring.

"Welcome home, my queen," Hiram says with a bow.

I slide the adveho ring of Umbra back onto its rightful spot on my left hand. The lore states that the gods created the rings to allow their divinus to travel quickly between two locations. They act similarly to the portals by creating doorways to the location the wearer chooses. They are very powerful trove items, giving the wearer access to any place they can picture in their minds. I often leave mine with my general in case something happens while I am away, opting to travel like a viator on the back of a horse. I know how dangerous the item can be in the wrong hands.

The metal of the ring is warm against my skin. King Oren was notorious for collecting and destroying trove items. He ensured he was the only mortal who could use the adveho power to appear anywhere he wanted. He claimed that he did this for Umbra's protection, but I know better. He used this item as a bargaining chip to hold over anyone he wanted to control. Now that he's dead, King Asher and I truly use it to protect our kingdom. I warn Midnight to behave, and thank Hiram as he leads the horses back to the stables. I turn to admire the powerful and beautiful waterfalls that tuck The Keep safely away within their stone. A secret castle hidden from outsiders.

The path into The Keep's front entrance is down a tunneled walkway on the other side of the pool. The onyx stone glistens in the moonlight as I make my way inside.

A black door hides within the stone. The etchings along the frame are only visible up close. Pushing it open, I step inside for the first time in a week. *Home at last.*

The Keep is quiet at this late hour. The sound of my footsteps on the black stone ground echoes through the hallway. The faint sound of the rushing waterfalls thunders in the distance, as well as the occasional noise from the guards on duty.

Stepping through the large wood doors of the dining hall, I head straight for the hearth on the far side, where a low fire burns with a pot set nearby. The moon glows outside the tall windows of the hall, its light filling the space. I pass tables of various shapes and sizes set with mismatched chairs. A hodgepodge of sorts, much like my kingdom. The sprawling serving table set right inside the large walnut entry doors allows for community-style meals.

A note addressed to me sits on the walnut mantel of the hearth. Inside the note reads,

Your Majesty, welcome home. I made one of your favorite meals to honor your return to us. I also prepared your favorite dessert and left it in the chilled box. Your faithful cook, Pyke.

Gods, I could kiss him. My people are always kind, but Pyke is another level of care and understanding. I would starve without him. Ok, maybe not starve, but I wouldn't enjoy eating as much as I do.

Opening the pot, I instantly drool as the scent of spices and herbs hits me and a delicious meal of salmon with potatoes and roasted vegetables in a buttery sauce with garlic, onions, and herbs is revealed. I take a seat at a nearby table to dig in. I moan a little as the flavors explode across my tongue.

I devour my bowl and quickly wash my dishes in the kitchen sink. I snatch my dessert from the chilled box. A sweet custard tart piled high with strawberries, blueberries, and cherries.

Sugar and honey coat the top. The balance of sweet and tart complement the fruit, creating a delectable treat to end any meal.

I devour my dessert as I head to our apothecary. The familiar scent of herbs reaches me as I enter the shop to find Loma behind the counter. Loma and the other healers are the most invaluable assets to my crew. As the mercenaries of Omnia, villagers of other kingdoms hire us to do their dirty work. That could be threatening someone, stealing items, or killing someone. You never know what could happen on a quest, so having our healers close is essential.

Loma's long gray hair is half braided back, allowing it to flow down her back. Her light-hazel eyes rise from her task and a sweet smile warms her face. Without Loma, more jagged scars would mar my body from my time with Oren. My wounds were expertly healed by her gentle hand.

"Our queen has returned," she says brightly.

She walks around the counter, arms outstretched, and pulls me into a tight hug.

"What brings you in this late? You're not hurt, are you?"

She pushes off me, snatching my arms in her hands, and turns me side to side, inspecting for injuries.

"I'm not injured, Loma," I laugh at her theatrics. "I need a lady's tincture, please," I say, looking down, and I glance anywhere to avoid eye contact with her.

"Oh, you dirty girl," Loma answers, lightly pushing my shoulder.

My cheeks heat with embarrassment. I can't recall the last time I had to ask for one. I've found myself in the beds of beautiful women more often lately than that of men. Women smell and, frankly, taste better.

Finally, I look back at Loma, who gives me a playful smile and heads to the wall of vials. She plucks a small violet one off the shelf and hands it to me.

The lady's tincture is a well-guarded secret in Omnia. Many kings have tried to eliminate it entirely under the pretense of needing heirs. Since the ingredients and the creators are unknown, their attempts have failed.

"Thank you for this and your discretion," I try to give her a stern look, but I know it doesn't faze her.

"Your naughty exploits are safe with me, Lily," she replies. She pulls me in for another hug before allowing me to leave the apothecary.

I hurry down the hall, back to my chambers, ready to bathe and slide into my bed. After a few minutes, I enter my quarters and strip off my clothes as I walk to my bathing chamber, leaving a trail on the floor as I go. The candles in my quarters were lit earlier in anticipation of my return, casting a soft glow.

As I enter my bathing chamber, I notice bottles of different oils and creams set along the counter. Picking one up, I head over to the spigot on the wall over the large, deep-set bathing tub in the center of the chamber. I turn the dial and water rushes from the wall. Placing the stopper in the drain, I let the water rise before uncorking the vial and dumping it into the water. The scent of roses fills the air. My favorite.

One major perk of living in a land overflowing with water is you can use it, allowing easy access with pipes and channels. With the turn of a knob, you can have water on demand. Something the other kingdoms don't know about and can't imagine. We work hard to keep it a secret as it is a great resource that some might just kill for.

I climb into my tub excited to wash away the past week of grime and filth. My back stings as it touches the water, and I flinch before settling in. I close my eyes, and let the luxurious bath ease my tense muscles. Suddenly, the hair on the back of my neck rises, and I feel as though someone is watching me. I crack open an eye to find I'm alone.

My shadows respond and tingle in my palms: the king senses that the queen has returned.

After scrubbing my body and hair clean, savoring the feeling of being back in my space, I step out of the tub and glimpse my back in the full-length mirror. Long scratches cover my upper back from where the alley wall dug into it. The red lines crisscross with the white scars covering my back.

I slip into fresh clothes from my closet before flopping into my bed. It feels like a cloud is swallowing me whole. My heart aches as I close my eyes. I miss Theo, but at least I got to have him for one amazing night. I'll always remember the feel of his calloused hands tracing my body and his soft snores as he slept.

I allow myself to fall asleep thinking of Theo, knowing that in the morning it's back to a life where a king and queen must hide in the shadows.

I'm forcibly pulled out of my sweet dreams of Theo and the alley by a loud knocking on my door. Whoever dares to disturb my sleep is going to regret it. I haul myself out of bed and storm to the door, swinging it open with as much authority as one can while wearing just a shirt.

On the other side is Kira. Her golden-brown skin is darker than when I saw her last. The summer sun has done wonderful things to her complexion, causing it to become richer as it tans and little freckles dot her cheeks. Her chestnut-brown hair frames her face with pale-orange streaks. Her light-brown eyes scan over me before meeting mine.

It isn't hard to tell why I continuously find myself in her bed, getting lost in the feel of our bodies together for hours. She's breathtakingly beautiful. But she wants more than the orgasms I can offer her: a genuine relationship that can never happen. While I can find pleasure with any mortal of my choosing, I can never break my bind to the shadow king and give myself fully to anyone.

Kira's motives have always been a mystery to me, but the need for power has always felt like her hidden agenda. I assumed she had been using me for physical pleasure in order to gain the favor of the queen, until she professed her undying love for me. I knew I had to end things then.

Since I've stopped letting her into my bed, things have been off between us. It's hard to go from an intense physical affair back to friends. The lingering arousal from my dreams of Theo and the sight of her this early has my body wanting to reconsider my decision. Desire ripples through me as I remember how good her body felt against mine.

Her gaze turns sour.

"Nyx sent me to fetch you for training. He said you're late," Kira says, crossing her arms in annoyance.

"I'm the queen. I'm never late. Everyone else is early," I answer in a playful tone that doesn't land. "Tell him I'll be there shortly. I need to get dressed and grab breakfast," I say with a huff.

She looks at me from head to toe.

"Hmm, not training in your undergarments today,

then?" I give her a sly smile.

"Wouldn't that be a little distracting for you?" I wink, and she blushes.

I can't help but flirt with the stunning woman, even though I know I shouldn't.

Kira turns on her heels to start back down the hall.

"I'll let the general know. Oh, and, nice legs, my queen." She winks over her shoulder at me before walking away.

I hurry to dress in a simple pair of black trousers and a loose-fitting black top.

Pulling my hair up, I tie it tight with a cord at the top of my head. I slide on my boots and head out the door within minutes of Kira arriving at my quarters.

Stopping in the dining hall, I shove several strips of bacon into my mouth and grab two biscuits to eat on the go. Pyke must have seen me run in because he hands me a warm mug of coffee to take with me. I thank him graciously for everything and rush out of the hall.

I push through the back door of The Keep, following the stone walkway in the creek, and step through the arch into the training field. Several of the crew are already sparring, their grunts and the crash of wooden practice swords fill the space. The air, still crisp from night, mixes with the mist from the waterfalls, keeping the yard cool into the late morning.

The guard of Umbra is mine to command—my brigade of warriors and spies to mold and train. Asher has never needed guards or help in any way. The dark shadow power he wields allows him to be an army of one. A last resort in desperate times.

As my feet touch the damp grass, I feel eyes burning into me. I snap my head up and meet the gray eyes of my general and best friend, Nyx Davey. I can see him clenching his jaw from across the yard.

What did I do?

He can't be that mad about me oversleeping. I had a long day yesterday.

I stare at him, shrug, and mouth, *"What?"* He walks toward me.

Great, just great. I love lectures in the morning.

His long legs eat up the distance between us at a rapid pace, and soon his towering figure is looming over me, blocking out the sun. I tilt my head back to look up at him properly. He's over half a foot taller than me, and the jerk is invading my space, making it uncomfortable to match his glare.

His olive-toned skin has darkened over the summer months, complimenting his black hair and accentuating his gray-blue eyes. If he weren't like a brother to me, maybe I would say he's handsome, but thinking of him in that way makes me want to vomit.

"Nice of you to finally join us, Your Highness," he says, crossing his arms, and I swear I see him puff out his chest. I don't even acknowledge it.

"What is with the attitude, General?" I bark back at him.

He is one of the only people who know my name. If he won't use it, I won't use his either. He uncrosses his arms and fists his hands at his sides.

"You're late, Lily," his words are clipped.

He can't really be mad at me for this right now.

"Seriously, Nyx? I traveled the entire day yesterday trying to make it back home. Sorry if that took a lot out of me and I overslept," I reply, taking a step back and trying to get distance from him, but he follows my step, remaining far too close.

"Besides, last time I checked," I look around the yard with exaggerated movement, "I'm the queen, and the most lethal warrior in all of Umbra. Gods, in all of Omnia! I think one day of missed training won't ruin me."

His eyes narrow into slits and he appears to be grinding his teeth.

"Training isn't just to keep you sharp. It's to show our crew you fight beside them both here and out on our quests. It isn't just about you, Lilith."

Damn. He got me there.

My shoulders sag, and I flop my head back in defeat.

"Fine. I'm sorry for being late, oh great general. It won't ever happen again," I say, and he relaxes his fists. "Unless I oversleep again, because we both know I like to sleep, so it's bound to happen," I joke.

I'm quick on my feet as Nyx lunges for me. I barely dodge his grasp, but when I do, I run to the table of practice swords, laughing the whole way. Nyx recovers and chases after me with an evil grin plastered across his face, which tells me this sparring session is going to be brutal.

I pick up a sword from the table and spin into a defensive stance, ready for whatever blows he's going to lay on me. I continue to walk backward, away from the table, never taking my eyes off Nyx. He grabs a sword of his own, twirling it in the air before securing a tight grip on the handle.

"Is this punishment for oversleeping or for being gone for a week without your knowing where I was?" I ask as we dance in a circle, each with our wooden blades ready for the first attack.

He tilts his head to the side.

"Why would I be punishing the dear queen for anything?" He answers in a mocking tone. "I'm merely the general of her guard. You know, whose entire life's purpose is to keep said queen from being harmed?"

He's always pissed when I leave, but this time I was gone longer, and I knew there would be payback when I returned.

Unexpectedly, Nyx starts to charge toward me like an out-of-control bull. I spin, narrowly escaping from his enormous body crashing into mine. I raise my sword, ready to deliver a blow to his side, but he blocks it.

We continue to battle in a flurry of strikes. The problem with training with the same person for ten years is that you know their moves just as well as your own. Neither of us lands any hits as we go back and forth until we are both panting. I bend with my hands on my knees, trying to catch my breath. Nyx is doing the same with his hands laced behind his head.

I huff, "We good? Got it all out of your system now?"

He doesn't answer me right away, seemingly thinking over the question and whether he wants to go a few more rounds to be sure he's done.

Thankfully, he nods and says, "Let's get some water."

We each grab a mug and gulp it down. I grab another and take a seat in the grass, resting my back on the cold, black stone. Nyx plops down beside me.

"What happened to your back?" He asks, and I choke on my water.

Shit.

Looking down at the ground, I stall, trying to gain as much time as possible to come up with a believable excuse. I lean my head back against the wall.

"I had a nightmare last night. I must have fallen out of the bed onto my back because when I came to, I was trying to crawl backward up the wall of my room," I lie.

I often have nightmares, so the lie isn't far-fetched. Anyone who has dealt with the pain and torture I have would have nightmares.

"Which one was it this time?" He asks, knowing me all too well.

I don't tell him all my nightmares. There are some things I don't even want to speak about.

"I can't remember. It felt like a few of them teamed up for one truly awful dream to welcome me back to Umbra properly," I reply as Nyx slowly nods his head in understanding.

I take the mug from Nyx and place both in a bin to take back in with us when we are done.

"Ready to do some actual training with the crew?" I ask, hitching a thumb toward our guards who are going through multiple stances in pairs.

"Yes, that sounds like a good plan," he answers, and we walk over to our crew.

As we near, they all pause and line up for our daily training exercises.

Their smiling, sweaty faces bring me joy I never thought I'd feel. My crew. My people—a group of misfits from all over the realm, here to defend the kingdom we all now call home. I lose myself in training for the rest of the day—a welcome distraction from the lingering pain in my heart.

CHAPTER 8

THEO

My heart pounds as air catches in my chest. A cold sweat covers my body while my hands remain warm, coated in her blood. My flower.

I shake my head, trying to change the sight before me, but it stays the same. Her frail body lies limp in my lap. I frantically brush the blood-soaked, red hair from her face, begging for those green eyes to open for me. But they never do. No matter how hard I try. Her curls remain plastered to her cooling skin, wet and shining.

Bright-red blood spreads out from her body, pooling around us. I couldn't save her. I let her die. Too weak to stop the man from driving the dagger into her over and over again.

Shouts ring in my ears as I let the tears fall, streaking through the blood splattered across my face. I scream into the storm raging above, wishing for the nightmare to end. She haunts my dreams, punishing me for failing her. She's constantly reminding me of how weak I once was. I'm sentenced to a life of never being able to see her face clearly again.

I jolt upright in bed as the shouts grow louder, and Nathaniel bursts through my chamber door.

"Someone broke into the castle and stole an item from the king's safe!" Nathaniel shouts through gasps for air.

I jump out of bed and quickly throw on clothes. My stomach twists into knots as panic floods my veins.

We rush from my chambers back to the main hall. The castle has erupted into chaos. My guards dart in different directions, lost to the fear of someone breaking into our home. My voice booms off the walls as I call for everyone's attention.

I get to work, assigning tasks to everyone and locking down Lux. Nathaniel maintains order within the castle while I lead four guards to the two gates outside. I leave them with direct orders to allow no one in or out until I or General Kincaid tell them to.

The echoes of shouted orders and thudding boots ring in the night air. I try to calm the anxiety retching my insides, but no amount of deep breathing is going to help.

I race back into the castle to find Nathaniel a few feet within its doors.

"Where is the general?" I ask.

"In the throne room with King Leopold. Good luck, Captain," he replies.

I turn on my heels and head toward the throne room on the other side of the hall. The door to the room is daunting on a normal day, but today it feels as though it will destroy me where I stand.

Pausing before the two ornate, solid-wood doors, I trace the scrolled details expertly carved to depict a scene of our goddess Astra, creator of Lux. Her long, flowing hair blows in the wind, billowing behind her as she raises mountains and cleaves rivers from the flat, untouched ground. Lightning shoots across the sky and strikes the new land below.

I take a deep breath and say a silent prayer for Astra's strength and guidance. I nod to the two guards stationed there, and they grant me entrance. I find my father, General Kincaid of Lux, standing at the steps of the dais, dressed in uniform, with his hands laced behind his back. Not a strand of his gray hair is out of place.

King Leopold paces on the dais in his long, cream nightshirt that brushes the steps as he walks.

Stepping beside my father, I drop to one knee and bring my head down, "My King."

Leopold eyes me but doesn't stop pacing.

"How did this happen?" Leopold demands, and I can hear the concern in his voice.

I rise, placing my hands behind my back, mimicking my father.

"We're not sure yet, Sir, but we are looking into it now. My men are searching the castle and kingdom for any sign of the thief," I say with faked confidence.

My father gives me a side-eyed glance, clearly unimpressed with my quick actions.

"You didn't answer my question, Captain," the king barks at me and stops pacing.

What am I supposed to say? Yes, this happened under my watch, but we have turned up nothing in our search so far?

My father responds before I can come up with a worthy answer.

"There was no stopping this, my king. We both know who stole from you," he declares.

Their eyes lock and understanding shows on the king's face. Neither of them says a word.

"Who? Who would be so audacious to steal from here? What did they want so bad and why?" I ask as they both eye me, but neither answer right away.

After a moment, the king lets out an exaggerated sigh, and I see his shoulders fall slightly. He paces the dais again, but at a more leisurely pace this time.

"They stole an amulet from my personal collection," he finally answers.

I narrow my eyes in confusion. The king's rare trove safe only opens for him and holds his most valuable possessions.

I start, "That isn't possible. How—"

My father cuts me off, "Umbra, that's how. Those damn thieves opened a portal into the safe and took the amulet. The only person capable of entering and exiting without being seen is King Asher with his adveho ring."

Hatred fills my veins at the mention of the dreadful King Asher of Umbra. Better known as the Umbra Brutus, he's a monster forged in darkness and released upon this realm to destroy it. If he is indeed behind this, we are all doomed. He's a hooded figure with coiling pitch-black shadows, a voice of nightmares, and a grip as cold as death. His ruthlessness knows no bounds.

"What would he want with an amulet? What's so special about it?" I ask.

There must be great significance to this item. A simple amulet would hold no value. Unless King Asher took it to prove a point and is gearing up for something bigger. He gets off on messing with people's heads. This could have been an intimidation tactic to show us that there is no place beyond his reach.

"It was a family heirloom, and it means a lot to our king. King Asher was probably made aware of this and took it. I'm sure his goons will be by within the week with his ransom demands for its return," my father answers while scratching his palm.

Why is he lying about this? A new pit opens in my stomach. My father is up to his schemes again. This can't be good.

"What is your order, my king?" I ask, wanting to hurry this conversation along so I can get back to duty.

I need to figure out what Asher wants with the amulet and what my father is hiding.

"We wait for now and see what Asher has to say for himself. I'll have a message sent to him at first light. We'll reassess in a few days," King Leopold replies, and I nod in agreement.

"We'll report back any findings we come across. Thank you for your time, my king," I say with a bow and leave the throne room.

My whole body is tense and in knots. Rubbing my shoulders, I try to release some of the tension as I walk back to find Nathaniel, but it does nothing.

I should return to the apothecary and see if the healer has anything that could help me relax. While I'm there, I can see if she's made any progress on finding a new potion that will clear the mind haze that has persisted in the month since my night with the barmaid. I have gone back to see the healer twice since my first visit after that night. Each time hoping a different elixir will clear the fog, but none have restored my memories. The haze veiling them has only lifted enough for me to see silhouettes with no discernible features.

Stepping through the front doors of Brightwick, I find Nathaniel in the courtyard scanning the grounds. He watches the guards scour the village below, looking for any evidence of a thief.

I stop beside my lieutenant and friend.

"They find anything?" I ask, even though I'm certain they haven't.

If it was King Asher who stole the amulet, we won't find any evidence. The king of Umbra and his mercenaries are known for their sneakiness. They could be beside you, and you'd never know. Just a perk of being in the favor of a shadow god.

"Nothing yet. What did the king and general say?" He asks, not taking his eyes off the guards.

"They think it's King Asher," I reply, and he cocks his head toward me with raised eyebrows.

"They are the only ones who could get in and out undetected. But what's the catch?" He asks, and I try to keep my face as neutral as possible.

"What do you mean?" I reply, trying to see if he came to the same conclusion as me.

"We both know they don't do things like this for fun. It's always for revenge, ransom, or to prove a point. I don't recall King Leopold speaking with Umbra's liaison recently. So, again, what's the catch?" Nathaniel asks, proving why he's my right-hand man.

He asks questions when events don't line up, and we share the need to find answers.

I grasp his shoulder, giving it a light squeeze.

"That, my friend, is what we need to figure out. Until then, let's investigate as we normally would. King Leopold said to hold off for now, but I think we need to get ahead of this before Umbra makes another move," I reply as we continue to watch over Lux.

In the week that follows the theft, I work hard to train my men to be better prepared for anything. We won't be caught off guard again. I force them through grueling hand-to-hand combat drills until I'm satisfied with the results.

As we near the end of training, King Leopold appears on the field with the general by his side. I step toward them, giving my father a questioning look, but he only motions for me to get my men into formation.

I call for the guards to get in line to receive news from our king, and they quickly assemble. My heart hammers in my chest as I stand at attention, waiting to hear what King Leopold has to tell us.

The king steps before his royal guard, giving us all an assessing look. His indigo-blue formal attire from court accentuating his dark-blue eyes.

"King Asher is refusing to answer our letters. I'm sure you have noticed the unease this is causing among the villagers," he begins, his voice commanding the space.

Word of the theft swept quickly through the village. The fear of an attack is causing borderline hysteria among the people, requiring more guards in the village to keep the peace.

"It's because of this I have decided to send a unit of guards to Umbra to retrieve the stolen amulet. The first group will leave in three days. I suggest you prepare," King Leopold says and turns to walk back into Brightwick.

My stomach twists as if I have been punched.

This is their bright idea? Sending men to their deaths?

The murmuring grows as the words sink in among my men.

I chase after King Leopold and my father, hoping I can talk some sense into them.

"General, may I have a word?" I shout, but he doesn't stop. "Arthur, I need to speak with you, now," I demand.

At the sound of his name, my father spins around, anger emanating from him. He hates it when I call him anything other than his titles, but I knew it would get his attention.

King Leopold continues toward the castle as I stop in front of my father.

"There must be another way. We can't send our men to be slaughtered by those monsters," I plead, hoping he will listen to reason.

"There isn't. We must strike before they attempt another attack," he replies and turns away.

I grab his arm, stopping him from walking away.

"Then shouldn't we keep them here? We shouldn't be sending our kingdom's protection to die for a worthless object," I say through gritted teeth.

He stares at my hand with disgust, and I pull back.

"You're not here to ask questions, boy. You are to listen to your divinus and follow his orders," he sneers, stepping closer to me.

I don't back down.

"Now prepare your men to leave, and may Astra watch over us all," he grumbles before turning and heading into Brightwick.

I stand at the edge of the training yard for long moments, trying to gather my thoughts. My men are going to die and there's nothing I can do to stop it.

CHAPTER 9

LILY

I read over the letter one more time, trying to gather more intel from its words. Annoyance flares in my chest as I read again about a lord needing help to retrieve items stolen by a man from Fati. There must be better use of our time.

Nyx sits across from me in the council room, waiting for my decision. He already knows I'm going to approve the quest. The payment for this request is double our usual rate. Also, at this point, I'm sure he only shows me the ones he knows I'll accept.

It's the same process with every quest that comes in. Nyx receives them from our messengers throughout the realm, reviews them, and brings the letters to me to have a final say. We receive countless requests to help with different issues in other kingdoms.

Now that we have a choice, we only take quests that will benefit us. King Oren accepted any paying quest, regardless of merit, and loved to unleash Asher on any unsuspecting victim, guilty or not. Now that Oren is dead, I choose the quests we accept, and we only request King Asher's involvement when it's absolutely necessary. "What's the risk with this one?" I ask Nyx.

He props an ankle on his knee, getting far too comfortable in his chair.

"There isn't one I can find," he answers.

"Why such a large payment, then? Is the man we are hunting dangerous or wealthy?" I ask, needing to calm the voice telling me something isn't quite right.

"Maybe people are finally paying us what we are worth," he replies with a shrug.

I pinch my lips into a thin line, unamused.

"I'll check into it before we go, if that will make you feel better," Nyx says, reading my thoughts.

"Go ahead and accept. We'd be foolish to say no. Just send in some spies before we head out. Asher will intervene if things get out of hand," I say, folding the letter and placing it back in its envelope.

I catch Nyx rolling his eyes, and I grin at his annoyance.

"I'll tell the crew that we leave in a few days," he says, getting up and snatching the letter from my hand. "You tell King Asher to be ready," he taps me on the nose with the envelope.

I swat him away, fighting back a smile before he turns and leaves the council room.

Dead grass crunches under our feet as we make our way through a wooded area on the outskirts of Fati. The seasons are slowly changing, but it appears summer wants one more round before it succumbs to autumn.

It hasn't rained in weeks despite several storms rolling across the realm. Astra hasn't felt us worthy enough to shower us with much-needed water. She's punishing mortals for something and is ignoring our pleas for forgiveness. Many people have resorted to old rituals to appeal to the gods to end the drought before it causes too much damage. Harsh conditions have been threatening the winter food supply, causing great concern among the kingdoms.

The gods never listen. They haven't in generations, and I doubt they are going to start now. *Selfish pricks.*

There's no smell of wet soil as we walk, which is unnerving. I silently thank Thalos for the endless supply of water in Umbra. We're the only kingdom that does not have to rely on rain to grow our crops.

We move silently through the trees. Nyx is beside me, ensuring he is between me and the scattered houses. Dressed head to toe in black with a hood covering my red hair, we are invisible as we move. Hiram and Kira have gone ahead to secure our mark.

Light flicks through the windows of our target's worn-down house. The hard smack of Nyx's bow across my chest stops me in my tracks, knocking the air from my lungs and causing my hood to fall back.

"Ouch! What was that for?" I choke out.

"Neither Hiram nor Kira is outside. It isn't safe to approach yet," he replies, not even bothering to look at me or apologize.

I pull my hood back over my head and survey the scene before us. To my dismay, Nyx is right, and neither of our spies are in their all-clear positions. *Where are they?* The house is silent, so either they are gone, or the target is.

The scent of freshly cut apples fills the air, and I know there is someone behind me. I release the hold on my power an ounce, allowing the shadows to intercept my spy. They lash out and grab the wrist inches from my shoulder, and I spin to face the culprit.

"Kira," I say, my voice flat and low.

Nyx startles beside me and jumps back, bow drawn.

"What gave me away this time?" She scoffs at me for ruining this little game of hers.

She likes seeing how close she can get to someone before they notice her.

I have to hand it to her. She's a spectacular spy. Quick-footed and deadly when the situation calls for it. She uses her petite frame to her advantage and can usually hide in places others can't. But I know every inch of her. Every little smell and noise that comes from her body.

"Maybe next time, don't use your bath oils before heading out on a quest," I motion for Nyx to lower his bow, and after a few breaths, he does.

I recoil my shadows, and they quickly respond. They don't want to linger longer than they have to in Kira's presence. They have never seemed to care for her. The best way to describe it is indifference.

But let's face it, they only ever really responded to Theo. Once when we first kissed and again in the alley. The thought of him brings an ache to my heart and between my thighs.

"He keeps demanding to speak with King Asher. No matter what we've threatened or done so far, he just keeps saying, 'King Asher,'" Kira debriefs as we step from the trees.

"Well, maybe we should just give him what he wants," Nyx says, looking over his shoulder at me.

I nod. While I'm highly skilled in getting what I want through the torture Oren taught me, the mere presence of Asher sends terror through anyone who's unfortunate enough to meet the shadow king. This man doesn't know what he's asking for. He will probably cave before Asher utters a word. I love quick and less messy results. It means we can get home faster.

I step aside to summon the king. Igniting the dark bond between us, I call upon Asher. Shadows swirl along the forest floor, flooding the space around us. Ash settles on my tongue as the king makes his dramatic appearance. The shadows thicken before revealing a towering, floating figure cloaked in darkness.

The Umbra Brutus, or beast of the shadows, steps from the grove of trees. His dark mass is so thick, not even moonlight pierces the surface. Nyx backs up to give space for the swirling black tendrils as Asher glides from the tree line. No words are needed. Asher knows what to do. I pull my cloak over my head, obscuring my hair, as the king and queen of Umbra set off from the trees.

We follow Kira across the grass and through the back door of the rickety house. The place looks worse on the inside and reveals its lack of upkeep. Holes and failed mending attempts dot the walls. A putrid smell of rotting food fills the air, causing my stomach to turn. I swallow down the bile threatening to escape.

Hiram stands near a table where he has tied a gangly, middle-aged man with thinning hair to a chair. Up close, the man's condition is vile. Dirt coats his skin, leaving streaks from where he has wiped the sweat from his face. He cocks a grin as we approach, revealing broken and rotting teeth.

"You don't look as scary as everyone says," he boasts with a fake arrogance that grates on my nerves.

It's easier when targets quiver at the sight of Asher and our crew. I hate when people weep, but I'll take crying over forced bravado.

The Umbra Brutus hovers over the man, forcing him to crane his neck to look up. The man scoffs. A tendril of shadow caresses each side of the man's face in a slow, placating draw. The man's breath hitches in his chest. As the shadow retracts, the man swallows hard.

Nyx steps forward, opening a scroll provided by the requesting lord.

"A lord of Terra has accused you of stealing several pieces of gold, silver, valuable gemstones, art, and clothing. How do you plead?" Nyx's voice is even and commands authority.

The man throws his head back in a hardy laugh. It's a reaction we rarely see in Asher's presence.

"That's real rich coming from the biggest thieves in all of Omnia," he says between laughs.

Nyx steps closer, bending to be even with the man's face.

"We are not the ones accusing you of theft. We're here to collect a debt. Give us the items you stole, and we will let you live to see another day."

This only makes the man laugh harder. His body completely relaxed in the chair.

"He thinks this is all a joke," Kira interjects.

He won't be thinking that for long.

"Silence," Asher's cold and menacing voice echoes throughout the home. The man stiffens and halts his annoying, condescending laughter.

"Where are the items?" Nyx's voice has more bite to it now, seeming just as irritated as I am.

The man shifts in his seat, suddenly uncomfortable. His eyes dart around the room.

"It's gone. All of it's gone," he shouts. "I sold them already. Made a pretty coin off of it, too. The lord had some good stuff," he says, boasting about his crimes.

A haughty smile slowly spreads across his face, and I fight back a groan. He leans back in his chair.

"But I have information for you. If you let me go, I'll tell you what I know," he declares, trying to bargain with us.

"What kind of information could you offer us that we don't already know?" Nyx says crossing his arms on his chest.

The man stares up into the black mass that is Asher with the confidence of a person not looking death in the face.

"Information about the Lux guards that are going to be at your doorstep within a week," he says.

My eyes flash to Nyx, who's just as shocked by this news as I am. We have several spies in Lux and within Brightwick, but none have mentioned anything about Lux guards coming to Umbra.

"Why?" The word is a snarl from Asher.

The man stiffens in his chair and gulps, hard.

"To get back the amulet you stole from King Leopold," he answers with hesitation.

"We stole nothing from King Leopold or Lux," Nyx says, his voice filled with irritation.

Besides our spies, none of my people have been to Lux since I left almost two months ago. We've been too busy negotiating new trade agreements because of the drought to even bother taking any quests until now.

"That's not what King Leopold and General Kincaid said," he quickly replies.

The shadows creep closer to the man and he stills. No one crosses the Umbra Brutus without the innate fear the darkness will consume them.

"And why would we do that?" Asher asks as shadows stretch across the floor.

The man shrugs.

"That's what I was hoping you would tell me. Information like that is a goldmine!" He answers with excitement.

He's trying to capitalize on this opportunity. Petty games for weak criminals.

"Like I said, we have stolen nothing from that man," Nyx says, irritation clear in his tone.

A genuine questioning look flashes across the man's face.

"Then who did? Because they are blaming you. They are saying your theft has angered Astra, which is why she isn't providing any rain. And that you've not responded to their pleas to return the amulet, which is why they are sending guards to Umbra," he says, clearly struggling with the conflicting information.

A chasm opens in my stomach. Theo. His men are being sent to their deaths because their king thinks we took something from him. They won't survive our beasts, and I have no way of stopping them.

Panic rushes over me, and I fight to keep my composure. We need to get out of here and figure out how to stop them from sending guards to Umbra.

Shadows slither along the floor toward the man, wind up his legs, and wrap around his face. He thrashes in the chair, but it's no use. Even if he weren't tied to it, the shadows wouldn't let him move from the chair.

I reach into my pocket, pulling out a vial of rowanberry, and for a brief second my heart breaks again for having used it on Theo. The shadows grasp the man's mouth and pry it open for me. He screams, as if anyone can help him. He screams louder as I pour the contents down his throat. He doesn't realize that we are sparing him in return for the information he's given us. The shadows cover his mouth and nose, forcing him to down the liquid.

"Did you just poison me?" He shouts after the shadows recoil themselves from his face.

"No, but you will wish we did," Hiram says nonchalantly.

"Take anything of value as payment for the items he stole from the lord," Asher commands to the crew.

Mischievous smiles spread across their faces, and I fight back a laugh as they ransack the house searching for things to take with us.

The shadows around Asher flicker and thin. The once thick tendrils fade into faint wisps of darkness as they skirt across the floor. When they reach the door, the dark void ebbs and disperses, and without another word, the king makes his exit. I can take it from here.

Stepping toward the wall, Nyx follows me as expected.

"We need to figure out why Leopold and Arthur believe we stole an amulet from them and what kind it is," I say as quietly as I can, and Nyx nods, clearly thinking the same thing.

"I'll reach out to our spies in the morning to gather intel. But what about the guards coming to the kingdom? If he's told us the truth, they will be there in a few days," Nyx replies.

My crew carries out Asher's orders as I contemplate the next best steps and how to handle Leopold. What does he have up his sleeve, and why is he targeting us?

"We have to let them in. If we stop them at the gate, they will know someone gave us information and could resort to more sinister tactics. The information made it to the people for a reason, even out of Lux, and we need to find out why," I reply.

Nyx is quiet for several minutes, and when he looks at me, there is sorrow in his eyes.

"They will all die, Lily."

The chasm opens further.

"I know, but we can't save them from their own king's poor decisions. We have to worry about our own people and keeping them safe. We can also send a messenger to Lux to see if we can discuss things before Leopold sends his own men to their deaths," I state.

Leopold is a cruel, violent man, just like Oren was—the two of them always secretly joining forces to terrorize all of Omnia. They were always scheming while I remained in the shadows, waiting for the chance to punish them.

Anger consumes every fiber of me, remembering what they did to me, how they broke me and took everything I love away from me. My mother's broken body hanging limp from the dungeon ceiling flashes in my mind. Blood pouring from the slit Oren sliced in her throat.

The air charges as my power intensifies with my hatred for the two men who destroyed my life.

"Is everything ok, Lily?" Nyx whispers so only I can hear him.

He watches me with worry lining his face.

"Yes, just frustrated with the blame being placed on us when we've done nothing wrong," I answer, thankful to him for drawing me back to the present.

"Let's send a raven to Lux at first light as well. See if they can catch anything," I say.

Nyx's face relaxes, and he nods his head.

Since becoming Queen of Umbra, I've commanded Oren's ravens. When I first noticed these soundless black birds flying above me and Theo on my last days in Lux all those years ago, I didn't know their true purpose. Although no one knows how the ravens came to be, they are invaluable spies. The viewing crystals attached to their chests capture movement that projects back to their owner, and they have helped me stay one step ahead many times.

I allow my crew to ransack the house completely before calling them off and saying it's time to go. The man has long passed out, and I have Hiram cut him loose before we leave.

We exit and head back to the cover of trees. As soon as the forest hides us, I drop the hood from my head, loose curls falling with it.

Lifting my left hand, the metal of my adveho ring flashes in the moonlight that cascades down upon us. My crew circles around me, Kira on my left, Nyx on my right, and Hiram directly behind me. They place their hands on my shoulders and the remaining crew does the same, creating a chain of Umbra warriors.

I envision the back entrance of The Keep clearly in my mind: a cave obscured by overgrown vines and thin lines of water, the sound of which trickles through the space, the small creek filled with rocks, and the crisp, fresh air.

A black mass rimmed in red appears in front of us, splintering at the center. I lead my crew through the portal, taking us all home.

CHAPTER 10

THEO

Through the arched windows along the corridor of Brightwick, the sun dips behind the horizon, painting the sky in vibrant oranges, pinks, and purples. Sunsets in Lux are breathtaking because the limestone buildings reflect sunlight, creating the illusion of a glowing kingdom.

I pass only a handful of people as I walk the gray stone halls heading to my father's chambers. Most servants are busy with evening tasks, and the guards are probably half-drunk by now.

I take a moment to draw in a deep breath before opening a set of heavy oak chamber doors. I prepare myself for the different possible outcomes of this meeting.

When the general found me earlier, I was stationed at the back door of Brightwick overlooking the river below, lost in the memories of laughter and love. A time when I was happy and dreamed of being a scholar.

My father's harsh, deep voice pulled me back to the present. I would have much rather been daydreaming about the day of my first kiss than dealing with him. He told me to meet him before sundown in his chambers to discuss new information regarding the stolen amulet.

I send up a silent prayer to Astra, hoping my father is going to tell me that we've received the break we need to get the amulet back and spare my men's lives. Gods know we've lost enough already.

Opening the doors, I step into my father's chambers. The quarters are sparse, with no personal items to be found— only a desk piled high with paperwork, and a large bed draped in elegant indigo sheets and far too many pillows for one person.

A long, dark wood table sits to the right side of his entryway, framed with four high-back throne-style chairs. My father has always been one for proving his status through extravagant possessions. He believes money and power can get you everything in the realm.

I take a seat in a chair along the side of the table, knowing my father will take one at the head. While I wait, I take in how cold and empty the quarters feel—fitting for my father.

There was a time when warmth poured from this space. My mother's lilac scent and gentle presence filled the quarters. I wonder what I would have become if my mother was still alive. She always said I could do anything, and that my destiny was beyond this kingdom. Maybe I could have been a scholar like I had dreamed. Teaching great minds all the knowledge of our kingdom. My days could have been filled with reading and researching a variety of subjects.

But the fates had other plans for me. Losing my mother at a young age was difficult, but even that didn't prepare me for losing the love of my life a few years later, and then losing her mother.

Eleanor Clarke, with her beaming smile, wavy auburn hair, and green eyes the shade of the pines along the mountains, was like a second mother to me. After my mother died suddenly from an unknown illness, Eleanor stepped in to ensure I still saw kindness and love as my mother would have wanted.

When we lost her daughter, we were both consumed with grief but found comfort in the time we spent together. Then she was gone, too. Someone evil took her from me three years later.

The castle seemed to tremble with grief the night of Eleanor's murder, and, as if by the cruel decree of the gods, I was left alone with my cold, heartless father.

The door swings open and General Arthur Kincaid steps into the room, interrupting my trip down memory lane. He's still dressed in his royal uniform from court earlier today, as regal as ever.

My father embodies everything of a true royal guard. After joining at age fourteen, he fought, deceived, and killed his way through the ranks. Eventually, he caught the attention of King Leopold, who saw his fierceness and knew he could use it to his advantage. Before the age of thirty, the king promoted my father to his current rank of general.

Now approaching fifty, he wears his battle scars proudly across almost every inch of his body. His gray hair and long beard add to the burly persona. Being an inch shorter than me and nearly as muscular as men half his age only amplifies his terrifying look.

My father's drive has always been a thorn between us. His long-set desire is for me to follow in his footsteps into the guard and rise through the ranks to be his second in command.

The general takes a seat in the head chair, as I expected. He's always so predictable. He sits with all the arrogance of a lethal warrior, practically lounging in the seat. I interlace my hands on the table.

"Why won't the king dig into food reserves to lessen the burden on the villagers?" I ask the question that's been burning in my mind since court this morning.

People from all over Lux packed the throne room, their body odor choking out the fresh air. Everyone wanted to know what King Leopold plans to do if the drought doesn't end soon. Farmers are losing sections of their crops daily now and dread is spreading.

The king, however, announced no plans to lessen the burden for his people. While I'm loyal to the divinus of Lux, I rarely agree with his lack of empathy or care for his people. One day, Junie will become our queen, and our people will be grateful for a kind ruler.

"The drought will end as soon as we get the amulet back. It's no coincidence it started right after those vile people stole from us. Astra is angry someone dared to steal from her divinus, and now we're all paying the price for their actions," he answers aggressively.

Distaste for Umbra and its hellion rings clear in his voice.

I shift in the uncomfortable, stiff chair, ready to be back in my chambers for the evening.

"You mentioned you had new information on the amulet. What is it?" I ask, not wanting to extend my time here longer than necessary.

He gives me the all-too-familiar assessing look, as if he finds me lacking.

Of what?

I never could figure it out, no matter how much I tried.

"We have a confirmed report King Asher took it," he says in his usual expressionless tone.

"How? From whom?" I ask as a mix of hope and caution blooms in my chest.

I want to believe one of my guards made it out of Umbra and got a message back to us. Even if only one survived, it would lift a weight off my conscience. But I don't trust my father, especially when I can't see his hands to confirm he's telling the truth.

"Don't worry about that. Just know it is from a reliable source," he replies.

Unease rolls through me. We don't have any spies in Umbra or within King Asher's crew, so where could he have received this information?

Before I can push him further on his source, he speaks, "But that isn't what I asked you here for tonight."

He leans forward in his chair, resting both hands in his lap under the table. Eyeing him, I raise an eyebrow in question.

"I have discussed our situation with King Leopold, and we have reached a deal," he states.

Unease grows within me. Something tells me that whatever deal he has made with the king, I want no part of it.

"What kind of deal, father?" The words come out as a grumble I can't fight back.

"Watch your tone, boy!"

He bares his teeth at me, but I don't back down. I'm used to his discontent. I don't take my eyes off him, and we are stuck for several moments in a heated staring contest. I have no plans to lose. If he is going to drag me into one of his poorly thought-out plans, then he is going to look me in the eye when he does it.

His audible sigh finally breaks the silence. "You'll lead the next deployment of guards to Umbra," he finally spits out.

This isn't shocking news. I expected to be sent with my men, but I figured it wouldn't be this soon.

"And?" I say with a wave of my hand, gesturing for him to continue.

The corner of his lip pulls up in disgust. I glare at him, squeezing my hands so hard my fingers turn white.

Through clenched teeth, he continues, "You'll go to Umbra, retrieve the amulet, and return it to King Leopold. As a reward, you will marry Princess Juniper."

Red, fiery rage surges through my veins as I shove back from the table so hard the chair flings to the floor behind me. The sound of wood splintering radiates through the quarters.

"What kind of deal is that?" my voice cracks as I yell down at my father.

He remains in his seat with the same look of disgust distorting his face.

"A damn good deal. You'll become the King of Lux. You should thank me for this opportunity. Be grateful for my sacrifices that have provided this for you," he says with self-satisfaction for a job well done.

"Thanking you? For what?" I scoff, "Sending me off to die and, if by some will of the gods, I survive, forcing me to marry my childhood friend? Oh, or should I be thanking you for making me a king when I have no desire to be one?"

He doesn't answer, but the veins in his forehead pulsate.

"I won't marry Princess Juniper," I say as I slam my hands on the table, causing it to vibrate from the force.

My father launches out of the chair, grabs me by the front of my uniform, and slams me into the wall. A jolt of pain shoots up my neck as my back takes the full force of the impact. I grab his wrists to push him back, but he pulls me an inch from the wall before slamming me back into it. I wince in pain.

"You ungrateful little shit! All I have sacrificed for you."

Slam.

"All the deals I've had to make."

Slam.

"All the things I've had to do for you to get where you are."

Slam.

"All I've—"

Shaking with fury, I finally find my voice to shout back, "All the things you've done for *you*! To gain power! I never asked for any of this! I wanted none of this! I wanted to be a scholar, remember?"

Pain shoots through my back, and I clench my jaw, hoping to hide my discomfort. His spit speckles my face, and I fight the urge to rip out of his grasp to wipe it away.

His head shakes with suppressed rage, and the muscles in his neck strain. Suddenly, he drops his hands from my shirt and steps back. I fall into the wall and bend my knees to stop from dropping to the ground.

We are both breathing hard, and he rubs at his jaw. He stiffens and turns back to me.

"This is a direct order, Captain," he says.

My title is a hiss of his tongue, laced with venom. I push off the wall, stepping toward him.

"No. You can't do this," I reply, shaking my head.

"I don't care what you want, Theodore!" He shouts, losing his briefly regained composure. "I have given you an order, Captain. Are you going to obey, or should I have them throw you in the dungeon for failure of duty?" He lifts his chin, knowing he's won.

Gods help me.

He may be my father, but he's my commanding officer above all. If I don't follow orders, he wouldn't hesitate to have the king torture me to prove his point. What he says goes, and I have no choice but to listen.

"Yes, sir," I raise my chin and take the stance of the soldier I am. It's a mask I'm so used to wearing at this point of my life.

"Good. You leave in three days. Have your team packed and ready to depart by lunch," he commands like a true general.

Never the father he should be. I walk past him, shoving my shoulder into him as I head to the door and exit his quarters without another word.

Anger clouds my mind as I hurry toward the back of the castle, searching for fresh air. I burst through the door, startling the guards on duty. I know this path like the back of my hand, even at night with only the moonlight leading the way.

Breaking into a sprint, I let my rage fuel me, my legs pounding faster and faster with each step. I race along the gravel path down the cliff, along the backside of the castle. Stones kick out in all directions as I go. The night air has cooled, and the clean, fresh scent of the river fills the air.

The cloudless sky above allows the stars to reflect in the water, making it appear to be glittering. Falling to my knees at the river's edge, I scream into the night, releasing all the anger and pain of the day.

Running my hands across my face and into my hair, I let my head fall back to stare up at the beautiful sky. I allow the water splashing on the rocks to help calm my nerves. I focus on the sound and not the emotions begging to be released.

Looking over, I see my ... our ... spot, and I head over to take a seat on the boulder, which holds so many childhood memories, both good and bad.

I think back to a time when I wanted to marry a different girl. *My flower.* I would give anything to remember what she looked like and not have the blood, hair, or haze always obscuring my view. But I'll never forget the feelings she instilled in me: love and happiness.

My heart breaks because there is no way of getting out of this. I'll either die in a failed ploy to steal back a worthless amulet or return and marry my friend.

"I'm sorry, I have no choice. I wish things could be different, but …" My head falls as I realize I'm trying to talk to a spirit. Maybe the gods or the fates will hear me and change my destiny.

"I wish it was you because it has always been you. Even death can't stop my love for you. The thread linking us will never break," I say into the night air.

A breeze caresses my face, and I swear it's her letting me know she's here—that she understands what I must do. A wistful smile curves my lips at the thought of her being near, though I'm certain it's all in my mind.

I hope she really would understand. The last thing I want is to marry, but at least Junie is a trusted friend. The thought of being king one day, however, makes my stomach turn.

I stare at the river for a long time, trying to figure out my next move, but my thoughts keep coming back to her, and my heart aches with betrayal. She would want me to stay safe and happy, but those two things are not exclusive. I know she would want me to move on. Even I know ten years is a long time to grieve the loss of your girlfriend, but she was more than that. I truly thought she was my fairytale love. *My Amari*. The threads of fate tied our hearts together as one through this lifetime and the next.

The trees across the bank rustle before the shadow of a bird breaks from the tops, cawing as it soars high into the sky. Standing, I brush off my trousers, giving the serene spot one more glance and whispering a goodbye to my girl.

I step carefully along the rocky bank to the gravel walkway. I allow my thoughts to wander as I make my way back to my quarters and hope tonight the nightmares of her stay away.

CHAPTER 11

LILY

Heat licks my cheeks as the burial pyres reach their peak of burning. The crackle of wood tears apart my heart with each snap. Four more Lux guards have been laid to rest in our soil, joining the five before them in the newly created cemetery.

We wrapped each one in the finest burial cloth of indigo, blue, and silver—custom-made by my weavers to honor the warrior's sacrifices. Knowing Lux traditions has come in handy over the past month. It would be disrespectful to bury their dead in anything other than their kingdom's colors.

Even though they are being sent to their deaths by their king, fueled by the idea of destroying Umbra or becoming martyrs, we make sure to treat them with honor and respect. Retrieving their lifeless bodies from the haunted forest and burying them with dignity is the only thing we can do.

The wood crackles again, and I shudder. After nine burials, you'd think my nerves would get used to such sounds. The smell of burning flesh and fabric is suffocating. I hope I never get used to it.

I'll never let myself become so callous that I no longer feel pain from this.

My eyes trail along the ten headstones made from their shields and weapons. I try to swallow the lump in my throat but can't. Tears moisten my eyes as I watch the last of the fires burn out.

Only one guard doesn't lie with the others, Creepy Gate Guard Jonathan. Lucky for him, he made it out of the haunted forest. Unlucky for him, he sprinted right into the pools surrounding The Keep, thinking the Cypres couldn't enter the water, which resulted in him being promptly eaten by a nobu. Fitting end for him to become fodder for my beasts.

I wipe away the stray tear rolling down my cheek while saying one last plea to the gods. If any of them remain, none are listening. I turn away from the pyres and head back to The Keep, my long, black dress dragging on the ground, gathering leaves and flowers as I walk. I don't have the energy to care. All this death and no way of stopping it has worn me down.

The first group of guards entered under the guise of a meeting with King Asher. The second group, however, beat my guard unconscious to enter through our portal. But even if we wanted to prevent them from entering, we couldn't stop them.

Leopold would view us halting them as a sign of weakness. Oren always said death is a sacrifice one must make to gain control. The greedy asshole murdered his own Amari chasing after that thirst for power.

Leopold isn't much different from Oren. His moves are predictable, as easy to read as a children's storybook. He's searching for cracks in our foundation to carry out whatever ridiculous plan he conjured up in his puny little mind. What he will find is monsters lurking in the shadows, ready to unleash years of pent-up rage, finally getting revenge so richly deserved.

The sounds of gravel crunching under my boots and birds singing from the tree branches above, provide a calming background for my walk back, but my mind still races.

Nyx follows a few steps behind, bow loaded and pulled tight. He has been on high alert since the Lux guards started arriving, convinced one is going to make it out of the haunted forest and attack when we least expect. But no one makes it through the trees, the Cypres make sure of it. Only those they believe are worthy survive.

The smell of burning overpowers the freshness in the air and clings to my senses and clothing. A rustling along the path has me squinting to get a better look, but Nyx steps in front of me, his bow ready to shoot.

A little, gray rabbit hops along the path perpendicular to us, and Nyx follows it with his arrow. Once it's safely on the other side, he lowers his bow but remains on alert.

"Oh, no! Help me, great General Davey! A rabbit is plotting to kill me!" I flail my arms above my head to emphasize my placating tone.

His eyes shoot daggers at me over his shoulder.

"No one is going to attack me in my own kingdom, Nyx. You can stand down."

As I pass, I jab him in the shoulder with my finger, which is met with rock hard muscle. Damn him and his chiseled physique. I can't even poke him properly.

He responds with an annoyed purse of his lips and returns a jab with the end of his bow. I dart out of the way, lessening the impact, and jog ahead. I catch him throwing his head back and shaking it with irritation before racing after me.

I slow as I approach the secret entrance to The Keep. To any outsider, it looks like a mass of vines cascading down the black stone brink with varying streams of waterfalls. At a glance, one might think the rocks in the small creek which flows to the back door are spaced at random, but they actually form a path leading the way home.

I step, light-footed, across the stones, the route second nature to me after all these years. Nyx does the same behind me. The black onyx door blends seamlessly into the rock wall. The etched symbols along the edge match the ones on the front entrance.

No one has ever told me what the symbols mean. Nor do any books in all of Omnia provide the details. But they are beautiful and could simply be an ornate design etched by an expert craftsman centuries ago.

Once inside, I breathe in the welcoming feeling of being home. As an extra level of precaution, we now have two guards stationed at the back door, and I give them a grateful smile as I pass.

A few feet down the black stone hall lies my old cell, and I pause at the open iron-barred door. I have made several adjustments to it over the years to wipe the horrors from the walls, but nothing has helped. I still see the young girl chained against her will as her father punishes her for simply wielding the same god-given power he possesses.

The chains still hang from the walls as a reminder. Their cuffs remain splintered from the night of my breaking. Nyx comes to my side as anger boils within me.

"You should be proud of all you've survived. Most would have given up or died from the torture," he says as he pushes his arm against mine, keeping me tethered to reality.

"What good has it done, though? He should have killed me a decade ago," I reply harshly.

More days than not, I wish he would have done just that. My life would have ended, and I wouldn't have to live while not truly existing. Forever being the nameless girl of The Keep. He may have let me live, but he killed who I was, and I can never get her back.

"Umbra and our people are safe because of you," Nyx says, looking down at me.

I scoff.

"King Asher keeps Umbra safe. I don't exist outside The Keep, Nyx," I say, staring straight into my cell.

His mouth opens to say something, but I refuse to listen anymore. I know what I am. Who I am. And nothing he says will change that. I turn and walk away. I desperately need time alone.

My quick pace eats up the distance to my chambers. Nyx trails right behind. As I round the corner, the onyx door of my quarters comes into view, and I break into a sprint. Nyx makes it around the corner, but he's not fast enough. I slide inside my chambers, turn, and stick out my tongue at him before slamming the door shut, locking it behind me.

A moment later, he is banging on it.

"Go away, Nyx. I'm safe in here, and we can talk later," I say, facing the door.

His knocking stops, but I know he is still there.

"I'm fine. I … I just need time to process everything. We can strategize later."

He remains silent.

"Unless you want to bathe with me, then I can gladly unlock the door," I say teasingly.

An audible gag comes from my best friend, and I let out a small laugh.

"I love you and will find you later." I say through the closed door.

"I love you too, even if you offer for me to bathe with you." His voice grows distant on the last words as he leaves me in my quarters.

After Oren died three years ago, and I became queen, I had the quarters completely changed. We removed his things and distributed them to anyone who needed them. Since I had no possessions, it was a simple move for me.

One of my favorite upgrades is my oversized, black wood bed with its massive headboard decorated with crimson gemstones and incredibly soft matching bedding.

As I go to the bathing chamber, I discard my dress into my dirty clothes pile and kick off my boots. The stone under my feet is cool. I turn on the water and dump in my oil, filling the chamber with the scent of roses. Climbing into the revitalizing water, I drop under the surface and stay under until my lungs burn, screaming for air.

I shoot up and gasp, drawing the rose-scented air into my lungs again. I scrub hard at my skin, trying to wash away everything. But no amount of cleaning can do that.

Dragging myself out of the water, I wrap my body in a fluffy towel and flop on my bed, not caring about soaking my sheets. I need to come up with a way to stop Lux from sending more guards. I have tried everything besides going to Lux myself to speak with King Leopold—or sending Asher but sending him would be a declaration of war.

We have sent letters to speak with the king of Lux, but he refuses to answer and has barred my messengers from entering Lux entirely. I rack my brain, trying to figure out why this would happen. What could Leopold possibly gain from this lie and the death of his guards? Why would he want to start a war with Umbra? There's no way I can allow that to happen.

I get dressed, throwing on black trousers, a shirt, and a vest with crimson stitching. Then I strap on my blades and secure my dagger to my right thigh, running my fingers over the hilt. I wonder briefly how Tobias would handle this situation. Would he see an angle of this that we don't? My heart pains at the thought of him and how desperately I wish he were still here.

Leaving my chambers to find Nyx, I stop dead in my tracks to prevent from running straight into him.

With eyebrows raised and arms out to steady me in case we collide, he asks, "Where are you off to in such a hurry?"

I crane my neck to look up at him.

"That rabbit from the forest tracked me down and was trying to murder me in my chambers, so I came to find you to save me," I answer, gesturing my thumb over my shoulder toward my door.

My face is blank as I stare into his gray eyes. He huffs in annoyance, but a soft giggle from me melts his resolve, and he answers with a deep one of his own.

"But seriously, what's up?" he questions.

"I may have come up with a wild idea on how to solve the whole King Leopold issue," I reply.

"Go on," he says conspiratorially, and I lean toward him.

"You know how he loathes," I draw out the last word, "being proved wrong?"

We nod together.

"Well, what if we prove ourselves innocent and put his lies on full display? Care to join in?"

Our faces split into the same devilish smiles.

"Let's grab some food and head to the council room to work out the details," I say, and we make our way to the dining hall to grab some dinner.

The hall is buzzing with activity. A chorus of conversation fills the space, laughter billows throughout.

The sight of my crew enjoying a meal together lessens the pain in my heart. Nyx is right. Our people are safe and happy. But I'll never tell him that.

Gods, I would never hear the end.

We cross into the hall, greeted by the scent of spices and cooked wine. My mouth waters, and I move to get in line for our meal. Several members of my crew take notice, and we share pleasant conversations as we wait.

Little children shower me with their messy hugs and ask me for the next story time. Their parents assure them it would be in a few days. My heart swells with the love I have for these people. My people. The only ones allowed to know part of who I am: their queen. Everyone in The Keep is sworn to secrecy in order to enter our band of misfits and protect the queen.

Only a few know my true name. When I arrived, I made the mistake of telling an older woman who I was. They buried her broken body the next day, after Oren was through with her. Others who slipped up met a similar fate. I learned the power of a name then and that it wasn't mine to hold.

Loma and Tobias knew my name from day one in Umbra but would never say it unless in private. Nyx learned shortly after but has been my anchor through the years. Without him, I would have lost myself completely a long time ago. It was risky to tell Kira my real name, but I needed it on her lips whenever we came together.

I look up and smile gratefully at Nyx. He returns a quizzical look. I shake my head and shove at him to move forward with the line. We pile our plates high with delicious pork cooked in red wine, coriander, garlic, and other spices I can't place. The aroma alone awakens my taste buds, and I am salivating.

Pyke pops out of the kitchen with a plate that holds a little round puff pastry. He bows, handing it to me.

"You don't need to bow every time, Pyke. How many times do I have to tell you that?" My words break through my laughter.

I swear this man bows even if he glimpses my red hair.

"It's a sign of respect and honor to bow before you. And I shall continue to do so until my body no longer allows," he says, stiffly standing straight.

Oh, my heart.

I close my eyes to let the words wash over me. I need this time with my people to revive me. All the death lately has been taking a toll on my soul, and they heal me with their kind words and shared respect.

Nyx and I sneak from the dining hall and head to the council room next to the throne room. He pushes open the heavy wood door and we enter. The room is simple, with large windows along the back that let the remaining beams of sunlight illuminate the space.

Before us is a dark wood half-moon table with five low-back chairs set around it. Positioned back from there is my desk in matching wood and a high-back chair with intricate lattice work framing the outer edges.

I walk to my desk and spy an envelope placed in the center. The elegant handwriting tells me the letter is from Amelia. Since my letters have to be diverted from Lux to Fati before coming to Umbra, it can take time for hers to reach me. I wrote to her a month after my return, as promised, and I'm interested to hear what she has to say about Lux.

Nyx notices the envelope too. "Who's that from?"

I trace her beautiful penmanship with my finger.

"A friend," I answer.

"You have friends? Well, besides me," he teases, and I narrow my eyes, causing him to burst out laughing.

"You think you're so funny?" I roll my head with the words, upping the sarcasm in my tone.

He takes a seat in the center chair across from me, shoulders still shaking with laughter. I take a seat in my chair, pulling my black dagger from the sleeve on my thigh, admiring the feel in my hand, and opening the letter in one smooth motion. Amelia's flowy script covers the page.

Thankfully, she's well, but there's unrest going on in Lux, which is worrisome. From her description, King Leopold doesn't seem to have a tight grip on his kingdom right now, which will make my plan work even better.

A lethal smile slowly curls my lips as I look up to Nyx, who is finishing his plate. He looks up to meet my gaze, food hanging out of his mouth.

"What?" A piece of pork falls back to his plate.

I shake my head.

"We should have our spies across Omnia focus on finding the amulet Leopold is accusing us of stealing. Then, once we find it, we can taunt him with it. My friend says discontent is growing in Lux, so it will be the best time to convince the people of his faults," I say, finally taking a bite of Pyke's puff pastry.

It's light and fluffy with a center of velvety chocolate cream. I melt into my seat at the satisfaction of it.

Nyx nods, his eyes bouncing back and forth, analyzing the plan.

"That could work. I'll contact our spies in the morning. But, Lily, what happens if we don't find it? There's a chance that nothing was taken and it's all a front," he replies.

I finish my dessert and wipe my mouth with the back of my hand.

"That's a risk we are going to have to take. At the very least, we'll gain valuable information which will help us be one step ahead," I answer, knowing this could be a lose-lose situation.

I can only hope that with time, we will find the amulet and the true intent of the cruel King of Lux. We'll come out on top. I'll make sure of it. Asher will make sure of it. The darkness in me stirs at the thought of finally getting our revenge.

CHAPTER 12

THEO

"Everything packed and loaded?" Nathaniel asks as I tighten the final strap, securing my bag to the silver mare I selected for the trip.

Looking over my shoulder, I check the field to see the other four men accompanying me are all set as well.

"I believe so," I reply as I run my hand down my horse's neck.

She responds with a loud huff, shake of her head, and hoof stomp. If the beasts of Umbra don't kill me, I'm sure this mare will. Snatching my hand away from my grumpy new companion, I stride to Nathaniel, who is wisely keeping his distance.

At least it's a beautiful day for our trip. Summer has finally released its tight grasp on the season, letting autumn's cooler days provide us with relief. The light breeze carries the scent of damp soil from the recent rains. Astra finally heard our pleas and broke the drought plaguing the realm.

For a moment, I wonder if my father was right, and King Asher angered her by stealing from her divinus, King Leopold. Maybe she saw the pain she was causing her people and gave up on the beasts of Umbra repenting for their sins.

Overall, we fared well compared to other kingdoms, saving us from a potential mutiny, but King Leopold's lack of action has caused tension in Lux and increased the need for patrolling to ease people's distress.

I catch Nathaniel eyeing me from head to toe.

"Are you trying to remember what I look like in case I die?" I ask, trying to lighten the moment.

He stops scanning me.

"Yes, but I was also checking your weapons in case you needed more."

I huff a laugh because we both lost count of the weapons as we packed them. We're as prepared as we can be, especially without knowing exactly what we will encounter within Umbra. We all know the lore of the land; but experiencing it is completely different.

"I think we have plenty, Lieutenant," I answer, but Nathaniel is more interested in something behind me.

I look over my shoulder to see Princess Juniper's somber face. A small smile tugs at my lips as I wave at her. She returns the gesture and motions her head to a bench nearby, silently asking for me to join her.

"Can you watch my horse? I need to speak to Junie before I leave," I ask, and Nathaniel simply nods his head.

He takes the reins of my mare as I head toward my childhood friend and now future wife. I push down the knot trying to twist my insides.

Junie sits on a low bench along the edge of the courtyard, facing where we have gathered to get ready for our travels. The bottom of her elegant indigo dress flutters lightly in the breeze.

Her light-blonde hair braided into a crown on her head gives her an even more regal look. She looks almost ethereal among the flowers.

As I approach, I drop to one knee and bow.

"As always, it's lovely to see you, Princess," I say before standing back to my full height.

There's a smirk on Junie's face, but her pale-blue eyes are filled with sadness and concern.

"How many times have I told you not to bow to me, Theo?" She playfully shakes her head. "You may be the captain, but you're still my friend."

I take a seat next to her.

"Ah, but you are still a princess, which means I'm required to bow," I nudge her arm.

Her bright chuckle is brief.

Junie lowers her head. "My father told me about the deal," she says, barely above a whisper. I bite my bottom lip, working on a response.

"We don't have to go through with it. When I return, we'll deal with our fathers together," I say, squaring my body to hers.

We don't have to get married. Neither of us wants to marry the other, so we won't. Simple as that.

Her gaze rises to mine and her shoulders sag.

She says quietly, "We both know there is no getting out of this. What our fathers say is final."

Grabbing both her hands in mine, I tell her, "We can make that decision later. We'll get through it together like we have our entire lives."

I must not be convincing in my tone because her wary expression doesn't change.

"It's not that I wouldn't be lucky to have you as my husband, Theo, so please don't think that. It's just … I've always seen you as family, and that makes for an awkward marriage," she says, and I can't help but laugh.

"The feeling is mutual, Junie. I adore you, but not in that way," I say with a smile. Releasing her hands, I lean back on the bench.

"Plus, I will feel like I'm betraying Lily. I know that sounds stupid. She's been gone for ten years and …" Junie starts, but I cut her off.

"It's not stupid," I lean forward, bracing my elbows on my knees. "Honestly, I've always felt like that, too. She was my one and only. She was my Amari. No one's Lily and no one ever will be."

"You want to know the worst part?" Junie asks, and I turn to look at her.

She moves forward, matching my positioning.

"My memories of her are so faded. I can only remember glimpses of her. Her details feel erased from my mind. Sometimes I can see her hair, but I wouldn't be able to pick her out of a crowd," Junie confesses.

I let my head fall between my arms. "I know exactly what you mean. But the worst part is the nightmares she plagues me with. I can never see her face. Just her red hair, even though I'm not even positive about the color anymore. The most vivid memories for me are from the day she died," I say grimly.

Junie inhales sharply, placing her hand on my forearm. An icy chill runs up my spine as if Lily's spirit is tracing the length of it, and I fight back the shiver.

"You know, there was nothing you could have done to stop King Oren. My father told you as much after speaking with him. He sensed her power after the nobu attack and came after her," she says reassuringly.

I place my hand on hers and give a gentle squeeze, but I don't look at her. I know by the sound of her voice that pity is etched across her face.

We both remain silent for some time, existing in our own grief over our lost friend. Raising my head, I notice Nathaniel looking in our direction, and I know we need to leave. Turning to Junie, I see she is staring back at him. A deep feeling of longing is evident between them.

I lean close to Junie, "Acted upon, or lusted after, Princess?"

My voice is only loud enough for us to hear in our little space. She jumps at the question, knowing I caught her staring at Nathaniel.

"What?" Her voice is soft and laced with embarrassment.

"You and the lieutenant, Junie. Have you acted on those feelings, or is it still in the wanting phase?" Her cheeks turn a shade of red I've only seen in flowers. I give her hand another squeeze.

"It's ok, Junie. Like I said, we don't have to get married. And even if we do, we won't have to be *with* each other," I say, hoping she understands my meaning.

Her only response is to let out a long breath while eyeing Nathaniel.

Out of the corner of my eye, a navy-blue figure enters the field.

My father.

I stand, knowing my time is up. I extend my palm to Junie. Her smooth, delicate hand slides into mine, and I place it in the crook of my arm. We set off toward the group, stopping at the edge of the field.

"Please come back Theo. I already buried one friend. I can't bear to bury another. I need you to come home," her voice cracks as she fights back the tears threatening to overtake her, and my heart hurts for her.

The pain of losing Lily a decade ago was the worst either of us has ever felt. If Junie loses me too, I'm not sure she would survive.

"I will. I promise. I will come home, Juniper," I say pulling her into the tightest hug I think her thin body can handle, and she squeezes me right back. The lavender scent in her hair gives me a lovely goodbye. She hides her face in my chest so no one can see the tears fall.

Releasing her, I place a kiss on her wet cheek. When I turn around, I find my father staring at me with a look I have never seen on his face—approval. As if my affection toward Junie was anything more than two friends saying goodbye. I stride right past him, not acknowledging he's there, and take the reins back from Nathaniel. Giving Nathaniel a pat on the shoulder, I mount my mare, ready to leave. Junie is still standing in the spot I left her, appearing frozen with fear.

"Take care of her while I'm gone, Nathaniel," I say without taking my eyes off Junie.

He looks over his shoulder at her. "Of course, she's the princess. I will keep her safe."

Staring at him directly in the eyes, I say, "I'm not asking as a captain to a lieutenant. I'm asking as a friend. Please keep her safe."

He nods.

"Words, Nathaniel! I need to hear you say it."

His posture tenses at my shouted command, and he stands at attention.

"Yes, Theo, I'll keep her safe."

"Thank you. I will see you when I return. Until then, the guard is yours."

I heel my mare and get her moving toward the exit of Lux, placing my father strategically in my path. I pull up beside him and pause.

"May Astra watch over you and keep you safe, son," he says.

I stare down my nose at him. "Now, General, you've never been good at being the caring father. Let's not start pretending now. You're the one who is sending me to my death, after all," I reply, my voice dripping with disdain.

I nudge my mare to walk, not allowing him to retort.

I don't look back as we make our way through Lux, down the cobblestone path out of the castle and through the village, passing by the small homes near the entrance, then out the gate toward the portal. My four guards keep close the entire way.

Our horses hesitate at the gray stone arch of the portal, and I don't blame them. It must be an odd sight, but we force them forward. Coming out the other side, in Fati, is a jarring feeling. The land differs from what I'm used to in Lux.

Our kingdom is lush with vast forests of green trees and gray snow-capped mountains, while Fati is mostly brown, with only patches of green fields in clusters plotted around sharp-angled plateaus. The results of a displeased god punishing and abandoning the people of Fati, leaving them to figure things out on their own. While they have found ways to survive over the generations, they're still poor and barely making it.

A shiver runs down my spine at the thought of being left by Astra and no longer having a divinus to protect our people. But we listen to our goddess, and she rewards us with King Leopold's power, saving us from any potential harm.

I say a silent prayer to the goddess to watch over my men on this ridiculous mission. They deserve more than this, but I must follow the orders of the king and general. Even if it means we are all going to die for nothing.

Pushing forward along the gravel path, we pass more small homes. Animal feces and something rancid waft in the air. I swallow hard to keep from vomiting at the stench. We need to get to the forest and into the fresh air.

I tap the side of my mare, and she takes off in an easy trot, straight for the woods. The chilled wind nips at my face as we race across the land, while the warm sun cuts through the bitterness, allowing the rest of our trip to be pleasant.

After a short trot, we make our way into the forest which runs along the mountains, and we slow to a brisk walk. The best path to Umbra is through the trees, and we use it to stay hidden, hopefully raising less suspicion.

The sun sets on our second day of travel as we near the portal of Umbra. The sky, filled with dark oranges and deep reds, adds an eerie feel to the scene before us. We pause at the edge of the woods before the gravel path leading to the portal.

There's one guard on duty, who we could easily subdue if it were required. We study the area until the sun sinks behind the horizon, night beginning in the realm.

I take the lead as we head toward the swirling portal before us. As we near, I take in the portal's intensity. Towering pools of water spiral at a realm-defying angle, straight up and down. The sight makes my stomach twist, and I grimace at the thought of having to walk into it.

We push our horses forward, the gravel crunches under their hooves, and the soft trickling of thin waterfalls greets us as we near. The entry guard sees us and steps onto the path, causing us to halt.

"Please turn around now before it's too late," he pleads.

The guard looks pained as he speaks to us, which doesn't sit well with me.

"We require a meeting with King Asher. Let us pass," I say, nudging my mare closer to the guard, but he doesn't move.

"I'm begging you not to enter. Turn around and go back to Lux. We've buried enough of you already."

I highly doubt they honored my men with proper burials. I let out a grumble at the thought of their desecrated bodies.

"We have direct orders from King Leopold to retrieve the amulet your king stole. Step aside and let us pass," I demand.

The guard stomps his foot. "Don't you get it? We don't have your stupid amulet, and we never have. You'll die for a lie!"

My guards whisper angrily at the Umbra guard's bold statement, and my patience wears thin by the delay.

"We're not liars, thieves, and murderers. You are. Unless you plan to try and stop us, let us pass." My words are a snarl through clenched teeth as I move toward the guard, unsheathing the sword from my back and pointing it down at him, showing we are prepared to defend ourselves.

He stares up the length of my blade as he raises his hands in defeat and steps to the side of the path.

"I'll pray to the gods your deaths are quick but know they won't be painless," he says.

Ignoring his last attempt to unnerve us, I place my sword on my back and heel the mare to step into the portal. I take a deep breath as she resists my command forward. The horses let out a collective whinny as we drive them toward the vortex of water.

Surely, no one has drowned in this portal before ... right?

I close my eyes as mist kisses my skin and we enter.

We're relieved to find the passage smooth and without peril. I'm finally able to let out the breath I was holding as we take our first steps into the dark kingdom.

Shadows blanket every surface of the land. We take a moment and light torches, emitting a faint glow around us. The darkness seems to overpower its reach.

Making out shadows and figures in front of us, I realize the only way forward is through the dreaded haunted forest that everyone in the realm is warned of. The overarching limbs of the largest trees I've ever seen block out the moonlight. At the edge of the forest, a thick fog dances as if it's alive. It moves in a hypnotic rhythm, beckoning us toward it. Unease washes over me at the sight.

We hesitantly move forward, expecting it to hurt us as we enter. Luckily, it doesn't, and we keep walking. The only sounds are our and our horses' heavy breaths. Where are the birds and small animals that usually roam the woods? Their absence causes the hair on my neck to stand.

My instincts flare, telling me to run, and I tap the mare to go faster, but she doesn't listen. She keeps her cautious pace. Her ears are at full attention, and I scan the trees nearest to us with my torch, its dim light barely breaking through the thick shadows around us.

My gaze catches on something seeping from the trunk of the trees, and I steer my horse closer to inspect. A thick, red liquid drains from the trees. Deep pools of what appears to be blood saturate the ground near the base.

Trees don't bleed.

My insides roll with dread and a breath lodges in my throat.

My men must have noticed the blood, too, because their faces are ghostly white, and their breaths turn shallow.

"Keep your eyes open," I warn.

We pick up our pace, each of us watching the trees for the beasts that are supposed to inhabit the haunted forest. In front of us, the trees thin into a clearing; the fog circles the barren space, appearing as though it's caught in a breeze, but the forest is deathly still.

We cross into the open space, the moonlight shines down on us through the broken canopy above. I sense movement out of the corner of my eye and snap my head to catch it. All I see is the dark forest looming, seemingly ready to swallow us whole.

The horses huff and pace nervously. We try hushing to calm them, but another dark mass cuts along the tree line, just out of sight. Raising our torches, we try to get a better look at whatever is circling us but see nothing. Two more masses dance around us. A moving wall of shadows, void of any shape. There are at least four of them; they appear to be hunting us.

We all swing our torches around the clearing, trying to glimpse what we are up against, but the shadowed masses are too fast. My heart quickens as they stalk the corners of my sight. The creatures dart along the tree line, using it as cover.

Wind picks up out of nowhere, engulfing us in a whirlwind of leaves and dirt. The shadows are racing around the circle, becoming a black blur as they swirl the space. The wind douses the torches, plunging us into complete darkness.

Our horses panic and buck wildly, trying to flee. I hold on to the reins as tightly as I can , but it's no use. I hit the forest floor hard, sending shooting pain through my back. From the sounds of their grunts, my guards didn't fare well either.

"Is everyone alr—"

Screams render me silent.

Oh, gods!

Bloodcurdling shrieks of agony tear through the darkness. It sounds as if the creatures are ripping my guards apart, limb from limb. My blood runs cold as I try to push down the terror clawing its way through my body.

I wince in pain as I scramble to my feet, my muscles protesting the sudden movement. Reaching over my shoulder, I grab for my sword, but it isn't there.

Damn it!

I unsheathe a dagger from my hip and try to ready myself to fight to the death with these beasts. More screams from my guards pierce my ears, and I spin, unable to find where they are in the dark.

Something massive knocks me on the shoulder, and I fall to the ground, my dagger flying out of my hand. The forest floor is wet and smells of iron.

Blood.

The blood of my guards covers the ground. Panic consumes me, and I fight to get my feet under me, but they keep slipping on the blood-soaked forest floor. A branch cracks, and I raise my gaze to find six sets of glowing yellow eyes staring back at me through the darkness.

I fall back on my ass with my hands slamming into the blood-soaked ground. I crawl backward, trying to get away. The eyes move with me, not letting me out of their sight. There's no escaping.

The forest falls silent. My men are no longer screaming. At least it's a quick death, even if it's painful.

Just like the guard said it would be.

A sliver of moonlight trails over my body, providing me with a thin view of my red-stained clothes. They feel sticky against my skin.

I pause my retreat and stare up at the tiny holes dotting the canopy. One last look at the stars. I close my eyes and take a deep breath.

One of my last ones, I suppose.

I'll finally join the women I love: my mother, Eleanor, and Lilith. My heart skips a beat at the thought of seeing my flower again. Being able to see all of her—the haze completely gone.

I'm coming Lily. Meet me at the gates of the Underrealm. We will be together again soon, my flower.

Making peace with my end, I look back at the creatures. Five sets of eyes stop just inside the clearing, while one set moves closer to me. My vision goes black at the edges the closer it gets. The pressure in my head is all-consuming.

I pull myself to sit on my knees and push my hands against my temples to counter the pain. I blink and look up again. The eyes are nearly to me now.

Another shot of pain sears through my head, and I fall to the floor, writhing in agony. My mind feels as though it's being shredded. Darkness comes in waves as my vision fades.

I won't cry out and give these beasts the satisfaction of my screams. I push through the pain and open my eyes again to see ...

Is that a giant rabbit?

CHAPTER 13

Nothing. There has been absolutely nothing reported back to us. It has been three days and not a single spy or raven has found anything of value.

Lux has always been bursting with gossip and tales to be told. It appears intentional that there are no rumors or hushed conversations about important information.

Whatever King Leopold has planned, we won't be getting ahead of it. Nor will we find the amulet soon. With the lack of details coming forward, we are stalled.

I let out an enormous sigh, my exaggerated breath ruffling the feathers of my raven, who is perched before me on the edge of the stone bridge. She tilts her head down to look at me suspiciously, and I resume scratching her chest. Her soft feathers caress my fingers as her head falls back, and she gives me a small warble of approval.

The black stone is warm beneath my bent arms, the light mist from the waterfalls preventing it from getting too hot in the sunlight. I peek over the wall at the grunts of nobu below. They've been restless the past day, and I haven't been able to figure out why, which makes my uneasiness grow.

My raven returned this morning after a few days scoping out Lux from the air. From the viewing crystal secured to her chest, there was little captured, only the regular comings and goings of the kingdom.

She did capture Theo sitting on the bank of the river, visibly upset about something. Unfortunately, she was too far away to pick up on anything other than his pained scream, which echoed through the forest on the opposite bank. The sound cracked off a piece of my heart and twisted a knot in my stomach, my instincts raging.

It feels like every nerve in my body is on a parapet expecting a fall. But all I can do now is wait. For what? I'm not sure. The endless possibilities have dominated my thoughts all day, and nothing seems to calm my mind.

I trained with Nyx and the rest of the crew shortly after reviewing the viewing crystal. Blow after blow, hit after hit, my mind still battled with what's to come. All day, each attempt at a distraction has been futile.

There is one last thing to try, drinking. Even though I know it will end badly, I will do anything to ease my mind.

Patting her head, I bid farewell to my raven and use my adveho ring to portal straight into my chambers as to remain unseen. I don't need a lecture about remaining safe, especially from Nyx or Hiram, when what I need is to not be myself for a little while. Plus, I can protect myself. If anything gets out of control, I can always call upon Asher, but that would only be if I were desperate.

Entering my quarters, I peel off my dirty clothes, dropping them into a pile on my floor. I slip into a cream, low-cut, long-sleeved dress, and lace a faded purple corset around my chest.

I give my breasts a once over, making sure they are on full display. They will help me get into someone's bed tonight, or I can fight someone for gawking at them. Either way, I will let out some of this pent-up frustration.

Is it the healthiest way to deal with my inner turmoil? No, but I wasn't raised to handle anything properly. Violence was Oren's preferred method of dealing with almost everything in life.

I retie my hair on top of my head, forgoing my usual wrap. I learned years ago that the villagers of Umbra don't care what you look like or if you have the gods' favorite hair color. As long as you're honest and fair, they'll accept you. Even if they don't know who I truly am to them or my real name, I'm free to be myself in this small way with my people.

I double check that the dagger on my thigh is secure, tracing the red gemstones with a finger before dropping my skirt. I slide on my boots and grab my coin purse from my desk.

Stepping into the middle of my quarters, I make sure everything looks like I'm in here for the rest of the night. The fire in my hearth is low but casts an inviting glow around the quarters. I lock the doors and pull the shades closed.

Satisfied with my cover, I raise my left hand with my adveho ring and picture my village. The black stone homes and businesses with their multi-colored slate roofs, long vines stretching across the tops, connecting everything together. The faint glow of lanterns shines through the windows, and the laughter of the tavern permeates the air.

The familiar red haze of the portal opens, and I step through it onto the gravel pathway on the outskirts of the village. My boots crunch on the stone as I hurry along to the tavern near the center square.

The air has a slight chill to it as autumn settles on the land. The nearly half moon is bright, shining down on us. The next full moon is in a few weeks, bringing monthly court and the autumn equinox. I'm sure the village is preparing for the festival, like it does every year. I hear it's a joyous occasion but have never had a reason to go.

I push open the large wooden door of the tavern to find it filled with villagers. My people are out enjoying the lovely evening and each other's company.

The soft glow of the lanterns hanging above warms the space. The smell of fruit and ale fills the air with an intoxicating aroma as I step through the door.

"Look what the beasts dragged in. You can come in, Margo, if you promise to behave. No fighting, you hear?" Otto, the owner and barkeep, shouts at me from behind the bar, using one of my many aliases.

Since Oren refused to allow anyone to know my real name to conceal my identity, I took it upon myself to create new ones whenever I traveled. Vivienne and Margo are the two I mostly use, and no one has ever questioned if I'm who I present to be.

"Do you promise to keep other patrons from making idiotic comments or touching others without consent?" I cross my arms and tap my boot on the wood flooring.

The last time I was here there was a man who thought making sexual comments toward me was a good idea, and I socked him in the jaw to prove a point.

"You nearly broke Leon's jaw the last time! He couldn't eat solid food for a week," Otto yells.

My only response is a shrug. I'm not sorry for punching Leon, and I would make no promises to not do the same tonight.

Wagging his finger at me, he says, "Best behavior, and I will get you the Fati wine you like."

I stride over and take a seat at the bar.

"I will do my best, but we both know you'll let me stay as long as my coin is good," I wink at Otto and place a few coins on the bar to prove my point.

He grunts and pours me a mug of wine. I take a long swig. The wine is smooth and goes down far too easily.

"Keep them coming," I say, placing more coins on the counter, knowing I'm paying well over the cost of the wine, but I need to win him over to stay. He happily takes the money and hands me more wine.

It's only after I finish an entire bottle of Fati wine and start a second that my thoughts become less frantic and my body eases. A few villagers who remember me from past visits stop to catch up, but otherwise, I'm left alone most of the evening and enjoy the solitude.

Otto brings me a tray of crackers, cheeses, and fruit, as I requested. Taking the first bite, I let out a small moan. I may be a little too drunk, and I giggle to myself at the realization.

As I take another sip of wine, the scent of apples surrounds me. I bite my bottom lip before turning to catch Kira taking a seat next to me. Her chestnut eyes meet mine as she settles.

"How do you always know it's me and not some predator?"

I eye her from head to toe, not missing the fact that she is wearing a revealing yellow dress, which is my favorite color on her. It makes her skin glow. Her long, golden-brown hair flows in tight ringlets down her back and over her shoulders. I take a strand, toying with it between my fingertips.

"Do you think after all these years I wouldn't recognize your presence even with my eyes closed?" I ask, staring into her glassy eyes.

She must be looking for the same thing I am tonight.

With the back of my other hand, I brush her hair off her shoulders and graze her soft skin. I watch, transfixed, as her breath hitches at my touch. It's been over a year since I've allowed myself to be this close to Kira, but the sensation still feels so familiar. The thought of her taste, her touch, and the sounds she makes ignite the old desire within me, which settles between my thighs.

I bite my lip again, lost in my filthy memories. Kira's hand slides up my forearm, and I realize I'm still playing with her hair. I let go of the strand and grab my mug of wine, finishing it. Her hand finds a comfortable spot on my leg, and I hate how easy it is for us to go right back to the same place we once were.

I set my mug back on the counter and blurt, "I need to get some air."

Pushing away, I stand wobbly on my feet and head out the door. Barely anyone bothers to look up. Just another inebriated woman leaving the tavern.

Stepping out into the cool night, I take a deep breath, trying to douse the fire igniting inside me. Using the wall to steady myself, I trudge to a cold iron bench and fall into it. My head spins from the movement.

Leaning my head back, I close my eyes, wishing things could be different. Wishing I wasn't bound to a shadow monster. And if I'm not free to be with my Amari, wishing that I could simply have a mutually beneficial arrangement with Kira, without her needing more. But I'm trapped. I can't have Theo or give Kira what she wants. I'm just stuck in the shadows with Asher until my dying day.

The bench flexes as Kira takes a seat next to me. The air around her is tense, and she huffs as she sits.

"Do I disgust you so much that we can't share a nice evening of drinks together in the tavern?" The anguish in her voice has me glancing sideways.

Kira pinches her lips into a tight line, emphasizing her frustration with me.

I let out a sigh, closing my eyes again.

"No, Kira, I needed fresh air for an entirely different reason." A snicker escapes me, but she remains silent.

Her apple scent invades my senses, reigniting the embers inside.

"I was having a hard time not picturing myself between your thighs," I declare. The wine has definitely loosened my tongue.

Kira shifts her weight.

"It was easier for me to step outside than worry about what I would do if I stayed. It wouldn't be fair to you if I acted on those thoughts, since we're not on the same page," I state.

The wine has removed all of my inhibitions and common sense. My clothes will surely be next.

I hear her gulp beside me.

"Oh," is her only response.

This is the most honest I have been with Kira in a long time. I want to say more, but my thoughts are a jumbled mess of words and sexual desire. We remain quiet for several long moments.

The distant sounds of birds distract me as I sink back into the bench. I could easily fall asleep right here. My brain feels muddled. Everything seems to swirl.

This may have been a mistake.

"What if we were on the same page?" Kira's voice startles me, and I jump, then settle back into my laid-back state.

My body feels too heavy.

"Are we though?" I ask, and even I can hear how slurred my words are becoming.

Before I can form any more words, Kira is straddling my lap. Her hands weave into my hair, tilting my face up, forcing me to look at her.

"Tonight, we're on the same page, Lily." She devours my lips hungrily, as if she had been starving for the taste of me.

It all feels like a dream, as if I'm simply watching the scene unfold. My brain has completely shut off, and I surrender to the dizzy and intoxicating feeling of her body pressing into mine.

Gods, she feels too good.

My fingers dig into her hips as I part my lips, trailing my tongue along her bottom lip. She opens for me, and we share the taste of the sweet and fruity Fati wine.

She grips my head tight, deepening our kiss and grinds into me, asking for more. Tracing my hands up her toned body, I slip a hand under the low-cut neckline of her dress and her bra, finding her peaked nipple. I tug on it gently, eliciting a little moan from her into my mouth. I smile at her noise and move my hand to her other nipple to do the same.

Kira bites my bottom lip, and it's my turn to moan. My body buzzes as I run my hands down her back to her ass and give it a firm pat. She jumps slightly, giving me full access to grip her ass with both hands. A surge rushes through me, and I push forward to stand but immediately fall back to the bench.

"I may be a little too drunk to attempt that," I slur and laugh too loudly.

She climbs off me and pulls me to standing. We sway, unsteady on our feet, drunk on wine and lust. We stumble toward the center of the walkway, and I close my eyes, trying to envision my chambers, but nothing happens. Laughing, I pull off my adveho ring and offer it to Kira.

"Will you please take me to your bed?" I stammer.

She eyes the metal glinting in the moonlight.

"Why can't you take us there?" Raising one perfectly arched eyebrow, she lifts her chin, and I hook my finger under it.

"Too drunk," I chuckle, "and I want to have you coming before I pass out."

Her eyes dance with what I think is anticipation, and I turn her toward the open space in the square, bringing her back flush to my chest. She slides the adveho ring on her index finger, lifts it, and closes her eyes in concentration.

I bend down, unsteadily, sliding my hand up the back of her leg and under her dress. She looks down at me, her shifted focus stops the red mist's formation.

"Pay attention to opening that portal, Kira."

She listens and goes back to work while I continue my path up her thigh.

I wrap my free arm around her waist, drawing her close to me as I fumble at her undergarments. I can feel a hint of wetness as my fingers trace slow circles on her clit through the fabric. She gasps at the sensation, breaking the mist again.

"Focus, Kira." I command.

Her eyes close for a moment, and she opens the portal once more.

As the red mist grows, I slip my fingers into her undergarment, playing with her warm, soft skin. Increasing the pace of my circles, her breaths quicken and hitch against me.

The portal finally opens completely, and Kira's chambers are visible within.

"Now, that's my good girl," I whisper in her ear.

She turns to me, and I pull my hand away from her pussy, letting her dress fall back to her knees.

Her eyes are ablaze, and her breathing is ragged. I bite my bottom lip as Kira's hands slide into mine. Walking backward into the portal, she leads me into her quarters and into her bed.

The sunlight beaming in through the window feels like razor blades on my eyes as I open them.

Gods, my head is pounding.

Rubbing the sleep from my eyes, I realize where I am.

Shit.

I glance over to see Kira is still sleeping soundly next to me. Her tightly coiled golden-brown hair frames her sleep-softened features. Her full lips are slightly parted. She looks delicate in this state. Not at all the expertly trained spy she is.

The bedsheet is under her armpits, wrapping around her body but allowing her breasts to peek out from the top. I look down at myself and realize I too am naked.

This isn't good.

I let my head fall back against her wooden headboard.

How did I let this happen?

I was drunk, lonely, frustrated, and desperate. That's how it happened.

After all this time avoiding close contact with her to prevent this exact thing from happening, I allowed my weaknesses to take over. I wanted to get lost in someone last night, but why did I choose Kira? I'll inevitably hurt her, and the cycle of resentment will continue.

After Oren died, I became queen and permanently tethered to the new king. I'm forever bound to Asher, forced to rule in secret, and cemented in my eternal loneliness. Kira was solace, giving me what Asher couldn't: companionship, warmth, pleasure. Spending most of my evenings with her legs wrapped around my head offered an escape. But as time went on, she became possessive, even getting angry with me when I spent time with Nyx, who had been promoted to general after we also lost Tobias. She wanted more from me, and I was already giving her all I could.

I know I should have ended it sooner, but I was being selfish for the first time in my life. I wanted her to accept the simple relationship I had forced her into. It wasn't fair and looking back, I would do things differently, but there's no changing the past. The gods know how much I wish I could in so many ways.

Right now, I would love to go back to last night and not come to Kira's quarters. I cautiously shift my weight and slip my legs out from under the covers over the edge of the bed. The movement is dizzying, and I grip the sheets, steadying myself.

After the everything stops spinning, and I successfully stop the bile in my throat from spewing, I grab my undergarments and dress from the floor. I look around for my corset, not remembering taking it off. Slowly and painfully, I put my clothes on and sit back on the bed.

Kira stretches and yawns behind me, causing me to freeze.

"Good morning." Her voice is soft and dreamy.

"Good morning," I say, turning to look at her as she sits up and tucks her knees into her chest.

"Last night was a lot of fun," she says.

A shy smile spreads across her face as she tucks her hair behind one ear. I adjust my position so I can see her better, placing a bent knee on the bed.

"From what I can remember, it was. But it shouldn't have happened, and I'm sorry for that," I state.

Her expression turns to stone.

"Don't do that. Don't act like I didn't want it just as much as you. Like I said last night, we were on the same page." Her words are harsh and clipped.

I never seem to know what to say to her anymore. It's as if everything I say is wrong, which is infuriating.

I turn and put my feet on the ground, entirely unsure of what to say.

"Don't … don't shut me out again, Lils. I can't take the cold shoulder anymore. Can we at least be friends?" she asks.

I rub my temples because it's too early, and this conversation is too intense for this severe hangover. A drawer opens, and Kira rummages through her side table.

"Here."

I look over my shoulder to see her handing me a vial with purple liquid in it.

"It's a hangover elixir from the apothecary. It will cure that pain in your head," she states.

I take the small vial from her hand, tilting it, watching the mixture roll from side to side. I've never had a hangover elixir before. Then again, I don't make it a habit to get this drunk. Thankful for the possibility of relief, I uncork the vial and down the tart liquid. I can't quite place the herbs I taste.

"Thank you. I'll get a replacement for you as soon as I can," I say.

She waves her hand at me. "Don't worry about it. I have plenty more from where that came," she says.

I nod and set the empty vial on the nightstand.

At least I was coherent enough last night to stash my dagger and adveho ring there. I pick them up, put my ring back on, and strap the dagger to my right thigh.

Suddenly, grunts and growls from the nobu filter through Kira's window. I raise my head as if I can see them from here.

"They've been agitated the past few days," she states with concern.

The unease that has been twisting my stomach returns.

"They have, and we haven't been able to figure out why," I say as the angry nobu sounds and the thrashing of water echo through the quiet chambers.

"I better get going before Nyx looks for me."

I stand from the bed, my dizziness already fading. That is a quick-acting elixir. I'll have to go buy some for myself.

Turning to face her, I see my corset hooked on a chair near the door and make a mental note to grab it on my way out. Kira has the bed sheet pulled up around her breasts and is pulling on a loose thread on the top blanket. Her face is a mix of sorrow and fear.

"Speak your mind, Kira. You've never been one to hold back, so why do it now?"

Her eyes come to mine, and they are cold, already knowing my response before speaking.

"Just don't shut me out again, Lily. It felt like I lost a limb. A piece of me. I'll take you in any way you'll let me. I can't lose you again," she says.

Unfortunately, I know Kira is lying. She can't handle just being friends. She'll always want more, need more, from me.

I soften my voice, "I will try my best, but—"

She finishes for me, "You are what you are and that won't change."

I've lost count of how many times I have had to tell her this.

"Exactly. Monsters don't change, Kira. And expecting one to do so is only going to leave you hurt. If you truly believe you can handle being friends, then I'll do what I can as well," I say.

Her eyes fill with hope as tears form. I lean across the bed and kiss the side of her head.

"I'll see you later."

She gives me a small nod, and I head to the chair where my corset hangs before opening the door to step into the hallway. I lift my hand and open a portal to return, unseen, into my chambers.

I undress and discard my clothes in the ever-growing pile. I stride into my expansive walk-in glass shower and allow the water to pour from the rainfall feature in the ceiling.

I quickly wash and dry before sliding on a fresh pair of black trousers and a white shirt. Using a thick cord, I pull back my wet hair and secure it in place. Lacing up my boots, I leave my chambers in record time.

The sight of Hiram leaning against the wall across from my quarters halts my movement.

"Captain." I narrow my eyes at him in question.

He pushes off the wall and dips into a deep bow.

"Good morning, Your Highness."

"What are you doing here, Hiram?"

He steps toward me, eyeing my door, before meeting my glare.

"I thought it would be better if I walked you to training this morning instead of the general, in case your guest was still around. Shall we?" He stretches his arm out toward the training yard.

A blush reddens my cheeks. How did he know I was with Kira last night? This is the problem with ruling a crew of highly skilled spies and warriors. They always know your business, no matter how hard you try to cover your tracks. He must have seen us in the tavern last night but not where we ended up.

"I know how Nyx feels about Kira, so I figured I would intercept before he made a scene about how you spent your evening," he states.

I stare at the black stones as we walk, embarrassed by being caught doing the exact thing I said a year ago I wouldn't do again.

"It was just one night. Nothing more."

He raises his hands in a placating manner.

"It's none of my business. Just be careful, my queen. While we all like Kira, she doesn't always have your best interests in mind. She has her own motives, and they tend to be troublesome."

His words are quiet, only for us to hear, but they still slam into my heart regardless of the volume.

"It was only a drunken hookup, Hiram. That is all," I reply.

He gives me a worried look before nodding. We are silent the rest of our walk to the training yard, and I remain that way the rest of the morning.

CHAPTER 14

LILY

The irritated bellows of the nobu have become the chorus of our days and nights. Standing at the edge of The Keep's pool, the water undulates, frantically splashing the shore as the beasts angrily move through it.

"They're worse today than yesterday," Nyx says next to me as we study the nobu.

Nothing seems to calm them. I've tried stretching my shadows through the water to ease their tension, which usually helps, but not this time.

Their glowing white eyes sprinkle the surface, matching the stars shining down from above. The knot in my stomach has only grown throughout the day, and my instincts are screaming at me, but I can't figure out what the alert is about.

"Did the male raven return yet?" I ask Nyx, raising my voice loud enough for him to hear me over the nobu.

"No. He was supposed to return yesterday, and no one in Lux has seen him," Nyx answers.

The raven's mate has to be worried with his longer-than-normal absence. I will have to check on her and their offspring tomorrow.

"What are we going to do, Nyx? This must be a warning, but of what?" My body buzzes with the alarmed screams of the nobu.

"I'm not sure. My best guess is King Leopold is preparing for an attack, so we'd better prepare, too," Nyx wraps his arm around my shoulder and pulls me tight to his side.

A wave of dread shoots through my body as if I've been struck by lightning. I sway in Nyx's grasp as my power tries to overtake me. Its strength threatens my balance. It feels like the first time all those years ago. That day in the river when I was a girl trying to protect the boy she loved from danger.

Nyx draws his dagger with his free hand as he grips me tight, sensing my alarm.

"What is it, Lily?" he asks, checking the field for an attacker.

"Something is coming. My power is reacting to it," I reply.

I double over in pain as the sensation of my heart being ripped apart flares in my chest. The thread twisted around it pulls tight, squeezing hard enough that it hurts to breathe. Nyx grabs my arms to stop me from falling.

As fast as it comes on, the pain is gone. And so are the agitated sounds of the nobu. We freeze and slowly turn our heads to the water, which is suddenly completely still. The moon reflects brightly on the glass surface.

"What in the realm?" Nyx whispers.

Thundering hooves come from behind us, and we whip around to find Hiram bursting from the haunted forest at breakneck speed, heading straight toward us.

"Queen!" He is shouting at the top of his lungs.

Renewed panic causes my breath to hitch. We run toward him to shorten the distance. He is flying off his Warlander before it even comes to a complete stop. We rush to him, and he stumbles, but I catch him in my hands, steadying him on his feet.

"What's going on, Hiram?" I shout.

He's panting and out of breath, his body shakes in my hands.

"Lux. Guards. In the haunted forest." His words break between gasps for air.

Great, more dead bodies to bury tomorrow.

"Four. Dead. Queen." He stares at me, clutching my arms.

His fingers dig into my skin.

"One is alive," he pants.

Shock overtakes me.

One survived? And we got to him before the nobu attacked?

"Where is he?" I ask urgently.

Hiram stands to his full height, finally catching his breath.

"Marcus and Silas have him. They are bringing him to The Keep for medical aid. It's hard to tell in the torchlight, but he's covered in either blood or the red sap of the bloodwoods. He keeps losing consciousness. They have to carry him," Hiram replies.

The thread around my heart vibrates softly as if a hand is gliding across it.

Thank the gods! Our prayers have saved one.

"He may need a physician. We should go get one," I say, turning to Nyx.

His eyebrows are so furrowed they are almost one.

"I'll handle it. Meet us in the throne room. We'll need Asher for this," Nyx says.

I look at my general and captain, whose faces both tense with concern.

"Of course. I'll go ready the king," I reply, stepping away and opening a portal to go prepare the Umbra Brutus.

Moments later, Nyx's stern orders echo in the stone hallway, and I hurry toward him. We nearly collide at the corner as he darts around it.

"How is his?" I inquire about our miracle Lux guard.

I notice what looks like blood on Nyx's shirt, and I feel the color drain from my face. Was he injured while trying to get the guard back to The Keep?

"It's the sap from the bloodwood trees," he reassures, "they bled everywhere. The forest ground is saturated with it. It's so strange. They have never done that before," he notes.

Just then, shouts come from the entrance of The Keep, announcing my guards' return with the captured intruder. We round the corner to watch as they carry the guard under his arms through the hallway as his limp legs drag behind. His clothes are tinted red, and his brown hair is matted. His head bobs back and forth as they carry him toward the open doors of the throne room.

I watch intently as they pass when, suddenly, the limp guard's head lolls to the side, and I catch a glimpse of ... *no. No. No. No.*

Theo.

It can't be him. They wouldn't send their captain to die!

Panic floods my body, and I can't think.

I can't breathe!

My vision goes black at the edges and tunnels. All I see is him.

My shadows rage within me as my entire body begins to shake. Darkness erupts, swallowing me whole. The air sparks as I give into it.

Strong hands slam me into the stone wall.

"What's going on, Lily?" The question is muffled, as if I'm underwater—all noises drowned out by the void engulfing me.

All I can do is stare at my guards standing frozen near the throne room door with Theo's unconscious body dangling from their arms.

"Lily!" The wall behind me shakes as Nyx roars for my attention.

But I can't take my eyes off Theo.

He can't be here. This isn't real. He's not safe.

My face is yanked away from the devastating sight of the man I love, and I'm forced to look into Nyx's gray eyes, which seem to be searching my soul.

"Look at me, Lily. Please look at me. The entire Keep is going to come down if you don't take a breath!" he screams at me.

But I can't truly see him through the black clouding my vision.

This is my fault. I'm the one who hurt him. My creatures. My forest. My kingdom. I did this.

A voice in the darkness whispers in response, *"Leopold."*

Rage blazes through me like a forest fire, consuming everything in its wake. The hallway seems to glow in response.

Leopold did this. He tried to kill what is mine, breaking our deal. Why? There's no way he found out about my slip up at the inn two months ago.

"Stop!" Nyx is begging. "This needs to stop. Lily, come back to me."

I try to bring myself back. I have to be present to help Theo.

Breathe. That's it. One more.

I gasp and crash, falling into Nyx's arms and sobbing. The wall of black evaporates.

Nyx pulls me tight to his chest, rubbing my back.

"Shh. It's ok. Just keep breathing for me. Everything's ok," he whispers into my hair.

"He can't be here, Nyx. It can't be him," I say through tears.

He pushes me back and holds me at arm's length with a firm grip.

"What do you mean he can't be here?" He demands.

I don't answer as the tears flow.

"Who is he, Lily? And don't you dare lie to me! You almost brought down The Keep. What in this realm is going on, and how do you know that guard?" Confusion and hurt line his face.

I've never told him about Theo or that I even thought I had an Amari. The pain was always too great to explain.

"He's the love of my life," I whisper as the guards carry Theo into the throne room.

Nyx's gaze narrows.

"Sure, because that explains everything," he says with exasperation. "We don't have time for this right now. Get it together. Summon Asher. We'll discuss all that just happened afterward."

He releases his hold on me and steps back. All I can do is shake my head. He grabs my face gently. His thumbs glide along my cheeks, wiping away my tears.

"Listen to me. You're the strongest person I have ever met. You have survived torture that would have killed others," he says, "you're the queen of the most feared kingdom in Omnia. Now go and summon your king so we can handle what needs to be done. Then we will go to your chambers, and you will tell me everything."

Nyx pulls the hood of my cloak over my head, hiding my hair. He places a kiss on my forehead and steps back.

I gather my thoughts and concentrate on my breathing. I tap into the dark bond between the monster and me and call upon the shadow king.

We're just gathering information. Theo won't be hurt.

The hairs on my arms rise as the air charges with increasing power. As if pulled from every dark corner of The Keep, shadows dance across the floor. They spiral and thicken until the towering, cloaked figure of Asher steps from the black abyss. The king has arrived.

We enter the throne room to see Theo, who is now conscious and kneeling at the steps of the dais, ready to meet King Asher. The lanterns emit an eerie glow around the space. The smell of iron wafts through the room, causing me to swallow hard. I swear I feel Theo's eyes tracking me.

Asher stands at the center of the dais. Theo's head lifts, eyes filling with fear as he realizes where he is. He fights against Marcus and Hiram's hold. From a kneeling position, he throws them off their balance before they regain control. Terror seems to sink in as they settle him back before the shadow king. His jaw clenches.

My shadows claw at my skin, begging to be released. They hum in his presence, seeming to be drawn to him.

I study Theo for a long moment. The stony, reserved face of a well-trained guard stares directly ahead at the wall of shadows. A simple, emotionless mask of indifference overtakes his expression.

"Just kill me already like you did my men so I can join them in the Underrealm," Theo yells.

Even though his face is resigned, the fury in his voice is palpable. I want to be relieved that he seems relatively unharmed, but his anger stirs mine. His sheer audacity to blame us for his men's deaths is laughable.

"Your king killed your men, not us. He's the one who sent you here uninvited, knowing death would take you all," Asher's voice hisses.

Theo lunges toward the dais in response, and Marcus and Hiram restrain him. Nyx steps in to hold Theo down by his shoulders to prevent him from trying to move again.

"You could have stopped all of this if you just gave back that damned amulet," Theo's shout echoes off the stone while he tries to shake off all three men holding him in place.

Asher brings his veiled face almost even with Theo's.

"As I've already told King Leopold, we didn't take his amulet, nor do we know who has it," Asher says before standing back to his full, towering height.

Theo's eyes dart back and forth as if trying to chase the words.

"What? He didn't tell you? Not surprised. He's a deceitful, lying king," Asher snips in response to Theo's reaction.

Rage fills Theo's face and he spits. It lands on the dais, just shy of Asher.

"You're the liar and murderer, not my king," Theo growls, baring his teeth at the shadow king.

Marcus draws a hand back to smack Theo across the face for his disrespect. Theo closes his eyes and pulls his lip inward, preparing for the impact. Shadows snatch Marcus' arm inches before it reaches Theo's face.

"Did I give you an order to harm my prisoner?" Asher's voice is cold and menacing.

Marcus tries to wrench his arm free, but the shadows hold on tight, not wanting to release him.

"If you lay a hand on him, I'll drive shadows so far down your throat they will come out of your ass. He's my prisoner, and I decide his punishment. Not you or any other guard. If someone dares to look at him the wrong way, they will meet an early grave," Asher says harshly.

The shadows release Marcus, who, having been put in his place, resumes his hold on Theo.

"You will allow my physician and healer to assess any wounds," Asher addresses Theo again, ignoring the spit.

The physician and healer step forward, and Theo flinches at their approach. A tendril of shadow lifts and the two stop.

Theo twitches with pent up anger.

"Rise." Asher commands.

Hiram, Marcus, and Nyx lift Theo. Only Nyx matches Theo's height as he stands.

Theo's eyes remain locked on the stone floor. I'm not sure if it's out of fear or defiance. The tendril of shadow reaches out and grabs his chin, forcing him to look at the void of darkness before him. My heart skips a beat. My instincts flare. I want to save him.

"Do you have something else to say, guard?" Asher demands.

He's the Captain.

Theo's nostrils flare as his lips twist into a snarl. "It's Captain." He says through clenched teeth, echoing my thought.

"Fine, Captain, speak before I make you," Asher matches Theo's tone.

The muscles of Theo's jaw flex, and he seems to debate with himself. The shadows squeeze his chin.

Not too hard. Just talk, Theo.

The pressure does the trick.

"Why are you doing this? Why provide me with anything if you plan to kill me? Isn't that a waste of your precious resources?" his words are a taunt.

An unnerving chuckle comes from the shadow king. "I don't need you dying from a festering infection before I figure out what to do with you."

Concern flashes across Theo's face, but only for an instant before it's back to the mask of a stoic warrior. Releasing his face, the shadow waves the physician and healer forward.

Theo allows them near him. Nyx, Marcus, and Hiram don't let go of Theo while he is being assessed. The physician checks him head to toe, lifting his shirt and pant legs to reveal unharmed tanned skin. I breathe a sigh of relief.

The physician and healer speak to Theo in low, gentle voices, and he nods or shakes his head to answer. Like me, his energy is waning after this horrendous day.

When they complete the examination, they turn to deliver their prognosis to Asher.

"A few cuts and bruises from what we can see, Your Excellency. We will bring him a salve to help with healing and any soreness he may have, " confirms the healer, and the two turn and leave the room.

"Take him to the cell by the back entrance," Asher commands the guards.

I try to push down all the emotions that erupt at the thought of Theo in my old cell.

"My king, do you think that is the best place?" Nyx lets go of Theo and walks up the steps of the dais, his face tense.

"Don't question me, General," Asher retorts. "There will be two guards posted outside his cell. Ask the kitchen to prepare a meal for him. Ensure the water in the cell is working and provide him with fresh clothes. Do I make myself clear?"

All the guards stiffen at the order and stand at attention.

"Good. Now go," the king dismisses everyone with the final decree.

Theo digs his heels into the stone floor, trying to halt Marcus and Hiram from moving him out of the throne room. The scuffing of Theo's boots on stone reverberates throughout the space as they haul him away and out of my sight.

The shadows surrounding Asher flicker, signaling that he is ready to move on. A moment later, they thin and skirt along the floor and out of the throne room, taking the king with them.

My resolve cracks, and a whimper escapes me. Nyx comes to my side, wrapping me in his arms.

"Let's get you to your chambers. I know you are tired, but we have a lot to discuss," he whispers into my ear.

We break our embrace and walk silently back to my quarters.

We cross the threshold of my chambers, and I fall into a seat at my table.

"Lilith, you better start talking now before I go down to that cell and ask our new guest how he knows you," Nyx shouts.

I stiffen at the thought of Nyx questioning Theo.

"That's the thing, though. He wouldn't be able to tell you," I reply.

Nyx scrunches his face in confusion.

"It's a long, painful story," I say, motioning for him to take a seat in the chair on the other side of the table, and he does.

I take a deep breath and tell my best friend my deepest, darkest secrets. The ones that plague the nightmares I have never been able to tell him about.

CHAPTER 15

LILY

"So, this guy watched you die and has no idea it was Oren using a trove blade to fake your death and kidnap you?" Nyx confirms the information he has learned this far.

I nod.

"He has no idea who I am. He doesn't know that Oren brought me here to use my god-given power as a weapon—to hone Thalos' shadows for his selfish reasons before I could learn to control them and use them against him," I explain. "You know that Oren brought me here to use as his weapon, but you don't know the extent of the torture he used to break me and force me to comply." I say, glancing over at Nyx.

Nyx's leg bounces anxiously as he grips the armrests of the crimson chair, bracing himself for more.

"Oren was good at deceit and lies," I remind Nyx, "and we did everything we could to hide how bad things were getting from you because we were afraid of what you'd do."

Fierce gray eyes snap to meet mine, and the anger within tells me we were right to keep it from him.

"We?" Nyx's question is a snarl. "Who are 'we,' Lily?"

The pain from my deceit clear in his voice.

"Loma and Tobias. They would heal me the best they could before I saw you. Tobias knew if you found out what was truly going on, you would have tried to kill Oren," I answer.

"My father knew and did nothing?" his words are mumbled.

Nyx stares at the black stone floor of my quarters, his eyes fixed and unblinking. The tapping of his boot as it bounces up and down provides a rhythmic thud to fill the silence. The muscles of his jaw flex in time with his leg.

"He was protecting you. If he could have found a way to keep both of us safe, he would have," I say as a small smile tugs at the corners of my lips, trying to calm him.

Nyx looks so much like Tobias it hurts sometimes, especially in moments like this. They share the same intensity for keeping those they love safe, and Tobias did all he could for me without angering Oren and putting Nyx in danger.

Gods, I miss him.

"I don't think either of us realized just how far Oren was willing to go to get what he wanted. Your father had to watch horrific things happen to me, and he couldn't interfere. But he always took care of me afterward, and during the worst of the torture, I would seek out his kind hazel eyes to ground me. I always knew he was right there with me, no matter what happened," I say, remembering the pain and all he had to witness happen to me, powerless against Oren's wrath. Nyx's face softens as I speak about his father.

Horrible memories cloud my mind and I'm transported back to my first day as Oren's prisoner.

"What do you want from me?" I asked, the cold cuffs digging into the soft skin of my wrists.

Oren scowled, and a disapproving look twisted his features. "I want to see what can come of you in the right hands. You will obey me and follow my every command."

I raised my gaze to his, baring my teeth. "And if I don't? You'll do what? Kill me? You already did that, remember?" I yelled, refusing to give in to a deranged man who stole me from my family.

Oren glowered at me with such contempt it caused the shadows to stir again. "There are far worse things than death, girl. It would be in your best interest to listen and obey."

I shake my head, trying to rid the memories from my mind.

"Over time, things turned into a routine. I would 'disobey' and Oren would torture me, forcing Tobias to watch. As soon as Oren left, Tobias and Loma would work together to heal my wounds. The pattern repeated itself over and over for seven years."

"We can't let him keep doing this, Tobias. He's going to kill her!" Loma harshly whispers from outside my cell.

"You don't think I fear that, Loma? We don't have a choice. Oren will carry out his plans, no matter what. We can't raise any suspicion, or she won't have anyone to help her. We stay quiet and hidden so we can save her. She must live," Tobias answer softly.

I let out a deep sigh, coming back to the present. Nyx's breathing becomes harsh as he grips the chair so hard his knuckles turn white.

"If Theo never arrived, would you have ever told me any of this?" Nyx asks.

The question stings because I know I wouldn't have. It was a secret Tobias, Loma, and I never wanted to share with anyone.

"No. I never wanted you to know how bad it got," I reply, feeling raw and exposed—the worst parts of my past on full display.

"The night The Keep shook seven years ago was also because of Theo," I say, ready to reveal everything.

Nyx's eyes are cold and angry. "He's the reason our home was almost brought down twice?" he yells.

I lean forward, bracing my arms on my legs.

"That night, everything changed. Oren chained me to the wall as usual, but this time he had opened a portal into the Lux dungeons where my mother hung from the ceiling," I say, rubbing the back of my head, remembering the pain from when Oren slammed it against the wall.

Nyx's eyes soften and his eyebrows furrow. I never talk about my mother. It's too painful.

"Oren and Leopold had beaten her before they woke me. It was punishment for both of us, I guess," I pick at my nails, trying to keep the memories at bay.

"She will end you all. You will fall and weep at her feet. She. Will. End. You." I can hear my mother's words as if she is here with me now.

"Oren offered me a deal. I was to listen to his every command and do what he wanted. In return, he would let her live. She begged me to not break, but all I wanted was for her to be safe, even if it wasn't with me," I say, wiping a tear from my cheek, expecting to see dirt covering my hands like it had back then.

I stare at the floor as the past and present melt into one. Hints of sweat and blood fill my nose as my mind fights to figure out what is real and what is a memory. Darkness creeps in, threatening to take me back.

"Listen to me, Nata. They can never truly break you as long as you follow the threads of your heart. They will always lead you to where you are supposed to be. The threads will lead you home. I will always love you. Make them pay, Lily."

"I tried reaching her, but I wasn't strong enough yet. And when I didn't immediately accept his deal, Oren slit her throat. He forced me to watch my mother die," I say, clenching my hands together.

My shadows swirl in the well at my core as I fight to keep my emotions in check. My skin buzzes as the darkness within me begs to be unleashed, to drag me into its black abyss.

"Lily," Nyx's voice is soft and low.

His eyes reflect the same heartbreak I feel. I swallow hard, preparing to tell him about my undoing.

"After they murdered my mother, I kept my resolve. I thought it was over—that Oren had taken all he could from me. But, somehow, Leopold knew that Theo was my Amari and offered him to Oren to try and use another person I loved to break me," I scoff.

Theo remains loyal to the man who so willingly offered him up for slaughter.

"At the threat, I cracked. And, suddenly, the well with my shadows erupted, flooding me with a power I had never felt before. It tore through my body, and I felt like the darkness was consuming every part of me. Then, I was no longer in my cell. My mind was pulled somewhere else," I say, trying to figure out how to explain it.

"What do you mean? What did you see?" Nyx tries to grasp what I'm telling him.

"A stone temple with three shapeless clouds colored blue, green, and purple hovering within. One pale man with black hair and solid-black eyes, as dark as the night, stood in the middle. He had a red-rimmed mist hovering around him. He was reaching for me. The air around him vibrated with energy. Then he spoke, and there was no denying who was with me: Thalos."

Nyx's eyes go wider than I've ever seen.

"Thalos was in your mind? Lily that is only heard of in lore! How? Why?" Nyx stammers, trying to make sense of it.

I'd love it if he could because it still doesn't make sense to me, even after seven years.

"He forced his shadow power into me. By the gods, it hurt," I say with a shiver. Thalos' deep, demanding voice rings in my head *"Now!"*

"When the power tore out of me, both Brightwick and our Keep trembled under the sheer force. The shadows went straight for Oren and Leopold, wrapping around their necks as if seeking revenge." I pause, remembering the feeling of their racing heartbeats through my power.

"After the shock wore off, they tried to fight back. It felt like Thalos was still in control of the shadows, demanding blood. But I couldn't do it. I had the choice to allow the darkness to consume me, but I knew that once it did, there was no going back. The power was too raw, and I couldn't control it. If I gave in, I would lose myself to the dark. Looking back, I should have done it," I pause, letting regret wash over me.

"Instead, before releasing them, I agreed to do their bidding but added some terms of my own. I would follow their orders, allow them to wield my power as they wished, and help them increase their control over the realm, but they couldn't hurt the ones I loved, including Theo. They agreed at first."

"You agreed to all of that … for Theo?" Nyx asks.

I look down at my hands. One day, I was fighting against Oren with every fiber of my being, and the next, I became part of the most destructive team in the realm—more and more blood covering my hands with each passing year.

"I thought if I kept my end of the deal, everyone I loved would be safe, but that's not what happened. If I even passively defied any of Oren's commands, he would open a portal into Theo's chambers to prove a point. Leopold was always all too happy to offer to torture him as a lesson for me. They would invent infractions to remind me that they held the real powers and could end Theo's life in an instant," I reply.

"You let them use you for a Lux guard?" Nyx grumbles. "How could you have kept this from me for so long, Lily? Do you know how it feels to know you went through all of that without ever letting me know what was happening to you?" He points at his heart, and I know I've hurt it.

"I know," is all I can say.

His jaw ticks. The pain in his eyes cuts through to my soul. He has put me back together for the past ten years. After every murder and torture Oren forced me to commit, he brought me back. Reminding me that there was still a bit of light in the darkness.

"You are good, Nata. Always remember that."

"Wait, you said he doesn't know who you are. If you're Amari, how can he not remember you?" Nyx asks in sudden realization.

"Leopold gave an elixir to Theo and Princess Juniper shortly after Oren took me. It veiled their memories so they'd never be able to recognize me. They remember Lily and my death, but they can't remember what I look like and have no idea I'm still alive and hidden in Umbra. I've tried figuring out what was in the elixir on my own but haven't been able to. Now that Theo is here, away from Leopold, I want to speak with Loma about an antidote," I answer.

"Let it be known," Nyx declares, "that I think that is a very bad idea, but I will go with you, anyway."

I reward him with a short-lived smile.

"Wait, you also said they accepted the deal 'at first,' what did you mean?" Nyx has started to put things together, and it appears his mind is racing.

"After the deal was made, I kept my power safely sealed within the well at my core. I practiced controlling it so that it would not consume me whole. At first, every time I cracked the lid, it would swarm out of me, trying to overtake me. It took me almost a year to wield my shadows properly. And that's when the deal changed."

"What do you mean, it changed?" Nyx asks apprehensively.

"I had started to fight back again and resist Oren's commands. My shadows and I grew stronger with each passing day. I was becoming more confident in my abilities, and it threatened Oren and Leopold's control over me. They worried I would use my skills against them. One afternoon, I was recovering from a brutal torture session, and Oren arrived to renegotiate our deal." I shudder.

"Oren told me that if I refused or ever tried to use my power against him or Leopold, they would torture and kill anyone dear to me. That included Tobias ... and you. He only allowed our friendship to continue because he knew he could use it as leverage against me."

Realization slowly dawns on Nyx's face.

"This time, though, Oren had an iron clad insurance policy. Twin trove warning stones. The lore states that gods made stones that two mortals could exchange, and if one were murdered, the other stone would alert the partner and let them know who did it. If I tried to kill one of them, the other would know immediately and would take revenge before I could stop them. I had no other choice. My fate was sealed. I did their bidding and never turned against them to keep my loved ones safe."

"Do you think Loma has a resurrection potion I could use? Because I'd like to bring Oren back just to torture him and let it be my blade that ends him versus the claws of a beast." Nyx's knuckles are white as he holds back his rage.

I lean over and pry his hand open. "If that were possible, you'd have to get in line." I sit back in my chair, exhaustion starting to take hold.

"When did Asher become part of the deal?" Nyx asks.

"Not long after that. Oren decided Asher would take over on quests. The Umbra Brutus was more intimidating than me. Besides, Oren didn't want anyone figuring out who I was, so it was an added layer of protection for him. He'd found a way to bind me forever to the darkness with no way of escaping. I allowed Asher to tap into my shadows; creating an unstoppable force. The torture became less frequent after Asher's arrival. I'm ashamed to admit it, but I was relieved. As long as I didn't speak and followed orders, I was safe. Asher kept me safe. It wasn't until Oren died that I became the first to protect, and Asher became a last resort."

We sit in silence for a moment, letting everything sink in. The hard truth of my past is not something I wanted to share. It feels nice finally telling someone, but these are supposed to be my burdens to carry, not Nyx's.

"Any other secrets you've been hiding from me, Lily?" he asks with raised eyebrows.

I grimace, wrinkling my nose.

"Those secret quests I would go on every few months? I wasn't always going to gather information on the other kingdoms," I confess.

He stares at me in disbelief. He wants the truth, so that's what I will give him.

His mouth falls open as the pieces fall into place. "Lily, please don't tell me you were going to see Theo," he pleads.

An uncomfortable smile pulls at my lips, showing far too many teeth. An irritated groan cuts through the room as Nyx drags his hands down his face.

"I was only going to watch him and make sure he was ok. I had to make sure Leopold was holding up his end of the deal even after Oren died," I say.

A condescending laugh comes from my best friend as he rolls his eyes.

"Yeah, I'm sure you were going to watch him," he says with reproach.

Searching for something to throw at him, I come up empty. I settle for narrowing my eyes until they are slits. "That's all I did … until two months ago," I retort.

With his head cocked toward me, he blinks slowly, "Why doesn't he remember you from then?" He asks.

A valid question, but an uncomfortable one.

I lower my gaze and tap my fingertips together in my lap.

"Because I gave him a rowanberry elixir," I confess. "I had a moment of weakness and tried telling him the truth, which was a huge mistake and dangerous—I know, you don't have to tell me. And he freaked out; his head was in so much pain, like trying to unlock the memory was killing him. I had to make him forget. Again. So, I did what I had to do."

Nyx rubs at his temples, appearing to have developed a headache from the information overload.

"You drugged the man you supposedly love? I get why you did it, but dear gods, Lily," he groans.

I sit back in my chair, letting out a sigh.

"I didn't like it either," I retort.

Crossing my legs at the ankles, I sink deeper into my chair. While my heart feels lighter after telling Nyx the truth, it remains heavy with worry about what to do next.

"I don't trust him, Lily. He sees us all as cruel monsters. Lux teaches their people that we live with no morals. We need to be careful. You may remember him, but all he sees is his enemy," Nyx warns.

"I know. I was raised there, remember?" I say teasingly, but a rough yawn breaks my words.

"Come on. Let's get you to bed, and we can talk more tomorrow. We both know how cranky you get if you don't get rest," he says, standing.

I laugh, knowing he's right. I'm worse than Midnight if I don't get enough sleep.

I slide my hand into his outstretched palm, and he helps me rise and draws me to his chest. Our embrace is filled with pain, frustration, and sadness.

"Get some rest, and I will see you first thing in the morning. And Lily," he pushes my chin up to meet his gaze, "please, no more secrets. I can't protect you if I don't know the threats."

I nod and squeeze him tight. A soft kiss to my head makes me smile into his chest. Nyx lets me go and looks at me warmly before turning to leave my chambers.

Locking my doors, I slip out of my clothes and crawl into the luxuriously soft sheets. It doesn't take long before sleep overtakes me.

"Please don't make me do this, Oren," I plead as a sob gets caught in my throat.

"Do as I have ordered, or he dies," Oren retorts, tightening the shadows twisted around Tobias' throat. Tobias claws at the black tendrils, but it's no use. His feet kick frantically as Oren slowly cuts off his air.

"They have done nothing. There's no need to kill them. Please stop." I beg again, hoping to break through to Oren. I look over at the three mortals tied to chairs in the middle of their home. A tearful mother and father with their sixteen-year-old son.

"You don't ask questions, girl. You do as you are told. Break the deal and you know what will happen." Oren steps closer to me as Tobias' lips turn blue. A tear slides down my cheek as our eyes lock. Tobias stops fighting Oren's shadows. He nods as if he's giving me permission to let Oren end his life. But I can't survive without him. Who would care for me after each punishment? Who would find Loma to heal my wounds? I need him to keep me mortal. Nyx needs his father.

"Fine. I'll do it. Put him down." I shove down every emotion trying to bubble to the surface. I won't make it through this test if I don't swallow every ounce of my mortality.

Oren places Tobias down on the rough wood floor of the home. He gasps as air finally returns to him. But Oren doesn't remove his shadows. One thick tendril still lingers around Tobias' throat in case I try to resist again. Tobias' eyes meet mine, filled with a deep, painful sorrow, knowing what he is going to have to watch me do. But I'll do anything to keep them all safe.

I step to the closest mortal, the mother. Her sob cracks through me, and I squeeze my eyes shut to compose myself.

"They have information I want. Start with their fingers, and we'll go from there. This all stops when you get them to talk," Oren commands. I take in a deep breath, praying to the gods to help, but they never answer.

A tendril of shadow spills from my hand, skirting across the floor and up the chair to the woman's hand. It coils around each finger, preparing to break them until Oren gets what he wants.

"With your hands, not your shadows. I want you to feel each snap of their bones as you do my bidding." I glare at Oren, who *smirks back, knowing he's won. I recall my shadows and step closer to the woman. "I'm sorry," I whisper as I wrap my hand around her index finger before breaking it. The cracking of her bones radiates through my hand, and I wince. Her screams pierce my ears, and I fight to not cover them. With each snap and break of their bones, every drop of their blood that splatters their home, a piece of my soul cracks off and falls away.*

I jerk awake, heart racing. Just a nightmare. I look around, trying to steady myself.

I'm not still trapped in that damn cell.

I close my eyes, taking a deep breath. Nyx is safe. Theo is safe. I open my eyes.

I need to keep it that way.

A faint glow beams through one of my windows. The sun is rising. I crawl out of bed and make my way to the bathing chamber. I strip off my undergarments and step into my shower. I allow the chilly water to wash away my worries and ground me in the present.

I dry and slip into a long, flowy dress of deep purple. There will be no training today. I will spend my day strategizing with Nyx.

Using my towel, I squeeze out the excess water in my hair, leaving beautiful curls as it dries. As I slide my black dagger into place on my right thigh, I smile, feeling better about revealing my secrets to my best friend. But my heart breaks remembering Tobias.

I'll never understand the secret quest he and Oren went on in Fati. I wish he had taken me with him. Maybe I could have protected him like he tried for me. Oren was running on borrowed time, anyway. Monsters can only lurk in the shadows for so long before enacting their revenge.

I step out my door into the quiet halls of The Keep. A whistle sounds, and I look over my shoulder to find Nyx striding toward me. It appears sleep escaped him as well.

His muscled arms wrap around me and squeeze me tight to his chest.

"You couldn't sleep either?" I ask, smiling up at him.

He simply shakes his head.

"Any nightmares after everything yesterday?" He asks with concern furrowing his brow.

I bite the inside of my cheek. But I promised no more secrets. I tell him all about my nightmare from my first ordered kills, and he stiffens. His fists clench at his sides, and I take one in my hand.

I look into his metal gray eyes and take a deep breath. Nyx holds my hand and does the same. No words required.

"Ready to go to the apothecary?" I ask, ready to change the subject.

He nods, and we walk the short distance down the hall.

We find Loma at the counter; she appears to be waiting for us. Her smile is broad as we enter the shop. The scent of medicinal herbs and spices welcomes us.

"Our fearless leaders." She says, walking around the counter with arms stretched wide, pulling us both into her warm embrace.

We laugh as she releases us.

"What brings you both to see me this fine morning?" She asks, far too cheery for the time.

I glance at Nyx before looking back into Loma's gentle hazel eyes.

"Have you ever heard of an elixir that blocks memories of a specific person? I know about rowanberry, but this would target one person and veil images of them only," I ask nervously.

She looks at me, puzzled, and shifts uneasily on her feet.

"I have, but it's an ancient and rare mixture. If I remember correctly, the ingredients were volatile and unpredictable. Why would you need such an elixir, Lily?" She questions.

I breathe a sigh of relief. I knew she could help. She's one of the best healers in the realm, and her knowledge is unparalleled.

"I don't need the elixir. I need the antidote. A way to unveil the memories and restore them," I answer.

Loma's mouth pinches tight as her eyes dart around the shop, seeming to look for something.

"I may find your answer in an old healer's journal, but I'll have to find it first. Then I can formulate the reversal elixir and gather ingredients. I'll need some time, though," she says, her eyes still searching.

"This wouldn't have something to do with our new guest, would it?" She asks.

My eyes go wide as I slowly turn my head to Nyx, who's just as stunned as I am. Both of us are unsure of how to answer.

"He's from Lux and your age. You two knew each other, didn't you?" She asks, already knowing the answer.

I avoid her gaze as I fight back the pain from all the years lost and focus on a purple gemstone on the counter. My silence answers for me.

"Understood, my queen. I'll work on this and find you when it's done," she says with a sigh.

I finally look back at her, and I'm positive she can see the pain in my eyes. She's always been good at reading me. Her soft smile lets me know she does.

"Thank you, Loma."

She grins at me with a sparkle in her eyes, which comforts me.

"Anything for you. This will be another one of our little secrets." She says with a wink.

Nyx groans loudly, and I stifle a laugh.

Nyx and I head to the dining hall next, following the smell of bacon. My stomach grumbles, and I quicken my pace. Hiram stands near the doors, and I hurry to him, wanting an update on Theo. He bends deeply at the waist to bow, crossing his arm on his chest.

"How is he, Hiram? Is he okay?" I ask anxiously.

I rub my thumb on my palm, trying to distract myself from the panic rising within me. My shadows dance nervously in their well. Nyx comes beside me, running his hand across my back to one of my shoulders, giving it a gentle squeeze. His silent reminder for me to breathe deeply, which I do as a natural response.

Hiram notices my agitation and his features soften.

"He slept through the night. I'm here to get him some food and water. He was still asleep when I checked on him a little while ago. I'll keep you posted if anything changes."

"Thank you, Hiram," I say, placing a hand on his arm.

"I follow orders, my queen." I release my hold, and, with a bow of his head, Hiram turns to the dining hall to gather breakfast for Theo. Nyx and I trail in after. The dining hall is quiet this early in the morning, with only a few crew members stopping in for a meal before starting their day.

Pyke steps out of the kitchen with a hot plate of food and a mug of coffee. He hands them over to me with one of his dramatic bows.

"Thank you, Pyke," I say.

His preening smile makes me smile back at him before he hurries back to the kitchen. "I'll meet you in the council room," I say to Nyx.

"You're not going to wait for me?" He asks with fake offense.

"And let my food get cold? Never," I huff before leaving.

I plop into the seat at my desk in the council room, staring down at my overflowing plate. My stomach rumbles loudly. I'm already devouring my plate before Nyx joins me.

 "Any idea what you are going to do about our new guest?" Nyx asks, picking at the food on his plate. I set my fork down and lean back in my chair.

"I'm not sure, but I know we can't send him back to Lux. They would try to kill him for failure of duty." I say, gritting my teeth at the thought.

Nyx leans forward, crossing his arms on top of the table.

"I have a theory. I went to Lux two months ago to investigate a rumor I heard in our village about Theo and Junie getting married," I say.

Nyx stares at me wide eyed. His jaw flexes, his annoyance palpable.

"Lecture me later about how it was unsafe. Right now, listen," I say sarcastically, and his face falls flat.

I fight back a laugh.

"We know big rumors typically come from the castle. What if Leopold planted it as a test to see if the villagers would accept Theo as their new king?" I ask, trying to work through the thought as I go.

"Possibly. But why?" Nyx retorts.

"I'm not sure yet. I don't think we are wrong about Leopold having a plan to attack Umbra. But I'm not sure why. I think Theo might be a pawn in his plan."

Nyx's head bounces from side to side lightly as he analyzes the different possibilities. Leopold is a man consumed by his hunger for power and often makes illogical decisions.

"So, how does that work with Theo being in Umbra? How is Leopold going to use him if he's dead?" Nyx wonders out loud with obvious distaste.

I interlace my hands under the table.

"I don't know, but I think Theo being here could be useful to us." I say, leaning forward.

Nyx crosses his arms on his chest and looks at me doubtfully.

"How? I see him as a liability to all of us, especially you. We should send him back before he can learn anything or do any harm," he practically throws the words at me.

"Leopold trusts Theo. He must, if he is willing to have him wed his only heir and the future divinus of his kingdom. I have to believe that if we can show Theo that we're not just monsters and beasts like they have taught him in Lux, if we can win him over, then maybe we can gain an ally in Lux," I answer.

Nyx rolls his eyes so hard they might get stuck in the back of his head.

"I know you don't trust him ..." I trail off.

"And you shouldn't either! You think you know him, Lily, but you don't. He's lived his whole life under the rule of lying, deceitful men who have done nothing but feed him stories about how cruel we are. He sees us as the enemy. He'll do anything to destroy us," he says, leaning forward, closing the distance between us.

"I have to try, Nyx," I say as he shakes his head. "He survived the haunted forest when no other guard has. The fates and the gods brought him to me for a reason," I continue.

I pray it isn't to have me die trying to protect him.

A knot in my chest twists.

"We have to listen, Nyx. Destiny brought him back to me in this kingdom. Let me help him see through the darkness. Let him see what Umbra truly is. We have worked so hard to make it something magical. I think it's time for everyone to see it."

"It's a terrible, dangerous idea. What happens when he tries to kill you? Because you know the first chance he gets, he will," he asks, tension rolling off of him in waves.

"Oren already tried that, remember? I don't die," I say with a smirk.

His face remains stony as the door to the council room swings open. Our eyes remain locked on each other. He's not done fighting this, and neither am I.

"An urgent quest has come in from Terra," Kira says, tossing an envelope on the table between Nyx and me.

"What's going on in here?" She pauses to look at each of us. The tension in the room is so dense you can almost touch it.

"Nothing," Nyx sneers, snatching the paper and sitting back in his chair to read.

I lean back in mine and look over to Kira. She eyes me suspiciously.

Without breaking eye contact, she reaches into her pocket and sets a viewing crystal on the desk near me. My heart skips a beat at the sight of its purple hue.

"Your male raven returned shortly before dawn. And before you ask, because I know you will, Silas followed him back to the nest. He is safe and unharmed," Kira says, and I breathe a sigh of relief.

I take the crystal and place it in a drawer to view later when Kira isn't around. You never know what the ravens may capture, and I don't need her finding out more than I'd like her to know.

"What's with the brute in the cage?" She asks, crossing her arms.

Her lips pinch into a thin line as she stares down at me.

Nyx peers up at me, waiting to see how I handle her question.

"He is a guard of Lux," I answer, not giving her more than she asks for.

"Obviously. But who is he?" She asks, tilting her head to the side, assessing my responses.

I pretend to think about the question before answering.

"I believe he called himself Captain," I reply, and Nyx huffs.

I push down a smile.

"Why is he here?" Kira continues with her line of questioning, sounding annoyed.

"He survived the haunted forest," I give another stunted reply.

"Seriously? How? Why?" Kira asks with confusion and surprise.

"That's what we're trying to figure out. Now, if you would excuse yourself, we could get back to it," Nyx says curtly.

Kira opens her mouth to speak, but Nyx cuts her off. He doesn't hide his annoyance.

"That was an order, not a request. Leave now, Kira."

"Of course, General," Kira says with faked sweetness.

She stares at me as if she's weighing my worth.

I glare back with indifference. Just another mask to block out the emotions twisting my insides. Kira shakes her head slowly before leaving the room with a slam of the door.

"What's the quest this time?" I ask Nyx, ready to move on after our interruption.

His eyes skim the letter once more.

"A lady of Terra is asking for our help regarding a lord harming several women. It appears their king isn't stopping the lord, and more women are being hurt," he says slowly, handing me the letter.

Fire flares through me as my shadows scratch at the sealed well. They crave the need to be judge, jury, and executioner of this horrid man. King Royce should learn to control his men better.

I wonder if it's hard for King Royce to rule over his people with his shard of remaining power. No one knows why Eos, the land and water god who created Terra, has found the Winfielde divinus line unworthy of his blessings. Many fear that soon the beautiful kingdom of wildflowers and rolling hills will be like Fati, with nothing left and another god lost.

"Accept it immediately. Send someone to Terra to gather information today, and we'll go in two days to handle the situation," I give the order to Nyx, fighting back the desire to go now and take care of things myself.

"Will the king have a soft spot for Theo as well?" Nyx asks with far too much attitude. "Or will he not appreciate someone trespassing in his kingdom and seek punishment for it?"

"I'm sure Asher will be neutral about the situation, as he should be. I'll ensure he visits Theo until we can figure out our next move," I reply, as my shadows buzz along my skin at the mention of the king.

This means Asher will need to walk the halls of The Keep, which we promised not to do after Oren died. He loved to parade Asher around as his weapon and threaten the crew with his power. The memory makes me clench my jaw to suppress the rage for our former king. I steel myself and push the memory down.

My people thrive on mutual respect, not punishment. But Oren never learned that. His motivation was always fear and power. His desire to use Asher as his weapon always dominated his thoughts. But now, Asher bends only to my will.

Nyx and I spend the rest of the day arguing about how to handle Theo. I try to get lost in my duties, but my heart won't allow it. The threads constantly tug, pulling me toward the cell, begging for me to go to Theo.

CHAPTER 16

THEO

My boots click on the black stone floor as I pace around my new cage. It's been three days since the hellions of Umbra captured me and locked me in this damn cell.

My days have become almost routine. The brown-haired one I've heard called Captain brings me food and water at least three times a day. I refuse to eat most of it, sticking with items least likely to be poisoned, like their fluffy bread.

I don't know why they insist on keeping me comfortable and well-fed when I know the horrors they inflict on outsiders. My father has warned us of all the tactics used by the beasts of Umbra. This fake generosity is only to give me a false sense of security before they either skin me alive or King Asher rips the air from my body with his shadows.

I'm sure part of my torture is forcing me to speak with the king daily. Each time, his shadows reach for me, aiming for my throat. I have no doubt they crave to wrap me in their darkness until I take my last breath.

They always pull back before they can touch me, prolonging the inevitable. I wish he would kill me and end this misery. The uncertainty is the worst part. The suffering of knowing my death is coming, but not when it will happen.

I pause my pacing and stare at the wall. Iron chains hang from it, strung through loops, the cuffs broken. I hate to think what kind of torture could have snapped the hard metal. The pain that person must have endured for simply being in the wrong gods-forsaken kingdom.

A throat clears behind me, and I turn to find their captain near the bars.

"Can I get you anything, Captain?" He asks, sounding genuine, but I know it's all an act.

I stare at him for a moment before striding over to him.

His brown eyes are fixed on me as I stop in front of him. I give him a false smile before fisting the front of his shirt and slamming his face into the iron bars. His nose cracks with the impact. The captain groans in pain as blood drips down his face.

"What in the realm are you doing?" A deep voice shouts from down the hall before the gray-eyed guard called general appears.

I release the captain and take a step back, smiling victoriously. He stumbles backward, his eyes watering from the hit. The general assesses his guard before telling him to go see someone named Loma. He turns his dark gaze on me and stalks to the cell like a predator. His long strides close the distance quickly, but I don't move. I refuse to back down.

"Why did you hurt one of my guards?" The general asks gripping the bars.

"I'm getting sick of the good mortal routine. Maybe now he'll drop the act," I answer with a shrug.

"If we weren't under direct orders not to harm you, I assure you Hiram would be the least of your concerns," he says with a snarl.

"I'm right here, General. We both know I'm the better trained warrior here. No sneaking around for Lux guards, unlike yours," I reply, knowing I'd win that fight.

The general presses his face closer to the bars, nearly touching them. "Don't worry, Captain. Once you mess up, and we both know you will, the protection order will be lifted, and we'll have our time. Then, I'll gladly beat you within an inch of your life. I have a score to settle with you," he says through gritted teeth.

I don't take my eyes off the general, hoping he sees he'd lose this battle. He glares back for a moment before stepping away and returning with my satchel. He shoves it through the bars, letting it drop to the floor. I don't move. I'll retrieve it once he leaves.

"Gather any useful information from my bag, General?" I ask, bringing my gaze back to him.

"You're not important enough for me to care what you brought with you, Captain," he hisses back. "Plus, I have no use for a propaganda filled book like *Battle Strategies of Omnia*." He turns and leaves, not waiting for my retort.

I grab my satchel off the floor and drop into the comfortable but too small bed. Searching through it, everything seems in place, but it is hard to be certain. I lean back against the headboard, trying to figure out my next move. Another day passes with me still trapped in the kingdom of beasts and monsters.

CHAPTER 17

LILY

We prowl quietly through Terra. Dressed in all black, we appear as shadows drifting through the night. We tuck ourselves close to the white stone buildings in the sleepy village, looking for our target.

Crickets play their evening song in the distance as fireflies twinkle in the meadows. The woodsy scent of the moss roofs makes it feel like we are still among the trees.

Nyx skirts the wall in front of me. Silas and Marcus lead the way. A small and discreet team for this in and out quest. No lingering or questions. We'll end the lord quickly and quietly. Punishment for the pain he has inflicted on the women here.

I pull my hood over my head to obscure my face and hair, not wanting anything to give away that I'm a woman. To remain inconspicuous, I will only summon Asher if necessary. I want my face to be the last thing this vicious man sees.

My shadows are tucked deep in their well with the lid secured tight, as always. They can be temperamental, and I've learned to hide them away to prevent them from spilling out whenever they please. If I need them, all I have to do is crack the lid.

We trail the wall along the row of houses lining the back side of the village. The light from lanterns flashes on our faces as we pass by windows. The alley curves along the edge of the town and leads directly to the lord's house.

This path provides stunning unobstructed views of the Terra wildflower meadows. I imagine the sunrise from this spot would be beautiful.

A chorus of laughter floats down the way, coming from the tavern. It's a perfect fall night with a slight chill in the air but still comfortable. The starry sky above adds to the pleasant setting for a cruel task.

We pair off. Silas and Marcus head into the alley first. The darkness provides better cover for us. Once safely concealed in the shadows, we advance quietly.

Marcus and Silas cautiously head down the rough stone walk. Various walkways branch out from the main walk, each leading to different homes along this part of the village. Small lanterns spaced at odd intervals provide dim lighting.

Nyx positions himself in front of me, scanning for any threat. We silently make our way closer to the lord's home.

There's a break in the silence as a large mass barrels out from one walkway, crashing into Silas and hauling him out of sight. A loud thud and a pained groan tell me he's been hit hard.

"Stay here and watch my back," Nyx says, holding his hand up, signaling me to stop.

Before I can protest, Marcus and Nyx are racing off to help Silas. The rhythmic thump of punches fills the air. I walk cautiously toward my men, checking for anyone approaching. My eyes scan the shadows and dark paths for an accomplice.

A hand grabs my hood, yanking me. My back and head slam into the white stone home on the left side of another pathway. I see stars from the impact, but the hand around my throat brings back my attention.

"What do we have here? A woman pretending to be a spy? You are far too pretty to be sneaking around in the dark, love," a grotesque man says, pressing me harder into the wall, and I realize we've been ambushed.

This is the lord we came here for, and somehow, he got the jump on us.

His large hand clamps down on my throat, shutting off my air. I try to remain calm and unseal the well holding my shadows, but he slams my head into the wall again. My vision goes black around the edges, and I claw at the man's arm, tearing at his skin.

I swing my legs up to shove him back, but he pushes his body into mine, pinning me. A lethal smile curves his lips as he leans in and rubs his pointed nose along my jaw. He inhales deeply, smelling my hair.

"Oh, I'm going to have fun with you," he whispers into my ear.

His warm breath causes my shadows to strike at the well. I reach up and dig my fingers into his eyes, hoping it will cause him to release my neck. My lungs burn from the lack of air.

The man's grip tightens on my throat. He lifts his body off mine enough to swing a fist back and punch me in the face twice. Warmth trickles down my cheek from the broken skin.

"Useless woman. All you are good for is fucking."

Another slam of my head into the wall has me limp in the man's hand. My vision is only a pinprick. His hand slides down my body as he pushes his hardening cock against me.

"That's more like it. Now hold still while we have some fun," he says as he fumbles with his trousers.

I try to reach for my shadows again, but my mind is too hazy to get to them. It feels as if I'm crawling toward the well, my fingers digging into the ground, as my power screams to be unleashed. If I could just make it, all this would be over.

My mind races as I watch a smile spread across the man's face. It's as if I'm watching what's happening from outside my body. *Asher, I need to summon Asher.* But my shadows are trapped, severing our connection. I scream without a sound.

In an instant, dim light fills my vision and relief floods my mind as the man is pulled off of me. I see Nyx tackling the man, slamming him into the stone path. They fight for control. Nyx's fists collide with the man's face as he overpowers him. He doesn't relent. Blow after blow, Nyx punches the man's face and the sound of his bones cracking splinters the air.

Long moments pass as I listen to Nyx unleashing his anger on this monster. My shadows stir and climb up their well. I throw off the lid, giving them what they want. They gain strength as they go until they burst from me in a tidal wave of darkness, devouring the light. They crawl along the path toward the man. With a light touch, my shadows pry Nyx from the man, setting him softly to the side.

The man swings at the dark mist climbing over his body. My shadows wrap around him, binding his legs and arms. Darkness digs into the man's skin, ripping and tearing it apart. A long, black tendril coils around his mouth, muffling his screams.

The fury within me rises. This man tried to violate me.

I'm going to make him pay. This one's for me—no need for Asher. This, I want to do myself. This, I will enjoy.

I unleash my fury and feel my shadows break every one of his bones. His ribs fracture, puncturing his lungs. His breaths come in ragged, pained shudders as the darkness continues its punishment.

I push my darkness harder into him for all the women he's hurt and violated. For what he did to me. A rich, unfamiliar voice hisses in my mind, "*Justice.*"

As his last breath leaves his body and his heart stops, my shadows recoil and vanish into my skin. This time, I don't close the lid.

Never again.

Nyx grabs me as I try to stand, but my head spins. He holds me up as I wobble on my feet. Marcus comes into view, grasping Silas firmly by his waist, allowing him to drape an arm over Marcus' shoulders. They are both bloody and bruised.

I look up at Nyx to assess his injuries. A smear of blood streaks his face. His cheek shows some faint redness, but overall, he's the least injured.

Nyx's gray eyes snap to mine, sheer panic darkens them. His jaw ticks as he looks me over.

"What happened?" He asks with barely contained emotions. I can feel mine rising in response.

"Caught off guard. The other guy?" My voice is weak and raspy. It hurts to get words out.

"Dead," Nyx's words are flat and final. I nod, but pain shoots from the top of my head to the middle of my back, causing me to yelp.

"Give me your adveho ring so I can get us home," Nyx demands. There's a tremor in his voice only I can sense.

"I'm fine. I can do it," I say, using him for support to stand up. I fall back into him as the village whirls. Something warm and wet trickles down my neck. I rub my hand along the spot, only to pull back and see bright-red blood coating it.

Nyx's breath catches. "Lily ..." His voice becomes distant as my head grows fuzzier and my knees collapse. Nyx catches me and pulls me to him.

"Lily!" His frantic calling of my name follows as darkness consumes me.

CHAPTER 18

THEO

A bead of sweat trickles down my brow as I force myself to rise from another sit-up. I've stopped counting my sets and do each movement until my body screams for me to stop, my muscles straining with effort. Exercise is the only thing that seems to put a dent in my growing anxiety.

Pushing up off the floor, I wipe my forehead with the back of my arm. My skin is grimy from not being able to bathe properly since being taken by this dreadful kingdom.

However, the general has not broken his word from a few days ago. No harm has come to me, unless you count being trapped in this cell all day. They still bring meals and water on schedule. This is not the treatment I was expecting from this vile kingdom. The horror stories and my training make me wary of their motives.

King Asher and his merry men of chaos left earlier, leaving only the captain to watch over me. He hasn't stepped close to the cell bars since I broke his nose a few days ago.

Looking at myself in the mirror, I rub at the beard growing in. It's rough on my fingers as I trace it. They don't permit the younger men of the Lux guard to have facial hair, so this is the most I've ever had. It feels foreign against my skin, and I long to shave it off.

Slipping out of my borrowed clothes, I pull on a pair of shorts, forgoing a shirt for bed. I prefer to sleep in my undergarments, but with someone always on watch, that would be awkward. The stack of clothes provided by King Asher upon my arrival only has one outfit left, and I wonder if it means my time here is ending. Either they have worked out a deal with King Leopold for my return, or I'll die at the same hands who killed my men.

I go through my evening stretches, hoping they will help me relax. My muscles are almost as tense as my nerves. I'm used to heavily regulated training that clears my mind and steadies my soul. Without it, I can't seem to calm my racing thoughts, especially tonight. I feel as if I can't take a deep breath, as though something's restricting the air.

Shouting comes from the hallway and the captain stiffens, his chest rises and falls rapidly, seemingly startled by the abrupt intrusion. Pain hits my chest and the knot in my stomach twists. The yelling becomes louder as if a floodgate has opened. I hear the sound of rushed footsteps heading down the hall.

"Hiram, get Loma now!" The captain's face pales, and I can see his lips plead the word *no* before he sprints away.

I hurry over to the bars of the cell and crane my neck to see what is happening. The quick thuds of boots on the black stone fill the space, and a groan follows the sound.

The dark-haired guard supports the weight of the blonde guard with an arm over his shoulder. They limp down the hall, bruises and drying blood marking their faces. Whatever they got themselves into must have been bad.

"Marcus, Silas, what happened?" A feminine voice calls from down the hall. Then, an older woman with long, gray hair steps into view.

"We'll be fine, Loma. But ...," the dark-haired guard says as he steps to the side, pulling the blonde one with him. The general hurries to the woman they call Loma.

His normally olive-toned skin is ashen and speckled with blood. A woman with curly, red hair hangs limp in his arms. Bright-red blood runs in lines from the woman's head and down the general's arm.

I blink, and I'm back in the meadow. *Red curls matted with blood as Lily lies unmoving in my lap. Lily's hair covering her face, much like this woman's.* I blink again, trying to clear the memory, but it digs in deeper, as if begging for me to watch it happen all over again. Red-stained daisies fill my vision. The ground and my clothes soaked in her blood.

So much blood.

"Lily ..." Her name is a whisper from my lips. I grip the bars tight, pleading with my mind to keep me here in the present. The general's gaze snaps to mine. His gray eyes are bloodshot and frantic. Whoever this woman is, she means a great deal to him.

"Help, Loma. She won't wake up," the general's voice trembles.

"How did this happen, Nyx?" Loma's words sound like a scold. She pulls at the general's arms to get a better look at the red-haired woman.

As Loma gently turns the woman's red head, I can see bruises on her face. There's a noticeable cut on her cheek and the start of a black eye. Her long, red hair falls over her shoulder as Loma inspects her injuries. There is an undeniable bruise around her neck. The distinct imprint of a large man's hand around her throat. Fingers dug in so hard to leave their mark.

"She was behind us. He came out of the shadows and just attacked," Nyx answers Loma with pain contorting his face.

The word *shadows* sends fury through me.

This must be Asher's work. The vicious shadow king.

Lux has well-documented King Asher's brutality toward women. It's the reason King Leopold doesn't allow women in the Lux guard. Being tortured and killed is one thing, being violated is another. But the Umbra Brutus is king here, and these monsters bend to his will and clean up the mess when he's through. I curse his name aloud, which earns me an odd look from both Loma and the general.

"Hiram, go get the physician and meet us in her chambers." Loma gives orders like a seasoned commander. "Marcus, take Silas to my shop and I'll be there shortly."

Loma walks to the side of the general and cups the woman's head with the gentleness of a mother. She nods, and they all hurry off out of sight.

I'm left alone to simmer in my anger and hatred for King Asher and his accomplices. They pass around women here as if they are nothing more than mugs of ale in a busy tavern. Everyone gets a taste until they've drained the last drop. Will they mend her only to use her again? I bet they will do exactly that.

I pace my cell, waiting for the guard to return so I can ask him about the woman. It feels like hours have passed before the familiar sound of his boots echoes down the hallway, and the brown-haired captain comes into view.

"Is she okay?" I ask, pushing myself against the iron bars.

He runs his hands through his already disheveled hair.

Is that a look of genuine concern on his face? He looks anguished.

He glares at me. "Mind your business, Captain," He snaps, and my rage returns, hot and unyielding.

I press my face against the bars, trying to get as close to the guard as possible.

"Why do you allow your king to hurt a woman you obviously care about?" I ask, needing to know how this can be justified.

He stares at me. His mouth opens and he blinks repeatedly.

"You don't know what you are talking about, so again, mind your business." He turns his back to me, trying to end the conversation.

The captain moves to the opposite wall. I project all my hatred and anger through my eyes as I stare him down. "You may tolerate his abuse of women, but I don't. Let King Asher know I'd like a word with him regarding that woman."

The captain lets out a low chuckle and averts his gaze, ignoring my demand completely. I mutter curses at him as I turn and head to my bed. This is futile. I must have misunderstood his previous look. He can't possibly care about anyone.

I lie down in my bed, trying to calm my rage. The black silk sheets are cool and soft on my bare chest. I lean back on the dark wood headboard and cross my arms. I glower at the captain until my eyelids grow heavy, and I fall asleep.

CHAPTER 19

I rub my temples, trying to counteract the throb setting in again. Nyx looks down at me from the other side of my desk in the council room, concern wrinkling his brow.

"I'm fine, Nyx. Just due for another tea to help with the headache," I say, bringing my gaze to him, but my words don't soothe his worry.

If I thought he was protective before, this is a whole new level of mother hen Nyx. He won't let me out of his sight. I had to lock him out of my bathing chamber to clean up this morning.

I barely notice the cuts on my cheek and my black eye. A handprint curves around my neck, five clear lines from fingers digging into my skin. I expected to wince when I did my assessment this morning but only a hint of tenderness remains.

I've always healed quickly, the shadows within me not allowing pain to linger too long. While my skin is painted in varying shades of purple and blue, within a few days, none of it will remain. Only the deepest scars remain. The ones inflicted by Oren.

But the headache persists. The throb pulsates, and I close my eyes, willing the pain away. Loma's healing teas have been the only thing to help.

Without speaking, Nyx cracks the door open. "The queen would like tea from Loma. Will you please go fetch it for her?" He orders and shuts the door.

"Marcus will be back with it shortly. Anything else bothering you?" Nyx says, stepping in front of my desk.

"Yes, a very overbearing general who won't stop hovering," I snip, cracking an eye open to look at him.

He sets his palms on my desk and leans into my space.

"Because the last time I took my eyes off of you, I almost lost you," the words come out as a rumble from deep in his chest.

I open my mouth to retort.

"Don't you dare say that you don't die. You may be willing to test that theory, but I'm not," he says, his gray eyes cutting into me. I wince down to my soul.

Unimaginable pain.

"I wasn't the only one hurt last night," I say, staring at the bruises along his jaw and his scabbed knuckles.

Gods, we all look a mess.

Marcus has a matching black eye to my own and a broken nose. Silas ended up with a large gash on his head from the impact on the ground and likely several broken ribs.

"No one else matters," Nyx stresses each word.

I give in and relax in my seat.

"Have we figured out how they knew we were coming?" I ask as he settles into his chair across from me.

"Not yet, but we will keep digging," he answers.

"Thank you," I say, picking up the now-vacant viewing crystal.

Its purple hue catches the sunlight through the high windows, reflecting the color across the floor.

"I find it odd that there was nothing out of place on the footage," I say, questioning what we just reviewed.

"I do too. It's peculiar that all the raven captured was a moment between the captain and the Lux princess. She looked pretty devastated watching him go." He finishes cautiously, watching for my reaction.

My heart breaks for Junie. I wish I could tell her he is safe with me, and I won't let anything happen to him, but she wouldn't believe me if I tried.

"But I think the strangest part wasn't what was captured," Nyx continues. "It was that there was nothing of King Leopold and his guards. There were no random outings to the market or strolls through the village. They seem to be holed up in Brightwick."

What are you up to, Leopold?

There is a knock on the door and Marcus steps in, holding a fresh cup of my tea. Nyx jumps up and retrieves it immediately, preventing Marcus from coming in any further. Nyx has not let anyone except Loma near me all day, and he's apparently not planning on it soon.

Nyx shuts the door then places the teacup gently on the desk. The warm, herbal scent sends a wave of anticipated relief through my body. I never ask Loma what's in her mixtures. I trust her and her wild remedies with my life.

Blowing on the hot liquid, I take a small sip and revel in the calming sensation flooding my system. I drink down the cup while trying to figure out an action plan for my kingdom. The throbbing in my head subsides.

"Have the letters revealed any more information about what's going on in Lux?" I ask Nyx. He spreads out two letters before him. I reluctantly push mine from Amelia toward him.

"They are more delayed than usual. It seems like our spies are having a harder time getting messages out to us. Maybe the post is being restricted as well?" He asks, looking up at me.

"That would make sense. Amelia's letter is from before Theo left for Umbra, so they are at least a week or more delayed. She said the villagers are becoming increasingly unhappy with the lost lives over the king's amulet. The turmoil and distress seem to grow daily. Leopold could be restricting movement within Lux, which is adding to the low morale among the people," I reply with my best guess about what the lightning king could be doing.

"What about the amulet? Were the spies able to gather anything on it?" I ask, hopeful that one letter holds an ounce of useful information.

"Nothing of real value. One said the amulet was still within the kingdom, hidden away to perpetuate the lie Umbra stole it. The other said the amulet never existed and King Leopold fabricated the lie to come after Umbra," he answers, leaning back in his chair.

"I find it strange that no information is coming out of Lux. It isn't normal," I say as dread fills my stomach.

"More reason for us to believe they're coming after us. We should remain on alert," he replies.

Commotion sounds from the other side of the door before Hiram bursts into the room. His eyes are wide and his nostrils flare in frustration. There's food in his hair and down his shirt. Small pieces of vegetables fall to the stone floor as he walks.

"Hiram, what's going on?" I ask, fighting to get the words out through choked laughter, earning me a scolding look from Nyx.

"The captain! He has gone mad. He threw his dinner at me and dumped a pitcher of water on Emery!" Hiram shouts, looking exhausted and fed up.

Nyx steps toward Hiram.

"What has him so upset he's throwing things at you?" Nyx asks.

Hiram's eyes snap to me, and he points. "Her! He saw her last night. He's been demanding to see King Asher. He wants to know what happened to her and why the king hasn't killed him yet. The captain has only become more agitated as the day has gone on," Hiram yells, throwing up his arms in defeat.

A pained groan escapes Nyx as I tilt my head at an awkward angle.

"Please tell me you didn't bring me in the back door last night, bleeding and unconscious, right past his cell."

He holds up his hands in defense. "I was a little preoccupied to worry about our uninvited guest," he reminds me. "It was the first place I could picture clearly enough to get the adveho to open a portal to," he defends himself as if that is a good excuse for his lack of thinking.

I lean back, crossing my arms. "Great. No wonder he's so distraught." My voice is harsh and annoyed at Nyx's lack of forethought when returning last night.

It had to be traumatizing for Theo to see that. A bloody redhead must be a very strong trigger for him. Maybe he remembers more than I thought.

"It's fine. Just summon Asher to go talk to him and then he will stop," Nyx says as if that is the right answer.

I rub at my temples again, my headache returning far too quickly.

"Asher has tried talking to the captain several times now, but he's refused to speak to the king. Why would the captain be demanding to talk to Asher now?" I ask as they both stare at me dumbfounded. "It's because he doesn't want to talk to King Asher. He wants to kill him. And if he doesn't, he will die trying. A hero's death, as they would call it in Lux."

"Besides, Asher wasn't with us last night. He wouldn't be able to explain what happened." I sigh in frustration.

No, Asher wasn't there. He can't get involved.

"All the captain knows is that he saw a woman who appeared to be beaten by a large man. Based on the horror stories Lux tells about us, he probably suspects one of our own did this. Maybe even Asher himself. Lux believes Umbra has a fondness for abusing women," I explain as Nyx's mouth falls open.

"He did curse Asher last night after Loma asked what had happened. So, what do you want to do?" He asks.

Go back in time and fix all our mistakes from the past day?

I rub my face and trail my fingers through my hair, twirling a strand. My heart tugs as a reckless thought comes to my mind. Only the fates know how this will work out.

"I have an idea, but you won't like it," I say, looking at Nyx. "I'll go talk to him as the Queen of Umbra."

Nyx and Hiram simultaneously declare, "No."

I point at them and raise my eyebrows. "Do you two have any better ideas?" When neither of them answers, I turn to Nyx.

"I told you before, they brought him here for a reason. He survived the Cypres for a reason," I say as he steps closer to me, his lips pinched tight.

"And I remember telling you I thought it was a bad idea then, and I still think it is," he answers, towering over me. I grit my teeth at his stubbornness.

"We have no other choice," I say up to him, "I have to show him that his assumptions about us are wrong. It's the only way we can get anywhere with him. I'll tell him I'm queen and no one here would hurt me. Especially not Asher."

I turn from him and head to the door, but Hiram halts my path with a raised hand.

"If you are going to do this, may I suggest changing?" His gaze runs from the top of my head to the tip of my boots. "Queens rarely wear trousers."

I look over my outfit. I'm wearing my usual black trousers, a shirt, and boots. I only wear dresses on special occasions. I'm a warrior queen, not some fair maiden.

Nyx places his arm around my shoulders. "Hiram's right. To make him believe you, you have to look like he would expect a queen to."

My eyes dart between both men. "But I am the queen," I reply, frustrated.

Hiram lifts both hands in front of him and steps out of the way. Nyx ushers me forward and out the door, steering me toward my chambers.

Panic twists my insides as bile rises in my throat. *Oh, gods, what am I doing?* I try to come up with what I'm going to say to Theo, but my mind is blank. I need him to see Umbra for what it truly is. The kingdom I have worked so hard to bring to life. Vibrant and full of possibilities.

As we approach my door, Nyx places a soft hand on my elbow, and I look up at him. His eyes move quickly, scanning the area from left to right, and his eyebrows are knit together in a look of concern. I reach out and place my hand on his, trying to reassure him.

"Last night, when Theo saw you ..." He takes a deep breath, as if he's unsure he should be telling me this. "He said your name,

Lily. I think it was him reacting to the sight of your red hair and the blood, but he said your name."

My heart skips a beat. I've been hoping that his heart remembers me even if his mind can't. If we're Amari, he will know me even through the veil.

I close my eyes, trying to calm my racing heart. Unable to form words, I nod at Nyx, and we enter my quarters to prepare for the Queen of Umbra to meet the Captain of Lux.

Looking over my choices, I ask myself what Junie would wear. I have always admired her regal grace and ability to pull off such stunning dresses. Drawing on memories of her outfits to court in Lux, I select a finely detailed black dress. The crimson stitching along the sweetheart neckline adds a pop of color to the garment, and the stitching continues down the long sleeves, wrapping around the cuffs.

Nyx helps braid my hair and twists it into a crown on my head. A splash of pink powder on my cheeks, and I look like a fancier version of myself. Except for the bruises and cuts marking my pale skin, I could pass as a lady of any kingdom.

My heart hammers and my breaths are rapid as we make our way down the hall to my old cell. Panic threatens to consume me the closer we get to Theo.

This is really happening. I'm going to speak to him as myself.

Theo's shouts echo down the hall as we get closer. The clash of metal on the iron bars tells me he's still throwing things in a fit of rage. Part of me wants to run toward him to comfort him, while the other wants to run as far away as possible.

My shadows dance under my skin as they sense him nearby. I tuck them in the well and place the lid over, leaving a small crack. Never again will I seal them away entirely.

Nyx comes to a stop down the hall from the cell and takes my hand into his. I face him, hoping he can help settle my overwhelming anxiety.

"I'm sorry you must hide who you truly are from him."

I nod at his words because he's right. I'm not fully myself, it's just another mask I must wear to keep the truth about my kingdom safe.

I close my eyes and take several deep breaths, repeating who I am in my mind. *I am the Queen of Umbra. A fierce warrior queen who will do anything to protect her people and her kingdom.* The little pep talk helps to ease my racing heart, and I roll my shoulders, fully embodying my role.

Theo's figure paces within the cell and I swallow hard to push down any last doubts. "Stay here and wait for me. I'm not sure how this will go, and I may need your help."

A small, knowing smile curves Nyx's full lips.

"Of course, my queen." He gives me a wink before pushing me down the hall.

Hiram and Marcus stand on opposite sides of the cell at a distance, so they don't get hit by any flying objects. I signal them to them to give me space, and they both quickly scurry away.

I pause for a moment, out of view, and say a quiet prayer to the fates and gods to show me the way and give me strength. *Please listen.*

I step out from the shadows and get a good look at Theo. His hair is disheveled as if he'd been pulling at it in frustration and anger. Sweat glistens on his skin, and I wonder if he has showered yet. He has trashed the cell. Everything we've provided him with is tossed about, with some items settling near the bars. Theo continues to pace the back wall of the cell near the chains from my nightmares.

He's muttering to himself, completely oblivious to my presence.

"Bring me King Asher!" Theo hurls an empty pitcher at the bars, and it bounces off with a loud *bang*, the sound reverberating through The Keep.

He freezes in his tracks when he sees me standing at the door of the cell.

"Is this how you show appreciation in Lux? And you call us barbarians."

A coy smile curls my lips as his honey eyes lock with mine, fracturing my past and present.

With a growl from deep within his chest, Theo says, "You."

CHAPTER 20

THEO

My chest hums as I practically snarl at the woman before me.

Gods, I am turning into one of them the longer I'm here.

I clear my throat, trying to shake off any lingering animalistic noises as I step toward her. My eyes trail over the cuts and bruises along her face before stopping on her neck. Her pale skin is different shades of purple with long lines from where fingers clamped down. I drag my gaze up only to be halted by soft, pink lips curled into a smile that causes my mind to stutter briefly.

"Are you ok?" I ask, unable to stop staring at her mouth.

Her delicate lips part, and I meet her gaze. Eyes the color of vibrant-green gemstones stare back at me. My steps falter.

Dear gods, who could hurt a woman as stunning as her? Monsters, that's who.

"I'm fine, Captain. I'd be better if you stopped trying to hurt my guards, though. What seems to be the problem?" She asks.

I'm mesmerized by every inch of her, and I fight back the urge to look down at her breasts, perfectly accentuated in her low-cut black dress.

"I asked to speak to King Asher. Where is he?" I answer through clenched teeth.

She watches me for a brief moment.

"You've had several meetings with our king but refused to speak. Yet, here you are, suddenly, trying to summon him. Why?" she asks, stepping closer to the bars.

I stare at her delicate bruised skin and fight back the rage that wants to boil over.

Save it for King Asher.

"I have my reasons," I reply in clipped words.

She takes another step toward the cell, well within my reach now.

"Would I be one of those reasons?" She asks, gently inquisitive.

I don't answer as she stares expectantly. Shadows dance across her face from the flickering lanterns.

"What? Does a nobu have your tongue, Captain?" She teases as if her injuries are a laughing matter.

She's taunting me.

I rush forward, slamming into the bars, expecting her to flinch or step back. She doesn't. She continues to stare at me like she's sizing me up for battle. I grip the iron tight and lean through the gap. I catch a whiff of roses as my face nears her hair.

The shuffle of boots sounds from down the hall. With a simple lift of her hand, it stops, halting whoever was trying to come to her aid.

A little late to be trying to protect her now.

"I asked to speak to King Asher because I finally have something to say. In my kingdom, hurting a woman is not tolerated. Even if the king is the one doing the hurting," I say through gritted teeth.

Her eyes soften for a moment but turn dark just as quickly.

"I wanted to tell him that if he needs a punching bag, I'm right here. That's if he's man enough to go after someone who can fight back, instead of ambushing a beautiful woman." I tell her.

She's probably never had anyone stand up for her.

Her eyes narrow as a sickly smile curls one corner of her lips. "Asher isn't the one who did this to me," she says, motioning to her face and neck.

"Then show me the man who did, so I can teach him a lesson," I say, her evasiveness stoking the anger within me.

She steps closer to the bars, and it's me who retreats, backing my face out from the gap. "That may be a tad difficult, seeing as how I killed him," she says, and her smile fills her face, dangerous and menacing.

I jerk away, thoroughly confused. Scanning her from head to toe, I try to figure out how a woman, so soft and fragile, could kill a man with hands large enough to wrap entirely around her neck.

"My guard and I were in Terra, seeking to punish a lord who had a habit of putting his hands on women. I ended him," she says, but my mind is chasing after her words, trying to piece together everything I know about Umbra.

Her guard? Punishing a lord in Terra?

"What do you mean by your guard?" I ask, my eyes searching hers.

"Well, Captain of Lux, I'm the Queen of Umbra. It's a pleasure to finally meet you," she answers, stretching a hand through the bars.

I stumble back, shaking my head.

That's not possible. What kind of game is she playing?

"There is no Queen of Umbra. King Asher never married. Surely, we would have known if he had," I say, my anger flaring at her lies.

This must be a ploy to unnerve me. They've sent her here to see what she could get me to believe, but I trust nothing said in this kingdom.

She withdraws her hand, adjusting the cuff of her sleeve. I glimpse white scars wrapping around her wrists.

Was she a prisoner here?

"Tell me then, Captain. What is a king's greatest weakness?" She asks, lacing her fingers together in front of her.

What kind of question is that?

A righteous king doesn't have any perceived weaknesses. This must be a trick.

What would be a weakness for King Leopold?

Realization hits me across the face harder than it should. My king would be devastated if he ever lost Junie or the queen. Their lives are ruled by his fear of losing them, always tucked away in Brightwick.

"His queen and heirs," I answer flatly, knowing we've missed a critical piece of information about Umbra.

Asher has a wife.

"Exactly. Because love is the death of peace of mind. A queen would be a target for the other kingdoms, looking for something to exploit to gain an upper hand on Umbra," she says.

That's why King Leopold doesn't allow Junie or the queen to travel much. He's afraid someone will try to kidnap them for ransom or to force a favor from him. But does King Asher truly care about anyone other than himself? Or is he hiding his queen so all the power remains his to wield?

"How? How does no one know about you?" I ask, needing to gain as much information as I can.

Her smile turns sinister, but her eyes flash with an emotion that doesn't match. Hurt, or pain maybe?

"Because I don't exist in this kingdom or anywhere else in the realm. The only people who know I'm the queen are oath bound to the divinus and will die before revealing our secrets," she says with coldness in her tone.

I blink rapidly, trying to process and figure out what all this means. How are these people so loyal to a monster of a king?

It must be fear of death or worse that keeps them in line.

"I'd like to make a deal with you," she says, interrupting my thoughts.

"Me? Why would you make a deal with me? You should talk to King Leopold about deals," I reply, my forehead wrinkling in question. "As your general so kindly pointed out, I'm no one of importance."

A small chuckle escapes from the queen, and her smile drops.

"No, I'd much rather make a deal with the future King of Lux instead of the current one," she retorts, and I freeze.

How does she have this information?

"Your information is wrong. I'm not the future king," I huff in annoyance.

She rocks back and forth on her heels.

"That's not what the villagers of Lux are saying. In fact, they're joyous at the announcement of your engagement to Princess Juniper," she says with a knowing smile.

I slowly walk backward, bumping into the bed and taking a seat. The king must have made the declaration after I left.

Still, how would she know?

She places her arms on the bars, leaning in. Her smile is gone now.

"It's my understanding that you love the people of your kingdom," she says, and I give her a small nod, lost in trying to figure out how Junie and I are going to get out of this betrothal. *If I ever make it home alive.*

"As do I, Captain. I think our lands would benefit from a powerful alliance between their rulers. I would like to propose that while you're here with us, you let me show you the truth about Umbra. Not the stories from rumors, lore, and legends. I want to show you what hides under Thalos' shadow veil. There's more to this kingdom than darkness and monsters. It's time someone from the outside got to see its genuine beauty," she says, her voice ringing with a love for her kingdom I never expected to hear.

My thoughts spiral, trying to figure out the underlying reason for this deal.

"What's in this for me?"

She taps a finger on the bars.

"You won't have to stay in this cell all day anymore," she answers.

I perk up at the prospect of not being trapped in here.

"And no harm will come to the people of Lux?" I ask, knowing I'm going to have to make this deal with my enemy's queen.

"As long as you don't harm my people, yours are safe," she answers simply.

"Why are you making this deal and not King Asher?" I ask, needing to ensure he's aware of this bargain.

"Because I'm one of the few who believes there is still hope for Lux. Just not under its current king. Many others don't hold such belief," she replies.

A queen defying her king. Interesting.

"Why should I trust you? Until now, I didn't even know you existed," I ask, trying to work through the mess of outcomes in my mind.

She lets out a haughty laugh.

"I don't exist, and you have no reason to trust me. But good alliances start with mutual understanding and love for one's people. I think we both want to do what's best for our kingdoms to ensure prosperous futures," she replies with what sounds like a sincere answer.

I doubt I could ever fully trust anyone from Umbra.

Knowing I will likely regret this, I nod and outstretch my hand toward the Queen of Umbra.

"For the future of Lux, we have a deal."

She's the best chance I've got to get out of here.

She smiles down at my hand. Her soft palm slides against my rough, calloused skin. Small pricks that feel like lightning flare where we touch, and I yank my hand back. I stare at my palm as dread settles over me.

Seems like Astra thinks I've made a terrible mistake.

CHAPTER 21

THEO

The hair on the back of my neck rises as I feel eyes boring into me. I snap my gaze up to see the queen staring at me with a softness that makes her look gentle and kind. An obvious attempt to trick me into thinking I can trust her—that she's not the queen of monsters.

As soon as her eyes meet mine, her gaze hardens to stone. The switch is so sudden it's as if a door slammed shut inside her, preventing any emotion beside cold indifference from passing through.

"Would you like to join me for dinner in the dining hall, Captain?" She asks, and I can't understand why.

I scan her face, trying to gauge how she would respond if I said no, but all I see is emptiness.

"You can say no. You make your own choices here. Just use your words," she says, as if reading my mind.

I open my mouth to decline, but my stomach has other plans. A loud grumble echoes through my cell, and I look down at myself, annoyed at my body for betraying me.

A stifled laugh comes from the queen. "I'm going to take that as a yes," she says with amusement.

When I look back up at her, the queen is standing at the door, lips pulled inward, trying to keep her composure. I nod, and a second later, the cell opens.

The queen gestures for me to exit and head down the hall to the left. I hesitantly walk forward, expecting this to be some sort of test. I check the hall and find only the guards waiting down the way.

The queen heads down the hallway, and I fall in step behind, as one does with any member of royalty. I continue to watch the onyx stone around me for any hidden traps or snares, which is why I miss the queen slowing to a near stop. I catch myself at the last moment before running into her.

King Asher would have definitely killed me for knocking over his wife.

"I know the view from behind is exceptional," she says with a wink, "but please walk beside me, Captain. My people need to see you as my guest, not my prisoner."

My mouth falls open at her assumption that I was staring at her ass.

She motions to the space beside her, and I reluctantly comply. She looks up at me smiling as if happy her little puppet did as it was told. I fix my eyes ahead, reminding myself I had no other choice.

For the good of Lux.

We stop before the ones called General and Captain. Both glare at me as if I'm nothing more than horse shit on their boots. I slip into the role that is second nature to me: stoic warrior. I lace my fingers behind my back.

"I'd like to introduce you to Captain Hiram Hale and General Nyx Davey," the queen says, and we all nod at each other. None of us extend a hand in greeting.

Even though she is almost a foot shorter, the queen shoulders through the towering wall of her guards, and we all follow suit. I return to my new place at her side, with Nyx and Hiram behind us. I peek over my shoulder to ensure the two men are not going to stab me in the back.

The queen's red hair snags my line of sight. It's twisted into a crown atop her head, but a few curls have loosened near her face, framing her features. If she were any other woman in any other kingdom, it would be easy to see her as a benevolent queen. Her regal façade is almost believable. But she's a woman of the shadow kingdom—so desperate for power she married the beast who rules it.

Her eyes catch me watching her. A smirk spreads across her face as I tear my gaze abruptly away, telling myself I don't enjoy the way her smile lights up her face.

She is messing with your head. Don't fall for it.

The clamoring of voices and dishes echoes through the hall as we near a large arched doorway. A small hand presses into my chest, forcing me to stop, and I suck in a breath as my heart seems to hum at the sensation. I grab the queen's wrist as our eyes meet. The scars marring her wrist are rough. Pinpricks skirt my fingertips where my skin touches hers. I shove her hand away from me.

Dark, gray eyes burning with pure hatred come into my view. Nyx steps so close to me our noses are inches apart.

"Don't touch her." His warning is stern.

"You should talk to her since she touched me first, General," I snap back.

Nyx looks like he's about to grab me, and I steel myself for the hit.

That's right, show me who you really are.

"Nyx," the queen's stern voice halts Nyx's movement, and I relax.

Nyx's nostrils flare as his jaw flexes. A breath later, he returns to his spot beside Hiram, who looks oddly entertained by the whole scene.

"There will be one rule for you, Captain," the queen says, drawing our attention back to her. "When you're outside your cell, you will stay close to one of us. I trust these two with my life and yours."

I make the mistake of looking over at Nyx and Hiram. Both have cocky grins spread wide on their faces.

"When we enter the dining hall, you will stay between Nyx and me. Understood?" The queen orders.

I nod before she starts toward the growing noise.

We step through the doors of the dining hall to a flurry of activity. People sit in mismatched chairs, carrying on conversations. The smell of parsley and rosemary mixed with something sweet wafts in the air as we cross the threshold, causing my mouth to water.

Eyes and heads turn in our direction as we enter, and the energy of the hall shifts. The crowd seems just as uneasy with my presence as I am with theirs. But after a pause, everyone returns to their meals.

I try to take in the hall, but my mind is warring with what I'm seeing and what I've been taught about Umbra. This is not like anything I've read. There are so many people here.

A shove at my back has me moving to stand in line behind the queen. In front of us stands a long table adorned with a line of food trays. Everyone is grabbing plates from a pile at one end and scooping portions before moving to the next station. I stare in utter confusion at the sight before me.

"Have you never seen a dining hall before?" The queen asks. She isn't looking at me, instead watching her people.

She's their queen, yet she waits in line with them.

"Not like this. It's …" I trail off, at a loss for words.

Nothing in all my years of studying and training in Lux detailed this type of community lifestyle in Umbra.

"Even monsters have to eat, Captain," her voice drips with sarcasm, "we just choose to do so as a family. Together as one."

We take a step forward and reach the table.

"Now grab a plate so you can eat," the queen instructs.

"Don't you even think about it, Your Highness!" An older gentleman yells, shuffling toward the queen. She tries to look annoyed but can't stifle her laugh.

The man drops into a deeper bow than a man of his age should attempt, sweeping an arm across his chest.

"I already prepared your plate. Please take a seat at your table, and I'll bring it out to you," he says, rising.

The queen reaches out, placing a hand on the man's arm and smiling so wide up at him my heart seems to falter.

How can a queen of shadows have a smile that looks like the sun high in the sky in the middle of summer?

"Forgive me, Pyke. What was I thinking? Will you please take the plate to my seat, and I'll be there shortly? I'm helping our guest with his food," she says, gesturing at me.

Pyke's joyous expression falters as his blue eyes land on me. "Yes. I heard the Captain of Lux stumbled into our kingdom.

What's he doing out of his cage?" His tone turns harsh, and the queen flinches as if his words hit her.

"I know your dislike for Lux better than anyone, Pyke, but you won't take it out on him," the queen says, stepping in front of me, blocking his path as if he would charge.

"Well, if he's as cruel as the man he looks like, we'd all be safer if you fed him to the nobu," Pyke hisses, peering around the queen, his eyes narrowing on me.

I fight back a shiver crawling up my spine at the thought of being eaten by one of those creatures.

"Pyke," the queen's voice booms through the hall, and everyone falls silent, all eyes on the unfolding scene. Pyke's face pales as he reluctantly drags his gaze back to his queen.

"The captain is my guest, which means you will treat him with exceptional hospitality and respect. That goes for everyone here," she looks over her people. They all nod and return to their food, the hum of conversation replacing the silence.

Without another word, Pyke bows and scurries back to the kitchen.

"Grab a plate, Captain," the queen says, pointing down at the stack.

I grab one with silverware and trail behind her as she tells me what each dish is.

After barely eating for the past week, all I want to do is pile my plate high and fill my depleted reserves. My body has been warring with me, and I know I need to replenish my energy.

But what if this is a trick and whatever I take will cause sickness or death?

"What is it now?" The queen hisses, turning around to face me.

I scan over the food on the table, trying to make sense of what's happening.

"Speak, Captain. Before I make you," her tone is so forceful, I take on a defensive stance in response.

"A word of advice: don't let her make you. While it would be enjoyable for us, it would be extremely unpleasant for you," Hiram warns.

The queen gives him a wink, and even though I relax, I'm annoyed by this banter they're clearly using to get me to do what they want.

"How do I know this isn't a trick?" I ask, gesturing at the table with my head.

"Trust," she answers, glaring at me.

I feel Nyx step closer to my back as a silent warning to tread carefully.

"As I said, I don't trust you," I say, staring down at her, ready to fight if it comes to that.

A string of angry mumbled words come from the queen before she snatches the fork out of my hand. She stabs it through some roasted potatoes and vegetables, then shoves it all in her mouth. She stares at me as she chews with her mouth open.

Not very queen-like, is she?

She swallows the mouthful of food and forces the fork back into my hand.

"There. Satisfied? Eat the damn food before I force it down your throat," she orders as she picks up a ladle of food, slamming it onto my plate, which nearly drops from my hands from the force. She steps forward, grabbing a chicken breast and tosses it on top.

She turns and heads to a table at the center of the hall. A set of hands crashes into my back, and I'm shoved forward. I stumble, trying to remain upright. I look back to see Nyx shaking his head at me while Hiram smiles.

I trail after the queen and take the seat across from her. She rubs her temples, and I wonder if she's in pain from her injuries.

No, she seemed fine before. She's playing with my emotions.

Nyx joins us in the seat beside the queen. He runs his hand up and down her back. I stare, assessing the relationship between these two.

Has the king seen them show so much affection? Maybe I can use this.

I pick at my food while observing the dining hall. The number of people here surpasses anything I would expect to see in Umbra. Our intel states they are a small group of outlaws who do the bidding of King Asher. But this looks like a normal evening in Lux, with families gathered together for an evening meal.

Families.

I stare in complete shock as a pregnant woman and her young daughter approach the queen, tapping her on the shoulder.

"My queen," the woman says with a shallow bow. Her belly getting in the way. The little girl drops into a curtsy of her own.

"Please, Charlotte, no bowing until after the baby gets here," the queen says, placing a gentle arm on the woman.

"Are you behaving for your mother, Grace?" The queen says, pulling the little girl into her lap and tickling her. The child's laugh freezes me entirely. Her blue-green eyes meet mine, and she smiles sweetly at me. All the innocence of youth shines brightly from her. No scars or bruises line her skin. She looks happy and healthy.

But how can that be?

I stare at the little girl, lost in the oddity of what's before me. There aren't supposed to be children here. No families. And definitely not a pregnant woman on the verge of giving birth.

How has our information been so inaccurate for all these years? How have they been able to hide these people from the outside realm?

Lost in thought, I miss the pair leaving and the queen's attention falling back to me.

"Is everything ok, Captain?" She asks, placing a hand on my arm.

Needles prick at my skin, and I jerk my arm out of the queen's reach.

"Where did all these people come from? And how have you been keeping them hidden from the rest of the realm?" I ask, unable to hide the surprise and disbelief in my voice.

"Being the most feared kingdom has its benefits. Thalos' shadow veil helps, too. As far as where they've come from, that depends on who you ask. Umbra is made up of those seeking a new life, away from the evil of the other kingdoms," the queen explains.

I scoff, "Evil? That's rich coming from the kingdom with the evilest divinus in generations. Where is the king, anyway? Off killing more innocent people?"

Things are not adding up here.

"Is that what your precious king tells you? A word of advice, Captain, King Leopold sent you to your death. I'd suggest questioning all the so-called facts he has given you over the years," she says, scorn lacing her tone.

"You seem to be the only one highly adept at lying," I reply curtly.

"Everyone lies, Captain. It's just the reason behind it you have to watch for. We lie to protect our people. Your king lies for his own self-aggrandization and desire to keep his people ignorant and compliant. We're not the same," the queen's tone is measured, as if she's speaking facts.

Nyx leans in, whispering something to the queen. She waves him off and reclines in her seat. Lifting her hand she prompts two people to immediately start clearing our table. She stands without saying another word. Nyx and I follow her out of the dining hall.

Nyx grabs the queen's arm, pulling her aside. They lean in close together, muttering words too low for me to pick up on. I scan the hall, attempting to orient myself and understand the layout of this place.

At the end of one walkway stands a figure, bathed in shadow that obscures any distinguishable features. Although their eyes are hidden, I can sense their unwavering gaze fixed solely on me. I feel as though I'm being scanned. Every inch of my body undoubtedly checked for weaknesses. I straighten my posture and stand at attention, confident and unafraid of whoever they may be.

"Let's go," the queen's voice brings my attention away from the shadowed figure. I resume my position at her side, and we walk back to the cell. We don't speak the entire way. Only the cadence of our boots on the stone floor echoes between us.

When we reach my cell, the door is already open, and two guards are positioned outside it. I step through and halt, realizing that the mess I left behind has been cleaned. A new pile of clothes and undergarments is set atop a freshly made bed.

"I had my cleaning crew stop by while we ate dinner. You'll find new soap, oils, a razor, and fresh towels for your shower," the queen says. "What is a shower?" I ask.

I've never heard this word. Does Umbra have its own dialect?

Her gaze travels from my creased brow down to my dusty boots, and her shoulders dip. She walks toward the bathing chamber and waves for me to follow. The space is tight, and my body is mere inches away from hers. She takes a step back into the wall as if trying to gain as much distance from me as possible. She gestures to a metal handle protruding from the wall.

"The dial on the wall allows water to flow through pipes within the stone, and it will come out there," she explains, pointing at a feature in the ceiling.

I lean in to get a better look at what she's talking about. Her rose scent consumes my senses, and I tell myself I don't like it.

Why does she smell so good?

"It will come out like rain, and you can bathe under it," she continues, and I stare up in amazement.

I've never imagined such things were possible.

My knowledge-seeking mind floods at this new discovery, and I can't help but smile.

I feel the queen's eyes burrowing into me.

She's studying me.

But when I meet her gaze, I see the same softness I glimpsed earlier.

"How?" I ask, my thirst for knowledge seeking more.

"We have a lot of water here. We've used it to our advantage," she says with a shrug.

I can feel the goofy, impressed smile on my face. The queen returns it with one of her own. I feel disarmed and vulnerable.

I can't believe I'm letting her get to me.

"King Asher is smart to keep you hidden. He's able to brutalize the realm while you rule in the shadows with kindness. It keeps his weaknesses veiled just like his kingdom," I return to my distrustful tone, stepping out of the bathing chamber.

"Darkness doesn't always mean brutality, and kindness doesn't always mean weakness, Captain. Your prejudices won't do you any favors here," she says, walking past me and pausing at the door. "Some things must remain in the shadows until it's safe to bring them into the light. You've only seen what we want you to see. Thalos' veil isn't the only thing blocking your knowledge of the truth. The sooner you realize that, the less painful this experience will be for you."

She stares at me for a long moment before leaving me with Hiram and another guard. Maybe there's some truth to what the queen is saying. Or maybe she is trying to mess with my head. I'm betting on the latter.

CHAPTER 22

THEO

I stand from my bed and finish lacing the fitted black trousers that were left for me. After my first ever shower, a shave, new clothes, and cleaning my boots, I look and feel like myself again. All the mental conflict I've been battling with seems to have washed away with the cascading water.

"The queen will be here shortly for you, Captain," Hiram calls from my cell door. I give him a nod and try to work through how I'm going to use this time with her to my advantage.

The conversation I had with the queen in the bathing chamber has repeated in my mind all night. If there are truths she wants me to learn about Umbra, then I will. All to provide Lux with more information.

Anything for my kingdom.

"All ready to go?" The queen's sweet voice asks from the hallway, stirring something deep within me. What? I'm not sure, and I'm not willing to acknowledge it.

The queen stands in the doorway of my cell wearing black trousers and a tight black shirt. Every inch of the fabric clings to her toned body, accentuating the curve of her waist and shapely ass.

Gods, I shouldn't be eyeing her like this.

She has a unique dagger strapped to her right thigh, and I stare at it for a moment.

"My eyes are up here, Captain," she says.

I slowly drag my gaze up her far too perfect body and meet her eyes. She winks at me, and it takes everything in me not to laugh or smirk. Those are the wrong reactions to have in front of your enemy.

Her jade-green eyes remain fixed on me as I walk over to her. My eyes catch a glimpse of her seductive pink lips and get stuck there.

I wonder if they are as soft as they look.

I shake my head.

No. Stop. Those are horrible, indecent thoughts I shouldn't be having about a married woman, especially when her husband is the Umbra Brutus. I'm sure if he could hear my thoughts, I'd be dead.

I step through the door of my cell and stop mere inches away from her. I watch as her breath hitches, and she steps back.

"What's with the outfit? Plan on adventuring today?" I ask, and she tilts her head up at my question.

"I thought we would do some sparring, and I didn't think a dress was the most appropriate outfit," she answers. "It would allow for effortless movement, but my undergarments would be on full display," she clarifies, wiggling her eyebrows at me as she heads down the hall.

I follow her, trying to force images of what's beneath her clothes out of my mind.

She's trying to disarm me.

Their hideout is quiet this early. We walk in silence as she leads me around a corner and down a long corridor leading to a set of large, dark wood doors. She walks to them, shouldering them open, revealing an expansive training room. The walls are lined with weapons of all shapes and materials. Body opponent bags for practice are set to the side. There are several marked sparring circles in the middle of the room.

How many ways is this place going to shock me?

Umbra is realm-renowned for their spies, but this training room is for warriors. It's far superior to our lackluster indoor space in Lux. We often choose to practice outside in the rain to avoid the poor conditions of our training room.

I walk to a table lined with wooden practice swords. The swords are intricately detailed and of excellent quality. I've been fighting with my father for months to replace ours. Some men had been getting splinters from the handles. Yet, here, in a kingdom we've thought to be too poor to care for its people, they have a training space that puts ours to shame. I can feel my face glowing with amazement as I take in the state-of-the-art space around me.

King Asher must be keeping his people poor to fund his army of brutes. How much of this was funded entirely from stolen items from across the realm?

"It's pretty, isn't it?" The queen says from my side.

I drag my eyes away from the room to see a smile on her face that makes her eyes glow with pride. She's absolutely stunning, and I fight the urge to tell her.

I need to stop looking at her.

"Pick out the one you like and let's get started," she says, rolling the sleeves of her shirt up and tucking back loose strands of her hair.

"I won't spar with you, Your Highness."

She has to be messing with me.

Walking to the table of practice weapons, she runs a finger gently over them, as if looking for the right one.

"Why? Are you afraid you'll lose?" She gives me a side eye glance before picking up a sword perfect for her height, and I hate myself for being impressed by it.

"Warriors fight for their queen, not with them," I say, trying to remember if Junie even knows how to hold a weapon.

The queen tests the feel of the sword in her hand. In a flash, she spins, and the blade is inches from my face. The tip grazes the end of my nose. I stare at her—awestruck.

A sly smirk curves across her delicate lips. "Well then, Captain, this is going to be unpleasant for you," she says with a step forward.

I jump to the side to avoid being jabbed in the face.

She gestures for me to follow and saunters away, her hips swaying side to side hypnotically. She stops at the center ring and turns around to face me. The candelabras from above cast an almost ethereal glow on her as she stares at me expectantly.

She surprises me every moment I spend with her. She seems to be a collection of contradictions. I've seen her be incredibly sweet to her people, and yet I'm sure she could kill me with the flick of her wrist. She probably wouldn't even feel bad about it, either.

Didn't she say she killed the man who gave her those bruises?

I swallow hard and reluctantly pick up a practice sword. I stomp toward her. The queen gives me a wicked grin, knowing she forced my hand and enjoying it.

The last thing I want to be doing right now is sparring with my enemy's queen. But I could use this time to study how they fight.

I'll take it easy on her and learn everything I can.

I barely have time to get into a fighting stance before she swings her sword directly at my head, as if to chop it off. I duck at the last minute, narrowly escaping the blow.

Popping back up, I can't help my approving look, and I take a few steps back. She licks her bottom lip, bringing to mind a predator ready to devour its prey.

I'd let her devour me. I shake my head. *Focus, Theo.*

I watch as she bends into a fighting stance. A strand of her long, red hair falls in front of her eyes. A tremor runs through me.

She shouldn't be so beautiful in this moment.

She lunges, and I block her blow with my sword. The wood clatters upon impact. She advances again, and I step to the side, trying to get out of the way, but she's faster than I expected. I feel the wind of her swinging sword as I barely avoid it, moving just in time. She is so much better than I imagined. If I stay passive, she will bury me.

She paces the edge of the ring, stalking me. All the while, a devious grin is plastered on her face. She is enjoying making me stay on the defense, giving her the upper hand. I need to find a move to switch to the offensive.

Her sword slices toward my right, and I move to dodge it, only to have her sword slam into my left side, causing me to grunt.

"Watch your left side. You keep leaving it open and vulnerable," she says in a tone that reminds me of a teacher trying to show me an area of weakness.

I rub my side, trying to soothe the sting. After taking a deep breath and loosening my shoulders, I take my fighting stance, preparing for another round. She answers my stance with one of her own, then lunges at me again. This time, I deflect and respond with a strike. She easily moves out of the way, light as a feather on her feet. We continue a sparring dance, each trying to find an opening to land a hit.

To my surprise, her skills are well-rounded. She can meet my blows with a defense most of my men couldn't handle; quickly sidestepping my swings and delivering her own right back. Our heavy breaths and quick feet reverberate off the walls. My body buzzes with the movement, seeming to have missed training over the past week.

I grin, enjoying the time out of my cell.

Enjoying my time with the queen.

Her sword jabs toward my right side, and I spin out of the way. My elbow connects hard with her face, and panic consumes me. I turn back to find her holding a hand to her mouth and blinking rapidly.

She pulls her hand away to reveal a busted lip and blood on her fingertips. She locks eyes with me and smiles, revealing crimson-coated teeth.

"Nice hit, Captain."

My blood runs cold.

My breaths come in fast huffs as I take in the sight. *I hurt her.* I have injured the Queen of Umbra. King Asher is surely going to kill me now, regardless of what she says. I step back, dropping my arms to my sides.

"What are you doing? Let's go," she goads, but the pounding of my heart in my ears drowns out her words.

She steps toward me, and I step back, shaking my head.

"It's fine, Captain. You're not the first man to hit me in the face," she says, wiping her blood on her pants.

Fury rages through me, and I tighten my grip on the practice sword, welcoming the bite from the wood into my palm. Her raising her sword, and returning to a fighting stance, is my undoing.

"You're a queen! You shouldn't be here fighting with me. Guards protect queens and princesses, not harm them. Not make them bleed!" I shout as I stare in horror at the blood staining her lips and rolling down her chin.

"It was an accident. We're sparring. People get hit when they spar. Not that big of a deal," she replies flatly.

I step to her, seething at her nonchalant tone.

What kind of kingdom forces its queen to fight? She shouldn't be used to being harmed.

"You're a woman of royalty. Married to the most powerful king of Omnia. You should be off doing queenly duties, not continuously putting yourself in situations where you can get hurt!" I yell at her, my voice bouncing off the walls.

Her normally bright-green eyes darken, nearly black. Stepping into my space, she glares up at me and I watch as her jaw muscles flex.

"Do you find me weak, Captain? Just another one of your fragile damsels in need of saving?" She hurls the words at me like daggers as the air around us charges, as if a storm is about to break.

"I think you're a queen, and you should act like it. Let your king do the fighting, not you," I answer.

A roar escapes as she slams her forearm into my chest, shoving me backward. I stumble a few steps, dumbfounded by her ability to physically move me. I have over one hundred pounds of muscle on her. She shouldn't have been able to do that. Staring at her, she bares her teeth at me as her nostrils flare in anger. She's a predator aiming for the kill.

Now she looks like the queen of Umbra I would expect.

I grit my teeth and take one step back to prove that I'm done. She lunges at me faster than before. Her movements like flashes of lightning in the night sky. The sword cuts through the air with a *whoosh,* and I barely bring my sword up in time to block the attempted hit to my chest.

She whirls, unleashing a barrage of strikes in quick succession. I'm forced backward with each blow, trying to find an opening to counter. My scanning misses her swing to the right, and she lands a hard smack on my ribs, matching the one from earlier.

The sting of pain has me wincing and arching away from her, trying to gain distance. But she doesn't let me have it.

Was she holding back earlier?

I bring my sword back up to parry another hit. The wood collides with a loud *crack*. The vibration shaking my arm. She continues to drive me backward when I notice a pattern. She hesitates after every few swings, not hitting as quick or as hard.

I wait until the next hesitation and use the opening to land a hit on her arm. Not too hard, but just enough to get her to stop.

As my sword barrels toward her side, she drops, moving under my swing, and pops up on the other side. Her fist makes impact with my left jaw, stealing the air from my lungs and thoughts from my mind. A *crack* echoes through my head.

I falter and stumble a step, but she swipes my legs out from under me. I slam into the stone floor with a loud *bang*, and I groan.

Then she's on top of me, pinning me to the ground with her blade to my throat. The black edge kisses the smooth skin on my neck. Her knees and legs trap my arms while her hips sit on top of my waist. I grit my teeth.

Gods, why does she feel so good?

A sharp pain shoots through my jaw, helping to clear my filthy thoughts about the shadow queen. Strands of her long, red hair fall in light curls from her face as she leans down.

"What about now, Captain? Do you still find me weak?" Her words are venom, cold and deadly.

The cut on her lip trickles blood down her gorgeous face.

Just another mark to add to her current assortment.

Her eyes scan me, landing on my lips for a moment before darting back to fix me with a stare.

Conflicting emotions surge through me, a blend of fury and fascination. She shouldn't have been able to take me down. I'm double her size and a trained royal guard. I hate the part of me that's aroused by this whole situation. A damn goddess of a woman is sitting on top of me after putting me in my place for assuming she was like all the other women I've encountered in Omnia. Or maybe that's just my feeling of failure rearing its ugly head. I've trained my entire life trying to protect the ones around me from the evils of this realm. *Of this kingdom.* And here I am, pinned by a secret queen.

The queen's voice brings me back from my racing thoughts, "It would be wise of you to remember this is Umbra. The land of beasts and monsters. We don't have the luxury of being weak. Power-hungry men forced us to become warriors. Men who seek to destroy everything good in this realm. I'll always be a warrior, regardless of my title. Do I make myself clear?" She hisses, drawing her face closer to mine.

I stare helplessly into those haunting eyes. They feel as if they are burning into my soul, picking every piece of me apart to remake me anew—forcing me to face those truths she's been preaching about.

I nod a response, which earns me a *tsk* of disapproval.

"Words, Captain," she says, studying me, waiting for an answer.

I swallow hard, causing the blade to nick my throat.

"Yes. Crystal clear. Can you tell me how you are doing this? No matter how much I try, I can't get you off me." I say, wiggling beneath her to prove my point.

Her face softens as she uses my chest to push herself to sit, creating more friction on my lap. I lock my eyes on the ceiling as I try not to think about her positioning. I get the feeling she knows exactly what she is doing to me right now.

"Were you never taught leverage, dear Captain?" Her voice is a playful taunt, which causes me to bite my lip to hide a smile.

"My legs are locking your arms and hands in place. This limits your entire upper body. As for your lower half ... well I'm sure you know precisely how I'm preventing that from moving," she says, licking her bottom lip before biting it slightly.

I close my eyes, halting the moan I instinctively want to make. Suddenly, the door clicks shut, and we both snap our heads in its direction. No one has entered, which means someone was watching us.

And the queen is currently straddling me. Shit.

I look to her for a reaction. As if unbothered, she slides the dagger back into the sleeve at her thigh with a flirtatious smile on her lustrous lips.

"Let's get going for breakfast. Pyke hates it when I'm late." She hops to her feet with the ease and grace of a cat.

Stepping to the side, she offers me a hand up. I prop myself on my elbows, debating on accepting or pushing her hand away. My instincts are screaming for me to run far away from her, but there's a faint tug on my heart. A pull I haven't felt in a very long time.

I slide my hand into hers. A tingle skirts across my palm as my calloused hand connects with her smooth skin. This time, I don't pull away. I tell myself it's nothing, but a small part of me feels the shifting of tides. An event the magnitude of which is only known by the fates.

The queen helps pull me to a stand, and I brush the dirt from my pants. Despite her playfulness, the air between us still hangs tense after our altercation. I long to break it.

"Your cook is an odd fellow," I say, walking past her to pick up my wooden sword from the ground.

An abrupt jab to my ass has me spinning around to face her. The queen stands with her wooden sword outstretched in front and a lighthearted grin on her face.

Gods, that smile is like the sunrise.

Bringing the sword to her side, she strides over to me, invading my space. "Watch how you speak about my chef, or you will find yourself on your back again."

Looking down, I study her. The busted lip I gave her breaks up the smile. The bruise under her eye and cuts along her cheek mar her pale, freckled face.

And she's still one of the most beautiful women I've ever met.

Her eyes fall to my lips as her smile fades. She shoves past, pressing her shoulder into me. The intoxicating scent of roses follows her toward the door as she hurries away. I scoop up the wooden sword from the ground and place it back on the table beside hers.

By the time we make it to the dining hall, it's alive with conversations and greetings. Everyone bidding good morning to their queen as we enter.

The queen's eyes land on General Nyx, who's already sitting at their table. They nod at each other before her delicate hand grazes the back of my arm, tingles erupting in its wake.

"Grab a plate and go sit with Nyx. I'll be right back," she says, leaning in close.

I look down at her, confusion furrowing my brow. She nudges me along before walking back down the hall. Every sway of her hips oozes confidence, and it's too tempting to stare as she goes. I force myself to look away.

I walk to the serving table, eyeing the spread before me. Small hands push at my legs as two small children scurry out from under the table. Their laughter makes me laugh as they chase each other through the hall.

My heart drops as I stare at the food, and worry opens a pit in my stomach.

How can the stories about Umbra's people starving be true?

The table before me is abundant.

I scan the hall as what I know and what I see battle in my mind. The queen's words about learning the truth ringing in my ears.

She's good. She already has me questioning myself. But what if this is all just a show for me?

To be safe, I add just enough food to my plate to make it until the next meal. I can't risk taking anything from the children who call this place home. I'll have to gather more information later about their supplies to stop guilt from tearing me apart.

As I take a seat at the table, Nyx's cold gray eyes scan me. I settle in, and his gaze focuses on my left jaw where the queen punched me. My injured pride has me wanting to look away. I can't recall the last time someone landed a blow on me while training.

Nyx's lips pinch tight but can't contain his laugh. It echoes off the walls. "Welcome to Umbra, Captain," he declares.

I look back at him in annoyance.

"She got you with her left hook?" He asks, gesturing to my face with his fork.

I nod, acknowledging my loss to their queen.

He laughs some more and shakes his head. "Wasn't expecting that," he says so quietly that I strain to hear him. "Hurt like a bitch, didn't it?" He raises his voice to ask.

I run my fingers over the tender part of my jaw, knowing I'll have a bruise by tomorrow. Nyx rubs his jaw similarly.

"It's her signature move. She does it to everyone."

"Everyone?" I ask, leaning in.

"It hurts and is unconventional, but it will help teach you to keep your left side guarded," Nyx answers.

I don't know whether to feel hurt or part of a club I have no desire to be a part of. What I do feel is relief that it wasn't her beauty that caused me to let my guard down.

"What did you say to get her to hit you? You're the last person I would expect her to do that to," he asks.

The last person?

"You two talking about me?" The queen plops into the seat next to Nyx, stealing a piece of bacon off his plate. He stabs at her hand playfully as she pulls it away, snickering.

"You punched him?" Nyx confirms, pointing his fork at me again.

"Maybe …," she says, flashing an unconvincing innocent smile.

He shakes his head and laughs.

"That's one way to win him over, I guess," he replies.

The queen winks in my direction. She slides a small tin can across the table to me.

"It's a healing salve that will help with the bruising. Loma said it will make your jaw feel better."

I nod and apply a thin layer, the tenderness decreasing instantly.

I dig into my food as Nyx and the queen begin to argue in hushed whispers. I focus on my plate not to give away that I'm trying to make out what they are saying. Their voices are too low. I can't make anything out. The queen's eyes drop to the table, and she takes a deep breath before she hones in on me.

"What's with the plate? Don't like the food?" Her words are harsh and agitated. She waits for my response as I plan my words carefully.

"From what I know, Umbra suffers from a low food supply because of limited trading. Since I'm an unexpected mouth to feed, I didn't want to take more than necessary." I answer, biting into a fluffy biscuit.

The queen's forehead creases. "Do you think I can't feed my people, Captain? First you call me weak, and now, you think I can't care for my own?" Her words sting, and I instantly regret mine.

Nyx chokes on his coffee, coughing in his seat.

"No," I reply honestly, "I just believe if you have limited resources, you could spend them better."

She sits back in her chair, folding her arms across her chest. "Care about my people that much already?" Her words are a taunt, but her eyes flare with hatred.

"I care about the wellbeing of all women and children in Omnia. You, of all people, should understand the evil and cruelty that plagues this realm," I snap back.

Her eyes soften as she looks around at her people before leaning back on the table with crossed arms.

"Let me worry about my people. Your information is another lie. We have enough resources to feed all of Omnia if they show up at our door. Now eat your fill, or I'll make you. We both know how easy it is for me to get you on your back." Her eyes take on a menacing look.

A traitorous image of the queen riding my cock flashes in my mind, and I shift uncomfortably in my seat. I prop my elbows on the table and lean toward her. "I wasn't expecting you last time. It won't be as easy if you try again."

She gives me a coy smile as she stares me down. "We'll see about that."

Our eyes lock as if drawn by a force beyond our control. I'm mesmerized, and I feel heat rising from my groin to my cheeks. She looks at me like she's about to pounce. *And I might let her.*

The sound of a throat clearing breaks our trance. The queen smiles warmly at my savior.

What is wrong with me?

Pyke stands beside the table with a plate piled high with food and a steaming mug of coffee. He sets it down before the queen and then drops into a deep bow.

"Please accept my apologies for my actions and words last night," he says as he straightens. His downcast eyes seem filled with regret.

The queen watches him for a moment.

"It's not me you should apologize to, Pyke. It's the captain," she says, pointing at me.

"I'm sorry, Captain. I … I have a history with your father and seeing you brought back a lot of memories. I hope you can forgive me," Pyke says, immediately following his queen's order.

What history does he have with my father?

"No hard feelings and nothing to be forgiven," I say, extending a hand. He stares at it for a moment before accepting the handshake.

"Pyke, I could use a favor if you would be so kind," says the queen. "Please bring the captain a plate of food, as you would for me or Nyx. He seems to have missed a few items and could use the energy after a tough training session."

Pyke fights to hold back a grin and coughs to hide his laugh. *Is there a running joke here about the queen kicking everyone's ass?* He hurries away and a minute later returns with a plate of food and mug of coffee for me.

We eat and have comfortable conversations. The queen catches up with her people as they walk by, and a few even acknowledge me. No one treats me as if I'm a prisoner here.

Their ploy is working. I'm playing right into whatever the king and queen have planned.

As the queen and I step out of the dining hall, a cool breeze blows strands of her curly, red hair over her shoulder. Even in trousers, she looks all the queen she is. Breathtaking. Radiant. Powerful. I shove my hands in my pockets to avoid the temptation of tucking a loose strand of her hair behind her ear.

It's like she's got me under a spell.

Her green eyes find mine, as they always seem to, and she gives me a dazzling smile, which I shouldn't enjoy.

But I do. Gods, I'm in over my head. I smile back, like the fool I am.

"Ready for a tour?" Her sweet voice rolls through me, sending a shiver down my spine.

I need to get my thoughts under control before King Asher finds me drooling over his wife. I'll be lucky if whoever was spying on us doesn't tell him what they saw.

It couldn't have been him or I'd surely be dead already.

I nod and follow beside her, keeping my hands in my pockets to avoid any accidental touches.

She shows me around her home, which they call The Keep. With every turn, she proves to me just how little I know about this kingdom. Our conversation is easy, and we never have moments of awkward silence between us. The more I'm around her, the more comfortable I become. Her presence calms me, and I find myself enjoying our moments together.

It's all an act, right? She's trying to make me feel welcome, so I become vulnerable to their manipulation. But why is that starting to feel like a lie I'm telling myself?

After a day spent learning more truths about Umbra, I get ready for bed in my cell. As I close my eyes, welcoming sleep, her face awaits me in my dreams.

CHAPTER 23

THEO

*H*er lips part as she moans in ecstasy. My fingers dig into her hips as she rides my cock up and down, chasing her orgasm. Her nails scratch my chest as her head falls back, her long, red curls cascading down.

"Theo." My name from her lips has my eyes rolling back with a moan. Her words are more of a gasp as she gets closer to the edge. "Theo." The pinch of her nails into my skin and her pussy clenching around my cock pull me right along with her. "Theo ..."

The tapping of metal-on-metal startles me awake, and I jolt up in my bed. I'm panting.

"Theo," a rough voice calls from the doorway.

I look over to find Hiram standing at the cell door looking serious. I pull the blanket up over my chest, feeling far too exposed.

"Sorry to wake you, but the queen will be here shortly for you," he says, eyebrows pinching together.

Blinking rapidly, I swallow hard, trying to gather my bearings. I take a long moment because all my blood is currently in my dick as it throbs against my undergarments.

All I can muster in response is a nod. He walks away with a worried look on his face, and I fear he knows what I was dreaming about.

Did he hear me moaning?

Thoroughly embarrassed, I look to see if anyone is watching before I climb out of bed, turning my back to the iron bars.

In the bathing chamber, I strip off my clothes and step into the rainfall of water. Maybe it will help douse the fire burning inside.

Images from my dream flash behind my closed eyes. I let my head fall back, the water runs down my chest to my hardening cock. Reaching down, I slide a hand from tip to base before slowly stroking myself.

Thoughts of the queen flood my mind. I imagine how her soft lips would feel as they wrap around my cock. The thought of her tongue circling the tip causes a snap of lightning up my spine. Increasing the pace of my strokes, I lean forward, bracing my other hand on the black stone wall.

Remembering the feel of the queen in my lap during our sparring adds to the scene unraveling in my mind. Her legs wrap tight around my arms, squeezing me into the position she wants me in. I remember the softness of her ass along my hips.

I imagine myself submitting and letting her take control, working us both until we are on the edge. Recalling her strength and power over me causes my cock to twitch. I've never had a woman dominate me, and the thought of letting her do so again has me quickening my strokes.

The thought of her gasping my name, her pussy clenching tight on my cock as she orgasms has my release blasting through me.

I groan as I cum, aiming for the shower floor, allowing the water to wash it down the drain.

It takes a minute for me to come down from my climax. My rapid breathing slows as I let the water fall over me. My thoughts are a tangled mess as I dry off and dress for the day. I run my fingers through my hair, styling it into place before slipping into my boots.

Shit. Why am I fantasizing about the queen of Umbra? Did they give me something?

I'm struggling with what I know about Umbra and what I'm seeing with my own eyes. People I've been told are cruel, vindictive, and filled with malice have been nothing but kind and generous. They have provided me with food and clothing, a gesture I'm not sure King Leopold would give to a prisoner of Lux.

Does King Asher have everyone in The Keep trying to manipulate me, or is this their true nature? Could all the information I've been given over the years be wrong? Between the stark contrast of Umbra and the queen, my mind is a knotted rope with no hope of being undone.

It's been days since I last saw the queen and there has been a strange ache in my chest since we parted. I've asked Hiram why she hasn't been around, and he's only said she's attending to her duties. Did someone catch us in the training room and tell King Asher about his wife straddling the prisoner? Has he punished her because of me? Is he the one who gave her those scars on her wrists?

I shake my head, reminding myself she shouldn't be a concern of mine. But I can't explain it. In the week I've come to know the queen, she has turned my life upside down. She has me questioning everything I think to be true. And I find myself wanting to learn more from her.

I should stay away—refuse to go on outings with her and keep my distance. But like a moth to a flame, I'm drawn to her. She's the most unique woman I've ever met, and it doesn't shock me that King Asher chose her as his bride. She radiates confidence, power, and doesn't shy away from violence. Between the red hair and smile, I could cave at any moment and swear an oath to serve her until my dying day.

I rub at the odd hum in my chest that's been growing since arriving in Umbra and reassure myself it's the hair color that's causing all these feelings.

"Ready to go, Captain?" The voice of a goddess calls to me, and I look up to see the queen leaning against the door frame with her arms crossed, emphasizing her breasts. One corner of her lips curves up as she catches me eyeing her.

Walking to her, I try to clear my mind of the images of her riding me as she cums. I stop before her, toe-to-toe. Her gaze roams over my body, halting briefly on my lips. Those striking green eyes seem to prick my skin as they trail over it, as if I were being hit with little bolts of lightning.

When our eyes finally meet, her breathing hitches and she squeezes her biceps as if she is fighting back an urge to touch me. I wish I could tell her I feel the same. It's entirely wrong, but it doesn't stop the feelings from bubbling up.

There are mere inches between us. The air feels heated and charged like a stormy summer's day.

"Are you ready to go?" my voice is deep and low in our shared space.

"Yes," her answer is breathy. Her gaze drops to my mouth again as her lips part.

Ask me for anything and I'll do it.

She looks as if she's holding her breath as she stiffly walks backward away from me. Her jaw flexes as she stares at me. I step toward her, concerned by her abrupt movement. I lift my hand reaching out, but she becomes rigid and takes another step back. I retract my arm as if she bit me.

"Let's go," she says, her voice is wavering as she walks away from me toward a large, black door.

I hurry to catch up and remain silent as she pushes it open, nodding at the bowing guard on duty as we go.

Through the door lies a small stream with oddly spaced rocks. I examine the cavern, which spins in a circle. The large, black door has strange etching carved into the trim. It practically blends in with the black stone walls, almost hiding it from view. The cavern is small, and through the opening, I can see the mist from the waterfalls.

Without a word, the queen walks to the stream and steps from rock to rock. Walking to the edge of the gravel path, I get a better view of the placement. The rocks are a secret path from the door to the opening at the end.

Clever.

I follow the queen, cautiously. She's light and nimble, hopping over the rocks. Having walked these stones her whole life, she can probably do this with her eyes closed. I walk unsteadily over the path, unsure of the stability of each stone I pick and not wanting to end up in the water.

With her back to the path, she waits for me at the opening. Blinking, I step into the bright sunshine beside her, but she takes off. I sprint after her, trying to keep track of her curly red ponytail bouncing along the trail. She leads me along a worn path between forests and what I assume is the brink which conceals The Keep.

I continue to chase her as my legs become tired from the prolonged speed. I'm used to running, but this is a faster pace than normal for me. She's quick in and out of sparring.

After leading me through a grove of trees and along a pool below a massive waterfall, she slows and stops in front of a stone path near the water's edge. I finally catch up, coming to a halt next to her.

I lean forward, bracing my hands on my knees, trying to catch my breath as she stands with her arms laced behind her head.

"Feel better?" I ask, practically gasping for air. I'm familiar with the need to push my body to clear my mind—trying to see how hard I can drive myself before either the thoughts ease or my body collapses.

I look up to find her staring at me with an unexplained sadness in her eyes. Her gaze follows me as I stand straight up, concern drawing my eyebrows together.

"A little," she answers. She gives me a feeble smile that is less than convincing. "Let's sit down for a minute before heading in."

She takes a gravel path down a small, tunneled walkway within the stone of the waterfall. The crunching of our boots and my heavy breaths bounce off the walls. A few feet down the way, there's an opening that breaks off from the main path we are on, and the queen turns into it.

Stepping through the arch, I realize it's the bridge that stretches across the pool. I look up at the massive waterfall plunging from the brink above, causing a light mist to form in the air.

Small grunts come from below, and I peek over the stone edge. Peering down into the pool, I'm met with several pairs of glowing pupil-less eyes. I jump away from the wall and the queen looks over her shoulder to check on me.

"There are nobu below us," I say, pointing over the edge.

The queen raises an eyebrow at me as I stand unmoving.

The day at the river with Lily plays in a loop in my mind. The gray beast charging after us as we frantically try to get away. Lily landing hard in the water as I turn to face my death, prepared to fight to keep her safe.

The queen takes my hand, and sparks ignite along my palm, causing me to jerk away. I stumble backward into the wall.

"It's ok, Captain. You're safe. They won't hurt you," the queen reassures softly.

The memories fade, and my eyes lock on the freckles speckled along her cheeks. My breathing is ragged, and I fight to take a deep breath.

"As long as you're with me, no harm will come to you," she offers me her hand again. I stare at it, trying to fight the instinct to run as far away from this monstrous kingdom as possible.

"Trust me?" The queen questions with a tilt of her head.

With my life. The realization hits me like a bolt of lightning.

"Not even in the slightest," I lie as I slide my hand into hers. Tingles erupt along my skin at the contact. She smiles as if seeing right through me.

She leads me to the center of the bridge and drops onto the stone bench carved into it, pulling me down with her. We sit in silence for several moments. The grunts from the nobu cut through me like daggers. *I need a distraction.*

"Have you grown tired of my presence already or simply ignoring me, Queen?" I ask, trying to shake off my panic attack and lighten the mood. Her green eyes trail over me, assessing.

"Maybe a little of both," she says with an amused smile. She leans forward, as if needing a closer look at me. "How did you put it? Ah, yes. I was handling my queenly duties," she says, taunting me with my words from our sparring session.

I pat my leg a few times to stop from smiling. "I deserve that. Well played."

She snickers in my face and sits back.

"Have any of those duties been talking to your husband about King Leopold?" I ask, emphasizing the word *husband* as a reminder to myself more than anything.

She's the wife of my enemy.

Her expression turns serious, and she shakes her head. "Nothing yet. It seems negotiations are more difficult than expected," she says, staring off into the distance.

"I'm sure King Asher is an excellent negotiator, all intimidating with his shadows." I wave a hand in the air, which earns me an odd look from the queen. "But maybe you should speak on Umbra's behalf? My king might respond better to your kindness versus your husband's bruteness."

She flinches at my suggestion. *Seems I've struck a nerve.*

Her eyes fixate on the stone wall. She doesn't blink for long seconds before speaking again, "Rest assured, Captain. I'm doing everything within my powers to ensure a positive outcome for all of us," she says, her voice lacking the warmth I've grown accustomed to.

I nod. When she speaks, I believe her. I realize that I've lost my wariness of her and can talk to her as a friend. *She's won me over. And then some.*

"Can I ask you something?" I decide to test my newly formed affection.

She tilts her head side to side like she is debating allowing me to ask, before looking at me playfully.

"Only if it's extremely inappropriate," she answers with a wink.

Seems her affections for me have grown as well.

"Why do you only call me captain? It's like everyone here refuses to say my name."

Her face falls, and I chastise myself for making her mood shift. I'm desperate for the lightness to return to her gorgeous features.

"You never gave me or any of us your name. Only stating you were a captain in the throne room the night you arrived."

Was she in the room when I was dragged in? I'd remember seeing her red hair. Her husband or Nyx must have told her.

She's right, though. When I think about all the conversations I've had since arriving in Umbra, I don't recall mentioning my name to anyone. Not even the beautiful and kind creature before me.

I extend my hand to the queen, and she looks at me quizzically.

"Name's Theodore, but my friends call me Theo."

I'm relieved to see softness return to her features as she slides her hand into mine. Those familiar sparks skirt my skin, causing me to shiver.

I can't get used to that feeling. Why does it happen every time we touch?

"It's very nice to meet you, Theo. But I have a confession. I already know your name. It's sort of my job." She shrugs her shoulders and drops my hand, looking away from me.

I shake my head in disbelief. "If you've known my name this whole time, why haven't you said it?"

All expression leaves her face, and vacant, green eyes meet mine, slashing at my soul.

"There's power in a name, Theodore Robert Kincaid. Power that wasn't mine to wield," she states.

Damn.

I can't help but be impressed. The spies here must do very in-depth research to get my middle name. Only those within

Brightwick have ever heard it. Mainly being yelled by my father in disapproval over something I did.

"What about you? Is there another name I can call you besides Queen?" I push the test of our friendship.

She inhales and takes in the view around us before answering.

"I have no name in this kingdom. One was never given to me. That was a power I wasn't granted." Her eyes are void of all emotion as she speaks.

The light breeze caresses our skin and lifts her curls softly in the air. She closes her eyes, letting it wash over her, seeming to carry away the pain in her words.

Bringing her gaze back to me, her eyes become bright and warm.

A carefully placed mask to push down all the hurt. I see you behind there, Queen, because I do it myself.

She lingers on the healing bruise her punch left on my jaw. Soft, gentle fingers trace the spot, and I close my eyes at the sensation. The queen rubs her thumb over my skin, causing sparks to radiate from her touch. There's a slowly building fire that will overtake me if I don't get control. I take a deep breath.

"I'm sorry," I hear her whisper.

Opening my eyes, I see there's pain in her expression. I fight the urge to reach out and scoop her into my arms to reassure her everything is fine.

I need to stop wanting to comfort my enemy's wife.

"It's ok. Not like you're the first woman to punch me," I try to lighten the moment by using her own phrasing. Thankfully, the intensity of the moment breaks, and she removes her hand from my face.

As she pulls away, it feels like she takes my heart with her—a slight tug. She turns her gaze back to the scenic view, and I rub my chest, trying to brush away the feeling.

Over the top of the bridge wall, a conspiracy of ravens bursts through the forest canopy and soars into the sky. I stand and walk to get a better look. They dart this way and that, as if chasing each other.

The black birds fly in hypnotic circles, and I watch them, entranced by their movements. A daunting sense of familiarity creeps up my spine, and I remember. These are the same soundless creatures we saw that day at the river, flying and watching us from high above right before the nobu descended upon us. The day King Oren took her from me. My blood boils with renewed hatred for this awful kingdom. A reminder of what they truly are.

And King Asher is worse than Oren ever was.

The queen comes to stand beside me, seeming to admire these horrid birds.

"Those are my ravens. The larger ones are a mated pair, and the three small ones are their offspring." She points at them as they circle over the forest.

I clench my jaw, trying to remind myself that Lily's death isn't her fault but King Oren's. She seems to notice the tension rolling through me.

"What is it?" She asks, concern peaking in her voice.

I debate not saying anything and letting it go, but I know she won't accept silence as an answer. Besides, something about her makes me want to tell her things.

"The ravens were in Lux when King Oren killed my best friend ten years ago. They stalked us the day she was murdered. I never knew they were creatures of Umbra, but it makes sense now," I reply, slowly bringing my gaze to her.

Sadness seems to overtake her. She is the embodiment of empathy, something I didn't think existed in this kingdom.

"Tell me about her," she urges gently.

How do I even explain Lily to this woman? How do I tell a woman who married for power that even at sixteen, I knew I had found my Amari and that Umbra's former king took her from me? She would never believe it. But I can't help but try.

"She was my everything. Her name was Lilith." My heart breaks saying her name out loud. Even after all these years, the pain still cuts as deep as Oren's blade into her flesh.

I look at my hand resting on the wall as the queen covers it with her own. I let the sparks fly between us. When I face her again, I find her eyes filled with tears.

"I can't remember much, only the way she made me feel. Happy. Loved. Whole. We were just children but already so much to one another," I say, not sure what more I can say about the love of my life.

I let out a breathy laugh and allow myself to stare at the queen's beautiful curly hair. Reaching out, I grab a strand and rub it between my fingers. Her eyes follow my hand as she swallows hard.

"The only feature I can distinctly remember is her red hair. Much like yours, but I think it was a different shade," I tell her wistfully.

"Ah, one of the gods' favorites. She was special," she says, watching my fingers twirl the lock of hair.

"You know the lore, too?" I ask, dropping the strand.

Her smile widens, and I want to commit it to memory. Warmth and joy beam from her, and I can see why she is so beloved in her kingdom, even in secret. She's everything a queen should be.

"You don't live with this color hair without hearing the story constantly, especially when you're young," she replies, and my own face brightens with a smile.

The fates sure have led me on a strange path.

A small laugh escapes me at the thought. I survived a treacherous forest and the wrath of a ruthless king who rules over a kingdom of thieves and murderers, only to find myself standing in a magically beautiful place enjoying my time with their secret queen. I hope the fates know what they are doing.

We stand in silence, enjoying the view of the haunted forest from the bridge.

It's actually quite beautiful from here and doesn't look like the terrifying horror inducing place I entered when I first arrived.

Pairs of yellow eyes glow back at me from within the forest's depths, causing me to startle. *Well, maybe it still is that.*

The queen leans toward me, her arm flush with mine. My skin tingles under her touch, causing me to flex my hand.

"So, it's Theo? Why not Teddy?" That awful name snaps me from my reverie.

"Please gods, never call me Teddy. Do I look like a stuffed animal to you?"

She looks me up and down, as if considering my likeness to a child's toy.

"No, I don't look like a teddy bear, Queen." I chastise.

She pushes into me, laughing, and I swear she wipes a tear from her eye.

"Well then, Theo," she over emphasizes my name, "we better head in for breakfast before Pyke hunts me down."

I laugh, knowing he would do just that.

She walks behind me this time, and I feel her fingers slide across my lower back. The tingles travel up my spine, and I fight back a quiver. Gods, it's like I am being zapped with tiny lightning bolts and set on fire in an entirely sinful way. The sensation stirring those forbidden feelings I keep forcing down. I take a deep breath, willing my cock to behave.

We follow the bridge back to the pathway and turn in the opposite direction from which we came. She turns around to face me, walking backward.

"So …" the queen drags out the word longer than necessary. "Do only lovers get to call you Teddy?"

I burst out into a loud cackling laugh. She joins my laughter, all sadness erased from her face, and she is glowing.

"Wouldn't you like to know? But unfortunately for you, I don't kiss and tell," I say, giving her a wink accompanied by a smug smile.

She laughs again, and it's the sound of home. My heart stirs, and I fight back the emotions trying to rise to the surface.

Following the queen through another set of black doors, these smaller than the back entrance, the smells of roses and apples fill the air, welcoming us inside.

We make our way through The Keep, and the queen points out new sections I haven't seen yet. As we near the large arched doors of the dining hall, the queen slows her pace. A petite woman leans against the door frame with her arms crossed, scowling at us as we approach.

"Another outing with the enemy, my queen?" The woman asks, her tight-black curls bouncing as she speaks. I aim to step toward her to introduce myself, but the queen places an arm out to stop me.

"What I do with my guest is none of your business, Kira," the queen replies, her tone harsher than I've heard her use with any of her people.

Kira's chestnut eyes dart from me to the queen as she glowers at us.

"I'm positive I'm not the only one interested in what you've been doing and saying to the prisoner, my queen." She hisses.

She looks like she wants to cut off my head, and knowing everyone here is a trained warrior, I'm sure she could.

Her figure looks familiar. I think hard, trying to place it.

Is she the one that saw us sparring? Is she reporting on my time with the queen to King Asher?

I'm shocked to realize that I'm more worried about not seeing the queen again than incurring the king's wrath.

Before I can blink, the queen is on Kira, forcing her to stand stick-straight against the door. The queen slams her hands on either side of Kira's head, causing her to flinch. Kira swallows hard as the queen leans to whisper in her ear. The words are too quiet for me to make out, but judging by the fear overcoming Kira's face, I'm sure I don't want to know.

The queen pushes off the door but doesn't put any distance between them. Kira's eyes flash to mine. They blaze with such hatred; I instinctively take a step back.

"Go now, Kira," the queen orders.

Kira's gaze returns to the queen as tears gather in her eyes, threatening to fall. She hurries out of sight. The queen's head falls back, and she takes several deep breaths. Her shoulders rise and drop in an even cadence. The queen doesn't look back or utter a word to me before walking into the dining hall.

CHAPTER 24

LILY

I stab at the last remaining food on my plate, lost in a mix of panic and anger. The interaction with Kira has my stomach in knots and my instincts on high alert. She's jealous of the time I'm spending with Theo, not understanding why I'm doing so. When she's like this, she lashes out and makes rash decisions that always end poorly.

"Any other plans for today?" The deep timbre of Theo's voice breaks my spiraling thoughts.

I resist looking at him. He just watched me intimidate one of my people. I'm worried I've reinforced his assumptions of the Queen of Umbra and all the progress I'd made with him is lost.

I force down my nerves and try to smile at him. "I'd like to show you more of the beauty of Umbra. I thought we could go for a walk around The Keep," I answer.

I'm ready for more fresh air.

He nods with a small smile, and the knot in my stomach loosens a notch.

Gods, I've missed him so much it hurts.

We clear the table and leave the dining hall, exiting through the front door. I lead Theo around the waterfall, stopping briefly at the pool with the nobu. I want to show him that he doesn't have to fear them and try to get him to stand near the water's edge with me. He refuses, but his body isn't as tense as it was earlier on the bridge. I consider it a step in the right direction and move on.

Autumn has descended upon Umbra, painting it in stunning shades of orange, red, yellow, and brown. The light breeze and warm sun are the perfect combination for a beautiful day here. Theo takes in all the sights and sounds of my kingdom. He asks questions as we go, wanting to know more.

Hope blooms in my chest as he seems to open up and see Umbra for what it really is.

If I can get him to see and accept my kingdom, maybe he will be open to me as well.

We come to a stop at the edge of the haunted forest. The bloodwoods' leaves have darkened to their crimson red of winter, intensifying the forest's eeriness.

"What creatures live in there?" Theo asks, pointing at the woods.

As he speaks, a pair of yellow eyes peek out from behind a tree. I don't have to see her to know it's the hare, the most curious of the four.

"They're called Cypres. They are creatures made of shadows that can infiltrate a trespasser's mind to show them their worst fears. They flood the mind with terrifying images, which results in the sensation of one's mind being ripped apart," I answer, scanning Theo for a reaction.

He swallows hard, most likely remembering his time in the woods.

"That's how they killed my guards, then? No wonder they screamed like that," he says, and his body stiffens.

"Sadly, yes. It's their job to protect Umbra from all trespassers. They can sense intent, which is why only a few survive the woods. If they find you worthy, you're granted safe passage," I say, hoping he understands that neither I nor Asher killed his men.

"Why did they let me live then? We all arrived in Umbra with the same intentions," he asks, eyeing me expectantly.

Because you're nothing like them.

"Maybe they saw something in you that you can't see," I say, choosing my words carefully.

Theo studies me for a long moment. His gaze examining my face.

I smile at him, feeling my heart nearly bursting with possibilities of what his being here means. Then I walk into the haunted forest. Theo, understandably, doesn't move.

He stands at the edge of the forest, still stiff and tense.

"They won't hurt you, Captain," I call over my shoulder.

He doesn't budge.

"Like I said before, nothing will hurt you when you're with me. Don't you trust me?" I ask for the second time and watch his internal debate play out on his face.

"Not even a little bit," he replies hesitantly, but I can feel that it's a lie.

He walks toward me. "If they kill me, I'll haunt you for the rest of your life."

"Don't threaten me with a good time, Captain," I say as he steps beside me, determination replacing the hesitation in his eyes.

He trusts me.

I turn and head into the haunted forest with Theo one step behind.

The sunlight speckles through the dense branches above, dimly lighting our way. It doesn't take long for the Cypres to sense someone in their woods. Shadows stalk us through the trees, staying just out of sight. Theo's head darts from side to side as they follow us toward the clearing. He comes to walk beside me.

The closer we get to the clearing, the more the Cypres circle. The black voids whirl through the trees, sending a breeze to stir the leaves underfoot. We stop near the center with patches of light dotting the space.

The Cypres continue to dance along the tree line at an increasing pace, as if unsure of what to do. Theo spins, as if trying to capture a glimpse of a creature, but they're too quick. I grab his arms and plant him in front of me. Small sparks flare across my palm from where it touches his skin. My shadows swirl excitedly in their well at each feel of him.

Theo's breathing is frantic as he tries to follow the shadows circling us.

"You're safe, Theo," I reassure him, hoping to ease his panic.

His eyes lock on mine. His chest rising and falling in quick breaths.

"I'm sorry. Like most people, I was taught to fear the dark. You may say I don't have to worry, but my gut says those beasts are out to get me," he says, pointing at the tree line.

As if in response, the wind picks up, lifting my hair.

"The darkness isn't something you should fear, Theo. Far worse monsters hide in the light," I reply, knowing one of the real beasts rules over Lux. A man who will destroy anyone who stands in the way of his power.

With my words, the Cypres stop. The wind comes to a halt and silence falls upon the woods. Theo's eyes nearly pop out of his head at the sudden change. He looks frantic.

"What's that?" Theo blurts, looking over my shoulder.

I turn to see the hare slowly hopping toward us.

What is she doing?

"That's one of the Cypres in their physical form. They only appear this way for me as they're bonded to me," I answer as the hare makes her way to my side.

I reach out and pet her soft fur as she nuzzles into me. Her tall antlers tilt out of the way.

"It's you," Theo says, staring slack-jawed at my creature.

"What?" I ask, confused by his statement.

"Before I passed out, when I was in the haunted forest, I saw a giant rabbit. I assumed I was hallucinating. But it was real," he says, his fear replaced with awe.

I examine my hare and see that she is looking at Theo with the same calm affection she does at me. *She knows.* My heart hammers in my chest as the hare pulls herself from my side and approaches Theo. She bows her head to the side, waiting for him to pet her.

I can't breathe as Theo runs a gentle hand over the hare's fur. She tries to scoot closer to him, but he jerks back as her antlers lift. She quickly drops her head and slides toward him, pressing against his legs. Theo smiles and resumes petting her.

I stare at the scene before me, completely flabbergasted by it. The Cypres have let no one but me touch them, always keeping their distance when someone else is with me.

Does she know he's my Amari? How can that be?

"What is it?" Theo asks, pausing his petting. I slowly bring my eyes to him and swallow down the lump forming in my throat.

"I don't think anyone but me has ever touched a Cypres," I answer.

A satisfied smile fills his face as he looks back down at the hare and strokes her soft fur.

"Maybe I'm special, after all," he jokes.

You have no idea, Theo.

CHAPTER 25

I thumb through the pages of *Battle Strategies of Omnia* until I find the section on Umbra. Leaning into the headboard, I settle in to make notes.

The details in the book are sparse and, after being here, I know them to be inaccurate. The book describes Umbra as a land devoid of anything but forests filled with monsters. The information regarding where the people live is vague, and I question if it is misinformed or intentional.

I take out the pencil Hiram retrieved for me earlier and make notes along the pages. I write everything I've learned so far and cross out the passages I know to be false. If I make it out of here, I'll have an accurate description of Umbra to share with the scholars of Lux.

As I read over my writing, double checking I haven't missed anything, I yawn and stretch to keep myself awake long enough to finish.

"Must be a riveting book there, Captain," Hiram teases from the cell door.

I finish reading the last of my notes before acknowledging him. Setting the book and pencil down on my bed, I stride over to the bars. Hiram takes a step back, out of my reach. He obviously hasn't forgotten me breaking his nose after I arrived.

"You can call me Theo, Hiram," I say, stretching my hand through the bars. Hiram stares at it as if trying to assess if it's some sort of trick.

"Well, Theo, the queen has sent me to ask if you'd like to join everyone in the library for story time," he remains at a distance and doesn't shake my hand, so I pull it back.

"You have a library?" I ask.

Will this place ever cease to amaze me?

"One of the best in all of Omnia," he answers, and my heart flutters at the prospect of new information to devour.

"Yes, I'd like to go, then," I say, unable to conceal the eagerness in my voice.

Hiram waves a hand, instructing me to step back, and I do. It seems I'm not the only one slow to trust around here.

Hiram opens the cell and motions for me to join him in the hallway. I follow him through the onyx stone halls of The Keep until we reach a large archway.

I step through the threshold and freeze at the sight. Rows and rows of bookcases span the massive space. Books as far as my eyes can see. This is easily the largest library in all of Omnia. Like so many of the things I've seen here, it puts Lux's to shame.

Walking over to the shelves, I run a finger along the spines. There's a mix of old and new books with varying shades of leather. A worn brown leather book sits next to a vibrant purple one.

The scent of old parchment warms my soul, bringing me back to my roots. I smile as sweet memories of days spent with Lily flipping through the pages of our favorite fairy tales flood my mind. *She would have loved this.*

"Finding anything you like?" The sultry voice of the queen asks from the other side of the bookcase. I bend slightly to see her watching me through small spaces between the books. The moment her green eyes meet mine, I grasp the wooden shelf to keep myself from stumbling backward. It always feels like she's looking directly at my soul.

Her stare leaves mine as she walks along the bookcase to step before my row. I track her movement, and my breath catches when she's in view. My gaze slowly travels up her body.

Her fitted, black trousers show off her expertly toned legs. I notice that she's not wearing her dagger tonight. A long-sleeved, emerald shirt makes her look like a forest on a fresh spring day. The sight is far too appealing.

"You don't seem to have many choices. Glad I brought something with me," I joke as I scan the expansive library.

"We have books to satisfy any taste. Everything from your dry battle strategy books," she replies, taking a step toward me, "to the filthiest novels in all of Omnia." She stops an inch away.

Her sweet rose scent causes my heart to momentarily forget its rhythm.

"Which would you like, Captain? Choose wisely," she says, and her voice sounds like seduction.

Gods, this woman is going to be the death of me.

Our eyes lock, and we're focused on one another for a long moment. The air between us is charged. Heat coils through my body as I battle to keep my emotions in check. Today, I feel like I'm going to lose the battle.

"We're ready for you, my queen," Hiram calls from behind her.

She breaks our eye contact but pauses on my lips for a heartbeat before turning on her heels. A chill rolls down my spine and everything in me screams to reach out and grab her.

I step out from the bookcases and, seeming to sense my movement, the queen glances over her shoulder. She points to a high-back, crimson chair near the center of the library. It sits next to a small table with a matching chair on the opposite side.

Walking over, I stare down at the queen, who stares right back. Even after I've passed, I can feel her eyes trailing down my body. I take a seat in the assigned chair, and she gives me an approving nod, as if pleased I've done what I was told.

The little girl from the dining hall, Grace, hands the queen a book bound in deep-red leather. The queen takes it with a beaming smile that seems to brighten the library.

Grace walks to the table beside me and sets down a worn yellow book. With a soft grin, she scurries back to her spot on the floor among the other children. It looks like everyone from The Keep is at the library tonight. The room is overflowing, and all eyes are on the queen.

I listen intently as the queen dramatically tells the first story about the lore of the end bringer. It's a realm old tale about a mortal created and favored by the gods. The one gifted with powers strong enough to bring an end to all we know and love.

Rarely looking at the book in her hand, she acts out the story with such ferocity it truly brings it to life. I vaguely remember it from my childhood, only bits and pieces sound familiar. There's something about hearing the legend here in this kingdom, being told by a hidden queen, that gives the story a new life.

After the queen finishes, the children ask curious questions, wanting to know more about the end bringer. The adults do their best to answer, but some things only make sense to the gods.

The queen turns around and sets the book down on the table. As she approaches, I give her a small, but silent applause for the show. She dips into a playful bow. She picks up the yellow bound book and returns to the children who are patiently waiting.

The next story is the tale of the Amari and how the threads of fate always lead you to those you are destined to be with, regardless of what life throws at you. Couples lean into one another as the queen eloquently performs the lore with dramatic flourish. A warm sense of love hums through the air as if the fates are here with us, listening intently.

The queen closes the book and returns it to the table beside me. She takes a seat gracefully in the vacant chair. Heat radiates from her and a light sheen of sweat dots her forehead. I want to reach for her and tell her how amazing she is but rub the back of my neck instead.

"I can't find my Amari," sighs a small voice from the center of the circle. The queen looks down at the crowd of children with so much love and kindness. My heart nearly erupts in my chest. This is the picture people should have of Umbra, not the harsh, murderous one set forth by their king.

The entire room looks back at the queen with adoration. I'm overtaken by the purity of the moment.

Is this the true Umbra she wanted me to see? This can't all be an act. A small voice of doubt enters my thoughts. But I take note of how much quieter and less certain the doubts have become.

The queen's sweet voice brings my attention back to the library.

"In time, you will find your Amari. And, when you do, stop at nothing to keep them safe and close," she answers, but instead of looking at the children, her sorrow-filled eyes flash to me. They moisten as tears form. But a breath later, they've dried. Pushed away like all her other emotions, tucked behind her carefully placed mask.

I wish I could tell her it's safe to let it slip with me, but that would make me a hypocrite. I've been wearing the same mask since meeting her. Neither of us is ready to deal with the reality of what revealing our full selves would mean for us.

My heart pings with familiar pain as our conversation from the bridge sets in. I'm trying and failing to reconcile this empathetic woman with the queen who married King Asher. It seems that they are not Amari, and their marriage is one of convenience, not love. What is she gaining from this? It's almost like she's his prisoner. The king wielding his power and hiding her away from the realm.

I slide my hand across the table and gently squeeze the queen's hand. A silent gesture of understanding and thanks for sharing an honest moment with me. Even if I don't know what it's truly about. Like me, the queen seems to be letting down her defenses.

A loud round of applause reverberates through the library, and the moment between us is lost.

"Time for bed, children," Hiram's voice booms as the children groan in protest.

Their parents usher them up and out, stopping to thank their queen before leaving.

Nyx leans down, whispering in the queen's ear before he exits the library, helping to carry exhausted children back to their beds.

We are alone.

The silence causes questions to whirl in my mind, and I have to know.

"Does King Asher not enjoy bedtime stories?" I ask.

I've been enjoying my time with the queen so much, it has barely registered that I haven't seen King Asher for a while.

How could he not want to spend every waking moment with this magnificent woman?

"It depends on who's telling them. Why, do you want to tell Asher a bedtime story?" She smirks.

"No," I answer quickly, trying to get the image of the terrifying mass of darkness looming as a sweet children's story is read. "It's just the king wasn't here tonight. He missed a great performance," I say with a grin.

The queen's expression turns inquisitive. "How do you know Asher wasn't here tonight?"

"The obvious lack of swirling black shadows trying to kill me was a bit of a hint," I say with a shrug.

The queen studies me thoughtfully.

"What do you know about Asher?" She asks, and I shift in my seat, trying to think of all the things I've learned about the shadow king over the years and during my interactions with him in my cell.

"King Asher has no known origin and is the strongest divinus in generations. He earned his name as the Umbra Brutus for being a murderous beast that lurks in the shadows. He has an affinity for killing anyone who crosses him. There are many people who believe he's a new god walking among mortals," I answer as if reciting from a textbook.

The queen smiles slyly.

"Here I thought you were a captain of the guard, not a scholar," she says and my cheeks heat. "But like most of your information from Lux, it's not entirely true. Yes, Asher is extremely powerful. But the shadow form is just another veil to protect our people. Underneath, Asher is as mortal as the rest of us," she says, watching me.

I swallow hard, trying to process the words.

Why is she telling me this?

If Asher is mortal, that means we can kill him. This has to be a gesture of trust. I've shown her that I trust her, and she is trusting me with Umbra's secrets.

Then, it hits me. If Asher is mortal, it means he could be around all the time in his mortal form, and I wouldn't know.

Has he seen my reactions to his queen?

Panic rises within me as I recall every glance, every touch, every moment that could give away my burning desire for the queen. Could he have seen it all? My mind screams one name. *Nyx.* He is always around; the queen is so comfortable with him. Their affection toward each other could be considered loving. He seems to be weary around me. I get the uneasy feeling that I should be a lot more afraid of Nyx.

Sparks skirt the back of my hand as the queen places hers atop mine.

"You're safe, Theo. No one will harm you," she reminds me.

"You can't protect me from everyone, especially your king," I reply, with more bite than I should.

I just feel so foolish. My entire life has consisted of half-truths about Umbra, and I never questioned them. I took the word of my king and scholars because I trusted them. But their lies have left me ill prepared. With all the things I've learned about Umbra so far, I never imagined that my knowledge of King Asher would be inaccurate too. How have I been here, walking around, seeing the kingdom, without realizing their king might be present all the time?

"There's no one in this realm that will get past me to harm you. You're under my protection until all this ends. You have my word," the queen repeats.

Her eyes are gentle and clear. If I didn't know better, I could easily believe that this woman would go to the edge of the realm, putting herself in danger to keep me safe. But I do know better, and that won't happen. If it comes down to me or her king, I know the choice she will make.

The now familiar buzz in my chest reminds me that the queen's hand is still on mine. A deep hum that seems to rise from the depths of my soul. The threads around my heart feeling as if they are being plucked one by one. The queen is the musician strumming away at the cords, creating a new tone only for her. A melody orchestrated by the fates telling me that I have everything all wrong.

CHAPTER 26

LILY

Theo seems lost in thought as the sparks between our hands intensify. My shadows and the threads around my heart are beckoning him. The two seem to rejoice at being united once again.

But I can't. Not like this.

I break the energy pulsating between us and sit back in my chair. Theo flexes his hand when I let it go, as if trying to make sense of what he's been feeling through it.

Theo looks like the library was made for him, and really, it was. When I made plans to renovate it, he was on my mind. He'd wanted to be a scholar when we were kids, and I wanted to build a library fit for a scholar. *Fit for Theo.* I wanted a place he would be proud of, but I never thought he'd be sitting in it—beside me.

"Where'd all this come from?" Theo asks, staring at the vast array of books lining the shelves.

"From all over Omnia. We traded for some books while others traveled here with those who now call Umbra home," I answer with pride.

Under Oren's rule, this library was nothing but a few rows of pointless literature. He believed that knowledge leads to power and there was no way Oren would allow for anyone to gain any power that he does not possess. *Pathetic.*

"You have books from Lux here?" Theo's eyes scan the shelves as if he could pick them out from the stacks.

"Several. We have a lot of former Lux villagers, and many of them donated their books. Pyke brought a few battle novels with him if you need more dry reading material," I reply, teasing him lightly.

Theo bounces his leg up and down. The rhythmic thud echoing through the library. His shoulders tense as he stares blankly at the floor.

"That's how Pyke knows my father? He's originally from Lux?" Theo is starting to ask questions about Lux and second guessing what he knows. My plan seems to be working.

"Yes. Pyke and his sister, Elizabeth, had left Lux and were viators when Oren met them. One bite of Pyke's food and Oren offered him the role as our head cook," I answer. Honestly, Oren bringing Pyke here was the only good thing he ever did in his life. One of the few times death wasn't his top priority.

Theo nods slowly, and I can almost see the pieces rolling around in his mind. Trying to put all of it together with as little information as possible. But he'll need more. Even though I'm not sure he wants to know all the answers.

"What did my father do to Pyke? I know it was bad, but I'd like to know. If that's ok? Pyke could barely contain his hatred for me, and I deserve to know what brought that on." He's definitely realizing that he needs more.

I let out a sigh, trying to prepare myself to tell Pyke's painful past. It's almost the standard here in Umbra. Heartbreak and loss forces people to risk everything to escape, even if it means facing new monsters. The depths people will go through to get away from the cruel, power-thirsty men of this realm.

"Pyke and Elizabeth lived in Lux with Pyke's husband, David. His Amari," I answer. Theo's face loses all color at the sound of the name. By the look on his face, he already knows exactly what his father did.

"David was Captain of the Guard. Your father wanted the position. He killed David during a training exercise and passed it off as an accident. One of their trusted friends told Pyke what happened," I continue.

Theo leans forward, bracing his elbows on his thighs. I wish I could tell Theo it was Breton who told Pyke everything, our friendly childhood guard. The one who knew us better than our parents sometimes. But I can't bring him up without getting emotional, and that won't make sense to Theo.

"Pyke attempted to retaliate against Arthur. But Arthur threatened Elizabeth. He told Pyke he was going to kidnap Elizabeth and do horrible things to her. Then he would let his men have a turn. Arthur told Pyke he would return Elizabeth as a ruined woman or a dead one. He didn't care which," I sigh, my heart aching for Pyke and Elizabeth and all they've endured.

Theo shoots out of his chair and begins to pace anxiously. He runs his hands through his hair, disheveling it. Even angry, he's still the most handsome mortal I've ever met.

"They got out, Theo. They packed and left the next morning. They traveled between the other kingdoms before Oren found them. Elizabeth has become one of the best seamstresses in the village. Pyke is here. They're safe. Arthur never got to harm them and never will," I say, hoping to ease some of the fury that is visibly rising in him.

"He did hurt them. He killed Pyke's husband! His Amari, for gods' sake!" Theo exclaims as he halts his pacing. He looks at me with a mix of fury and shame. This is his father we're talking about, and his commanding officer.

"Pyke did everything he could to rescue his sister from the man who murdered his husband. Only for the son of the murderer to show up in his home years later. The pain I must have caused him by showing up. I know if things were the other way around, I would have had a much worse reaction," Theo admits. "I know my father has always been ruthlessly ambitious. But knowing what he's done to them … I hate him," Theo whispers the last words.

"We're not responsible for our fathers' sins, Captain. Pyke knows that you're not Arthur. He wouldn't have said he was sorry if he didn't mean it," I tell him honestly. He looks at me doubtfully.

"Is your father as bad as mine?" He asks as the word *our* clicks into place. Memories claw at my mind, trying to pull me back into the darkness.

"Worse. You're not the only one with father issues. It seems to be relatively normal around here," I say, flat and hollow.

I fight back the urge to tuck at the sleeves of my shirt to keep my scars from showing.

My past and present meld in a harsh onslaught. Flashes of being chained to the wall of my cell, hungry and filthy, fill my vision. Then I'm back to the present with Theo standing in the library I built for him. Suddenly, I'm pulled back to the past by the memory of a hand closing around my throat. Oren stares at me as black fills his eyes. A smile laced with malice tells me Oren knows what I'm planning—even from his grave. I'm thrown back into the present, gasping for air, feeling as though I've been punched in the gut.

Rough fingertips wrap around my hand, prying it open. I feel a sting in my palm, and I register that my own nails are digging in. My heart races as my breathing becomes ragged. Theo kneels before me and rubs the palm of my hand, trying to calm my panic.

"Breathe with me," he whispers. The same words he used to say when I was his flower, and my anxiety got the better of me. He always knew how to talk me through it. I yank my hand away from him, swallowing hard and fighting back a flood of emotions. Theo stares at me with a mix of shock and concern as he examines me.

He stands, crossing his arms over his chest. This time, I'm the one who can't meet his gaze as I try to steady my racing heart.

"Do you ever let anyone see the real you under all those masks?" he asks with a hint of annoyance in his tone.

"I could ask you the same thing, Captain. I'm not the only one who hides behind one," I answer, glancing up at him through my lashes.

His features soften as he looks away, and I return to my staredown with the floor.

"Do you sometimes feel like you don't know who you are without the masks? That it's hard to tell where they start and you end anymore?" Theo asks. He looks at me, face relaxed and a twinge of sadness furrowing his brows.

My breath hitches as I look into his gentle, honey eyes, completely void of the stoic façade of a royal guard. A small crack to show me how we're not that different after all. I swallow hard, trying to gather a coherent thought.

"I think sometimes we spend so much time protecting ourselves or the ones we love that we lose pieces of who we once were," I answer. A smile tugs at the corners of my lips as I remember what my mother always told me. "But we're never truly lost. The threads will lead you home. You just have to listen and follow."

"Why does that sound so familiar?" Theo asks as his face twists in hard concentration.

"I'm sure I read it in a book or something," I say, hope erupting in my chest.

The likelihood of him remembering me without the antidote is slim but cracking the veil clouding his mind will help clear it faster once we find it. He gives me a small nod, but by the crease in his forehead, I know he is still pondering my words. *Please remember, Theo.*

"Would you like to pick out a book or two to take back to your cell?" I ask, wanting to break the somber feeling in the air.

"That would be great. Thanks," Theo says, relaxing his features. "Can I take the end bringer one you read tonight? It, too, sounded familiar, so I want to read it for myself."

I can't fight back the smile as it spreads across my face. Our mothers once told us a similar story when we were children, but with less death and devastation. Their version felt more uplifting about love and the power that it holds.

Sliding the crimson bound book forward on the table, I pat the top a few times. "Let me know if you need me to read this to you, Captain. I'd be happy to read you a little bedtime story," I say with a wink. His jaw snaps shut as his eyes blaze into me.

My gaze gets stuck on his plump lips, remembering how they felt on mine. I bite my bottom lip at the thought before dragging my eyes back to his. Theo stares at me with an intensity threatening to burn me alive.

"Anything else I can get for you, Theo?" I ask, leaning back in my chair and crossing my legs. His jaw ticks as he watches me. A few rapid blinks seem to clear his mind.

"Do you have anything on the creatures of Umbra? The nobu and …" his eyes dart side to side, trying to remember the name of the beasts in the haunted forest. "The Cypres. I would like to learn more about them," he recalls.

"You want to learn more about your friend the hare? You don't have to be shy about wanting to know more about her," I reply, standing from my chair and scanning the library for the book.

"Yes, I would like to learn more about my new friend," Theo says, and his words fill my heart.

I get lost in him for a long moment. Dreaming about a different life. One where we could spend afternoons in our library reading through all the books of the realm. Because this is where Theo should be. Walking the rows of a library dedicated to his curious mind.

"The book is in the lore section," I say, nearly breathless. I walk toward the shelves, trying to compose myself.

As we walk down the row, I run my finger along the spines, their leather bindings soft on my fingertips. The scent of cedar and old parchment swirl together. I slow as we near the spot where the book should be located, and I study the shelf.

Searching the bookcase for the distinguishable purple etching of the Cypres book, I spot its worn edges a few shelves up and out of both of our reach.

"Give me a boost," I say with a tap to Theo's chest and point up toward the book. His eyes follow my finger, squinting.

"No, that's a bad idea," Theo replies, looking down at me. I shrug and place a foot on the edge of one shelf. Grasping a ledge, I pull and find another foothold before pushing upward, scaling the shelves.

Strong hands grab at my waist, yanking me back down to the ground.

"Excuse me! I was climbing that!" I exclaim as I pivot to face Theo. His hands are still tight on my hips. My shadows hum under my skin at his touch. *They only respond to him.*

I spin, and we are nearly nose to nose. My breath hitches in my chest. I'm close enough to see the varying flecks of amber in his eyes.

"Did you not hear me? That's a bad idea, Your Highness," Theo says curtly.

"If you don't want to help me, how else do you suggest we get the book you asked for?" I huff, annoyed, and point at the shelf.

"Oh, I don't know, maybe a gods damn ladder? You have those here, right?" He groans the words as his eyes flare in frustration. "You don't need to hurt yourself trying to climb these old bookcases." His fingers dig into my hips before he releases me.

There's a tug on the threads around my heart as he pulls away, always taking a piece of me with him.

"You know how hard it will be to find one here. They are never where they are supposed to be. It will take too long. My plan is much easier and faster. I'll be fine," I say, patting his chest and turning back to the shelf.

Theo grabs my wrist, but I jerk away before he can tighten his grip. I slam my forearm into his chest, causing his balance to falter. I spin to the right, snatching his wrist. With my other hand, I push him into the bookcase and pin his arm behind his back. I lean my hip into his ass, keeping him in place.

He huffs as he turns his head to look at me over his shoulder.

"I said I would be fine, Captain. No need to worry your pretty little head over me," I tease.

A sinister smile tugs at the corner of his lips as I loosen my grip and step back.

That is as far as I make it before Theo snatches my wrist again, but this time with a decidedly firm grip. *Fast learner.* He tosses me into the shelf, using his arm to cushion my impact. I grasp his shirt tightly as he pins my other wrist to the shelf. His arm slowly slides out from behind me, only for his hand to find a familiar spot along my hip, pushing me more into the bookcase.

His eyes blaze with a dangerous mixture of victory and desire. The memory of him between my legs in the alley flashes in my mind. Theo on his knees, devouring my pussy as he watched me with a similar heat. I choke on a moan as it tries to escape.

He leans in close, which is more seductive than threatening. I try to keep my breathing steady as his enormous frame presses into me. "Do you ever stop putting yourself in risky situations? Do you ever listen to logic and do as you are told?" His breath tickles my neck, and I shiver in his arms. He smirks, seeming to get the response he wants.

"Not usually," I say as my gaze trails from his lips to his eyes. A fire flares within me and my shadows seem to stoke the flames. His hip applies the right amount of pressure to make it impossible to get out from under him. But he's not hurting me. I test him by shifting, as if looking for a way to escape.

Theo responds by planting his foot between my feet and leaning his thigh into me. The unexpected contact with my clit sends tingles of pleasure through me, and I whimper. His eyes lock on my mouth and both our breaths quicken.

"If you knew what was good for you, you'd listen," he says as he leans in. His body flush with mine is entirely too much. His stiffening cock pushing into my leg and the desire to stroke it is overwhelming.

I can't think.

I can't breathe.

I need him like I need air to survive.

"Tell me, Theo. Do you know what's good for me?" My words break as I pant for air.

He runs his nose along my jawline. His lips faintly brush my skin as his breath teases me. My lips part as I try to draw in air. I'm burning alive under his touch. I dig my nails into his chest and a low rumble comes from him.

Touch me, please. I need you, Theo.

"Mmm ... roses," he says, taking a deep breath.

The sound vibrates through his chest and into mine. A man sniffing me would normally disgust me, but when Theo does it, I'm weak in the knees. I want him to take all of me in.

Gods, I need him more than I've needed anything in my life. I'm dying of thirst, and he's the water to quench my desire. He moves his head out from my hair to look at me. His eyes scan my face as his lips part. Our chests rise and fall in time with one another.

"Theo." His name is a raspy plea from my lips.

Theo steps back so quickly I think someone has pulled him away from me. I fall back into the bookcases, my ass smacking into a shelf knocking books to the floor. He adjusts his pants, trying to get his hard cock more comfortable.

"Your husband," he barks. "That's who's good for you."

My mouth falls open as I stare, utterly confused by his words.

"What?" I yell, causing my voice to echo off the walls.

Theo glares at me, his jaw tight and his nostrils flaring.

"The king," he shouts back before he turns, heading back toward the center of the library.

I stand, trying to wrap my head around what just happened. How did we go from the verge of coming together again to him turning away from me? His words finally cut through the lust haze in my mind. He stopped because of Asher.

Oh gods, no.

"Theo, stop. You don't understand," I shout, sprinting after him. I catch up near the crimson chairs and table at the center of the library. I grab his arm, and he spins to face me, anger darkening his eyes.

"Will you please let me explain?" I plead, still holding his arm, hoping the sparks will distract him from trying to escape again.

"There's nothing to explain. Does King Asher really think all of this is going to work?" He demands, yanking his arm out of my grasp.

"What?" I don't understand.

"He's smart, I'll give him that. Sending his beautiful queen to seduce me. Did he really think I would cave and give him whatever he wants for you?" His upper lip curls as if disgusted by the idea.

That hurts. A lot.

My desperation is replaced with anger.

"Is that what you think of me? That I'm just a pawn for a man?" He has some audacity to think I would allow a man to use me to gain power. I've only ever done that to protect him. And now he thinks I'm some puppet for Asher.

"Aren't you? I see what you're doing. Using your carefully crafted lies to get me to think you care about me and what I have to say. All the while you're just a temptress luring me in for your king to use," he says with pure disgust.

I shake with a rage strong enough to destroy.

"If you still believe all of this," I gesture wildly around me, "everything we've done together and said to each other," my voice escalates to a shout, and I smack my hands on his chest, causing sparks to ignite along my palms, "has been to serve a devious ploy by King Asher, then you're the liar here, Captain."

He grabs my wrist, trying to push me off, but I don't let up. His grip tightens as lightning flares up my arms. The threads around my heart are vibrating with new intensity. He lets go and steps back, noticing the change.

I fist his shirt and pull him back toward me.

"I don't take orders from anyone. You got that? What I do, I do because I want to. For me!" I scream, inches from his face.

He opens his mouth to respond, but I'm not done.

"If you would shut your mouth and use your mind for a moment, we could talk about what's really happening between us and what we can do about it." His face begins to change as his anger seems to subside.

The musky, smoke scent of leather hits me too late.

"I told you not to touch her!" Nyx shouts as he enters the library.

"Again, she's the one touching me, General," Theo says without breaking our eye contact but raising both arms in surrender.

Nyx reaches us and shoves Theo hard, breaking my grip. Theo stumbles into the table, knocking the books to the floor. Nyx steps toward him, but I put myself between them.

"What do you think you're doing?" Nyx's voice is dark and low.

Before I can discern whether he's addressing Theo or me, Theo charges forward at Nyx. Grabbing Theo's arm, I yank him backward until he's back behind me, and Nyx lunges toward Theo in retaliation.

"Knock it off, now!" I shout, pressing a hand into each of their chests, attempting to force them apart. If they get their hands on one another, they'll end each other. A strange pulling sensation tugs at my heart as I bridge the space between them, as if the cords are strung together as one.

"Care to explain why you're still here with him when he is supposed to be in his cell?" Nyx demands, pointing at Theo and staring at me. Theo swats his hand away, drawing Nyx's glare to him.

"Put your finger in my face again, and I'll break it off," Theo threatens.

The two men stare at each other as if hurling silent insults at one another. They're in full attack mode.

"That's enough," I say with a smack to their chests. They both wince.

The crisp crunch of an apple breaks the tension in the library, and we all turn toward the sound. Hiram stands leaning against the door frame with a smirk on his face.

"Please don't stop on my account. This is very entertaining," he says and takes another bite of the apple.

"Hiram," I say through gritted teeth, trying to control my frustration at the entire situation.

"Come, Theo. Let's get out of here before these two really start fighting and we are caught in the crossfire," Hiram says, pushing off the frame to stand.

Without a word, Theo backs up, picks the crimson book up off the floor, and walks to Hiram. I dare bring my gaze to Theo, hoping to see a sliver of the spark that was growing between us. But all I see is confusion and annoyance wrinkling his brow. Hiram leads Theo down the hall and out of sight.

"Care to explain yourself now that he's gone?" Nyx asks, forcing my attention back to him. I drop my hand from his chest.

"Explain what? That I'm doing exactly what I said I was going to do, trying to win him over?" I answer curtly.

"Sure, and how well is that working out for you? We both know you can't break through the mind veil Leopold placed on him without the antidote. And he seemed pretty agitated when I got here," he retorts.

"I don't have to break the veil when the threads of fate are still there. He knows, Nyx. Even if he doesn't want to admit it to me or himself. He knows," I say, emphasizing the words. "No elixir can stop the cords from calling out and leading you back to your Amari. I've been seeing signs. He's feeling the tug."

"And what if he's playing you? What if everything you think you are seeing is just him messing with your head?" He asks, stepping into my space.

"That's a risk I have to take, but I know I'm right, Nyx." I try to step around him to leave, but he stops me with an outstretched arm.

"And if you're wrong, it isn't just your heart he could destroy. You're playing a risky game," he says with less bite in his tone than before.

I push at his arm, and he drops it. "I'm not wrong. He's coming back to me, Nyx. I know it," I say, heading toward the door.

"I hope you know what you're doing, Lily. Because I'll kill him if he hurts you," Nyx says, and I stop at the threshold to look at him.

"I know you will, but I promise I can handle this." I give him a soft smile before leaving him in the library to stew in his irritation.

As I fall asleep, I run through every scenario of how this can go. But they all end with Theo hating me for one reason or another. Nyx is right about one thing: he'll destroy more than just my heart. When all this ends, I know I'll never recover. I'm bound to be forever broken by the man I've always loved.

CHAPTER 27

Gray eyes bore into me as I square off with Nyx.

"It's not happening," he murmurs through gritted teeth. We've been stuck in this staring contest for far too long, neither of us budging.

"Ok then, let's go to your chambers to get some clothes for Theo. You're the only one close to his size. Or we could just let him walk around naked. You won't hear any complaints from me," I say, wiggling my eyebrows.

His face pinches in disgust at the image, and Hiram gags at his spot against the wall.

"Then it's settled. I will take Theo to the village to have him fitted for new clothing." I lean back in my chair. Nyx doesn't budge. It seems his arms have become permanently attached to my desk in the council room.

"Like I just said, it isn't happening. It's too risky. He could try to escape. He could take advantage of the situation and try to harm you," Nyx counters.

I roll my eyes at the implication that Theo would hurt me.

"Honestly, I'm more afraid of her hurting him than the other way around, General," Hiram chimes in with a smirk.

I smile brightly at my friend for having my back.

"He can't keep wearing the same donated clothes he has been for the past few weeks. They're too small, and the seams are already ripping. We need to take him to the village to get some properly fitting ones," I say, trying to soften my tone, but doubting it will work.

We've been at this for so long the sun has begun to set. The whole time, Nyx has been fighting against any idea of Theo leaving the Keep, and I can't tell if he truly thinks Theo will do something wrong, or if he is still pissed at me from the other night in the library. He's been putting himself between Theo and me ever since, preventing us from having any type of meaningful conversation.

"I don't trust him not to take advantage of the opportunity. He will run at the first chance of freedom back to Lux and take all our secrets with him," Nyx says, finally leaning back in his chair.

"Hiram, what are your thoughts on this? You've been oddly quiet during our little debate here," I ask, tilting my head at my captain.

He pushes off the wall and steps toward us. He runs a hand through his hair, seeming to ponder over his response.

"I think we haven't given him much of a chance to gain our trust. Besides the few times he's been out of his cell with the queen, we've kept him locked away. Maybe we should see what he does," Hiram answers with a shrug.

My smile is so wide it hurts.

I turn my gaze back to Nyx and see him trying to grind his teeth down to nothing.

"Listen, Hiram and Marcus will be with us the whole time. If anything goes awry, I'll summon Asher. Then any plan of Theo's would be foiled." I lean forward, folding my arms on my desk. "But I don't think you have anything to worry about."

He stares at me for a long moment before his head falls back to the chair in defeat.

"We'll leave in a few days, then. Hiram, will you let Marcus know for me?" Hiram nods and leaves the room.

"You're going to have to trust him eventually, you know?" I say with a smirk.

Nyx cracks one eye open to peer at me.

"Unlikely," he snorts, closing his eye again. I stand from my desk and walk over to Nyx, wrapping my arms around his shoulders.

"Can you at least try? Just a little bit? For me?" I ask sweetly, causing him to groan in irritation.

"Do I have to?" He leans his head into me.

"You kind of do. He is my Amari, after all," I answer.

"Don't remind me," he says with a huff. "I'll try. That's the best I can do."

"That's all I ask. Now go manage our spies so we can find that amulet and humiliate King Leopold."

We've been slowly gathering information leaking out of Lux for the past few weeks. We're getting closer. I can feel it in my soul. We're close to figuring this out and what the lightning king has up his sleeve. The intel is out there, and it's going to get to us.

I grip the book tight as I stride through the hall of The Keep toward Theo's cell. I stopped by the library to retrieve the book about the Umbra creatures. Someone had suspiciously placed a ladder nearby, and I wonder who could have moved it.

I'm hoping I can use the book as a sort of truce between us. When he left the library, things were tense, and they haven't improved with Nyx's constant presence. I need to pull him back to where we were if I hope to break through to him.

Rubbing a thumb over the purple etching of the book's binding, I take a deep breath as faint wisps of cedar fill the air. Hiram and Marcus stand ready at the back door. They both bow as I approach, and I wave them off. We're done with the formalities. I'll be just another viator when we go to the village, so the bows need to stop before we leave.

Theo lies outstretched in his bed, leaning on one elbow, flipping through the old pages of the end bringer story. I watch him for a moment, enjoying the look of him so relaxed in my kingdom, as if this is truly his home.

Sorrow claws at my heart because he may never accept this as his home. Even after everything he has seen so far, he's still loyal to Lux and their dreadful king. Nyx's words echo in my mind that he'll always choose them over us. *Over me.*

"You must be enjoying that if it has you so distracted," I joke, leaning against the bars.

His head snaps up, and he pushes off the bed, startled by the sound of my voice. His eyebrows rise and his mouth parts as he realizes it's me without my brooding shadow.

"Or maybe I wasn't expecting someone to rudely interrupt my reading," he responds with a raised eyebrow.

I look over at Marcus and Hiram, who feign innocence. They never told him we were leaving. I shake my head, knowing they did it on purpose to see how he would react.

I turn back to Theo, and he's nearly to me at the doorway, moving silently through the cell. *Quick learner.* I give him a smirk as he stops a few feet from me. Those pools of honey lock on me, devoid of emotion. His mask is firmly in place to protect himself from me.

"Here's the book you asked for," I say, handing over the lore book.

Our fingers graze as he takes it, sending small sparks along my skin. He pulls it to him, running a hand over the black leather.

Theo studies it for a moment before looking at me without lifting his head. A small grin curls the corner of his lips.

"Please tell me you did nothing reckless to retrieve this book," he says as his eyes fully come to mine.

Interlacing my fingers in front of me, I lean forward on my toes, closing the gap between us.

"When am I not doing something reckless?"

His smile unravels, and I smirk as I settle back on my feet.

"My gut tells me never," he says, turning and placing the book on his bed.

The white shirt he's wearing stretches tight across his back, and I admire the view, longing to drag my nails along it.

When he turns back around, my gaze gets stuck on his perfectly shaped lips. His cupid's bow looks as if the gods themselves etched it on his face. His jaw flexes as I drag my eyes up to his.

"If you came to continue our conversation from the library, you've wasted your time. We have nothing further to discuss," he says, crossing his arms over his chest.

The fabric of his shirt strains, and I briefly debate if I want to get him new clothing.

He's annoyed me, and I move toward him quickly, stopping inches away. He doesn't move.

"That conversation is far from over. But until we can speak without others eavesdropping, it will have to wait," I whisper.

"There's nothing more for us to talk about, so if that was your plan, then you may leave." He leans forward, narrowing his eyes.

"This," I say as I grab his arm, immediately feeling the pinpricks erupting along my palm. Theo grits his teeth.

"And this," I lay a hand directly over his heart. "Says we have plenty more to discuss."

Theo's eyes widen as sparks flare between our skin.

"Do you think your husband would appreciate you touching his prisoner?" He asks as his breath hitches.

"My husband doesn't tell me who I can touch, Captain. I do what and who I please when I want to. I may be bound to the shadow king, but it's a marriage in name only. Nothing more," I sneer at him.

I see a breath lodge in his chest before he lets it go.

"You can lie to yourself all you want, but you can't hide from this," I say as my power hums within me, increasing the sparks. His lips pinch into a thin line as he glares down at me.

"Are you ready to go?" Hiram's deep voice beckons from the doorway.

Theo's gaze darts up, and I drop my head at the interruption. I lower my hands from him, letting them fall to my sides.

"Where are you going?" Theo asks, eyes bouncing from Hiram to me.

"To the village. I need to order some clothes that fit all of this." I gesture at his enormous frame and hear a small snicker from Hiram.

Theo looks at me with an arched eyebrow.

"Care to join, or would you rather run around naked?" I ask with a sultry smirk.

Theo's answer is an eye roll before a small nod.

"Lead the way," he says with an outstretched arm.

I turn and leave his cell to find Hiram wearing a smug smile.

We leave out the back entrance across the stepstones. I watch Theo navigate the path with more confidence than last time. We walk through the hidden archway into the warm sunshine. The crisp autumn breeze brings notes of the musky falling leaves. The fading colors paint Umbra in orange, red, and yellow as the leaves change. Winter will be upon us in a few weeks, stealing the color from the land, but right now it is a picturesque scene.

Hiram leads the way across the sprawling field toward our waiting horses. Midnight lets out a loud whinny as I approach, and he stomps at the ground.

"You have my horse?" Theo asks, eyebrows pinching in confusion.

"The little gray mare with Midnight?" I point at the horse, and he nods.

"Well, she's not my horse, but she's the one I arrived with from Lux." The mare must know we are talking about her because she lets out a huff of annoyance.

"We have all the horses brought by the Lux guards, Theo. They live in our stable, on the outskirts of the village," I answer honestly.

Theo's eyes darken in anger.

"Why? You kill my men but keep the horses and me alive? Your tactics don't make any sense," he says through clenched teeth. I step toward him, putting my face as close to his as he'll allow.

"How many times do I have to tell you we didn't kill your men? They died because your king failed to heed the warnings of Umbra. The Cypres protect this land from all intruders and Leopold knows that. He killed your men, not us," I say, barely containing my frustration.

"What about me, Your Highness? Why keep me around? Why are you really doing all of this? Did your king send you to seduce me, or did you do that on your own?" He asks, tilting his head to the side.

My heart cracks as I stare up at him. His face twists in suppressed anger toward me and my kingdom. Nyx was right. No matter what I do, he isn't going to listen. His mind is too clouded by all the lies fed to him by Lux.

"Have you been listening to anything I've been telling you over the past few weeks?" I ask, fighting back tears.

"Listening to your lies? No, I haven't been," he answers, taking a step back.

I've had just about enough of his erratic moods.

I glare at him as I try to figure out what could break through to him.

The cemetery.

If he's so concerned about his men, then let me show him how we respected them, unlike his beloved king.

"Ready to leave, Captain," I order Theo as I turn to find Hiram to discuss our stop. He stands talking with the handler. I whisper in Hiram's ear about stopping at the cemetery before heading to the village, and he nods.

Before we go, the handler gives us an update on the status of the stable. They need some minor repairs and adjustments, but overall, things are managing well with the additional fifteen horses. He informs me Midnight seems to enjoy spending time with the gray mare, and I look over to observe them.

I find Theo dangerously close to my overly aggressive horse, his outstretched palm ready to pet him.

"Theo, no!" I yell, sprinting toward them.

But I'm too far away. Midnight might just take Theo's arm. He only allows me to touch him. All I can do is watch in terror as my horse walks to Theo with his head slightly lowered, appearing to stalk toward him. Midnight sniffs at Theo's hand as if he's assessing his flavor. Midnight's black eyes scan to see if Theo is worthy of his time.

I stop dead in my tracks, causing Hiram to slam into my back, and we stumble forward. We watch as Midnight pushes his snout into Theo's hand and closes his eyes, enjoying the feel.

"What in the realm?" I gasp, panting from fear as I walk hesitantly toward them.

My horse—straight from the Underrealm— who hates everyone except for me, is allowing the love of my life to pet him. Theo moves beside Midnight to pet both of his cheeks, and a deep rumble escapes the horse's chest as if purring.

"Well, that's … strange," Hiram says, just as shocked as I am.

I step over towards them, slowly.

"You have the biggest horse I've ever seen. For his size, he's very gentle," Theo says with a smile, the anger less noticeable now.

Hiram's laugh booms through the open air, and I snicker as I step in front of Midnight, petting his face.

"His name's Midnight, and he has bitten every person who has dared to touch him, except for me … and now you."

Theo's eyes go wide, and he stops petting. This earns a very disgruntled snort from Midnight.

I give Midnight a kiss on his muzzle, and he returns it with a caress to my face. Theo's gray mare steps beside Midnight, and he turns to greet her with a gentle nose touch.

"The handler said these two have been quite fond of each other since her arrival," I say to Theo, and Midnight nods his head as if in agreement. I reach over and give the little mare a small pet on her cheeks.

"She's the one you should be worried about. She tried to bite me the entire trip here," Theo says with a huff.

I laugh as I rub gentle circles on her face.

"So, you got yourself a feisty girlfriend, Midnight? I love her already." He gives me a happy whinny.

Hiram, Theo, and I climb atop our horses. We watch as Marcus tries and fails several times to mount his own. He's a terrible rider, and we all fight back our laughter. Marcus finally makes it, and we all give him a round of applause. He rolls his eyes at our teasing.

"Lead the way, my queen," Hiram says, and I heel Midnight toward the tree line, heading toward the cemetery.

Theo's head swivels back and forth as he takes in this new part of my kingdom.

When he arrived, I had such hope he would see this land and fall in love with it like I have over the years. My stomach drops, realizing that dream may never come true. I close my eyes, saying a silent prayer to the gods.

Please open his eyes and let him see the truth. I need him to see.

We head down the stone path toward the cemetery. We stop several feet from the burial plots. Theo's eyes dart all around as if not understanding where we are.

"Hiram, Marcus, wait here. Theo, come with me," I say as I dismount.

My guards nod and get comfortable in their saddles. Theo hesitantly drops from his mare.

Walking side by side, we follow the path and pause by the gate created for the Lux guards. It's a lovely burial site, with massive trees surrounding it and beautiful flowers dotting the forest floor.

Theo's face dances through several emotions as if he doesn't know how he should feel.

"Why did you bring me to a cemetery?" There is slight apprehension in his voice.

I take a deep breath to prepare myself for this heavy conversation.

"This is the burial site for your men," I answer, turning to look at him.

Theo's breathing quickens, and he stares at the plots before us.

"You buried them?" He looks at me, confusion pinching his eyebrows together, and I nod softly.

"We buried them according to Lux rituals. We sectioned this area off and had the soil blessed by a Lux cleric before we performed their burial rites. I commissioned our weavers to make traditional burial linens in Lux colors to wrap them in. Pyres were lit, and we laid their ashes to rest in individual plots. Identifying items adorn their headstones. We burned anything else they had with them to take into the Underrealm." I take a deep breath, remembering the heat from all the pyres.

"Why?" He sneers, staring at the headstones.

"Because they deserve respect. They had a warriors' burial, Theo. We honored them for their sacrifice, even if it was for of a cruel king," I answer.

He turns to me with a mix of pain, sorrow, and hatred twisting his face.

"Why didn't you just give their bodies back to Lux so we could bury them?" He asks, but his face falls flat as if realizing why we didn't.

"You know why. Leopold would never have given them a proper burial. He would have seen their deaths as failure and thrown their bodies in a hole to rot," I say harshly, allowing too much of my hatred to bleed through.

"Your men deserve better than that. They deserve to be welcomed into the Underrealm as warriors with Astra by their side. We gave that to them. Not your king. Your men rest peacefully because of us. We protected them after Leopold sent them to die for nothing," I say, not holding back my anger.

"Your king knew what would happen to all of you when he sent you here uninvited. He knew and sent you anyway. If he respected you or cared about you, he wouldn't have sent you all to die from your own nightmares at the hands of my beasts!" I shout.

Theo's look seems to burn with rage.

"He sent us to get back what you stole," he yells back.

"We didn't steal the damn amulet, Theo! He sent you to die for nothing! Why can't you see that?" I say, pointing at the graves.

"Think, Theo! Think of all I've shown you, of the people you met, of the things that don't add up with what you've always known!" I can't restrain myself.

I need you to get it, Theo.

Theo turns his gaze back to where his men are laid to rest. His breaths are quick as he tightens his fists at his sides.

"Go pay your respects and remember, it's something you wouldn't have gotten to do if we sent their bodies back to Lux. Remember who actually caused their deaths and who treated them with respect," I say in exasperation, turning away from him.

I take several steps away, needing the distance. If this doesn't break through to him, nothing will, and everything has been a waste of time. Loma needs to find that antidote before I'm forced to send him back to Lux.

Theo walks slowly toward the graves, stopping at each one and kneeling before it, lowering his head. I let him spend as much time as he needs going from headstone to headstone. The cool breeze cuts through the trees, soothing my agitation.

After a long while, Theo turns and makes his way back to me. The anger that was blaring in his eyes is now gone.

"There are only thirteen plots. One's missing." He asks as he approaches me.

"There was one guard who made it out of the haunted forest. But he ran into one of the pools in front of The Keep, thinking the water would shield him from the shadows. The nobu promptly ate him," I answer, fighting back how I really feel about Jonathan being eaten by the nobu.

Theo's head turns back to the plots, going over each one carefully this time. His laugh startles me.

"Fitting end for such a vile man," he says with a shake of his head.

When his eyes return to mine, there's a new light in them. Hope blooms in my chest at the possibility that this finally broke through to him.

"Even after you leave here, Theo, you're welcome anytime. And so are the families of those who were lost," I say, and a soft smile tugs at his lips.

I turn and head back to the horses with Theo trailing behind me. Theo grabs my wrist, spinning me. He pulls me tight into his chiseled chest. I fight the urge to melt entirely into him as his muscular arms wrap around my back. My body and power flare in response, igniting the fire I've been fighting.

"Thanks for this. You did what was best for my men, even though they meant you harm. You treated them as your own when you didn't have to. I have no way of repaying your kindness and respect. Just know I'm forever grateful for it," he whispers into my hair as I tuck into the crook of his neck.

I wrap my arms around him as far as I can and squeeze him into me. He doesn't fight it or try to pull away. Cedar engulfs me, and I breathe it in deeply, allowing it to bring me a sliver of hope. My power hums under my skin and little pricks of lightning skirt it, as if dancing at the sensation of him around me.

We part, and he gives me another soft smile, though it doesn't warm his eyes. Giving one more glance at the burial plots, we continue our way back to the horses. Hiram sits on his brown Warlander and gives me a suggestive look. I roll my eyes but can't hide the pink on my cheeks.

CHAPTER 28

THEO

We ride silently along the path, the beautiful autumn day providing a comfortable ride. Birds chirp from the forests as we make our way to the village.

I find myself constantly searching out the queen, as if some force is drawing me to her. She closes her eyes and tilts her face up to the sky, soaking in the sun's warmth. Her long, red curls cascade down her back and bounce with each step of her massive horse.

My mind struggles to process everything from the cemetery. They didn't have to bury my men. They could have let their bodies rot in the haunted forest and become carrion for their beasts. But they didn't. Instead, they used their collective knowledge of Lux to give them the burial they deserved. Would King Leopold and my father have been as kind? Or was the queen right, and they would have thrown them away as if they were worthless?

Jade-eyes meet mine, and I should look away. I shouldn't let her catch me watching her, but something tells me she'd know anyway. The one corner of her lips turn up in her smirk.

I hate how much I love her smile.

I battle with myself the rest of the way to the village. Everything I've learned growing up is how ruthless and heartless the people of Umbra are to any outsider. Ask anyone in Lux, they will all say the same. Only the most brutal and monstrous people live in Umbra. A kingdom ruled by one evil king after another.

Being here, though, that's not what I've found. While I'm certain Nyx, or Asher, would kill me at the first opportunity, everyone else has been caring and kind. How is there such a stark difference between what I've learned in Lux and what I am seeing here? I feel as though I can't trust myself, or my mind.

A small stable comes into view, and we slow as we approach. We all dismount from our horses. A young man strides toward us before halting at the sight of the queen's horse. His shoulders slouch and he groans loudly.

"Not Midnight. He tried to eat me the last time you were here, Margo."

The queen laughs and hands over the reins, causing the man to flinch.

"Keep him with the little gray mare, and he won't be an issue for you this time," she says, pointing over at me. The man mumbles aggressively as he takes Midnight and then my mare. The two grumpy horses follow the man without a fight, pressing close together as they go.

I step toward the queen, a scowl on my face. "So, your name is Margo? You could have just told me your name."

She turns to face me, tracing the wrinkle in my brow with her eyes.

"That's not my name, Captain. It's a name I go by here," she folds her arms across her chest. "Remember, they don't know who I am. They only know me as a viator—here to do business like everyone else."

"So why can't I call you Margo?" I ask, frustrated by others being able to call her by a name. She talks about trust but refuses to give me a name other than the queen to call her.

She laughs and places a hand on my arm. My muscles flex as the sparks skirt my skin.

"You can call me any name you like, Captain," she says with a smirk before heading down the gravel path.

Hiram cackles loudly as he watches us.

Glad one of us is entertained.

The crunch of the gravel turns to clicks as the path changes to cobblestones. I walk in my spot beside the queen, with Hiram and Marcus close behind us. I freeze at the sight of the village.

Dark stone buildings with multicolored roofs line both sides of the path. But the most shocking part is all the people. There's a massive crowd filling the center square. Their voices echo off the walls. There are shops with doors swung open, inviting shoppers and the rich autumn air inside.

Various merchants from all over the realm have set up small booths in the square with their goods. Vibrant colored artisan depictions of the landscapes of Omnia, aromatic baked goods, any kind of trinket or clothing you can imagine, and a blacksmith shop forging new items for buyers dot the street.

"If you see something you like, please let me know, Theo," the queen says, breaking my shock.

I look at her. She looks just as dazzling as a viator as she does as a queen.

"There are goods from every kingdom here. How's that possible?" I ask, refocusing on the awe-inspiring scene before me.

There shouldn't be a village here. There shouldn't be a village where people from all over the realm gather to sell goods. No one has trade agreements with Umbra.

But the queen said that they did. And it looks like they do.

There is no way that this is a ruse to get me to cooperate. Not even King Asher can create an entire village just to get me on his side.

How have we been so wrong? Is anything I've been told in Lux true?

The queen slides an arm into mine, and I don't resist it this time. I let her force me into escorting her through the village. I try not to think about how she fits perfectly in the crook of my arm as if she was made to be there.

"I told you we have treaties, and that extends to merchants as well. They must remain honest and fair to continue their sales here, and most are more than happy to make the trip," she explains, leading me into the throng of people.

"I don't see a ring on your lady's finger, good sir. I have some mighty fine ones, so you can make an honest woman out of her." A middle-aged man with a plethora of miscellaneous goods comes up at my side with every finger donning a different ring in every color.

My cheeks redden at the implication, and Hiram practically falls over, laughing hysterically.

The queen shoves Hiram playfully, which only makes him laugh harder, and he stumbles away to Marcus, who's at a table on the other side of the row.

She waves the man away from us. "No, thank you. I like to keep my options open. This one is just pretty to look at," she says, patting my arm and pulling me along the path, heading closer to the buildings.

She stops us near an alley leading to another section of the village. The market is a flurry of energy, and I scan the crowd, trying to take it all in. A few people stop and greet the queen as Margo.

I watch the villagers through the eyes of a guard and not the prisoner I am. Easily slipping into the same role I would if I were with Junie at the market. Strangely, her guards don't seem too concerned about her safety since they're on the other side of the market—out of eyeshot.

A gentle squeeze to my forearm has me shutting my eyes as my skin tingles from her touch.

"Care to share your thoughts, Captain?" She asks, and the use of my title tells me she's messing with me. "Do your guards often leave you unattended when on outings?" I ask as Hiram rummages through the different paintings, appearing to need a new one.

I look over to Marcus who is at a baked goods table accepting samples from the attractive ladies running the booth. He seems more interested in the women than the food.

"As you know from firsthand experience, I can protect myself. I often travel alone and rarely have any issues," she answers simply, as if that gives her an excuse to be unguarded.

King Asher allows her to travel by herself? I thought he had her locked away at The Keep. Does she go without his knowledge?

I release her arm from mine and turn to her fully. My body tenses as I remember the moment we met. Her face was covered in cuts and bruises. Her neck was purple from a man trying to hurt her. Anger burns at my core, and I struggle to explain why protecting her is consuming all my thoughts.

"What about the night you were attacked? You may have walked away from that, but not unharmed, Your Highness. What about then? Shouldn't your guards be there to keep that from happening again?" I ask, trying to dampen my frustration at her blatant disregard for her own safety.

She purses her lips and narrows her eyes at me. "They were getting their asses kicked, too. And remember, I ended that fight. I killed the man who attacked me. Not my guards. Me." She jabs a finger into my chest as she walks past, heading toward another row of shops.

I take a step to follow her but halt. No one is watching her or me. I look down the alley, debating my options. Looking over at Hiram and Marcus, I confirm they're still distracted by their shopping. The queen's curls blow in the wind as she walks away from me.

Time to teach you why you should always keep your guards close.

I slip into a crowd of people, easily blending in as a shopper looking at the various goods set along the tables. I hover around near the edge to keep an eye on the queen. Waiting for the perfect moment to attack.

The queen stops and turns around with a smirk on her face but freezes when she doesn't see me behind her. Her chest rises and falls quickly as she spins around, looking for me. "Theo," she calls out, panic shaking her voice.

She turns away from me, and I make my move. I slither through the crowded village to get behind her while she's distracted looking for me.

"Th—" I cut off her call by slapping a hand over her mouth.

I grab her by the waist, easily lifting her off the ground. I pull her tight into me as I walk backward into an alcove completely obstructed from view.

Her light kicks tell me she knows exactly who has her, but that doesn't stop me. My whole body hums with her tucked so close to me. Her rose scent swirls around me, and I try to calm my racing heart.

I spin her and push her back into the stone wall, pinning her down with my body.

"Now, you're going to be a good girl while I teach you a lesson," I say with my hand still covering her mouth.

She bites her lip and I feel it along my palm. I stare at the back of my hand as if I can see through it, perfectly picturing her nibbling on her lower lip.

A mischievous smile curves across my face, thinking about all the things I could do to her in this alley where no one would find us. I drop my hand from her mouth, and she surprisingly doesn't make a sound. *Such a good girl.*

I trail my hands down her arms before lifting them above her head, pinning them to the wall. Her breath hitches, and I drag my eyes to meet hers.

"This is why your guards should always be by your side. You never know when someone could stalk the shadows, waiting to strike. How would you defend yourself now?" I lean in closer, trying to prove my point.

She strains to look up at me, her back arching off the wall. Her breasts push into my chest, and the desire to find out how they feel in my hands is almost too much.

"No one else would get this far, Captain. I have enough blades to halt any man before he got me into this alley," she answers, challenge lacing her voice.

I drag my eyes down her body, enjoying every dip and curve.

I need to stop. I should stop.

Instead, I switch to looking for weapons, curious about how many she can hide on her body while wearing a dress.

"Let's see about that," I say as I slide a hand along her side.

My gaze falls to her breasts, and I can't stop my tongue from sliding along my bottom lip. Imagining what it would be like to lick every inch of her, enjoying the taste of her skin, has my cock hardening.

I ease off her a little, not wanting her to feel what she's doing to me. She arches her back off the wall, more in offering than an escape attempt. I clench my teeth, pushing down all the traitorous things I'd like to do to her. If only she wasn't married to the shadow king. If only she wasn't my enemy's queen.

I trail light fingertips along the side of her breast, finding blades hidden in her corset vest. I count them slowly, watching as her breath hitches with each touch.

"Three on this side," I say as I move to the other side.

My fingers skim the underside of her breast as I go, and I close my eyes to keep in control.

I want to rip this damn vest off her.

"And the matching three on this side. Is your black dagger strapped to your thigh as usual?" I ask.

She swallows hard as she stares at me. Her leg swings up and hooks around my thigh. The hem of her dress riding up to her knee. Her soft, pale skin exposed. I want to drop to my knees and lick every inch of her until she tells me to stop.

"Maybe you should check. Just to be safe," she asks breathlessly.

My cock twitches at the thought of running my hands across her bare skin. Her eyes go wide as she sucks in a breath.

There's no hiding her control over me. I'm lost. I can't bring myself to stop, even though I need to. My whole body is a flame needing to be doused.

I lock eyes with her as I place a hand on her knee. Hesitantly, I glide along her thigh until it meets the holster of the dagger. I watch her face for any warning to stop. She shifts in my grasp, rubbing against my cock. I can't stop the deep growl that comes out of me as a fire blazes within me.

Her lips part as she whimpers, and her breathing quickens. I tighten my grip on her wrists and dig my fingers into her thigh above her dagger. It would be so easy to continue the path, sliding my fingers beneath her undergarments.

"Did you wear this dress just to tease me, temptress? Knowing how it would make your eyes shine like vibrant gemstones, and I wouldn't be able to resist? Do you have any idea what you do to me, and how much I hate you for it?" I ask as I grind into her.

She moans as her eyes roll back.

"Yes. And you don't hate me. You may try, but you fail every time," she says, panting. Her muscles flex beneath me as if she's fighting the urge to continue rubbing herself against me. I close my eyes, trying not to give in to the temptation and allow her to.

When I open my eyes, hers are scanning my face. The air around us grows heavy, like the moments before a violent storm breaks free. She pushes off the wall, her arms straining from where I hold them. Her lips brush against mine in the faintest touch, but it sends a bolt of lightning shooting from my head to my toes.

I stare at her lips, frozen in the moment. My breath lodges in my chest as I war with myself.

What are we doing? This is wrong and reckless. I need to back away and run as far from her as I can, but why does my gut say I'll regret that the moment I leave her side?

No one has made my heart sing like this since Lily. My chest aches at the thought of betraying her, even though I know she'd want me to be happy. Would she wish for my happiness if she knew it was with our enemy's queen, though?

"Theo," the queen's voice cracks as she looks up at me with unshed tears in her eyes. The pain and sadness plastered on her face doesn't feel like an act.

Has all of this been real and not some kind of trick to win me over?

If I give in, I could lose everything I've worked for and stand for.

Is she worth it?

Yes.

My heart races as I stare down at the queen. Her lip quivers as she holds back her emotions.

Screw the gods, the fates, and even King Asher. They can damn me to the Underrealm because it doesn't matter. None of it matters because she's mine.

Releasing her wrists and thigh, I grab her face with both hands, slamming my mouth into hers. It's a fiery explosion fueled by the past weeks of light touches between us.

She gasps as I press hard against her. She moans as she feels my cock, and I slide my tongue into her mouth. Her nails dig into my back, and I groan as lightning trails down my spine. *I need more of her, all of her.*

I grab her ass, rubbing her along my length. She adjusts her hip and whimpers as I slide against her clit. Too much clothing is between us, and I debate ripping her dress off right here in the alley.

The queen feels utterly perfect in my hands. I could get lost in her touch, her taste, and her sounds. I grind harder into her, chasing the pleasure that shoots through me with each movement.

She moans louder, and I capture the sound with my mouth. I pull my lips from hers and both of us are panting.

"If you keep moaning like that, we won't leave this alley until you're screaming my name," I say in warning.

The queen bites down on her bottom lip and nods enthusiastically.

She's going to be the death of me.

"Where did she go? My queen? I mean …, shit, Marcus, what's her name in the village?" Hiram's shaky whispers come from the pathway leading to the alley.

We freeze as footsteps echo around us. I reluctantly release her and take a step back. I adjust my cock uncomfortably in my trousers as the queen smooths out her dress.

"What do we do?" I whisper from our little hiding spot, trying to keep the concern out of my voice.

We were so close to being caught. The queen grins at me. Her lips plump from our kissing. She nods to some low pallets set along the stone wall.

"Take a seat. We'll say we were taking a break or something." She slides her hand into mine to lead me over. I sit down beside her as she situates herself, wiping moisture from around her lips.

I stare at her finger as it trails along her skin. The whole scene feels oddly familiar, as if I've been here before. But that's impossible since I've never been to Umbra or their village. The dark stone around us makes the queen's red curls and green dress stand out. They appear as if they're the only color in a sea of darkness.

Footsteps and harsh whispers grow louder.

"Is everything ok, Theo?" The queen asks, placing a gentle hand on my leg.

I drag my gaze to hers only for the sense of déjà-vu to grow. My mind claws at itself, trying to remember. A pang of pain spikes across my head, causing me to wince.

"Yes. It just feels like I've been here before. Must have been a dream or something," I answer, forcing a small smile. The queen's lips part.

"There you are. What are you doing?" Hiram's husky voice comes from the opening of the alcove.

We both turn to find Hiram and Marcus glaring at us with daggers in hand. I instinctively reach out to pull the queen behind me. She pats me on the back, and I sit back on my pallet. Hiram raises an eyebrow at the interaction.

"We were taking a break. The crowd was a little unexpected for Theo, so we thought we'd step away for a moment to get some air," the queen says selling the lie so easily.

If it's this easy for her to lie to her men, what about to me? I shake my head, trying to force away the thoughts.

Hiram slides his dagger into his belt, but Marcus keeps it aimed at me. Hiram walks to the queen, offering her his hand to stand.

"A word, your majesty," he says, more as an order than a request. The queen's lips pinch tight together before she slides her hand into his, and they step to the side.

Marcus doesn't take his eyes off me. Glaring at me with the same disgust I normally have, but after today, I'm not sure if I have it in me anymore.

I pretend to be studying the alley while eavesdropping on Hiram and the queen. He tries to keep his voice low, but among all this stone it still echoes.

"What do you think you are doing? This is exactly what Nyx was talking about," Hiram says, frustrated.

"I told you we were taking a break," the queen answers innocently.

Hiram huffs in annoyance.

"Was this break his idea? A way to get you secluded and out of our sight?" Hiram retorts.

"No, it was a mutual idea. I'm fine, Hiram. I told you both to trust him. When are you going to listen to me?" The queen answers curtly.

Nyx and Hiram don't trust me, but the queen does. That must mean something, right?

Marcus takes a step closer to me. His grip tightens on his dagger.

Let's add Marcus to the not trusting Theo group.

I shift back on the pallets, attempting to put distance between us.

The queen steps to Marcus, whispering in his ear. His face pales as he sheaths his dagger.

"Let's get going to Elizabeth's before it gets too late," the queen says, looking directly at me. I stand and give her a nod.

I step over to her, offering my arm to escort her to the shop. Hiram shoulders me, forcing me to stumble back. The queen glares at him as he passes and comes to me, sliding her arm into mine and leading the way out of the alley.

The queen instructs Hiram and Marcus to wait outside while she takes me into Elizabeth's shop. A woman with graying hair is bent over the counter writing something down in a notebook. When her dark-blue eyes lift from the paper, she stands stick-straight and hurries over to us.

"My queen. What are you doing here?" She asks with a small bow and her voice low. The queen smiles at her, taking one of the woman's hands in hers.

"I need to order some clothes for my friend here. We've been struggling to find clothes within The Keep that will fit him," the queen says, gesturing over her shoulder at me.

The woman peers over the queen to me and her face goes stark white. She tries to take a step back as if retreating, but the queen keeps hold of her.

"Kincaid," is all she says. The queen wraps an arm around her back and rubs, trying to calm her.

"Yes, but I promise I'm nothing like my father. My name's Theo. You must be Elizabeth," I say, stretching out a hand. "Your shop is lovely. You're a very talented seamstress. Umbra is lucky to have you and Pyke."

She looks at her queen for reassurance. The queen speaks softly to Elizabeth, who takes a deep breath before accepting my hand in greeting.

"It's nice to meet you, Theo," Elizabeth says with a hard swallow. "I'll need to measure you to get the best fit. Will you please follow me?" She drops my hand and heads over to a small box on the floor.

Elizabeth works quickly to get all the measurements she needs. When she takes my inseam, I squirm on the box, which results in Elizabeth telling me to hold still, and the queen laughing at the whole situation.

I wonder about the store while the queen and Elizabeth head to the counter to finish up the order. The queen had asked what colors I wanted, and I told her to pick. She seemed surprised by this answer, but since I'm here, I may as well embrace the opportunity to wear other colors for once in my life.

A sudden burst of excitement comes from Elizabeth, and I snap my gaze to her. The queen is trying to hush her, but the smiles on their faces make me wonder if they are up to something. Whatever it is, I hope it involves more time spent with the queen.

CHAPTER 29

My foot slips in the damp grass and I narrowly dodge Hiram's wooden sword from smacking me in the face. He groans at the missed blow as I rise back to standing.

"We good yet?" I ask, getting tired of avoiding his jabs of frustration.

Hiram and Nyx have been grumpier than usual since our trip to the village a few days ago. Hiram has decided the best way to work out his irritation with me is by sparring. And by that, I mean him charging at me on an endless loop while I parry his blows.

"Are you going to tell me how you ended up in that alley?" Hiram asks for the umpteenth time through harsh breaths.

I spy Nyx over Hiram's shoulder. He's wearing a cocky grin. These two are enjoying punishing me way too much.

I narrow my eyes at Nyx, tilting my head to the side.

No more games, boys.

Hiram lunges for me again, and this time, I don't step back. I counter his blow with one of my own, catching him off guard. His arm jerks back, and I take the opening to ram my shoulder into his chest, knocking him to the ground.

Landing on top of Hiram, I press my wooden sword into his throat. Not enough to cut off his air but enough to tell him that I've had enough. He grits his teeth with eyes fixed on me. Light chuckles surround us as members of my crew watch me put Hiram in his place.

"Whatever grievances you have, speak them now. This whole game you two are playing to reprimand me is over," I say leaning close to Hiram.

I snap my eyes up to Nyx. "You got that, General?"

Hiram taps my legs twice, letting me know he surrenders.

I climb off him and offer him a help up. He smacks his hand into mine, and I pull him to stand. Hiram dusts himself off as I peer around Nyx to watch Theo sparring with Emery. She was more than happy to pair off with him.

I think she underestimated his skill based on her slowing movements and sweaty brow. Theo grins at Emery as they circle each other, waiting for the other to strike. My heart flutters at the sight of him blending in with my crew so seamlessly.

"I'm struggling to believe that it was your idea to go into the alley. Nyx said Theo would use the village trip as an opportunity to test boundaries, and I think that happened. Please tell me I'm wrong," Hiram says, stepping beside me to watch Theo and Emery.

Nyx comes to my other side, crossing his arms on his chest.

"I'm with Hiram. We gave him an opening, and he took it. We don't know his true intentions, and you need to stop putting yourself at risk like that," Nyx says, glaring at Theo.

I pinch the back of his arm and he flinches away.

"First off, stop staring at him like you want to stab him," I say, mimicking Nyx's glare.

"But I do," he retorts. I pinch my lips together and jab him in the ribs for good measure.

"Second, we sat in an alley and talked. You both are overreacting like always," I say. These two don't need to know the details of what really happened, and I hope they never find out.

"Third, if he had ill intent, why would he be doing that?" I point at Theo now, helping to walk a newer member of our crew, Prim, through some training exercises. Emery and Theo work together to ensure Prim is in a proper stance before she strikes at the air with her wooden sword. Her long, black ponytail swings as she moves.

Hiram and Nyx both seem to huff at the same time. I roll my eyes and groan at these two insufferable men, who care a little too much about protecting me. It's like they forget who I am.

"They trust him. I trust him. Maybe you two should see what the rest of us are seeing and not what you want to see."

Nyx sucks in a deep breath, and I already know he's working on a retort. I put up a hand to stop any back talk.

"This conversation is over. Figure it out. We have too many other things to worry about. Now, let's finish up training. I have a celebration to plan." I say before walking away to join Theo, Emery, and Prim.

I pace anxiously outside the dining hall, waiting for Hiram to bring Theo down the hallway. Nyx obviously didn't take any of my advice from yesterday and has continued his chaperone nonsense. This has provided zero opportunities for Theo and me to be alone together, resulting in increased irritability from me.

Chewing the inside of my cheek, I send another silent prayer to the gods that tonight will go smoothly. Today is Theo's twenty-seventh birthday. I never thought I would get to celebrate another with him, so I've secretly been planning a party in his honor. Everyone thinks it is a celebration to thank Thalos for a bountiful harvest.

Two days ago, we received word of our better-than-expected crop numbers for this year despite the drought that killed many crops in other parts of the realm. The timing had to be a sign from the fates or the gods to celebrate. This may be my only opportunity, so I want to make it a night he will remember.

The clothes I special ordered from Elizabeth arrived this morning, fresh and ready to wear. I asked Pyke to make something extra special for tonight. Based on the vanilla infused air wafting from the hall, I know he baked something delicious.

I planned a bonfire with several musicians from the village coming out to play. Astra must be blessing us today because it has been exceptionally beautiful and clear. This evening is bound to be the same.

Now, if I could only get rid of the extra limb I seem to have grown. But unfortunately for me, Nyx is persistent and knows me too well.

As if he can sense I'm plotting against him, he eyes me suspiciously from his perch against the door frame. His muscular arms crossed over his chest, stretching his white shirt tight. He put extra effort into his appearance tonight by expertly combing his hair in a swooping pattern away from his face. He looks very handsome, even if he is a pain in my ass.

Footsteps sound from down the hall, and my heart skips a beat as Theo walks with Hiram toward me. An irresistible smile curves Theo's exquisite lips. The new black trousers and gray shirt fit him perfectly. They hug his muscles in the most delectable way, and I bite my bottom lip at the thought of them being on the floor of my quarters.

Hiram bends into a bow, and Theo flinches as if his instincts take over, telling him to do so as well.

"How do the clothes fit?" I ask with a smile.

Theo brushes his hands down his chest, feeling the soft material clinging to him.

"Better than my clothes back home. Thanks again for them." His smile is warm, and I have to turn away from him to stop myself from kissing it.

Nyx pushes off the door frame and steps in front of Theo to stand beside me. I look up at him with annoyance. He pays me no attention and continues his path into the hall and into the serving line.

Pyke waves me over to my table where two plates and mugs already sit. He points at Theo and my heart warms.

"Theo, Pyke has your plate at the table. Come with me," I say, looking over my shoulder at Nyx, who clenches his fists so tight that his knuckles turn white.

Theo walks to me, placing a hand briefly on the small of my back before pulling back.

"How pissed is he right now?" Theo asks with a hint of satisfaction.

"Furious," I say with a laugh.

Pyke pulls out a chair for me with his usual bow. Theo takes the seat across from me to allow Nyx to take the place at my side.

"Ale?" Theo asks, sniffing the mug.

I nod, taking a sip. The bold hops burst on my tongue, leaving notes of chocolate and spices in their wake. Its warmth calms my nerves instantly, so I take several gulps.

Lowering my mug, I glimpse Theo watching me, eyebrows raised and mug to his mouth. He chuckles and drinks his ale. When he places his mug down, he starts to look about the hall.

The hair on the back of my neck rises. Slowly, I glance around the hall but stop when I find Kira glaring at me from where she sits with Marcus and Silas. Her cold, unblinking stare causes a sense of unease deep in my stomach.

Watch yourself, Kira.

I give a slight shake of my head, trying to convey a warning. I don't know what she's thinking, but the look of disgust on her face tells me everything I need to know. She doesn't want to know or understand what's happening with Theo. She wants to hate him.

We dig into our meal of thinly sliced beef with green and red peppers, all piled atop fluffy rice covered in brown sauce. The flavors complement each other, melting in my mouth.

A moan of approval comes from Theo, and I watch him eat, enjoying the movement of his mouth. He swallows and clears his throat, his cheeks reddening in embarrassment.

"It's fantastic." His words are clipped as he digs into his food.

I nod in agreement and return to my meal as Nyx joins us.

I struggle to keep my eyes off Theo throughout dinner. He looks truly happy, a sight I never expected to see during his time in Umbra. His smile is bright and all-consuming. His laugh is genuine, and he seems to get along with many people within The Keep.

I'm hoping this means that our little outing broke through to him, and he's finally seeing Umbra how I want him to. My heart sings at the thought of him being here like this with me forever. But he's not mine to keep, regardless of the fates pulling us back together.

Pyke serves us a dessert of small, rounded chocolate cakes, only big enough for one person. Each topped with cream and chocolate shavings. Theo stares at the oddity, assessing it before picking it up and shoving half of it in his mouth.

I gawk at him and the ferocity with which he's eating the cake. He catches me watching and pulls his mouth away from the dessert. My laugh booms through the hall as I look at Theo. He has cream smeared from cheek to cheek as if he has a new smile.

Nyx's eyes shoot toward me, confused by my outburst, but when he notices, he laughs too. Theo fakes annoyance as he wipes his face and finishes his cake.

"Where are they going?" Theo uses his head to gesture at a group of people who are heading outside.

"Let me show you." I push past Nyx, who is standing far too close, and follow the crowd outside through the back door and over the rocks.

In the clearing, a bonfire lights the space. People sit around the fire enjoying the heat on this cool evening.

Two tables bearing various fruits and nuts for late night snacking are set off to the side. Mugs of ale and Fati wine are being carefully poured by one of the kitchen crew at the other table.

Musicians have set up on the other side of the clearing, playing a mix of songs to keep people dancing for hours. The energy is lively and jovial as everyone comes alive for a night of celebration. Light and shadows dance in rhythm with the music. I smile at the thought of Thalos joining us for tonight's festivities.

Laughter and the crackling of the fire fill the air and warm my heart. Nyx continues to put himself between Theo and me at every opportunity. While I understand his concern, that doesn't decrease the desire to shove him into the pool of nobu.

Occasionally I'll feel eyes on me, and I know it's Kira, somewhere in the crowd, grimacing at my proximity to Theo. I'm sure she has seen the two of us sneaking glances at each other.

Theo leaves to grab a mug of ale and stops by a tree on the edge of the clearing. A member of the crew waves at Nyx to come to him. After giving me a lecture to stay put, he leaves the clearing.

I scan the crowd to see if anyone is watching me. Hiram's busy flirting with a stunning brunette, so the answer is no. I stroll over to the beverage table, picking up a mug of Fati wine. Taking a sip, vanilla and nutmeg swirl on my tongue, and it tastes as if I'm drinking autumn. The flavors and scents create an almost euphoric ambiance. I allow the wine to give me some extra courage as I walk to stand beside Theo.

He greets me with his dazzling smile, and some of my bravery falters. I stand beside him, watching the celebration.

"Are you having a good time?" I ask, taking a sip of my wine to distract from my nervousness.

It's been days since we've been able to be this close. The feel of his lips on mine consumes my thoughts all day and night.

"It has been a wonderful evening. Where did your handlers go?"

I roll my eyes and elbow his side, causing his ale to splash.

"I'm not entirely sure, and I don't care. As long as they're not following me around, they can do whatever they want." We clink our mugs and drink to that.

A moment of silence passes between us, the music blending with the crickets from the forest to provide ambient sound.

"Has King Asher heard from King Leopold about negotiations?" Theo asks, and my heart pings with guilt.

Despite our best efforts, nothing has worked to get through to Leopold. He has made up his mind. We're guilty and that's final.

All talks have stopped, but we continue to look for the amulet he claims we stole.

"Nothing yet. I'm sorry. I wish there was more I could do to get you home."

He looks down at me, his expression sorrowful. But I can't risk sending him back. Leopold's an evil man who will undoubtedly torture Theo, believing he's a traitor, if he were to return to Lux.

"Don't be sorry. I'm sure you're helping King Asher as much as he'll let you. If you say he has it handled, then I believe you," he says with a smile.

I believe you. These three words flood me with relief and joy.

I want to tell him that King Leopold has refused to speak with King Asher, effectively putting a stop to any possible resolutions … including bringing an end to the lightning king.

"Plus," Theo's voice interrupts my thoughts, "you've given me the best birthday I've had in years, so the stay is worth it."

I let my mouth drop in fake surprise.

"It's your birthday?" My voice is mildly convincing.

I've never missed his birthday in the decade since Oren took me from him, always celebrating in whatever way I could—wishing on the stars for him to be happy and safe. Tobias would sneak me a piece of dessert and celebrate with me after Oren went to sleep.

Tobias knew there was something special about Theo and reminded me often to keep tugging on those threads wrapped around my heart. He said they would lead us back to each other, and he was right. The fates brought him back to me, even if only for a short while.

Theo gives me a simple nod, and we both look out at the cheerful people dancing the night away. I realize Nyx hasn't returned and Hiram's nowhere to be seen.

"Can I show you something? Consider it my birthday present to you," I ask, looking up at him.

"What do you have in mind?" He retorts, raising an eyebrow.

An enthusiastic smile curls my lips as I formulate our plan.

"First, we are going to have to be Umbra spies. Up for a lesson, big man?"

His face becomes expressionless in playful annoyance, and I cover my mouth to stifle my laugh. I go over a few details with Theo about placing our empty mugs in the bin one at a time and then slipping into the tree line directly behind.

Tucked into the trees, I wait anxiously for Theo. My heart pounds in my ears, and I'm bursting with anticipation. My shadows seem to hum with excitement under my skin.

Moments drag on, long and agonizing, but suddenly I hear heavy footsteps in the trees. It's dark with only slivers of moonlight peeking through the treetops, and Theo stumbles, hitting something with a groan.

I don't need the light to tell me where he is. I can find him in complete darkness. My shadows call, and the thread draws me toward him. Following the pull, I find him and lay a hand on his back, startling him.

"It's just me. Take my hand. There's a path a few feet away with more light," I whisper.

His callused hand slides into mine, causing tiny sparks across my skin. If I look close enough, I'm positive I could see light bouncing between us.

He closes his hand around mine, and I lead us out of the trees onto the worn path leading up to the brink. Once safely in the light, I let go of Theo's hand, even though I don't want to. We walk quietly up the hill under the clear sky. The stars and moon shine brightly upon us, lighting our way.

As we near the crest of the brink, I grab Theo's arm, halting him.

"Close your eyes. I want this to be a surprise."

His warm, honey eyes look down at me with skepticism.

"You're not going to throw me off the cliff, are you?" I release his arm and give him an irked glare.

"I don't know. Are you going to be a good boy and do as you're told?" I mimic his words back to him.

He shakes his head but follows my directions and closes his eyes. I take both his hands in mine and walk backward into the clearing at the top of the brink.

Stopping at a safe distance from the edge, I release his hands and stand beside him.

"You can look now. Happy birthday, Theo."

He opens his eyes, and they instantly go wide at the view in front of him. His mouth falls as he takes in the sight. I smile and look out at the realm before us.

This is one of my favorite spots in all of Omnia. From here, you can see the other three kingdoms. Each appearing to glow in the distance. I've searched the realm for another view like this, but there isn't one.

I allow Theo time to enjoy this view while I enjoy mine. There's one more place I want to show him tonight, and my heart flutters at the thought of sharing my secret spot.

CHAPTER 30

THEO

"If you're up for it, I have one more place I'd like to take you." The queen's voice is soft and muffled as I stare blankly ahead at the entirety of Omnia. I didn't know there was a place in the realm where you could get an unobstructed view of everything. There are the harvested fields and sky-reaching plateaus of Fati. The glow from the moon is the only light across the harsh land. The rolling hills with overflowing flowers of Terra. Fireflies dot the landscape, making it appear as if they're stars blinking in the night sky. The snow-capped mountain tops of Lux, massive and unyielding. The flicker of lights from the lanterns and candles across the village cast a warm glow, making my heart ache for home.

I swallow hard, trying to clear my mind. My mouth is slightly dry from being open in shock for a little too long. I can't take my eyes off the spectacular sight before me.

"Thanks for this. The view is unlike any I've ever seen." I feel her gaze shift to me, slowly trailing up my chest to my face. My skin heats where her eyes slide along my body.

"It's just one thing that makes Umbra so special. True beauty lies under Thalos' shadow veil, if only you know where to look," she explains. Turning to look at her, my heart skips a beat as I finally take her in.

Her porcelain skin almost glows in the moonlight while her hair is aflame as if embers of a fire yet to smolder out. Her luminous jade-eyes stare softly at me as the corner of her lips curl up in a smile. She's stunningly beautiful—looking like a radiant goddess under the glow of her kingdom.

I need to get it together.

Blinking several times, I try to clear my thoughts. Obviously, it doesn't work. I take in a shaky breath to calm the anxiety rising within me.

"Yes, please lead the way."

I stretch my arm out toward the path back down the brink. She nods and walks past me toward the tree line on the opposite side. Her hair lifts on the breeze, swirling the intoxicating scent of roses around me.

There's no path in the trees, and I hesitate to follow. She pauses, looking over her shoulder at me. Only the outline of her face peeks through her curls. "Do you not trust me, Theo?" she asks.

I search for that nagging voice in the back of my head that usually questions all of her motivations and actions, but it's gone.

Yes. I trust her. She might be the only person left in this realm that I can trust.

I walk toward the queen and catch sight of a brief smile curving those sensual lips.

When we get closer to the tree line, I glimpse a small path, but it's barely visible through the darkness. The forest canopy scarcely allows light to penetrate through the overgrowth.

"Do you want help, Theo? I can lead if you're worried about tripping again?" The queen asks noticing I have halted before the path.

I'll never understand how she seems to read my mind.

"Yes, please. I'd hate to get injured out here and become carrion for your monsters," I say.

The queen cackles as she slides her delicate hand into mind. Flashes of lightning dance across my skin, more intense than the times before. Little pinpricks scatter along my fingertips into my palms.

The queen leads me through the shadowy woods along a path only she knows. She slows, and I step beside her, not releasing her hand from mine. The cloak of darkness enhances my bravery.

"Are you ready to see something truly magical?"

There's wonder and joy in her voice. I give her hand a little squeeze before she drops it and steps forward.

"Welcome to paradise, Theo." As she speaks, light floods the space around us.

She pulls back a curtain of thick, leaf-covered vines which act as a wall hiding a glowing waterfall with a small pool below. The moonlight reflects brightly off the water and stone, chasing away the shadows.

Cascading water mists the air where it crashes into the pool below. Rock walls form a half circle with caverns along the underside of the cliff snaking behind the waterfall and out the other side. Stepping into the light, the peaceful roar of the falls provides a soothing melody for my racing heart. The scent of fresh water and rich soil permeates the space.

The path tucks tightly between two large boulders, and we walk onto the soft green coastline of the pool. Standing side by side, we take a moment to enjoy the view. This is the second time tonight she has shocked me, and I wonder what other mysteries this captivating woman holds within her. She smiles radiantly at her hidden spot as her eyes fill with delight.

How many people know about this place? Nyx, King Asher? I highly doubt there's anything he doesn't know about his beautiful queen.

A deep pain erupts in my chest at the thought, and I run my hands through my hair to distract myself. When I look back at her smiling face, warmth spreads through me.

"Do you want to go for a swim?" Her sweet voice snaps me back to reality but doesn't erase the need growing inside me.

That's a terrible idea.

"I would love to," I say. Her smile grows at my words.

Gods, that smile may be my undoing.

If she asked, I would fall to my knees and denounce my king to align with her. I would bow to her and only her for the rest of my days just to see that damn smile. *Pathetic.* She's been able to break through my resistance too easily. All I want to know now is if her skin tastes as sweet as her lips and if she moans the same as in my dreams. My cock hardens at the thought.

Her smile falters, and I worry I said something out loud. She backs away, and I fight the urge to reach for her. She pulls at the bottom of her maroon shirt, untucking it from her black trousers. Walking toward the waterline, she takes a seat on a boulder and unlaces her boots.

The image brings back memories of a time long ago with another beautiful red-haired girl and our first kiss by the river. The fates have a twisted sense of humor.

Standing, she pulls her shirt over her head, exposing her pale, lean body to the night air. Her eyes dance as she sets the shirt down on the rock. My body hums with anticipation. I watch as she pulls the laces of her trousers and wiggles out of them, placing them atop her shirt.

She stands there for a moment in her undergarments, looking directly into my eyes. Her body is more divine than my wildest dreams: supple breasts with the hint of peaked nipples showing through her thin bra, a toned stomach lined with old battle scars, and long legs that would look perfect wrapped around my head.

I trail my gaze up her body as she turns to the water. The moonlight catches the scars marring her back. They crisscross in long, harsh lines. Several of them are raised and jagged, as if a rough knife were used to carve at her skin. Others are smooth, white lines with strange uniformity. A deep, primal rage boils within me at the thought of someone hurting her bad enough to leave those marks.

The splashing of water cools my fury as I watch the queen glide slowly into the water, causing the faintest of ripples. She ducks under the surface for a moment. When she emerges, she pushes the hair from her face as the light bounces off her skin, illuminating her freckles. Another set of white scars wrap around her wrist.

Who hurt her so deeply?

The queen stares at me as if she's a water goddess beckoning me to come join her. I willingly comply. Repeating her movements, I drop my boots and clothing on the boulder and stand on the shoreline in nothing but my undergarments.

When I look back, she's watching me with a mask of calmness, but fire burns in her eyes. Not removing my gaze from hers, I ease my way into the pool and swim out to her, treading water in the middle. The water is cool against my heated skin, and I hope it helps to quell this desire. I have to get a hold of my thoughts before I do something we will both regret.

"Isn't it the most beautiful thing you've ever seen?" She smiles, looking around her little piece of paradise, but I can't take my eyes off her.

"Yes." I'm not talking about the scenery.

Her eyes lower and when she looks back at me through her lashes, all I can see is lust burning into me. That last bit of hold I have on my desire snaps. I reach for her, wrapping a hand around her throat and pulling her toward me. The flicker of lightning skirts my skin as she grabs my wrist.

Water ripples around us as her lips part in a ragged breath. I pull her close, keeping several inches between our mouths. The queen tries to break the distance, but I hold her back. She narrows her eyes at me, then leans hard into my hand, biting her lip. I add the slightest amount of pressure, causing her eyes to roll back with a low moan. My cock immediately stiffens at her noises.

"You told me before that your husband doesn't dictate who can be in your bed," I say as her eyes refocus on mine. "Is that true? Because I want you. I need you, Your Highness. But I won't act on anything if it puts you at risk. I need you to reassure me that King Asher isn't going to come out of the shadows and taint this water red with our blood."

"I've told you Asher won't hurt you, Theo. It's not a marriage of love. I may be bound to Asher, but our union is in title only. I'm free to do as I please," she says, an emotion I can't quite place flashing in her eyes.

My hand loosens on her throat, my fingertips settling on her collarbones.

"You don't love him?" I ask, needing to be sure before I act on the desire burning its way through me.

"Can anyone really love a monster?" She asks.

That's all I need to hear. I kiss her hard and hungrily, as if I'm starving and she's the only one who can satisfy my need. *Because she is.* She kisses me back without resistance and melts into me.

My hand glides from her neck down between her breasts. I slide my hand under her breast, allowing my thumb to graze her peaked nipple. She sucks in a breath at the tease.

My hand trails down her back before I grab her ass, rocking her along my length. She gasps as I groan from the sparks flaring through my body.

My other hand wraps around her waist, keeping her close as her legs settle on my hips. The queen's arms move from my chest to my shoulders. Her fingers tug at my hair, sending a jolt down my spine and to my hard cock.

I part my lips and swipe my tongue across her luscious mouth. She opens for me and lets out a little moan that I capture with my mouth. My hand trails up her back into her hair to give it a slight pull back, exposing her throat to me. She whimpers into the night air as her fingers dig into my scalp and shoulder.

I smile against her skin as I kiss and nip at her jawline. She shudders in my arms and my pulse skips a beat. I need more of her. I need all of her. She's like a drug, and I just took my first hit. I can't get enough of her, and I fear I never will.

I pull back from her neck, loosening my hand in her hair to scan our surroundings. She sighs at the sudden withdrawal. When her gaze comes down to me, her brow wrinkles with concern.

"What's wrong?"

I halt my evaluation. My hands grip her waist, and I kiss her again. She hums at the move and grinds down on my hard cock. The thin undergarments barely create a barrier between us, and I feel her soft pussy pressing into my length.

"I need to find a spot with a little more privacy."

She smirks before kissing my jawline and traces her way to my ears, nibbling slightly on my lobe. I groan in frustration.

"Behind the waterfall." The queen's words break as she kisses my neck.

I tilt my head down, causing her to stop exploring with her mouth.

"Do you know this from experience or fantasies?" I ask.

She shrugs at me. "I'm not one to kiss and tell, Captain." Winking at me, she places her hands on my chest, pushes off, and starts swimming backward toward the shore. I let out a small chuckle before following her.

I quickly catch up, and we step out of the water together. Grabbing her hand in mine, I bring it to my lips and kiss it sweetly. She smiles at the gesture, warming my heart in ways I haven't felt in years.

The moon hits her wet skin, and it sparkles in the light. She's a goddess standing before me, and I want to drop to my knees to worship her. I lead us toward the cave set behind the waterfall. The stone walls of the cliffs create a walkway between the forest floor and the stone mass above.

There's heavy mist at the entrance, and we hurry through it to the other side. The waterfall plunging from the cliff above creates a breeze that blows through the cave. The smooth stone beneath our feet is cool upon first touch but warms quickly as we go. As her familiar scent of roses reaches me, my heart skips a beat.

When we reach the center most point behind the waterfall, I notice the stone bows away from the water. It disappears into a hole cut into the rock and reappears on the other side several feet down. In here we're completely out of sight.

We reach the cutout, and I stop, pulling her beside me.

"Another one of your secret spots?" I turn and bring her flat to me.

Her hand slides along my chest, sparks flare in its wake. I grip her hip with one hand and bring the other under her chin, tilting her head toward mine. Her skin has a slight chill on it, but I'm sure I can warm her up.

I gaze into her pleading eyes and bring her lips to mine to kiss her softly. Her lips open immediately, and our tongues mingle once again. I groan at the sensation and kiss her deeper. I reach down to grip the back of her thighs, raising her to my hips. She wraps her legs around me.

She fits perfectly against me.

I walk us further into the cutout. The feeling of her wrapped around my body is exhilarating. Coming to a halt in the middle of our little hideaway, she pulls her lips from mine. Missing the contact, I lean my head forward to kiss her again. She quirks her lips and releases her legs from my hips.

I lower her to the ground gently but don't release my hold. She looks up at me with palms flat on my chest. She raises up on her tiptoes to place a soft kiss on my mouth. I reach for her, but she stops me before I can grasp the back of her neck.

Placing my hand on her shoulder, she trails delicate kisses on my chin before running her lips over my skin to my jaw. I tilt my head up and back, giving her full access to my throat. Her smile against me says I satisfied her with my response.

I long to touch her, but she seems to want control right now, and who am I to deny her? I dreamed about her having complete control over my body and using it for her own pleasure.

She continues her light kisses down my throat, letting a hint of her teeth graze over my skin as she goes. I rest my hand on the small of her back as she works her way down my chest, encouraging her to continue her trail toward my throbbing cock.

Her hands glide to the band of my undergarments. She lowers herself to her knees as she kisses my stomach. Her fingers tighten around my undergarments as her mouth inches toward my waiting cock. All I can do is watch as this beautiful woman tortures me in the most salacious way possible.

This is not the torture I was expecting when being captured by Umbra. Especially not from their queen. Looking down into those green eyes that always find mine, I realize we can't do this. Not here. Not like this.

I grab her wrists, stopping her from tugging my undergarments down. Her gaze snaps to mine. Despite how much I want this, I know once I get a taste of her, I'll never want to stop. And how would that work? She can't be mine here. Not while she's bound to the king.

I take in a deep breath. "We can't do this."

Confusion and concern wash over her in a wave.

"Why not? Did I … did I do something wrong?"

The insecurity in her voice breaks me, and I fall to my knees to be level with her. Grasping the back of her neck and bringing her forehead to mine, I breathe in her rose scent. "No. Trust me, there's nothing I want more than for you to take my cock in your delectable mouth," I say, kissing her forehead.

She pulls back to look at me, and I release her neck. She stares at me in confusion.

"Once I have you, there's nothing else. You're mine, and I don't want to hide in the shadows. I can't be your secret. I'll slip up and then who knows what King Asher will do."

"I told you it's not like that, Theo," she says recoiling and leaning back on her heels with one arm braced against the stone floor.

I too sit back on my heels, placing my hands in my lap, aching to bring her back into my arms.

"I know, but I doubt he would like his wife fucking his prisoner. It doesn't paint him in the best image among his people."

CHAPTER 31

My mind spins as I try to make sense of Theo's words. How did we go from us about to come together to him worrying about Asher, again? I shake my head in frustration.

"No one within The Keep will care or bat an eye at us being together, Theo."

He stares at me, seeming to study my face as I rack my mind for a way to explain everything better to him.

"How do you know he won't see it as a betrayal and lash out? We could leave before anyone finds out. You could be free. No longer living a life in secret," he says with such hope and determination it makes my heart ache.

"No one knows we're here. We can sneak away, grab Midnight and the mare, and head to Lux. We'll be long gone before anyone notices." He stands and offers me a hand up. I take it, but a knot twists my stomach at the thought of leaving Umbra.

"You want me to leave? Run away from my kingdom?" I ask, knowing I could never do that. Not anymore.

"Yes. Let the king finally do what he's supposed to do and rule over Umbra. We could be free in Lux together. You would no longer be his little secret. A new life. A new identity with a name," he cups my face. His eyes glow with the idea of a fresh start in another kingdom.

"I don't want that, Theo. This is my home. This is my kingdom. I worked to make it what it is today. I helped my people create a place they could be proud of, and I won't leave them to fend for themselves. You know I can't do that," I say, taking a step back. His hand rubs the back of his neck as if in deep thought.

"We'll go talk to King Leopold. You know King Asher's weaknesses so you can help King Leopold figure out a way to kill King Asher. After the shadow king is dead, you can come back and rule over your people again. But we need to leave now." He grabs my hand, trying to pull me after him.

Rage coils within me, hot and unyielding.

"If you think that's what Leopold will do, you don't know who you serve. Leopold would never allow that. If he saw a chance to kill Asher, he would take over Umbra and slaughter any who opposed his ruling."

"My king may be far from kind, but he's more merciful than yours," he turns to me, fists clenched at his side. "What about yours, queen? Do you truly know who you serve and who you're married to? What kind of monster he really is?" His voice grows in agitation, echoing off the stone walls.

He stands rigid, tension rolling through his body. His hatred for Asher burns deep from all the lies told by his precious king.

What happened to believing me?

"Yes, I know exactly who Asher is. I also know what lies under your king's stoic façade. The evil that lurks there. If you think Asher is the monster, you still haven't opened your eyes," I sneer, letting parts of my anger and frustration boil to the surface. Even now, he stays loyal to a king who offered him up as a sacrifice.

"Do you know how many innocent people have died at the hands of King Asher? Because if you did, I don't think you would be defending him so fiercely. I think you're the one who doesn't want to face their king's cruelty, not me, queen," he shouts back. His nostrils flare with anger as he stares down at me. His eyes burn with all the hatred he has for Asher.

All the years of pain and suffering wash over me like a wave. But this time, all that's left is a burning rage. The carefully placed mask I use to keep everything pushed deep down in the darkest parts of me falls, and I don't stop it. I welcome the fiery anger ripping through me.

"Yes, I know exactly what Asher is, because I *am* Asher," I seethe, taking a step, causing him to flinch. I tilt my head to the side, staring up at him. My shadows hum under my skin, itching to be released from their well.

Shock flashes in Theo's eyes.

"What? That doesn't make any sense. You're not King Asher. I've seen him. I've talked to him. He's a monster. That's not you." His face pinches as he continues to deny the truth.

"No, Theo. I'm the monster that lurks in the shadows. The one with blood-soaked hands." I say, unleashing some of my power. Shadows swirl around me in agitated circles, lifting me to eye level with Theo. He stumbles backward, his eyes wide in fear.

"No, that's not possible. You're kind and caring. You'd never do all the horrific things King Asher has done," he says, narrowing his eyes.

"Do you think I wanted to do any of those things?" I ask as the shadows lower me to the ground. "Are these the scars of someone who willingly did all those things?" I turn with my arms stretched out, letting him see every inch of marred flesh.

Theo's jaw flexes as he clenches his teeth. "Who did that to you?"

The hair on the back of my neck rises as the air becomes charged with our growing anger. "The man who created the monster to enact his vengeance upon this realm. The one who spread all the lore about Asher to ensure no one would cross him."

Theo looks away and his lips press into a thin line. "King Oren," he answers his own question, finally seeing the whole picture.

"Yes. I was the unfortunate soul who got Oren as a father. Lucky me." The depths of hatred reflecting in his eyes match my own.

"Why did you get to live, while so many others had to die? Why did she have to die?" Theo shouts. His anger vibrating through him.

I let my head fall back as his words bounce off the walls. "You don't think I wished for him to kill me every single day? Death would have been merciful. The gods and the fates never granted me that salvation."

Theo stares at the scars along my stomach and legs. Oren may have stabbed me with a trove blade, but the wounds were real. Daily reminders of how he ripped me from my life only fueled my desire to end his.

"You've been lying to me since I got here. This really has been a ploy all along. I should have known better. Was your speech about trusting one another nothing more than a lie to get me to agree to your deal?" Theo asks, a hint of pain flashing in his eyes.

"I may not have told you Asher's true identity, but I have not lied to you. No one outside my crew knows I'm Asher. You know that, especially after our visit to the village. I couldn't tell you without putting my people at risk. The only reason I'm telling you now is because I trust you, completely," I say, trying find the man who would have followed me to the ends of the realm just moments ago.

"You're nothing more than a liar and murderer. You're just like the ones you claim to despise. Like father, like daughter," he sneers at me. His nostrils flare as his breathing quickens. A quiet calm rolls through me. All sounds and thoughts narrow to a fine point.

I step toward Theo, and he counters with a step away from me. "Do you think I wanted to do any of those things?" I take another step as I stalk him. My mind focuses only on him. "Do you want to know what caused all these scars?" He continues to back away from me until he collides with the stone wall. He stares at me wide-eyed and panicked as if he's prey stuck in a predator's trap.

Theo's breaths are quick as he tries to find a way out, but he knows he can't outrun shadows.

"I've experienced depths of torture even the strongest warriors haven't survived. I was nothing more than a vessel meant to be a weapon for Oren, and he reminded me every time he punished me for disobeying his orders." Theo's brows pinch together, as if unsure of how to handle my words. His rage falters for a moment before he forces it back.

"Oren loved to whip me until I passed out from the pain, allowing my limp body to remain shackled to the chains on my wall. The cuffs dug into my wrists, leaving a constant reminder of his handiwork." I raise my arms, showing him the ring of scars. He flinches, as if expecting me to hurt him.

"If the whip wouldn't get through to me, he would carve at my skin until it was more blood than flesh. Some days, he would pick his fists over tools. Do you know what it feels like when your ribs break and puncture your lung?" I ask, staring up at him. He doesn't move, frozen to the wall. "The worst part was the constant feeling of suffocation until a physician could figure out how to fix it."

Theo's features soften as I continue my confession. Baring myself to him should feel freeing, but it only makes me feel raw and exposed, as if my soul is on display for his approval.

"After a while, you get used to the stomach pains of hunger or the exhaustion from lack of sleep. Days blend into one another in a cascade of pain and agony no one should have to experience. But just like those chains, I eventually broke. I didn't have a choice. I could continue to fight, and he would kill everyone I loved one by one in front of me, or I could obey. I made the ultimate sacrifice, losing myself so they could live. So my people could live," I shout, my voice dark as it echoes harshly through the alcove.

The tightly wound spool of my anger is on the verge of completely unraveling. The edges loosen, and the darkness threatens to consume every fiber of me. I force it down with all my control. Wrapping a mental string around it to keep it in place.

"You stuck me in your cell, didn't you? Those chains on the wall. You broke them?" He asks, unclenching his fists, but frustration still darkens his eyes.

"Yes," the words are a growl, feeling more animal than mortal. "A reminder of the day I fully gave into the darkness and let the monster consume me."

In a flash, Theo is upon me. His large hands wrapping around my wrists. As his fingers run along my scars, a burning sensation like hot pinpricks flares down my arms. I pull back, trying to yank out of his grasp, but he tightens his grip.

"Let go of me, now," I snarl, glaring up at him and baring my teeth. He stares at me, jaw tight. Theo assesses me as if he can see every mark on my soul. I want to run. I want to fight, but he doesn't release me.

"I'm sorry I let my fear blind me so that I couldn't see what you were trying to tell me. I didn't want to believe the kind, gentle queen I've come to know is the nightmare that plagues this realm," he says as the last of his anger ebbs. Mine still rages within, needing a release.

My shadows spread from my hands, coiling around Theo, winding their way up his arms. I can feel every flex of his muscles and quick rhythm of his heart as they trail along his skin. He stares at the darkness slithering its way up his body, and his breath hitches.

A hum vibrates through my shadows as if they are purring under his touch. Theo seems to relax slightly at the feeling.

"Since I arrived, you've stressed the importance of me having a choice because you never had one," he says, more as a question than a statement, so I nod curtly.

"I'm sorry," he says again. His eyes soft as he looks at me. But my anger isn't ready to yield yet.

"I don't need your pity," I say, trying to pull out of his grip. He doesn't let me have even an inch. I stare at his chest, not wanting to look at him.

"Look at me, queen." I reluctantly raise my gaze to him. "You did what you had to do to survive and keep everyone you care about alive. It's not pity I have for you, it's respect. You fought the darkness and won. Changing it into something beautiful. You should be proud of that."

His calmness is grating. "Such pretty words don't change the fact that I'm a monster, Theo. They don't change the things I have done." I try to use my shadows to pry his hands off me, but they don't seem to want to potentially harm him. I groan in frustration.

Theo pulls me flush to his chest, pinning my arms behind my back. He wraps one hand around both my wrists while the other lifts my chin, so I have to look at him.

"Oren forced you to become a monster. You are not one. You can be mad and rage all you want about the things that happened to you. But you don't get to take it out on yourself. You're not what he made you. Even in the darkness, you created light, shining bright like a star, leading everyone to safety. You are good."

"You are good, Nata."

My mother's words combine with Theo's, finally breaking my anger. I sag in his grip as my shadows fade from his arms. When his lips touch mine in a gentle kiss, I melt into him. His coolness calms my blazing fire, only to reignite the embers of desire.

His hand loosens from my chin and slides down my throat, stopping over my heart. The tips of his fingers rub the edge of my collarbones, sending flickers across my skin. I slide my tongue along his bottom lip, needing more. His lips flex as he fights a smile before happily opening for me.

Theo releases my wrists and trails his hand to my hip as his other hand trails down my chest to meet it. He toys with the hem of my undergarments. Breaking our kiss, I drag my eyes up, digging my nails into his arm. On the outside, he's calm, but his ravenous look says he's ready to devour me.

His fingers hook the band of my undergarments, pulling them to my ankles in one smooth motion. He kneels before me and taps the side of my leg while offering me his hand for balance. I lift my legs so he can put my undergarments aside.

Using his hand as leverage, I climb on top of him on the stone floor, wrapping my arms around his neck. His strong hands find my hips as our lips meet again. With only his undergarment between us, I can feel his hard cock press against my pussy, and I grind down on his length. I need more of him, now, before I go mad.

Theo's hands trail up my back, unclasping my bra and removing it. He breaks our kiss to admire my breasts on full display. One of his hands finds a breast, palming it, while his mouth finds the other. His tongue makes delicate circles around my nipple, eliciting a moan from me. He switches to give my other nipple the same treatment.

Holding on to his shoulders, I rock my hips back and forth along his dick, my clit aching to be touched. I arch my back, trying to get the right angle. His mouth leaves my breast as his hand slides along my back. He leans forward, and I cling to his shoulders, trying not to fall.

A grin spreads across Theo's face as he braces an arm on the stone floor behind us and he lowers us to it. He lays me on the ground, sliding his arm out from under me. I wrap my legs around his hips, pulling him into me. With his forearms braced on each side of my head, I reach up, wrapping my hand around the back of his neck and pull him in for a rough kiss.

My shadows hum under my skin as my need grows more impatient with each passing moment. His tongue dances with mine as our breaths become heavier.

I trail my hand from his shoulders down his chest, needing to feel him in my hand. Before I can make it to the band of his undergarment, he grabs my wrist and places it above my head. He grabs the other and does the same. I whimper into his mouth, causing him to break our kiss.

Theo plants light kisses along my cheek and down my throat. He moves down my body painstakingly slowly. He nips and kisses my collarbones on each side before tracing over the spots with his tongue.

He continues down my body, stopping at a peaked nipple and circling it with his tongue before sucking it into his mouth. I moan at the feeling of his mouth sucking and licking my skin. He repeats the move on my other breast, and I arch my back from the pleasure rippling through my body.

My shadows vibrate under my skin with frustration, wanting to be released. I shove them back and focus on Theo's lips trailing down my stomach to my hips.

"Theo, do something now before I flip you onto your back and take matters into my own hands," I demand.

His lips curl into a smile as they brush against my skin.

"Let me enjoy myself. I'll make it worth your wait." His words are a purr against my skin as he removes my legs from his hips, pushing them apart.

The feel of his tongue on my clit sends a wave of fire flashing through my body. I moan loudly as he draws circles around it. He licks my pussy, and a hum of enjoyment rumbles his chest. His noise vibrates into me, and my shadows pulsate in response.

As I try to push them into their well, he lightly sucks on my clit, sending the sensation of lightning all the way to the top of my head. A breathy whine escapes my lips as I arch off the ground. My hold falters and my shadows slither from my hands, skirting over Theo's back in long-black tendrils. He pauses his delicious licking and glances up at me from between my thighs. *Gods, I love the sight of him there.*

Looking up at my shadows, he withdraws slightly from his position.

"I'm sorry. They have a mind of their own," I say with a grimace, propping up on my elbows. I call them back, but they seem reluctant to stop touching his bare skin.

He raises an eyebrow at me, and a smirk curves the corner of his lips. "They are warm and tingle a little. Do they know how to play? Maybe something like scratching?"

As if he commands them, my shadows lightly dig into his back like nails would. His eyes close, enjoying the sensation. When he opens them again, animalistic desire courses in them.

"Oh, this is going to be fun."

Theo slides all the way to the black stone floor until his chest is flush with it. He places my legs over his shoulders before his tongue returns to my clit in tantalizing circles. I gasp as he continues to lick and suck, sending waves of pleasure from the tips of my toes to the top of my head.

His tongue glides along my pussy as he feasts from me. I can feel the muscles of his back flexing through my shadows, increasing my desire to touch him. The combination of licking and sucking drives me closer to the edge. He teases my pussy with one finger before slowly slipping inside. I whimper as he moves in and out of me in quickening motions.

Goosebumps erupt along my skin from his steady pace.

"Theo." I pant his name through unsteady breaths.

"Be a good girl and cum for me."

Oh gods, that filthy mouth.

I dig my hands into his soft hair and rock my hips on his face, chasing my orgasm.

His other hand slides up my body to play with my breasts. He rolls each nipple tenderly between his fingers. Each one sends shocks through my body. I shudder as the edge of my climax inches closer. I rock my hips faster along his mouth while the fire threatens to consume me.

"That's it. Take what you need from me." His voice is low and vibrates my already humming body.

He adds another finger as stars gather in my vision. My pussy clamps around his fingers as my shadows pulsate along his back. The sensation of him both on me and within me heightens my arousal to levels I've never experienced.

He curls his fingers, hitting just the right spot. I scream his name as I fall over the edge of my orgasm, hard. It shoots through me like an arrow striking its target. I grip his hair tight, and my shadows dig into his muscular back. The air around us heats. It feels like time has slowed down to draw out this moment a little longer. The space around us glows as he continues to lick every ounce of pleasure out of me.

CHAPTER 32

LILY

When I finally come back to my body, the faint sound of pebbles across the stone floor has us both halting. Theo peeks his head out from between my legs with a sinister grin. His lips glint in the moonlight. I draw my shadows back to me, and they caress his face as they return. He doesn't flinch or withdraw from their touch, which makes me want him even more.

He licks his lips, enjoying the taste of me. "You taste divine, queen. The best dessert in Omnia." He climbs up my body until he reaches my face and kisses me. His large arms cage my head in, with one on each side. I wrap my legs around his waist as he sets his hips into mine. His hard cock rubs against my sensitive clit, reigniting the fire burning inside me. This man is going to destroy me in every way, and I'll probably thank him in the end.

I run my hands down his chest, itching to touch him. To give him all the pleasure he gave to me. My hand reaches for the band of his undergarments as we break our kiss. We are both breathing heavily as my hand slides down.

"Li … Queen? Are you back there?" Nyx's voice booms off the walls of the cavern. Theo and I freeze, not making a sound. *Oh, gods, why? Why now? This can't be happening.*

"My queen! I know you're here. We found your clothes on the shore. Answer me now." My best friend's yell reverberates through the space. The anger in his voice is palpable.

Theo groans above me, and his forehead leans into mine.

"You better answer him before he charges in here. Neither of us are decent enough for that." A loud huff of irritation escapes from me as I turn my head toward his voice.

"Go away, Nyx!" My words come out as a hiss through gritted teeth. My annoyance with him is at an all-time high.

"Get. Out. Here. Now. Both of you," he shouts, emphasizing each word.

I turn back to Theo, who is looking down at me, his eyes soft as they trace over my face. Leaning down, he kisses me sweetly. I bring my hands to his cheeks and deepen our kiss, our tongues dancing briefly.

He breaks our moment, and I miss the feel of him already. All I want to do is stay here in this hiding spot, in this dream, forever with him. Footsteps click on the stone near the entrance to the cavern, and I know it's Nyx coming to retrieve us.

"We're coming, Nyx. Just give us a damn moment," I yell.

His footsteps stop but don't turn around as he waits.

Theo stands and offers me his hand to help me up. I soak up as much of his warmth as I can before Nyx is between us, again. I know my best friend means well, but right now I could kill him.

Theo adjusts his undergarment before picking mine up from the ground. He kneels, sliding them back on me. His fingertips graze my skin as he goes, threatening to reignite my burning desire for him. He motions for me to turn, and he secures my bra back in place.

I lean my head back as he runs his hands through my hair, gently breaking up knots and removing leaves. We give each other one last look over before walking side by side down the walkway out of our hidden spot. His hand slides into mine as we go, and we smile at each other despite what's waiting for us.

When we exit through the misty entrance, we're met with the cold, gray gaze of my general. Angry is an understatement. Nyx is fuming and looks murderous. I step in front of Theo to act as a shield. I know he can protect himself, but Nyx won't hurt me. After their little shoving match in the library, I'm certain Nyx would throw the first punch at Theo.

Nyx takes in the sight of us in our undergarments and lets out an exaggerated sigh while rubbing his temples.

"What do you want, Nyx?"

His unnervingly empty eyes snap to mine. Nyx, in this rare territorial form, shows off the fierce warrior he is. He earned his title as general through training and skill. Alone, he's a force to be reckoned with, but with me and my shadows, we're the monsters in all the stories.

"What are you doing here? And with him?" He yells. His hand flies up to point at Theo, but I quickly smack it down. He might lose a finger if he keeps shoving it in Theo's face.

"That's none of your business, Nyx. Unless you came here for something important, I suggest leaving before I make you." He's ruined my post orgasmic high, and I don't appreciate it.

Nyx steps toward me, and Theo shifts behind me. Reaching out my arm, I halt Theo as he tries to come around. Nyx and Theo lock eyes in another staredown.

Tension thickens the air around us, charging our little bubble. I shove at Nyx's chest, trying to break this standoff, but he doesn't budge. I snap my fingers in front of his face, finally getting his attention.

"What was so important you had to ruin my evening?" I ask, allowing my annoyance to be heard. He stares down at me, fury darkening his eyes. I stare up at him with the same amount of rage.

"We received urgent news from our spies. I went back to the bonfire to get you to head to the council room, and you were nowhere in sight. No one knew where you had gone. I took a lucky guess at where you may have taken him." His gaze trails up to Theo, who pushes into me.

The air is thick with smoldering anger, and I have had enough.

"Both of you knock it off, now, or I'll silence you myself." I release my shadows from my hands in long spirals, taller than both of their hulking forms.

My power vibrates wildly, responding to the tension.

Nyx's eyes widen in shock as my shadows twirl before returning to my hands. I take a deep breath, trying not to smack the two men around me.

"What was the message, Nyx?" I groan.

He cocks his head at an odd angle, pure rage rolling off of him. "That's not something I'm comfortable discussing while others are present."

It must be about Lux then, and I briefly wonder if they found the amulet.

I lean my head back to rest on Theo's chest and look up at him, knowing our night together is over. A tight smile crosses his lips letting me know he had the same realization. I soak in our closeness for a moment longer, before shoving all my desire deep down and allowing only frustration to remain. Standing up straight, I grab Theo's hand and push past Nyx, shoulder checking him for good measure.

We walk the gravel path back to the coastline, heading toward the boulder with our clothes. I freeze when I see Hiram and Marcus near the vine wall. Theo bumps into my back, wrapping his arms around my waist. I stand tall, gathering my confidence and walk to the boulder.

I grab Theo's clothes from atop mine and hand them over. Theo quickly dresses as I stare down my guards. Hiram meets my gaze with pinched lips.

"Lovely evening for a swim, my queen."

Marcus' face burns bright red in the moonlight as he fights his laugh. He turns away to hide his amusement. I'm glad they are enjoying all of this because I want to strangle every single one of them.

I pull on my clothes, the moisture from my undergarments causing everything to stick together. Nyx steps to my side, gripping my arm and pulling me toward him.

"What were you thinking? This is exactly what I told you not to do," he whispers harshly.

Before I can retort, Theo pushes Nyx off me, causing him to stumble backward.

"Don't you grab her like that. What's your problem, anyway? Don't like someone taking the queen's attention off you?" Theo teases Nyx.

"You're the problem. You have been nothing but a threat to our kingdom's safety since you arrived here. I should have sent you back the moment you survived the Cypres," Nyx shouts, pointing at Theo.

"I told you not to put your finger in my face, General," Theo snarls. Nyx takes a step closer with his hand still raised.

"And what are you going to do about it, Captain?" Nyx asks, taunting Theo. Baiting him. In a blink, Theo shoves Nyx's arm to the side before punching him in the face. Nyx's head flicks to the side and when it returns to Theo, his eyes are colder than snow. An icy, burning rage flares through them. Nyx lunges at Theo, slamming a fist into his stomach. Theo grunts and hunches over in pain. Nyx swings for another punch, but Theo dodges it, landing his own to Nyx's ribs.

"You two knock it off already!" I shout as Hiram and Marcus rush past me, eager to join the fight. Theo and Nyx dance around each other with Hiram and Marcus closing in on Theo.

Hiram and Marcus make eye contact with Nyx. The slight raise of Nyx's eyebrow gives me all the warning I need. As the three men charge at Theo, I unleash my power. Shadows burst from me in long arches, stretching for all four men. They coil tightly around each one, raising them off the ground as if they are on display for me.

Nyx stares at me with nostrils flaring. Unless masked as Asher, I rarely release my power. It's always been more of a weapon, and I've never needed that around my crew.

Until now.

Hiram and Marcus are rigid and wide-eyed. Their racing heartbeats vibrate my shadows that are wound around them.

Theo looks at me with soft eyes. No fear or anger to be found. He sees me. Not the monster I've always been. Just a queen keeping her guards from hurting the man she's madly in love with.

"I hope you have all of it out of your systems because this ends here. No more petty arguments. No more standoffs trying to prove who's the broodiest of you all. It's done." My guards flinch against the shadows while Nyx and Theo remain calm.

I set them all back on the shore, recalling my shadows to their well.

"Shall we?" I stretch a hand to Theo.

He smirks before taking it. I lead us out of my ruined paradise, with Nyx, Hiram, and Marcus trailing behind.

We make our way to the back entrance of the Keep in complete silence. I push open the doors without acknowledging the guard on duty and halt in front of the iron bars of Theo's cell. My slow-burning anger causes my shadows to hum under my skin.

Hiram and Marcus don't make eye contact as they wait by the back door for me to leave. Nyx leans against the wall behind me.

"Get lost, Nyx. I'll meet you in the council room." I look over my shoulder at him, and he shakes his head.

His predatory gaze fixates on Theo. "Not happening after all that."

I shake my head in irritation. My shadows shoot from me in waves, creating an expansive wall around Theo and me. Nyx growls on the other side, but it's barely audible. Theo stares at the black mass surrounding us, a flash of panic in his eyes. I grab his hand, bringing his attention back to me. His face lightens with a small smile curling his lips.

"I'm sorry about tonight," I say. Theo's hand cups my cheek as his thumb rubs my bottom lip.

"I'm not. You gave me the best birthday gift."

I fist his shirt and pull his lips to mine. He holds my face in his hands as he kisses me, slow and steady.

He pulls away and scans my face before leaning his forehead to mine.

"Don't kill your general tonight. Even if we both want to," he states.

A sharp laugh escapes me at Theo's words because I'm debating on Nyx's punishment, and death is on the table.

"I can't make any promises. I'll see you in the morning for breakfast." Taking one more look into those honey eyes, I give Theo a kiss on the cheek and step back. He bows his head to me as I drop the wall of shadows. Nyx stands at my back where the wall came down.

My smile falls as I turn and make my way to the council room. Nyx trails behind. We don't speak for the rest of the walk.

CHAPTER 33

LILY

Before the council room door clicks shut, I'm turning, ready to unleash my anger on Nyx. "What is wrong with you? Why do you continue to put yourself between Theo and me?" I demand. He stares down at me with cold, narrowed eyes while stepping into my space.

"Me? What are you doing unleashing your shadows in front of him? Do you want him to figure out who you are?"

My lips curl into a scowl as my shadows pulsate with agitation.

"He knows who I am, Nyx. I told him all about Asher," I tell him.

His breath quickens as he towers over me.

"You did what? Please tell me you didn't tell the Captain of Lux the most guarded secret of our kingdom," he pleads.

I cross my arms on my chest, digging my elbows into him.

"No, I told my Amari the truth about me not being married. What's he going to do? Tell someone? He's here. Leopold has made it clear he doesn't want him back." Nyx runs his fingers through his hair and steps away from me.

"It's one thing to put yourself in danger Lily, but you have now put Umbra in danger. What happens when he goes back to Lux and tells Leopold the truth? Then what? We will lose the lore that keeps everyone away, all because you caught feelings for a man," he shouts, turning back to me.

"It's not like that at all and you know it. He's more than just a man. Stop acting like I'm throwing my people into the line of fire for him."

He launches at me, and my shadows respond to the threat, creating a wall on each side of me. Nyx shows no reaction to them.

"You may claim you love him, but we both know he doesn't love you back. Right now, you're a convenient piece of ass for him. A pretty, naïve little queen ready to give him whatever he wants. And then some. He's using you," he sneers.

I slap Nyx across the face, stinging pain shooting across my palm.

"You don't know what you are talking about, and you won't speak like that about Theo. Before I told him I was Asher, he was trying to figure out a way to get me out of here. To give me freedom. Does that sound like he doesn't care about me, Nyx?" I say through gritted teeth.

I fight back tears as his words sting more than I'd like to admit.

He stares at me, face reddening from my smack and Theo's punch. My shadows grow and vibrate in the air around us.

"Put the shadows away, Lily."

They respond by undulating like a wave and growing bigger, causing him to grit his teeth at their movement.

"I can't. You pissed them off, too. Ten years, Nyx. I have missed him every day for ten long years. I have suffered so much loss and pain trying to survive so one day the fates would let me be with him again. Anything to stop the constant pain in my chest from our thread being pulled taut. I have the chance now, and I'm not passing it up." My shadows deflate with my words, becoming a cloak wrapped around me, warm and comforting.

"I don't trust him," he retorts.

I pinch my lips at him.

"Really? Because even Midnight trusts Theo. Are you telling me you are more temperamental than Thalos' horse?" I tease.

"He's still loyal to Lux. He would pick them over us. Over you. He would sacrifice you for what he sees as the greater good. Until I'm certain he won't, I can't trust you alone with him," he says.

I lean on my large desk, bracing my hands atop it.

"I understand that, but you know I can handle myself. Besides, if I were that easy to kill, I'd be dead already."

He glowers, and I stick my tongue out at him, hoping to break the tension. My shadows slowly recoil into me but remain near the surface, ready to act if needed.

"Can you please loosen up? You're teetering the line of overprotective brother, and it's annoying."

Nyx walks to me and cups my face in his powerful hands, forcing me to look into his warming gray eyes.

"I'll cross any line if it means keeping you safe. I'll always put your safety and well-being above all else. I'm bound to you by duty and soul. You're my Amari, too. There's no length I won't go to protect you, even if the one you need protecting from is the one tied to your heart." He leans forward to press his forehead to mine.

My chest stings at the memory of the first time our cord showed itself. A deep trill resounding from within. A string being plucked, tethered to my soul, so different from the one I felt with Theo.

Confused, we asked Tobias what it meant since Amari was only for your true love, and Nyx always felt like the older brother I never wanted but was glad I had. Tobias reassured us it was about the fates showing us our destiny, bringing our souls together. Bound to one another through all lifetimes.

I look up at him with a soft smile, placing a hand on his chest. The trill has grown stronger throughout the years—a feeling of comfort and love.

"I know, but he won't hurt me. Can you at least try to trust him and be less overbearing?"

He looks at me with a widening grin.

"Good, because I'll kill him if he tries anything."

I shove him away as he laughs. "I promise I'll try to trust him more. I guess I should get used to him since we're kind of stuck together, since we're bound to you," he answers with a shrug.

"That's all I ask of you, Nyx. Now, what's this important message from our spies you interrupted me for?"

Nyx takes a seat on the desk beside me. He opens his mouth to speak, but the door to the council room flies open. Hiram storms in with eyebrows creased and lips pinched tight.

I startle, jumping off the desk to stand. My stomach twists with concern that Theo, Marcus, and Hiram continued their fight once I was out of sight.

"What in the realm were you thinking?" Hiram stops a few steps from me, and I take a seat, realizing this is a lecture, not a warning.

"You left with no one knowing where you went. If Nyx weren't your Amari, we would have never found you, and who knows what Theo could have done. Thank the fates for their threads," he says, crossing his arms over his chest.

I glance at Nyx, who fights back a smirk at my being scolded. I elbow him in his side.

"Clearly, I'm fine, Hiram. Thank you for your concern, but it's misplaced. Just like I told Nyx, you're going to have to trust him like I do."

Hiram huffs and takes a deep breath as if readying to speak his mind. "That's enough, Captain. Also, if you were so concerned, why did you leave Marcus alone with Theo?"

"I didn't. Kira is helping Marcus stand guard right now," Hiram answers as if that's an acceptable response.

A pit opens in my stomach at the thought of Kira watching over Theo.

What is she doing?

"Why?" I ask, fighting back the desire to run down the hall to save Theo from Kira, but I know she wants a reaction from me. I need to remain calm. I grip the edge of my desk to quell my rising panic. Nyx leans against me, sensing the shift in my mood.

"She's been asking to be more involved within The Keep, including guard tasks, so I've been letting her help with different things," Hiram says with a shrug.

"If she wants a job, she can go to Lux for us then," Nyx chimes in.

I snap my gaze to him with an arched brow.

"That's what I wanted to discuss," he answers my question without my asking. "Our spies may have found the amulet but have conflicting intel on where it's located. They are requesting for someone to come help find it."

We're close to getting answers, and my shadows hum at the prospect of this all being over. I relish the thought of proving Leopold wrong. The look on his face will only be the start of my revenge against the lightning king.

"Send Kira and Emery. Kira is our best recon spy. No one else has the skills to get in and out of places without being seen. If the amulet is hiding in Lux, she'd be the one to find where they have it stored. Emery can go in case they run into any trouble." I give the order and both men nod in agreement.

"When do you want them to go?" Nyx asks.

The desire for answers makes me want to send them tonight. But that wouldn't be fair or wise.

"Wait until morning to tell them. They can leave the next day. That will give them a few days to gather information before returning in time for the autumnus festival," I state.

Hiram drops into a bow before leaving the council room with the new orders for his guards.

Nyx stands, offering me his hand. I rise from my desk, drained from the day. "We'll handle everything in the morning. Now get to bed." He pulls me to his side, and we walk out of the council room back to my chambers. My clothes smell like cedar, and I fall asleep comforted by the feeling of Theo with me.

CHAPTER 34

THEO

The yellowing pages of the old book are brittle under my rough fingertips, and I do my best not to damage them while I read. The scent of old parchment and leather wafts in the air, warming my soul. I delicately turn the page for another read through of the end bringer story that captured my attention over a week ago.

I've read it at least five times since then. Something feels off about the story, but I can't seem to figure out what it is. It's like it was told to me in a past life, but my mind is struggling to put back all the pieces. The book abruptly stops as if someone forcefully ripped the pages from the binding. But the lack of torn edges or markings prove that hasn't happened.

I shift in my new deep-crimson chair in the corner of my cell, getting more comfortable for another read. A gift from the queen so I can have a small reading nook complete with a table. I must have given her a wonderful orgasm behind the waterfall to receive furniture as a thank you.

Trailing my fingers across my lips, I remember her sweet taste and intoxicating noises. It's only been days since our outing, but it feels like a lifetime. We have zero privacy with Nyx always putting himself between us at every opportunity, earning a disgruntled noise from the queen each time. She has also seemed preoccupied, and I wonder if it's because of the message they received that night.

The scent of roses drifts into my cell, and I smile, knowing without even looking that the queen's standing at my door. A flutter forms deep in my chest at her presence.

"Are you still reading the end bringer story?" she asks.

She's leaning against the bars inside my cell wearing her usual attire of all black, showing off her exquisite body. I want to memorize every inch of her, learning each curve and the sound she makes as I touch it.

Her bright smile makes my heart skip as she studies me. "Maybe I need your help to read after all." A small snicker comes from her as she looks down at the floor. When she brings those radiant green eyes back to mine, it takes everything in me not to drop to my knees for her.

She pushes off the bars and slowly steps toward me.

"I was stopping by to make sure your new chair is big enough." Her gaze trails over me as she steps closer, barely out of reach.

"It's a little uncomfortable," I say, lifting my ass off the cushion as if it's the root of the problem. This causes the queen to lean in closer to inspect the chair.

I snatch her wrist in a firm grip, learning from my mistake in the library. Pulling her hard to me, I sit her down on my lap.

"Ah, now that's more comfortable."

She lets out a breathy laugh as I wrap my arms around her while still holding the book in one hand. I lean my head into the side of hers.

"Thanks for the chair. It's perfect."

She leans her head back into mine. I set the book down on my leg and reach up, placing my hand on her cheek. With the slightest amount of pressure, I turn her face toward me, and she leans back into my chest. I capture her lips with mine, and she melts into me. Her fingers slide into my hair as our tongues dance. We restrain ourselves from deepening the kiss.

The warm caress of her shadows trailing up my arms brings memories of being between the queen's thighs. I pull away and stare into those captivating eyes, wishing to know all the secrets they hold. She relaxes into me as her shadows fade away.

Wrapping my arm around her waist, I draw her tight to me.

"I missed you." I whisper into her ear so no one else can hear.

She shifts slightly in my lap.

"I missed you, too," she answers softly. I savor the feeling of her soft body against mine, and I rub her arm, trying to satisfy my need to touch her more. "How did you convince your jailers to give you freedom tonight?"

She reaches across me to pick up the book from my lap. Her enchanting scent causes my heart to skip a beat.

"Because we're not alone, Captain."

Hiram clears his throat from the hallway, out of sight. The queen settles herself in my lap, and I relax back into the chair.

"I guess I will have to settle for a bedtime story, then."

Her soft giggle causes me to smile. I could easily get used to the sound.

The queen reads me the story of the end bringer. The smooth timbre of her voice rolls into me in comforting waves. With each line spoken, the sensation of the story being on the fringes of my mind intensifies. The memory hidden deep within, waiting for the right moment to be released.

When she's done, she places the book on the table before settling back in my lap. Being with her like this feels as if it's how we're meant to be. Trailing my gaze over her, I get snagged on the sight of the thin band on her left hand.

"If you're not married, why do you wear a wedding ring?" I question.

She lifts her hand, the metal glinting in the lantern light.

"It's a family heirloom, not a wedding band. It happens to only fit that finger," she says.

A fleeting feeling washes over me of wanting to replace the ring with one of my own, but I push it away. That's an irrational idea, especially since we haven't even known each other for a month.

I've tried to force down the growing feelings I have for the queen, but it's becoming harder to do. After a decade of thinking I'd never find love after losing my flower, it's hard to realize that I may have found it hiding in the darkness. How poetic of the fates to have me fall for the daughter of the man who murdered my Amari.

I pull the queen tight into me, needing her presence to slow my racing heart. I'm not sure I'm ready to admit my affection for her, but I'll gladly enjoy the way her body feels against mine.

The hair rises on the back of my neck, and I look up to see Hiram peeking around the wall. He quickly darts out of sight when he realizes he's been caught.

"Nyx and Hiram don't like me very much, do they?"

An audible growl comes from the queen, and I fight back a laugh.

"It's not that they don't like you, they don't trust you. They're afraid you're going to hurt me."

I give her a squeeze.

"They realize you're the most powerful divinus ever seen in Omnia, right?" I question.

She shifts in my lap, trying to get a better angle to look at me.

"Yes, I reminded them both. For Nyx, it's different though. Princess Juniper and you have been friends since childhood, right?" she asks, leaning on the armrest and bringing her gaze to mine.

"Yes, and you can call her Junie," I answer.

She gives me a warm smile. I picture her with Junie. Two queens with opposite personalities, but I feel that they would be good friends. My heart beams at the thought of them together.

"Ok. If Junie were spending time with someone you didn't know, wouldn't you be concerned about her safety?" she asks.

I think this over for a moment and realize I would act like Nyx if the shoe were on the other foot.

"I would do anything to keep her safe."

The queen nods slowly.

"You two are not very different. As for Hiram, you broke his nose when you got here, so he may hold a little grudge," she says with a smirk.

Hiram peeks his head around the wall again to nod at me.

When I bring my gaze back to the queen, she is watching me. Her eyes are soft, and I pray the emotion behind them matches my own. I wrap a hand around the back of her neck, pulling her to me. The kiss is slow and passionate, and the desire burning through me rages.

She breaks our kiss and places her forehead against mine. I slide my hand down her back to settle around her waist. She takes a deep breath as her fingers move to twirl a strand of her hair.

"Go to the autumnus festival with me," she asks, her voice low.

I pull back to look at her. Thinking over all the stories I have been reading about Umbra traditions, I don't recall one about a festival.

"What is that? I've never heard of it."

"It's a celebration of the autumnal equinox. Under the full moon, we thank and honor the gods for their many blessings through music, dance, and feasts. They decorate the village with lights and beautiful colors."

I smile down at the queen as she describes what sounds like a lovely evening.

She fidgets with a curl as if overtaken by nerves. I don't know why she would be nervous, though. I doubt I can say no to her, even if I wanted to. She has captured all of me. I look into those gemstone eyes that take my breath away. Reaching out, I take her hand in mine, rubbing slow circles along the back of it.

"I would love to go with you." I bring her lips to mine for a brief kiss as her other hand rests on my chest. Her beaming smile nearly causes my heart to burst.

Hiram steps into view from the other side of the iron bars. The queen looks at him and with a simple nod, I know our time together is over. She stands from my lap, and I join her. Sliding her delicate hand into mine, I walk her to the door.

"What does one wear to this festival?"

She halts at the threshold, turning back to me. I don't let go of her hand and briefly think about yanking her back into this cell with me.

"Don't worry about that. Your outfit will arrive the day of the festival."

I arch an eyebrow, wondering how she has already arranged clothing for me.

"I will wear clothes, right? This isn't one of those dances-in-the-moonlight-naked type of festivals?" The queen bites her bottom lip, and I squeeze her hand at the thought of being naked with her again.

"Clothing is always optional with you, Theo." Pushing up on her tiptoes, she kisses me again, and I slide my hands down her back, savoring the feel of her body.

I pull her closer, deepening our kiss. It may be days before we get to be alone together again, and I greedily want to soak up every piece of her I can.

The need within me grows with each passing day. Thoughts of her consume my mind even in dreams. She pulls out of our kiss and steps back. I reluctantly release her and stare at her bright smile as she walks backward out of the cell.

"Goodnight, Theo."

She exits, and I glimpse Hiram with a huge smirk on his face. The queen nudges him playfully, and he rolls with her push. I watch as he wiggles his eyebrows at the queen, walking backward down the hall. She shoos him away, and I see a faint hint of pink warming her cheeks as she strides out of sight.

CHAPTER 35

LILY

I groan in frustration as my fingers get tangled in my curls again. Why can't I make more than a simple braid? Nyx can create beautiful braids in my hair with minimal effort while I've spent half my time getting ready, trying to get something to work.

As if I summoned him, the clicking of his boots resounds in my quarters. He enters my bathing chamber, and his eyebrows furrow with concern.

"What's wrong? Why are you not ready yet?" Nyx asks.

I let my hands fall to my lap in defeat.

"I can't braid my hair. It keeps getting caught in my fingers. Will you help me, please?" I plead.

He gives me a knowing smirk and steps behind me, quickly getting to work. He weaves intricate braids with masterful skill, and I watch him in the mirror. His eyes raise to mine with an expression of apprehension.

"What is it, Nyx?" I ask. He continues his braiding.

"I spoke with Kira and Emery. They found the amulet, Lily." My jaw nearly hits the counter. We were right, those damn liars.

"Kira said it's at a trade post in Lux. After a few drinks, the owner wouldn't stop talking about it," Nyx continues. Hope surges through me at the prospect of finding the amulet and figuring out Leopold's motives. This one item has caused so many problems and deaths, I'm ready to be rid of it.

"How soon do you want to go?" I ask as Nyx twists and twirls my hair, pulling it across the back of my head.

"We should be able to leave tomorrow night. Kira and Emery scoped the shop out before they left Lux last night. I had them write everything down for us to review."

My heart thunders in my chest with vindication, knowing we've been right this whole time.

"Will you please tell everyone at dinner? We can organize first thing in the morning. The sooner we retrieve it, the better. Less time for them to move it," I say. He nods behind me as he finishes placing pins in my hair, securing the right pieces in place. Taking a step back, he admires his work, and I grab a hand mirror to do the same. Half my hair is down, allowing long, flowing curls to cascade down my back. He braided and twisted the top half together, giving the illusion of a full moon.

I smile brightly up at Nyx. "Thank you! It's perfect. Will you help me get into my dress, too?"

He rolls his eyes but lightly shoves me toward my closet. I hurry and slip into the gown Elizabeth made for me.

Holding the front around my chest, I walk back to the bathing chamber. Nyx turns to get a better look and stares at me with shock on his face. I turn so he can button the back. He places his hands on my shoulders to spin me toward the mirror. Even I'm stunned by my appearance.

The dress hangs loosely off my shoulders before dropping into a sweetheart neckline, accentuating my breasts. The bust fits snug against my body before it flares into a long skirt that billows from my hips. There's a slit up the right leg, stopping at the top of my thigh, giving me easy access to my dagger. The coloring is something I have never seen before. The top is a deep-black as if it is night. The skirt slowly fades into a rich crimson-red, appearing as though it has been drenched in the blood of my enemies.

How fitting.

"You look beautiful," Nyx says, wrapping his arms around my waist. I smile at him, placing my hands over his.

"Thank you for everything, Nyx." I squeeze him close, and he plants a soft kiss to my head before releasing me.

"I may not like this, but I trust you. Even if I don't think you know what you're doing," he says with a smirk. "Let's get going before you're late to the party." He offers a hand, and I take it.

I slip on my boots and strap on my dagger before we head out of my chambers. The Keep is alive with laughter, and music booms throughout. Cinnamon floats in the air, causing my mouth to water.

We head toward Theo's cell and my stomach twists as my nerves increase with each step. We stop down the way, and I take a deep breath, trying to calm myself. Nyx turns toward me, giving me a head-to-toe look-over one last time.

"I wish father were here to see you like this. You look like … you. Whole and happy. It's been a long time since I've seen that light in your eyes. I've missed it, Lily."

My heart breaks with his words, and I choke back tears. I'm not sure if Tobias ever saw me in a dress or truly happy. We never got that chance. Nyx pulls me into him, and I grip him tight. When he releases me, his hands cup my face and steely gray eyes cut through me.

"Please be careful with Theo. For me. I love you so much. I can't lose you, too." I place my hands on his, leaning into him.

"I know, Nyx. I promise I will be. I love you too," I answer, placing a hand over his heart, feeling the cords trill between us. He kisses my forehead and steps away, heading back toward the dining hall.

Turning, I gather myself before heading the short distance to Theo's cell. Walking along the iron bars, I watch as he braces one foot on the edge of the bed, checking for dirt. He looks ridiculously handsome in the outfit from Elizabeth.

The black trousers hug his toned legs and perfect ass in the most sinful ways. The black vest over a long-sleeved, black shirt emphasizes his broad chest. Crimson stitching on the vest trails down, drawing the eye with it.

I run a hand over my dress, double checking how I look.

"Theo." My voice is soft and sweet, even to my ears.

"Yes, my flower." My stomach drops at the use of my old nickname, and I can't breathe.

Theo bolts straight up, appearing shocked by his own words, and coughs, clearing his throat. "I mean, yes, queen."

He turns and freezes. I take in a breath, trying not to show how his slip has affected me. Theo stares, blinking slowly. Stepping into his cell seems to break the trance, and he swallows hard as his gaze trails up my body.

I saunter over to him, my dress fluttering around me. His eyes get snagged on my thigh, peeking through the slit with each step. I smile up as I stop in front of him. "You look very handsome, Theo."

He takes a step, closing the distance. I lean my head back to keep my eyes locked with his. "There are not enough words in this realm to describe how breathtaking you look tonight." His voice is low as he leans closer.

My heart nearly leaps from my chest.

He grabs me by the back of my neck and pulls me in for a heated kiss. I dig my fingers into his chest as our tongues mingle. His cedar scent consumes my senses. I'm drowning in him, and I can't get enough.

He releases my lips, both of us breathing heavily. His hands roam over my body as he leans back for a better view.

"Stunning."

Taking my hand, he twirls me around, causing my skirt to float in the air.

"I like what you did with your hair." He brings me to a stop, facing him.

I run my hand softly over my locks.

"Thank you. Nyx did it. I can only do simple braids, but he's mastered them over the years."

Theo's eyebrows go up with this new information about Nyx.

"Maybe he could show me sometime. It might come in handy," he says.

I look up at him, imagining the scene. There would be lots of yelling and pushing if that ever happened. I laugh at the thought.

"Wow," Hiram's scruffy voice sounds from behind us.

I smile at my captain as he drops into an exaggerated bow, and we walk toward him.

"My queen, you look absolutely radiant tonight. I've … I've never seen you like this. It's a good look for you."

"Thank you, Hiram. You're too sweet."

He gives me a warm smile as he backs out of the doorway to let us through, motioning for us to lead the way.

Theo offers me his arm, and I look up at him, taking it. I feel the need to pinch myself to ensure all this is real. Even in my dreams, I never imagined I would be here with Theo staring down at me with heat simmering in his eyes. The gods have never been kind to me, and I fear what the cost will be at the end. Right now, though, I want to focus only on him and the way he looks at me as if he's all mine.

We stride down the hall with Hiram behind, heading to dinner. The atmosphere during autumnus is cheerful. Everyone is wearing their finest clothes, ready for an evening of celebration. We step through the doors of the dining hall to a wondrous sight.

I have always avoided celebrations of this magnitude. Their energy, while exhilarating, can be overwhelming, causing my shadows to become agitated under my skin. But tonight, they seem to dance to the sounds of my people.

Theo escorts me to our table and pulls out my seat. As soon as we are situated, Pyke brings out our plates, setting them down before us. Then he drops beside me, and I reach for him, fearing he has fallen. His gentle hands take mine, placing a soft kiss on them.

"We're truly not worthy of your beauty and grace, my queen." I smile down at him as a man to my left cheers, "Hear, hear!"

I raise my gaze to look at him, toasting to me.

"To the queen!" This time it's a woman to my right, and I draw my gaze to her as mugs around the hall rise. The love of my people flowing all around makes my heart nearly burst with pride. I watch as they all bow from their seats. These people have welcomed and trusted me with their lives long before I became their queen.

While Oren ruled with fear, I have ruled with dignity and respect. These are my people, and I'll do anything to keep them safe. As they all raise their heads, I place my hand over my heart, bowing my head to them in mutual honor.

I help Pyke rise from the ground, placing a kiss to his cheek before he strides back to the kitchen, and the hall resumes its flurry of activity.

Turning back in my seat, I see Theo watching me, his lips parted and eyes soft. He closes his eyes and bows his head. My heart flutters at his gesture, and I do my best to keep my breathing even. Not wanting to delay our trip to the village any longer, I dig into my plate, savoring the rich flavors fusing on my tongue. Dinner conversation consists of shared stories and laughing at Theo's terrible jokes.

True to his word, Nyx sits with Hiram, which causes me conflicting emotions. I'm so used to him being with me, but it's nice to have time alone with Theo, allowing us some form of normalcy. Even if I know Nyx is watching me from his seat.

For dessert, Pyke brings us something he calls baked apples. It looks like a ball of flaky pastry covered in a caramel drizzle. Sweet vanilla and cinnamon drift with the steam as it rises from the dish.

Picking up the spoon, I slice into the mound to find a soft apple at the center. Taking a bite, the warm flavors melt in my mouth, giving the feeling of a cool autumn evening. The perfect dish for tonight. Theo closes his eyes, relishing the taste.

We devour our food and say goodbye to everyone before stepping out of the dining hall. I lead Theo out the front entrance of The Keep, into the field between the haunted forest and the waterfall pool. Stopping us near the middle, I bring Theo to face me.

Rustling in the forest draws our attention, and we find six sets of glowing yellow eyes watching us. I suddenly fully realize what it all means. Just like me, my creatures are tied to Theo. The nobu sensed he was in danger long before he arrived on our soil, and the Cypres eliminated any threat to their kingdom. *And their king.*

I stare up at Theo with pure amazement. If he knew any of this, would he embrace it or run away? Soon, I think I'll need to figure that out, but tonight I want to enjoy the moment.

He stares at the haunted forest with curiosity lighting his eyes. The moonlight bounces off the golden streaks of his hair, making him appear to glow. Love doesn't describe the feelings I have for him. It goes beyond this realm and this lifetime.

He looks down at me, still smiling.

"Do you trust me, Theo?" He scans my face before kissing me.

He rests his forehead on mine. "More than I've ever trusted anyone."

I take a deep breath as I hold one of his hands in mine. Raising my other, I open a portal to the edge of the village. The red-rimmed mist appears and opens faster than normal. I can't help but wonder if it's because of Theo. My power seems to change the longer he's here. The well within growing deeper than before.

He squeezes my hand as the portal opens and his lips part.

"Oren didn't destroy all the adveho rings. He kept Umbra's and we use it to travel throughout the realm."

Holding his hand, I walk us through the portal. Theo hesitates briefly as we break the surface. Our boots crunch on the gravel walkway as we cross onto the other side. As the portal closes, I check Theo for any hint of unease.

"That's an interesting family heirloom," he says, turning to me.

I shrug and give him a playful smile. We walk hand-in-hand toward the village, causing my heart to thunder in my chest. Music and revelry ring in the air; the festival is in full swing. I marvel at the scene before us. Lanterns hang like falling stars between the buildings, casting a warm glow on the space. Pumpkins and colorful gourds are in decorative towers along the pathway where various vendors have set up small booths. A group of musicians is playing near the center, and the villagers dance to the rhythm around them.

Theo pulls me tight, wrapping his arm around my waist as we enter the flow of people. We both gaze in wonder at the joyous celebration playing out. I grab Theo's hand and tug him toward the tavern. People step out of our way as we go.

We push through the door, laughing with the lively energy. Spice and sweat fill the warm air of the tavern. We sit at the counter, and I take everything in. Bringing my gaze back to the bar, I spy a familiar face.

"Good evening, Leon. Harassed any women lately?" The older man slowly turns to look at me, his mug frozen in mid-air, eyes wide with panic.

He aggressively shakes his head before backing away from the bar. I snicker as he runs away like a terrified animal, tail between his legs.

Otto stands behind the counter, arms crossed and a scowl on his face.

"I knew my night was going far too easily. You're a menace alone, Margo. Did you really need to bring a beast with you?" I turn and look at Theo, who's staring at Otto, flabbergasted.

"Me? I just met her outside. Can we get some ale, or is this not a tavern?"

I pinch my lips, holding back a laugh as Theo's hand slides up my back. Otto rolls his eyes and brings us two mugs, for which I promptly overpay. I lean back into Theo, enjoying the evening out in my village with him.

We drink and revel in the festival fun around us while constantly finding reasons to touch each other. When we step back out into the throng of people, Theo takes my hand and drags me toward the dance circle. He pulls me close, wrapping one arm around my waist and placing my arms around his neck. As both his arms enclose me, we sway to the rhythmic beat.

For a moment, we get lost in the music and each other. Theo looks at me as if I'm the only person in all of Omnia. I wish this could be our life. Evenings in the village enjoying all Umbra offers. I close my eyes, soaking in everything and committing it to memory.

Silently, I pray to the fates and gods again, begging for this to be my happily ever after, like in the fairy tales. When I open my eyes, warm pools of honey watch me with a hint of what feels like love reflecting in them. *Please let this be real*.

Theo leans forward and kisses me sweetly. My hand slides into his hair as our tongues dance. We break apart, fire raging in both our eyes as they meet. Theo trails his hands along my arms, taking my hands, and leads us out of the crowd.

We exit the circle near Elizabeth's shop to find Loma behind a small table with various rocks. I tug Theo toward her. She spots me through the crowd and comes around the table, arms outstretched. I hug Loma tightly before she places a hand on my cheek.

"My girl, you look radiant tonight." I lean into her as Theo steps beside me, causing her hand to fall from my face.

"Loma, this is Theo. Theo, this is our healer, Loma." He reaches out, and the two shake hands. Loma locks her eyes on him, studying him intently.

"What's with all the rocks, Loma?" I try to get her attention off Theo.

Unease rolls my stomach at the way she is looking at him. Her eyes come back to me as a soft smile curves her lips.

"These are wishing stones. Pick the one that calls to you, and I'll help you infuse it with a wish. Tomorrow, with the rising sun,

I'll bury all the stones in blessed soil to allow everyone's wishes to grow." Loma returns behind the table as we step in front.

The stones are in a variety of colors and shapes, but each one has a distinct line wrapping around it from the top to the bottom. One continuous cord, unbroken near the center. I select a dark-green stone while Theo selects a white one.

"Now place it in your palms and enclose it in your hands." Loma's voice is gentle and kind as she instructs us through the wishing steps. "Now close your eyes. Connect your mind, heart, and soul. Use them to push your wish into the stone."

I do as I'm told and take a deep breath, looking inward. My shadows tingle under my skin as I draw into myself, tethering all the pieces together. As I concentrate on the stone, it heats and rattles in my hand.

"That's it. Very good. Now dig a little deeper to set the wish fully in the stone." I look further into myself, pulling everything into a ball at my core with my well. My shadows vibrate harder as I feel the fragments of myself slipping together. Sparks skitter down my arms to the stone. Light flashes behind my eyes as my power roars under my skin, aching to be released.

Loma's hands clamp around the top and bottom of my hands, causing my eyes to open, fearing my shadows had unwillingly flowed out from me. Loma's face is practically glowing with joy, her eyes bright as they pierce into me.

She releases my hands, and I pass her my stone. Theo does the same. He smiles excitedly at me as we look at each other. I try to match his joy but can't seem to shake the sense of dread. My shadows swirl back into their well at my core, comfortable once again.

We thank Loma and walk through the village, stopping at the different booths. All the little touches and kisses feel so natural between us, as if we're nothing more than a couple helplessly in love.

As the evening goes on, we find ourselves back near the entrance of the village, leaning against one of the black stone buildings. Theo's shoulder presses into the wall as I tuck in close to him with my back flush to it.

He leans down to whisper in my ear. "What did you wish for?"

I look up at him, scanning his face, debating my answer. I decide I no longer want to hide my true feelings for him. The time we have left is growing shorter every day. I can't keep pretending like he's just another man passing through.

"I wished for you to love me." I hold Theo's eyes, bracing myself for the possibility of rejection.

He leans his massive frame into me, tucking a loose strand of hair behind my ear. His finger hooks under my jaw, pulling my face toward him.

"You don't need to wish for that. I already do." He kisses me hard as his hand slides to the back of my neck.

I grab his shirt, pulling him into me. His other hand glides down my back, grasping my ass. I arch off the wall as his hands roam my body, begging for more.

Theo presses into me, pinning me in place. The feel of his hardening cock makes me moan into his mouth as our tongues explore. I push on his chest, separating our lips. We are both panting. He gets the silent message because he grabs my hand, dragging me out of the village. I laugh as I try to keep up with his long strides toward the tree line where we arrived.

Once out of view, he pulls me in close, capturing my lips. Theo slowly raises my left arm into the air, and I follow his command by opening a portal to my chambers. Grabbing his vest, I walk backward with Theo's hands on my hips and lips on mine.

Once within my chambers, I break our kiss to close the portal and lock all the doors. This time, we'll have no intruders. Theo looks around my quarters, and I realize how long I have been waiting for this moment. *A lifetime.*

My boots click on the stone floor as I walk back to him. He stops his observation and turns to me. I kiss him softly, wanting to draw out this time together for as long as possible.

Slowly, I unbutton his vest and he pulls it off, letting it drop to the floor. Our tongues dance as I work on each button of his shirt before pushing it off his shoulders. I trail kisses along his cheek, down his throat, and to his collarbones.

My fingers trace down his chest, and my lips follow their line, watching his breath quicken as I go. I lower myself to the floor as my hands brush over his hard cock, eliciting a deep moan from him. I kneel before him and unlace his boots, tossing them out of the way.

Watching him, I rise, kissing his chest again while I loosen his trousers. They fall to the floor with a click as I run my hands down him. The thin fabric of his undergarment strains under the hardness of his cock. As I slide my palm along his length, I bite my lips with anticipation.

He grabs my wrist with a groan. "Your turn."

He spins me so my back is flush to him, rubbing against my ass. My head falls back in a soft moan at the thought of him being inside me again.

He brushes the hair away from my neck and plants kisses down it, slowly leading to my shoulder. His hands make quick work of the buttons on my dress, and it falls to the floor in a puddle of fabric.

Lifting one of my arms, Theo trails his kisses down before taking my hand, leading me to the bed. He sits me down on the end, the soft sheet cool on my skin. He kneels and brings my foot to his chest to unlace my boot. His fingers are gentle as he goes, but the fire in his eyes when he looks up shows he's ready to devour me.

After tossing my boots to the side, his hands trail up my legs before halting at my dagger. He unbuckles the straps and places the dagger gently on the floor under the bed.

His hands resume their glide up my body, stopping at my undergarment. One hand pulls the thin fabric to the side as the fingers of his other slide over my wet pussy to my clit. He makes slow circles there, and my head falls back at the sensation.

Theo grabs my thighs and yanks me down the bed until my ass is teetering on the edge. He drops to his knees as his eyes focus solely on my pussy. Positioning himself squarely between my thighs with my legs over his shoulders, he pulls my undergarment off before burying his face in my pussy. He licks and circles my clit, causing me to whimper as he builds up my climax.

"I've missed the way you taste." He says with a deep growl, sending a shiver to the top of my head.

I moan as he alternates between licking, circling, and sucking. I grip his hair as my shadows drift from my hands, trailing down his back. They coil around his body, trying to touch every piece of him. He slides one finger inside me as my shadows skirt lower on his body. His finger slowly works its way in and out of me, causing a whine to pass my lips.

I coax my shadows toward his cock and stroke the length of him through his undergarments. Theo lets out a shaky breath onto my heated skin. He slides another finger inside me and curls them, hitting that perfect spot. His tongue flicks and circles my clit, pushing me off the edge of my orgasm. I shake as waves of pleasure roll through my body.

Before I can come down, Theo is climbing up my body. My shadows pull his undergarment off as he goes. I grip the hair on the back of his head as he hovers over me, forcing his mouth to mine. The lingering taste of me is sweet on his lips.

Theo breaks our kiss to look down at me with a hint of hesitation in his eyes. I slide my hand down his chest, taking him fully in my hand. His breath hitches, and he shudders above me. A sly smile curls the corner of my lip as I stroke him from tip to base. He presses his forehead into mine as his breath quickens.

He sets his hips fully between mine, and I bring my legs up around his waist. I tilt my head to capture his lips again and our tongues dance. My heels press gently into his ass, urging him forward. I rub him through my wetness before slowly guiding him into me. Inch by inch, he pushes deeper. I grip his back as the pressure from the fullness causes me to gasp.

"That's it. Take all of it, my queen."

Oh, gods, him calling me his queen causes my heart to skip a beat. He withdraws slightly before sliding further in than before, sending tingles along my skin. The feel of him consumes me as my shadows find their place on his back and my hands trail to his shoulders.

"Such a good girl," he growls near my ear, and I rock my hips, begging for him to move. He draws his hips back before slowly pushing into me again.

I whine in frustration at the languid pace he's taking, and I use my heels to speed him up. I'm teetering on the edge, still reeling from my first orgasm, and I greedily want another.

Theo pushes off the bed, sitting back on his heels. He hooks my thighs in his arms while looking down at me with a sinful smile. He slides out before slamming hard back into me. I grip the sheets as my breath catches and sparks flare under my skin. He does it again, and I arch my back off the bed in a loud moan.

"Tell me what you want. Use your words." He pushes slowly back into me while using my wording against me.

"Hard, Theo. Now. Please." I'm panting, my voice broken as I try to speak.

"That's my girl." He doesn't hesitate and slams into me.

His thrusts are hard and unruly as he drives in. The sensation of lightning shoots through my body as his finger works delicate circles on my clit.

A strangled cry comes from me as I stumble closer to the edge of another climax.

"Oh, gods," I moan as I rock my hips in rhythm with his thrusts, painfully close to toppling over.

He pauses to lean forward, dropping my legs to the side, and brings his hand to my neck. "It's not the gods worshiping your body right now, my queen. My name is the only one that will cross your lips ever again. It's my name you will be screaming loud enough to wake the gods as you cum."

I gasp as he towers over me. Gripping my neck, he resumes his punishing thrusts into my pussy. I grasp his biceps as my eyes roll back, my nails nipping his skin.

My shadows coil around us in waves, seeming to leave sparks in their wake across our bodies. His other hand slides between us to make circles on my clit. I moan his name as tingles trail from my toes to the top of my head. He quickens his pace, sending shock waves throughout my body.

I scream his name as I plunge off the edge of another orgasm. Light flares behind my eyelids, and my pussy clenches tight around him. Theo groans loudly as he finds his release too. His cock spasms inside me as he cums. The air seems to vibrate as my shadows pulsates around us.

Our breaths are heavy as we bask in our shared euphoria. Theo's hand slides up my neck to my cheek. His thumb gently rubs as he stares into my eyes. I smile brightly up at him.

Running my hands up his arms, I pull his lips to mine for a sweet, passionate kiss, silently wishing this night would never end.

CHAPTER 36

LILY

The bed shakes under me as I am jostled awake. Theo flinches side to side and a low growl escapes through his clenched teeth. He's having a nightmare and isn't coming out of it.

His face flashes through terrified emotions as his eyes pinch tight together. The muscles of his arms flex as if he's fighting someone in his dreams.

I sit up, letting the sheets fall, exposing my still naked body. After our realm-shattering sex last night, Theo helped to clean me up and then pulled me tight into his powerful arms. Between the multiple orgasms and him wrapped around me, I was asleep in moments.

I stroke Theo's chest, trying to wake him as easily as possible. I don't know how he reacts when awakened from nightmares.

"Theo, it's ok. You're safe," I whisper.

His thrashing increases, and I know his horror is reaching its peak. I need to get him to wake up before it consumes him. "Theo, please wake up." I raise my voice a tone higher and push at him. I lean closer, looking for a way to break this nightmare's hold on him.

His large hand clamps around my throat as he sits up, pushing me back. His eyes are empty. My shadows seep from my hands, unsure of what to do. They won't hurt him, but they know they must protect me.

I urge them toward his head to pull as I attempt to pry his fingers from where they dig into my skin.

"Theo," my voice is weak as he cuts off my air in his tight grip.

I use my shadows to wrap around and shake him hard. The light in his eyes returns as he pants from fear. His face pales in the dim glow of the room as he realizes his hand is around my throat. He drops it immediately and I fall forward, gasping for air.

Theo pushes back, slamming into the headboard. "I'm sorry. Oh, gods. I thought … I'm so sorry."

The agony in his voice is palpable. I raise my head as my breathing eases, and I rub my neck. I crawl toward him and sit in his lap. Cupping his face, I bring his pained eyes to mine.

"I'm fine, Theo. You didn't hurt me." I plant light kisses on his cheeks, forehead, and then his lips.

A weak sigh comes from him. I grab the back of his neck and place my forehead on his, taking an exaggerated breath. He understands the meaning and takes one with me. I make him take several deep breaths before I release my hold.

Sitting back, I look at him with a soft smile, letting him know everything is alright. "Do you want to talk about it? I know a thing or two about nightmares," I ask, hoping he will share with me. His eyes fall to the bed, and he adjusts the sheet, fidgeting.

"It was about King Oren. It's the same nightmare I've had since he killed Lily, but this time I caught up to him." His eyes slowly rise to me, and I fight back my emotions.

He has nightmares because he thinks he failed to save me, and I loathe Oren for what he did to him. Hatred boils under the surface, and I curse the fates for not letting me be the one to take Oren's life.

"You were strangling him for what he did to her?" I ask, already knowing he was. He nods lightly at my question as I shrug. "It seems we share our dream of killing Oren as well." I let out a breathy laugh and Theo huffs. I shift off him and take a seat on the bed, wrapping a blanket around us.

"Can I tell you something no one else knows? Not even Nyx." He nods, and I swallow as I prepare to divulge a secret I've never spoken out loud.

"I was plotting to kill Oren before he died," I say quickly, getting it out. Theo's eyebrows raise at my declaration. "A few years before he died, he did something I couldn't get over."

I gaze at the reason this plan started. Those sweet honey eyes stare back at me in wonder.

"I took little responsibilities from him and began acting on my ideas to improve Umbra if I were to become their queen. The trade agreements were my idea." His hand slides into mine for reassurance, and he rubs his thumb lightly over the back of my hand. "The crew stopped listening to his orders before he died. I was slowly driving him mad by taking away the one thing he loved the most—power. I was days away from killing him. Unfortunately, whatever creature was in Fati got to him first."

I scoot up the bed until my back is against the headboard beside Theo. He watches me, taking in my words. I get comfortable and lean my head on his shoulder. Theo wraps his arm around me, drawing me close. I snuggle into him, enjoying his warmth and tantalizing scent.

"Oren died in my arms," I say, and Theo flinches beside me. "He opened a portal back here, thinking we would save him. Oren stumbled in, gasping for air as blood poured from long slashes across his chest. His skin was gray, and red stained his fingers as he tried to stop the bleeding. There was also this ... odor."

Theo pulls back to look down at me. "What do you mean, an odor?" he asks with confusion lacing his tone.

I take a moment to remember the day Oren died. *Probably the best day of my life.*

"Rancid but sweet. He smelled like his flesh was rotting off his bones already, but there was this undertone of a sweet, tangy scent. It smelled so unnatural and putrid," I answer, wrinkling my nose as I remember the way the scent lingered after they removed his body.

Theo settles back into my side with a shudder.

"Do you want to know what I told him as he took his last breath?" Theo doesn't answer, but I'm too deep in the memory to stop now. "I told him I was going to wipe our history of his name. That I'll make him the forgotten, no-name King of Umbra. He never allowed me to have one, so it's only fitting that I take his away," I say, and Theo gives me a little squeeze.

When Oren took his last breath, I smiled down at him, knowing I finally won. I was free from him and his demands. His cruelty. As his soul left his body, I knew the gods were waiting to hold judgement for all the wrongs he committed in this lifetime. I pray every day that my mother is helping with his punishment. *Goodbye Oren. I hope my mother tortures you in the Underrealm.*

Sunlight skirts across the floor, and outside my window the sky glows in beautiful shades of blue and purple. "I'm going to shower. Would you like to join me?" I say, lifting my head to Theo, and I watch as a seductive smile curls his lips.

Pushing off him, I slide out of the bed, letting the blanket fall to the floor as I walk, exposing my naked body. I reach the doorway to my bathing chamber and pause, looking back at Theo. His eyes trail along my body as he bites his lower lip.

When I slip into the chamber, his feet scramble across the floor, rushing toward me. As I turn on the spigot, allowing the refreshing water to pour out from the ceiling, Theo presses into my back as his hands enclose me. He lifts me off the ground and walks us into the shower. I laugh as he sets me down and tilts his head back under the spray, letting it wash over him.

I follow the droplets as they travel down his chiseled chest. I trace my gaze slowly back up his delicious body to find Theo's eyes on me, lust blazing through them. He steps toward me and lightly touches my neck where he grabbed me earlier. His eyes soften, and his jaw flexes as he grits his teeth. I reach up and adjust his hand, so it is flush to my skin. I lean my head back as I grip his wrist.

A low growl comes from him as his fingers dig in slightly, and he pulls me to him. His kiss steals my breath, hard and demanding. His hand leaves my neck, sliding down to my breasts. Theo circles my nipple, causing it to peak before pinching it and then moving on to do the same to the other. My breath hitches as tingles erupt along my skin.

He pushes me against the glass wall of the shower. My ass slamming into it with a thud. His mouth leaves mine, and he kisses down my neck as his thumb circles my clit in a rhythmic spin. Teeth graze my throat, and two fingers slip inside my pussy. I'm breathless as he curls his fingers inside me, hitting that extra sensitive spot. I grab his biceps, digging in my nails as he pinches my nipples again. He's building my pleasure at a punishing pace, and my legs tremble.

His fingers leave my pussy, and he leans back, creating a gap between us. I'm panting, on the verge of cumming already. Glistening fingers enter Theo's mouth as he fists his hard cock. My eyes dart between the two movements, not knowing which one I want to see more.

"You taste even better for breakfast, my queen," Theo's voice is rough as he stares at me like I'm his next meal. I nearly melt into a puddle on the shower floor.

Bending down, he picks me up by the back of my thighs, using the glass for support. My hands wrap around his shoulders. He lowers me onto his cock, allowing me to feel every inch of him as he buries himself deep. I gasp as he pulls me the last bit before being fully set. There's a small twinge of pain as he hits spots never touched. "You take my cock so well." His voice fills with praise as I rock my hips, using his shoulders as leverage.

My shadows trail down his back, coiling around his legs. His hands pull my legs apart, widening for him. He withdraws nearly all the way before slamming back into me. I cry out as he thrusts into me, mercilessly.

Shadows spiral up my legs, and I feel my weight settle into them naturally. Theo notices the shift and releases a leg to circle my clit with the perfect amount of pressure. I grip his shoulders tight as waves of pleasure blast through me in endless succession.

Sparks flare in my vision as lightning skirts from my head to my toes. Theo pounds into me in a wild frenzy. A choked scream bursts out of me as I'm flung over the edge of my climax. Theo lets out a loud, guttural moan as he cums with me.

Our breathing is ragged, our skin wet with the mix of sweat and water. I rest my head against the glass wall as my shadows recoil, and Theo sets my feet back to the ground. His hand braces the glass as his arm wraps around me, keeping me upright. He leans down, placing soft kisses on my lips.

After a moment, he pulls me into the water and washes us both. I let him clean me as I bask in sweet orgasmic bliss and being cared for by the man I love. I want this to be our life forever, and I hope he does too.

Once I'm thoroughly cleaned to Theo's satisfaction, we step out of the shower and wrap ourselves in fluffy towels to dry. I grab fresh clothes for the both of us, setting them down before Theo. He stares at his set with eyebrows raised in question.

"I had hoped you'd stay the night eventually, so I got an extra to keep here." I shrug at him as I pull on my clothes.

Using my towel, I squeeze out the excess water from my hair before sitting down at my vanity to braid it back. Once dressed, Theo comes to stand behind me as I finish brushing out all the tangles from my hair. "May I?" I look at him through my mirror as he runs his hands over my hair.

"You want to do my hair?" I ask as he stares in deep concentration.

"You said Nyx braided your hair last night, so I want to try. Can't be that hard if he can do it," he says. I lean my head back, allowing him full access to my hair.

He gets to work splitting my hair into three sections before waving them together to form a braid. Well, what is supposed to be a braid, anyway. It looks terrible. Pieces of hair stick through breaks in the twists. The end is at an odd angle after he ties a cord around it.

He examines it with a pained expression as he brings his eyes to mine in the mirror.

"It's perfect," I say as I smile brightly at him, and his face falls.

"It looks terrible." He grumbles, reaching to undo it. I duck out of the way and slide off my seat to face him.

"Well, I like it. Now, let's go because I'm starving." I leave the bathing chamber and pick up my dagger from under my bed and place it on the entry table.

"Please let me try again. I can't let your people see you like that." He asks grimacing, and his nose wrinkles.

Walking to him, I place my hands on his cheeks. I kiss his nose and forehead, trying to smooth out the worry lines. "I love that you did my hair, Theo. I'll wear it proudly." He sighs, knowing he won't win this battle no matter how much he protests.

We slip on our boots and waltz out of my chamber doors into the breezy hallway. A faint scent of apples wafts in the air. My stomach drops, and I look to see if I can find Kira hiding nearby, but I know it's useless to try. I swallow hard. I think it's time I have a talk with her about watching us.

Theo's hand slides into mine, and we head toward the dining hall. I scan the hallway as we go, hoping to glimpse her. The scent of bacon and sausage floats in the air as we near the dining hall. The clinking of plates and silverware lets me know breakfast has already started.

We walk through the doors, and it's much quieter than usual. Looking around the hall, there are not as many people up and eating. The ones who are here show the remnants of last night's celebration on their faces. Many are rubbing their temples as they nurse mugs of coffee and nibble on thick biscuits. Simple meals seem to work the best when nauseated from a hangover.

Theo and I head to our table, taking our seats. Pyke walks out of the kitchen, slower today than usual. He places two heaping plates before us, and another kitchen staff member brings mugs of coffee.

Pyke attempts to bow to his customary depth, but wobbles on his feet. Theo leaps up to steady him.

"Are you ok, Pyke?" He questions as he places my chef back upright, not letting go. Pyke pats Theo on the arm.

"Yes, I may have over-celebrated last night. Just like everyone else, it seems." Theo and I both laugh as Pyke slowly turns and walks back to the kitchen.

Theo rejoins me at the table just as Nyx slides into the chair next to me with his own plate and coffee. The fresh roasted scent reignites my hunger, and I dig into my food.

"Have issues braiding again, my queen? This time is worse than usual." Nyx's fingers snag the end of my braid, picking it up as if it were something rotten. I swat at him.

"No, Nyx, I didn't. Theo braided my hair for me today," I retort with a smile. Nyx wrinkles his nose in disgust before shaking his head and returning to his food.

"Looks like another thing I'm better at than you, Captain." Theo's face is void of all emotion as he chews his food, open-mouthed and exaggerated. I fight back a laugh at my two favorite men poking jabs at each other.

Nyx breaks my enjoyment with business. "We will be a few less on our quest tonight. Apparently, the festival was one for the ages, and everyone is still drunk from last night." I look around the sparsely filled hall, confirming we may have all over-celebrated in our own ways.

I turn my gaze to Theo and smile, remembering how we worshiped each other last night instead of the gods. He returns my smile, making me think he was having the same memories. "That's fine. It may work out better with a smaller crew. Easier to maneuver and less suspicious," I say. Nyx nods as he takes a bite of sausage.

"You have a quest to go on tonight?" Theo asks, and I realize I never told him I would be gone this evening. I reach across the table and grab his hand.

"I'm sorry. I forgot to mention it earlier. Yes, we do. Hiram and Silas will remain with you here. I'll come find you when I get back." His eyes come to mine, and he gives me a small nod before taking a bite of his remaining eggs.

After breakfast, we spend the rest of the morning together, enjoying each other's company. At lunch, I leave Theo with Hiram and Silas, promising to stop and say goodbye before we leave. I hate having to be away from him, but we need to strategize for tonight.

Nyx and I plan in the council room for a few hours. Deciding simple is better. We aim for a quick in-and-out trip to retrieve the amulet. We don't need Leopold or Arthur finding out we are in their kingdom. They would see it as an invasion and use it as an excuse to attack us.

I leave Nyx and head to see Loma in the apothecary. The herbal scent of the shop provides a calming effect as I walk through the doors. Loma looks up from her notebook with a warm smile.

Reaching under the counter, she places a small violet vial on top. I pinch my lips together as I pick it up. Popping the cork, I drink the liquid like a shot before setting the empty vial back down.

"I figured you'd be needing a lady tincture after last night. This new batch is stronger, so you'll only need to drink a vial once a week," Loma says as our eyes meet. I smile at her and admire her constant work to improve her tinctures. This one will help so many women and be more discreet.

She reaches under the counter again and sets down a vial filled with a thick, black substance. My eyebrows pinch together as I stare at the repulsive-looking liquid.

"I found the antidote to the elixir you asked about. I had to make a few changes to cover all bases since we're not sure who made the original. This is powerful, and only a small amount is needed to lift the veil." Loma clarifies as I lean in for a better look. I pick up the vial. It feels oddly warm in my hands.

"It won't hurt, will it?" I question, concerned about Theo and Junie's safety.

I've spent the last ten years trying to protect them, and I won't risk them now.

She shakes her head. "No, it's safe, I promise. There might be some discomfort as memories are restored, but it should feel more like a headache." I turn the vial in my hand, the liquid coils like my shadows.

"Thank you for this, Loma. I know it wasn't easy to make, and it means so much to me." She walks around the counter and pulls me into her arms. She leans back to cup my face. "Help them see the truth, Lily. They must know the depths of the secrets stolen from them. All will be revealed in due time."

I nod, but a knot forms in my stomach at her words. She has been cryptic lately, and it has my instincts flaring. She's always been forthright with me, and I'm questioning what my healer knows that she isn't telling me.

CHAPTER 37

Back in my chambers, I hide the vial in a lower drawer in my bathing chamber, knowing no one will look there. I take a moment to come to terms with what this all means. The time to awaken Theo's memories is quickly approaching, and I need to come up with a plan.

Readying for the quest, I gather my gear, strapping my dagger to my thigh and pulling on my vest with hidden blades. I grab my hooded cloak before heading out the door.

Evening has settled in within The Keep, barely any noise echoes through the halls. I walk to Theo's cell. It's the safest place for him while I'm gone. While he has been making a home here, I can't risk something happening to him. With two guards always watching him, no one could get to him without going through them first.

Theo is seated in his chair with a good book, completely relaxed. I could get used to seeing him like that, comfortable and content in my home.

He looks up from his book when he hears the clicking of my boots from the hallway. Placing the book down, he stands to greet me with a breath-stealing kiss. I melt into his arms as his hand grips the back of my neck.

A clearing of the throat stops our kiss from progressing further. "I shouldn't be gone long, and I'll come straight here when we get back." I promise, looking up into those gorgeous honey eyes. He pulls me tight to his chest, and I wrap my arms around his waist, soaking in the warmth of his body.

"Please be safe tonight," Theo's words rumble from his chest and into mine. I give him a squeeze before backing out of our hug. I kiss him softly as his hands cup my face. Taking one more look at him, I step away and join Nyx in the hall. I give Hiram and Silas a nod before we step through the back door.

The red-rimmed mist of the portal appears immediately, revealing gray stone. Our boots clank on the cobblestone walkway as we cross the portal into the alley behind the shops. *Our alley*. The pallets and boxes are long gone, but the memory of Theo remains.

We walk down the dimly lit pathway of Lux. Stopping at the end, Nyx peers around the wall, checking for any concerns before pulling back. I draw my hood over my head.

For now, we will act as tradespeople in town looking for a good deal. I serve as Nyx's obedient lady, and the rest of our crew are bodyguards. We take formation, with Nyx leading us and the other three members taking up each side. I walk behind Nyx with my head down and hands laced in front of me.

Villagers walk past, not paying any attention to us. Based on their uneven footsteps, I would bet many of them are drunk as they stumble down the path.

The door of the shop chimes as we enter. The space is lit with several lanterns along each wall, making it too warm. Boots thud on the hardwood floor as a heavy-set man walks out from a back room. He's as short as he is wide. The vile smell of ale and sweat enters the room with him. I fight back a gag.

"What can I help you with?" The man asks our group. Nyx steps forward and scans the room as if looking for something.

"Word across the realm is you're the man to see if one is looking for a trove item to purchase."

The man's jaw clenches as he studies all of us.

"Those items may be out of your price range." He says with self-righteousness. Nyx scoffs at the man while digging in his pockets for a satchel of coins. He drops it on the counter with a loud *bang*. The man eyes it with newfound interest.

He gives us one more glance before saying, "This way," and heading into the back. We follow in a line and enter a space with an assortment of items lining the walls. My shadows stir under my skin as a faint chime rings in my ears.

Nyx gradually closes the distance between him and the man while admiring the collection. Nyx inquires about an item on the shelf, and the man gleefully gives him information about it.

With the man distracted, Nyx grabs him in a headlock and lifts him off the ground, cutting off his air. Nyx's biceps strain against the fabric of his shirt as he hauls the heavy man to a chair placed near the middle of the room. My crew ties the shopkeeper to it before Nyx allows him to breathe again. The man gasps and coughs as air enters his lungs.

I drop my hood and step to the man. "Where's the amulet?" I hover over him, forcing him to look up at me. The color has returned to his face as he scowls. "You're wasting your time. I have no amulet." His raspy voice can't hide his lie.

I check the room as I pace around him. The chime turns into bells ringing, and my shadows beg to be released. I flinch, trying to clear the sound growing in my ears. "We know you have it, so save yourself by telling us. We don't want to hurt you."

He rolls his eyes at me and cranes his neck to Nyx. "Do you always let pathetic little bitches speak for you?" Nyx laughs to himself as he steps toward the man.

I backhand the shopkeeper hard across the face before snatching his chin in my hand. I squeeze his face, digging my nails into his skin, hard enough to draw blood.

"Seeing as how this bitch is their queen, I would say they do," I sneer, inches away from his face. I release tendrils of my shadows to trail over him as his eyes go wide. Darkness dances around him, coiling him like a snake holding its next meal. I release him roughly, allowing my shadows to circle around him, increasing his panic.

"Tell me where it is before I rip you apart." My words are a hiss as he remains frozen with fear. My shadows squeeze the man, emphasizing the threat.

Bells ring, harsh and loud, in my ears, briefly drowning out all other noise. I cover my ears, trying to block the sound, but it doesn't work. My shadows vibrate in response. A sense of urgency washes over me, and my heart races.

"What's wrong?" Nyx is at my side, gripping my elbow as I pull my hands away from my ears.

"You don't hear the bells?" I ask, as dread creeps over me. He shakes his head.

"What bells are you talking about? I don't hear anything," Nyx answers, concern wrinkling his brow.

Bells chime again, louder and more insistent, as if yelling at me to find them. Another tendril of my power skirts along the floor toward a painting along the back wall, seeming to be drawn to it.

The painting is a picturesque scene that looks like a fairytale. Large mushrooms seem to touch the sky as the branches of massive weeping willows dust the top of sparkling ponds. Flowers glow like stars along the rolling landscape lighting up the scene.

Nyx's hand wraps around my arm as I stare at the painting, completely lost in the familiarity of it.

Have I read this in a storybook from our library?

"What is it?" he whispers.

"Help me take it down, Nyx," I say in a rushed breath. My heart thunders as my shadows trail under the purple and gold frame.

"There's something behind it," Nyx says as he releases my arm and goes to one side while I go to the other. Together, we lift the painting off the wall, revealing a small metal box.

"Get away from there!" The man shouts from behind us, and my shadows draw tighter around him to shut him up. I stare at the safe, everything around me fading away. Bells ring cheerfully, as if excited by my find.

I release my shadows into the lock. Metal grinds and snaps as they destroy the locking mechanism, keeping the box closed. The ringing stops as the last piece is severed.

I step to the safe, and Nyx places a hand on my arm, halting me. I look up to see his expression mirroring mine. After a moment of hesitation, he nods and releases my arm. I can barely breathe as I slowly open the door. My stomach drops as the light reveals what's tucked safely inside.

Time freezes as I carefully lift a delicate piece of jewelry out of the safe. The metal is untarnished despite its age. Beautiful, multi-colored gemstones shine brightly as I pull the piece into the lantern light.

Dread bursts through me as I stare down at my necklace. The last thing my mother gave to me before Oren destroyed our lives. The only piece of her I have left in this realm.

Nyx stares at it as I tremble. "All this over a necklace?" He asks apprehensively. I trace the intricate metalwork with my fingertip as tears slip down my cheek.

"It's mine, Nyx. It was a necklace from my mother," I answer, my voice shaky as I fight back the flood of emotions rushing through me. Nyx's breath hitches as his hand finds my back to tether me to the present. But I'm spiraling, and I'm done controlling it.

"Who gave this to you?" I scream, yanking the man out of the chair and bringing him to me. He yells in pain as the ropes that bound him shred against his skin, tearing apart his flesh. My shadows swirl in a vortex around the room, knocking items off the shelves. Bottles shatter and items snap as they slam to the floor.

"Leopold," the man says through sobs. "He gave it to me and told me to keep it safe. To put it somewhere no one would find it."

"And you just took it?" I shout at the man.

"I was doing what my king asked of me. Please let me go," the man pleads as Nyx tugs at my arm.

"Put him down so we can go. We will give him the rowanberry elixir, and he'll forget everything that's happened. They will never know we were here," he says, trying to reason with me, but I'm too far gone.

Darkness overtakes me. The monster lurking deep within the shadows, clawing its way to the surface. I can't hide what I truly am. *I'm the Umbra Brutus. I'm the beast of nightmares. The destroyer of all.*

"You followed a command from your corrupt king without question," I begin to lay out his crimes. He swallows hard. "People died, and you did nothing to stop it. You had the power to stop the unnecessary deaths of the Lux guards, and you did nothing!" I yell, causing my shadows to coil aggressively.

"Queen," Nyx calls as the man's sobs grow louder.

"May Astra deny you at the gates of the Underrealm for your sins," I deliver the final judgment before throwing the man at the wall of his shop. Bones snap as his body slams against the stone.

He hits the ground with a sloppy thud. I grit my teeth, festering in the depths of my anger.

"By the gods!" Nyx chides from my side. "That's not keeping a low profile." My shadows slowly fade back into me, revealing the destroyed shop. I stare at the man's lifeless body as blood leaks from his head.

"He deserved what he got," I say, trying to quell the anger still blazing. Years of carefully controlled rage begging to enact revenge.

Nyx cups my face. His skin feels cool against mine. "I'm not saying he didn't. Kill them all for what they did." He shares my hatred for this wretched king and his kingdom. "But you need to let me be your anchor to keep you here. To keep you from losing yourself."

He presses his forehead to mine. "You were right. There's something going on with your power. We'll need to figure that out, but right now, we need to get home."

"He's taunting me, Nyx. This is all about me. It's a message of what he's capable of and what he has done," I say, fighting the urge to storm into Brightwick and behead the lightning king.

"It could be, but I think there's more to it. This necklace called to you. Why? These are answers we will not get here. We need to go home and figure this out."

I nod as my anger cools to its usual smolder. In its wake, remains the uneasy feeling of no longer being in control of my life. The freedom I've felt for the past three years feels at risk of being taken. *I'll burn this realm to the ground before I let that happen again.*

Raising my hand, I open a portal to the backdoor of The Keep. In a flash, it appears, and we step back into our kingdom at last. My shadows calm as my boots hit the soil of home.

CHAPTER 38

THEO

Rubbing my eyes, I yawn loudly, causing Hiram to look at me over his shoulder. I shake my head, fighting off sleep while I wait for the queen to return. It's strange being the one waiting for their warrior.

Part of me wishes she would have asked me to join them while the other part questions if that's truly what I want—to be an Umbra soldier, forced to remain in the dark.

This time away from the queen has caused my mind to run through the various potential outcomes of our torrid love affair. Do I return to Lux and risk being labeled a traitor? My punishment would be death, but I know she would never allow that to happen.

Do I throw everything away for a woman I've known for a month? If I stay, will I end up being the secret king of Umbra? Our lives forever hidden from the rest of the realm.

My heart pains as I wonder what Lily would think of my betrayal of her and our kingdom. I hope she'd be happy that I finally found someone who pulls my heart like she did. Even if the new threads link me to the queen of our enemy.

The back door slams open as loud footsteps thunder through the hall. Hiram and Silas quickly bow. *My queen has returned.*

I set the book I wasn't reading down on the table and stand, anxiously waiting for her to come into view. Flashbacks of her covered in blood and bruises knot my stomach as the fear of her being injured again races through my mind.

When her curly, red hair pops into my line of sight, I take a deep breath in relief. The scowl on her face says their quest didn't go as planned. The hair on my arm rises as if she's charging the air around all of us.

The queen stops in front of my cell with Nyx on her heels. They speak in harsh whispers before the queen shoves something into his chest, obviously frustrated.

She walks into my cell. Her face twists in agitation as she takes large strides toward me. She slams into my chest, engulfing me in her arms. She squeezes me tightly while burying her face in my chest.

I close my eyes as her rose scent invades my senses, and I wrap my arms around her, holding her close. I look to see Nyx's face mirroring hers. His expression is tight as he grips the item in his hand. Whatever happened on their quest isn't good.

The queen's shadows pour from her, creating a wall in the shape of wings. I trail my eyes along the black mass as it moves and encloses the cell. The tips of what look like raven wings skim the edges of the space as they flutter as if in mid-flight.

I pull her away from my chest to get a better look at her. Those jade-eyes stare at me with rage, burning hot inside. I kiss her softly, trying to balance her anger with calm. She grips my hair tight and deepens our kiss with fury.

We pull apart, breathing heavily as fire sparks in her eyes. Her shadows recoil in a flash, and she opens a portal to her chambers. I have no time to object or hesitate as I'm dragged across the threshold. She yanks me into her for a rough kiss as she fumbles with the buttons of my shirt. An irritated groan comes from her right before she rips my shirt open, buttons scattering across the room.

I grab her wrists and push out of our kiss, holding her away from me. "Are you ok? What happened tonight?" I ask as she struggles in my grip.

"I'm fine." She speaks through gritted teeth. I release her wrists and grab her face, forcing her to stop.

"Answer me honestly or this ends," I refuse to be kept in the dark any longer.

Her eyes narrow as she glares at me, and I add a little pressure to my hold. She huffs in frustration before her body relaxes slightly.

"Yes, I'm ok and not hurt." Her hand grips my arm. "We found out some new information that changes things." I stare down at her as she finally takes a deep breath, and I nod in approval.

"What do you need from me? How can I help?" She digs her nails into my skin, and I growl deep as my cock stiffens.

"I need to be in control," she says, and sparks seem to flash in her eyes. I pull her face to mine as her lips part.

"All you had to do was ask. Use me, my queen. Take what you need from me. I'm yours to do with as you please." A wicked smile spreads across her face, and I know I'm in the best kind of trouble.

She pushes me backward, forcing me closer to the bed. She watches me as she pulls her shirt over her head. I try to walk toward her, but get pulled back by my wrist. Shadows wrap around me like a rope tethered to the bedpost. I turn to find the queen naked before me. My cock hardens at the sight of her perfect body. *Gods, she's the most exquisite thing in all the realm. And she's mine.*

I tug against the shadows as she walks toward me. She flicks her wrist and pulls my arms upward, putting me on display. Her eyes roam over me as she unlaces my trousers, letting them fall to the floor with a *click*.

Her lips find my neck, and I roll my head to the side as sparks dance along my skin. She's intoxicating and knows exactly how to drive me wild. The queen's lips trail over me as she makes her way down my body.

Her fingers hook in my undergarment, and she slides it down my legs, unleashing my throbbing cock. She licks her lips and drops to her knees. I look down at her as my breath quickens in anticipation. *My queen.*

Her soft hand glides over my cock as her eyes rise to meet mine. She stares at me as she strokes me up and down, enjoying her power over me. My eyes roll back as tingles spread across my skin, and I pant at the sensation.

When I drop my gaze back to her, she smiles softly up at me. Her lips part, and her tongue trails along the head of my cock, swirling around it. My breath hitches as she licks along my length, teasing me. She draws back to the tip as her eyes lock with mine. Her lips slide over my cock, taking me into her mouth as her tongue flicks along the way.

I moan and my head falls back as I feel the back of her throat on my tip. She glides her warm, soft mouth back up. Her cheeks hollow as her hand encloses me. Sparks trail up my spine, and my knees shake as she continues to have complete control. She watches every move I make, learning what causes the biggest reaction from me.

The queen's hand and tongue work in tandem to push me closer to my release at a punishing pace. I growl as she takes my cock deep in her throat. Another wave of pleasure ripples through my body as her tongue slowly slides back toward the tip.

My legs tremble, and I grab onto the shadows, trying to steady myself. She arches her back in a whimper, a faint hum vibrating into me. I tug on her shadows again and she shudders around me. I groan as I become dangerously close to the edge of release.

My breathing is ragged as I try to hold off as long as possible. The queen releases me from her mouth, drool running down her chin. Her lips are slick and swollen as she smiles up at me. *Gods, she's absolute perfection.*

"What do you want, Theo?" She asks, slowly stroking me.

"You. I need you. Please." My words are broken through ragged breaths.

"Are you going to be a good boy for me?" She says, teasing the tip of my cock. She drags her tongue along my length before staring up at me.

"Yes," I answer, panting harder as I try to keep control.

"Are you only going to cum when I say you can?" she asks. Her lips brush my tip as she speaks. She takes me deep in her mouth again, and I moan as fire blazes through me.

"Yes, my queen," I answer obediently.

"Such a good boy." She praises my willingness to be controlled, and I know my reward will be glorious.

The shadows drop me to the bed and slide me back until I'm close to the headboard. They pin my arms by my sides, restricting my movement. The queen crawls up my body, taking me into her mouth one more time, before continuing upward.

She hovers above me with her knees on both sides of my head. I arch up, trying to reach her, but her shadows pull me back down. "Do a good job, and I'll give you what you really want," she commands, staring down at me. I nod, ready to return the favor.

The queen sits on my face, and I greedily devour her. I slide my tongue through her wet pussy, causing her to sigh and relax further into me. I circle her clit in quick rotations before sucking on it lightly. She moans and rocks her hips, needing more.

I lick, swirl, and suck until her legs are shaking. "Right there," she says, riding my face hard as she grips the headboard. I increase my pace, focusing on her clit, pushing her closer to the edge. My cock throbs, aching to be inside her, but the desire to have her cum on my face is greater.

The queen's head falls back as she cries out my name. I suck on her clit, drawing out her orgasm as choked moans escape her. As her trembling slows, I slide my tongue through her pussy and curse at how delicious she tastes.

I look up to find her smiling at me. Her chest rises and falls in rapid breaths. She raises off my face, backing down my chest. Her shadows lift my arms above my head, preventing me from touching her. She straddles my hips and rubs her slick pussy along my length. I groan in frustration, my need nearly an inferno blazing inside me.

"Say you're mine, Theo," she orders as she halts her teasing.

"I'm yours, my queen. My shadow goddess," I answer, meaning every word.

"And you'll bow to me and only me," she says, raising up to fist my cock. She strokes me agonizingly slowly. I groan as lightning flares up my spine.

"Until my last breath and in all lifetimes, you'll have me," I answer honestly. I'm completely lost in this woman, and I'll let her destroy me, if that's what it takes.

She smirks as she lines herself up on my tip. Sliding down my length, she takes as much of me as she can. Her breath hitches as she shifts her hips for a better angle.

Her soft pussy wrapped around me nearly sends me over the edge. I clench my hands into fists and take a deep breath. Placing her hands on my hips, she moves up and down, taking a little more each time. She whimpers needily as she buries my cock deep inside. Her pussy flutters, and I moan deep at the feel of her taking me fully.

The queen uses my hips to slide up and down my cock, becoming rougher as she goes. Adjusting her knees for better leverage, she rides me hard and picks up the pace. She trails a hand down her breasts to play with her nipples. I pull against her shadows right as she pinches, causing a strangled whine to escape her parted lips.

She continues down and rubs circles on her clit as she slams down into me. I try pushing my climax back for as long as I can. But my self-control is wavering. I need her to cum for me. I need to feel her fall over that edge because of me.

A strained whimper comes from the queen as she quickens her pace, chasing her orgasm. "Please. Let me cum with you," I beg. "Please, my queen. I need it. I need you."

"Hard, Theo. Now," she orders, and her shadows fall away instantly. I grip one of her hips with one hand while the other grasps her thigh. Lifting her up almost to the tip, I slam her down and thrust into her. Her head falls back with a high-pitched shriek. She circles her clit in fast swirls as her pussy clenches tight around me.

Even my dream couldn't prepare me for how good this is. I could live a thousand years, and I'll never tire of this with her. I'll never be able to get enough of her.

Sparks skirt across my skin with each thrust. Stars dance in my vision as tingles flood my body. Her pussy clamps down on my cock. Her back arches as her orgasm blasts through her. She screams my name as she flies over the edge.

I grab both her hips and thrust relentlessly, chasing after her release. She whimpers as I draw hers out, relishing the feel of her tightening around me. A guttural groan rips through me as I cum harder than I ever have in my life.

A fire erupts throughout my body, blazing hot. Lightning flashes in my vision as I shake with my release.

Exhausted, she falls forward onto my chest. Our bodies slick with sweat. I wrap my arms around her, our breathing rough. After we catch our breaths, she slides off me, and I pull her close to my side. Brushing the hair from her face, I pull her in for a sweet kiss. A soft moan comes from her as our lips touch.

I break our kiss and stare into the stunning green eyes that have changed my life forever. "You have me, my queen. Every piece I can offer to you, I'm yours. I love you." I suck in a breath, shocked by my own words.

She smiles at me while examining my face. "I love you, too. I'm yours through this life and all that comes after." Her lips return to mine with renewed passion, and I smile against them.

I've never heard of a person having more than one Amari in their lifetime, but I know she's mine. She has to be. There's no other explanation for the way my heart hums when she's close. I could find her in the darkness by the cord stretched between us.

I say a prayer to Astra asking for a favor and to bless me with this warrior queen as the one who has my heart forever. I silently ask Lily to give me a sign that she's happy for me. That this is what she wants for me. I've waited so long to find someone who makes my heart sing like she did.

CHAPTER 39

"*Never take it off. It will protect you.*" My mother's words echo in my mind as I run my fingers along the delicate ironwork of the necklace. I always thought they buried it with me, but she must have kept it.

Nyx and I have spent all morning in the council room trying to solve this mystery. We've discussed the potential origins of the necklace and the reasons my mother would have said it was for protection. Neither of us comes up with a definitive answer.

We can't seem to figure out why Leopold claims we stole it either. The only thing we've been able to determine is he's targeting me and my kingdom. *He'll die before I let him step foot on my land.*

We've been debating for hours the different tactics we could take against Leopold. Right now, the best we can do is increase the guards at our entrances and halt any viators from entering. Business will be down for my people, but I'll make it up to them. I need to keep them safe.

"We need to get someone within Leopold's circle if we ever want to figure out what he's planning," Nyx says with a furrowed brow. I close my eyes and squeeze the necklace in my hand. What would my mother tell me to do? *"Make them pay."*

"Do we still have a spy within Brightwick?" I ask, my mother's words ringing in my ears. Nyx answers with a nod. "Good, because we need to get a message inside the castle."

His gray eyes stare into mine as he tilts his head to the side. "What are you thinking?" I take a deep breath and open the drawer of my desk, pulling out a piece of paper and pen.

"I'm going to write a letter to Junie asking her to meet with me in Terra. I have to go there in a few days to speak with Royce regarding the new trade agreement. It would be on neutral ground with fewer concerns about being overheard or watched." My words are flat as I look down at the blank page.

Nyx steps closer to my desk, placing his hands atop it. "Do you think she will help us and go against her father?"

I bring my gaze back to Nyx.

"I think she will once she learns the truth. Once Theo and Junie have their memories back, there's nothing Leopold can hold over me anymore. I'm done hiding, Nyx. For Theo. For me. I'm no longer hiding in the shadows. The time of Asher is behind us." Rage boils deep within me, craving the revenge I so rightly deserve.

His hand squeezes mine. "I'm with you until the very end. Write it and I will portal a messenger to Lux right away," he encourages, before releasing my hand and leaving me alone with my thoughts.

I stare down at the paper, willing the words to come to me. What can I say to convince her to meet with me? What will I say if she does? I take another deep breath to calm myself, and I write.

Princess Juniper,

Theo is safe. He's alive and unharmed, finally living like a scholar. There are many things your father has been lying to you about. Things forced to hide in the dark are ready to see the light. If your curious mind still seeks to know the truth, meet me in the tavern of Terra in three days when the sun is at its peak.

Sincerely,

What lurks in the shadows

Satisfied with my letter, I fold it, placing it in an envelope and sealing it closed. I write Junie's name in script on the front, like I did when we were children. Holding the letter to my chest, I say a prayer to the gods that she will listen and meet with me.

When I leave the council room, Nyx is waiting for me outside the dining hall. I hand over the letter and my adveho ring. He gives me a kiss on the cheek before he's off to handle my errand. I stroke a strand of hair, trying to ground myself. My anxiety twists my insides like a knotted rope.

The scent of fresh apples drifts in the air, and I find Kira leaning against the wall. I clench my jaw at the sight of her, knowing she's stalking me. Taking long strides, I storm over to her. A coy smile curves her lips as I near.

"Where's pretty boy at?" she snarks. My shadows swirl with agitation beneath my skin as I step into her space, towering over her. She stares up at me, disgust twisting her features.

"You're to stay away from Theo, Kira. That's an order," I sneer. Her lips curl back in a snarl, exposing her teeth.

"So protective of a traitorous, pathetic man. I thought you were better than that," she says, taunting me. I grab her by the throat, shoving her hard into the wall. A mocking smile spreads across her face as I apply pressure.

"If you harm even a hair on his head, I'll kill you." I bark at her as my shadows seep from me. They vibrate with annoyance, sending sparks along my skin. Her chestnut eyes don't break from mine as she glares at me. I want to wipe that cocky smile right off her face.

My shadows ripple as my temper rises. Pebbles roll along the stone as my power surges, hot and untethered. My breath quickens as new depths of my well glow brightly in my mind. It calls to me, asking to be opened. *To be set free.*

"My queen?" Hiram's raspy voice sounds from behind us, laced with uncertainty. I drop my hand from Kira's neck and take a step back. My shadows reluctantly recoil, not finished with this fight.

Kira's look is sinister, and I hope she doesn't make me keep my word. A large hand slides along my back as Theo steps beside me. I look up to find him glaring at Kira, jaw flexing. "Go, now," I bark the order at Kira. She pushes off the wall and strides away, never taking her eyes off Theo.

"Is everything ok?" Theo asks, turning to face me. Hiram joins us, confusion furrowing his brows.

"Where were you?" I look him over, noticing a gleam of sweat on his forehead.

"He was with me, my queen. I'm sorry. We wanted to get a run in before the rain started," Hiram answers quickly. Theo rubs the back of my hand as I take a deep breath, trying to calm my racing heart. *He's here with me. He's safe.*

Theo's eyes trail over me, and he pulls me into him. I bury my face in his chest, inhaling his sweaty cedar scent. Tears threaten to fall as he rubs my back, trying to soothe my panic.

"I'm going to take her back to her chambers, Hiram. I think she could use a break." Theo says as he turns us toward my quarters. He holds me tight to him as we make our way down the hall. My arms wrap around his waist, focusing on my breathing. My shadows hum in response to Theo's touch.

Once in my chambers, Theo sets me down in one of the entry chairs and kneels before me. He lifts my chin gently, so my eyes meet his. "What happened with Kira?" I try to lower my gaze, but he pushes back, preventing it. He stares at me, waiting for an answer.

"Today or in general?" I huff my reply. He blinks slowly at me, not amused. "She's been stalking us, so I confronted her. It didn't go well, as you saw." His hands slide from my chin and rest on my legs.

"Why would she be stalking us?" His question sounds genuine, and I know I should have told him about this before now. "She's my ex-lover. We had an on and off again, … um … relationship, for the past few years. I ended it over a year ago when she said she loved me," I answer hesitantly but honestly.

Theo's eyebrows raise as he slowly nods. I take his hands in mine as he seems to process this information. His eyebrows and lips pinch together. "Men and women then?" He asks while narrowing his eyes. I give him a small nod, causing him to let out a sigh.

"Why do I have a feeling you've been with more women than me?" He sits back and crosses his arms on his chest. I laugh and lean back in the chair, unease releasing its firm grasp on me.

"Look at me. Who could resist?" I say, flipping my hair behind my shoulder. Theo shakes his head before rising to stand. He scoops me out of the chair into his muscular arms. I yelp as he hoists me into the air and walks toward my bathing chamber.

I rest my head on his chest, smiling. He sets me down near the tub and turns on the water. The calming scent of lavender fills the air as Theo pours oil into the tub.

"Arms up," He commands, and I comply. Theo pulls my shirt over my head, dropping it to the floor. Goosebumps erupt across my exposed skin. He unlaces my trousers, letting them fall down my legs. His muscular arms wrap around me to unclasp my bra and slide it off my body.

He stares appreciatively at the sight of my breasts. I reach for him, but he grabs my wrist to stop me. "While I would love to worship every inch of your body, right now you need to relax," he says while his eyes trail over me.

I step to him, placing my hands on his chest. "But that's relaxing," I purr the words at him, hoping he'll see my side and give in. His hand leaves my wrist and slides to the back of my neck. He pulls my head back, forcing me to look straight up. "Be a good girl and listen, then maybe later I'll give you what you want."

I groan in frustration as he releases me to pull off my undergarment. Theo helps me climb in the tub and kneels next to me as I slide into the water. "I'm going to grab a few things and a change of clothes. You stay in here until I return," he says.

He tries to stand, but I grab his wrist, sitting up in the tub, panic twisting my stomach. After our fight, I really don't trust Kira to not harm Theo. She's hurt by my love for him, and I wouldn't put it past her to do something foolish to get back at me for rejecting her.

He places a hand over mine, staring down at me. "Hiram's right down the hall. He never goes far. I'll stay with him until I'm back with you." His voice is soothing, and the knot uncoils in my stomach. "But I can also defend myself." He smirks and leans down, kissing me on the forehead.

Theo's call for Hiram and Hiram's response assure me he's being guarded. Sinking into the tub, I allow the water and oil to consume me, easing the tension in my body.

I'm not sure how much time has passed before Theo returns. I can faintly make out Hiram and Theo's low voices as they discuss staying in my chambers for the rest of the evening. The door shuts and the lock clicks into place.

A loud *thud* and clanking echo through the quarters. Theo steps into the bathing chamber, and I look up as he nears. He holds open a big fluffy towel, and I stand for him to wrap it around me. With one arm around my waist and the other under my knees, Theo lifts me from the tub and carries me to bed. He sets me down gently before stepping away to grab something off the entry table.

He returns with a large white shirt. I lift my arms, letting the towel fall to the bed, and he slides one of his shirts over my head. Grabbing the fabric, I take in his cedar scent and smile as it warms my soul.

Theo walks to the head of the bed, pulling back the sheets, and I scoot up to rest my back against the headboard. Theo covers me and walks back to the entry table. When he comes back, he's holding books in one hand and dessert in the other.

"I asked Pyke if you could have your dessert now. I had to force him to let me bring it back to you."

I laugh as he hands me my favorite fruit tart. Giddy with excitement, I wiggle in the bed, staring at the delicious sweet.

"I grabbed a few books from the library for your reading enjoyment as well," he says while placing them on the nightstand. Taking a quick glance at the covers, it looks like he found a few romances and fairytale books I haven't read yet.

Placing his hands on the bed, he leans in to place a soft kiss on my lips. I melt at his tenderness. He pulls away and stands. "I'm going to shower and be right back. Eat up." He plucks a berry off the top, and I swat at him. A smile curls his lips as he pops it into his mouth and walks to the bathing chamber.

As the shower turns on, I settle into the bed and dig into my dessert. The creamy tart and sweet berries melt on my tongue in perfect harmony. I devour the plate long before Theo returns.

He steps out in a pair of loose gray pants and a white shirt. Picking up his own book, he climbs into bed with me, relaxing against the headboard, and I tuck in close to him.

We spend our evening in bed cuddling and reading. Theo brings dinner back to my chambers and we enjoy eating in private for the first time since he arrived.

I want to believe something grand is on the horizon for us. I've dreamed of nights like this—the two of us relaxing in our shared space. For a moment, it's as if Oren didn't rip apart our lives, stealing a decade from us. We would have a life like the Amari in all the stories we used to read.

I feel the dream of a lost, forgotten girl within my grasp, but still just out of reach. A storm, cruel and wicked, stands in the way. I can sense that this is the calm before its violent onslaught. I have to figure out how to stop it before it wipes away everything I hold dear.

CHAPTER 40

The hardwood floor creaks under my boots as two guards lead me to the throne room of Oakwell Castle. King Royce of Terra has requested King Asher's presence to renegotiate our trade agreement. So, here I am. Well, Margo, the snarky liaison of trade for Umbra, but that makes no difference.

The white stone hallway has beautiful bouquets of flowers dotting it, filling the space with their scent. Towering dark wood doors swing open to reveal Royce sitting upon his ornately carved wood throne on the dais. His beige skin is dull with age. Beside him on a smaller throne is Princess Violet. Her glowing tawny skin looks as radiant as ever, reminding me of the dahlias in the fields. Her dark-brown hair falls in soft waves around her face.

As I step to the dais, her rich-brown eyes widen in surprise. I drop into a deep, over-exaggerated bow because it annoys Royce, and I love irritating men who think they hold the power. I return to standing to find him glaring at me.

"Where is King Asher? I specifically asked for him to come. Not you, Margo."

I rock back and forth on my heels, unfazed by his agitation.

"I don't know. Probably off terrifying someone into submission, as shadow kings do. He's a little irritated with you for delaying this agreement, so I thought it would be wise if I came instead. People usually end up dead if they annoy King Asher," I say, arching a brow at the Terra king. Royce shifts uncomfortably in his chair while Violet pinches her lips together, fighting back a smile.

"What seems to be the issue with the agreement? Nothing has changed since the last one," I ask, staring down Royce. He rolls his shoulders back to sit up straight on his throne. He brushes the front of his trousers as if covered in dirt only he can see.

"I want to change the deal," he says with far too much confidence. My eyes dart to Violet, who stares at the white stone floor. She swallows hard, and my stomach sours.

"What kind of change, Sir?"

Violet's eyes slowly rise to mine and fear steals their warmth. She picks at her nails as her lips tremble.

"As a show of goodwill and a strong union between our two kingdoms, I would like to gift my daughter, Violet, to King Asher," he declares with satisfaction. "She'll be an excellent wife, mother, and queen for Umbra." I glare at Royce as a wicked smile spreads across his face. *If only he knew who he was offering his daughter to.*

"My king has no interest in a wife. No matter how absolutely stunning she is." I give Violet a wink. Her cheeks turn pink as she blushes. The fear in her eyes momentarily breaks. Royce clenches his jaw at the exchange. His wrinkles dance as his muscles flex.

"He may not want one now, but soon he'll desire an heir. While she doesn't wield any of Eos's power, Violet can still provide children for King Asher. His legacy will live on with her help," he states, as if her only worth is producing heirs for men.

I scowl in disgust at him. I want to rip his throat out for thinking she's a piece of property for him to auction off. She's smart, funny, gorgeous, and feisty. She'd be a better queen for this kingdom than Royce or his two worthless sons.

"It would be highly controversial if he took your darling princess as his wife. There has never been a child of two divinus before. The results are unknown and risky. You're willing to put your only daughter's life in danger for a veiled attempt at diplomacy?" I say, questioning his motives.

Royce looks over at Violet with disdain, nose wrinkling. My shadows knock on the well, asking to be released. Over the past several years, I've become fond of the sweet princess of Terra. It took one exchange with Violet in their village tavern for her to captivate me. And one more exchange for her to go back to my quarters with me.

"As I said, she holds no power, so there's nothing to be concerned about." Disappointment bleeds from him like an open wound. He's disgusted by her. But he sired her, which means it's his weak power not manifesting. As always, though, a pathetic man is blaming the woman for his shortcomings.

Violet's eyes are soft as she stares at me. I want to run to her and tell her I'll save her. Get her out of this awful place and bring her where she can be herself and not be a bargaining tool for her father. Or I could always kill the stone king and eliminate the issue altogether. My shadows hum at the thought, agreeing.

I take a deep breath to quell my rising thirst for murder. I take a moment to consider Royce's offer and how to get around it. "If I'm going to bring this back to my king, I need to speak privately with the princess. I will need to discuss certain lady things to ensure I know what he's getting into." Violet nips at her lip and narrows her eyes at me. I know the look all too well. She's trying to figure out what I'm getting us into.

"Violet is pure. I've made sure she has remained that way," he states with confidence. My lips pinch into a thin line as I fight back laughter. *If only you knew the things I've done to your daughter.*

"I'm sure you have, Your Highness. However, if I don't ask the questions myself, King Asher will have my head, and this deal will end with my life." He lets out a loud huff and motions for a guard to open a door to the right of the dais.

I drop into another dramatic bow as Violet rises from her throne. She strides toward the quarters, and I trail directly behind. As we walk through the door, I shut it in the guard's face, stopping him from following us in.

Violet stands in the middle of the room with her arms across her chest. I walk to her with a large smirk on my face. "Margo, is it? You said your name was Vivienne?" She pushes on my chest but can't move me.

"Does it really matter what my name is? You don't moan it anyway," I say, taking a step closer to her. She shakes her head as the corner of her lips curl.

"There's the sweet-talking V I know. What are you doing here? Is this why you were always in town every autumn?" Her doe-like brown eyes stare up at me, making me smile. I tuck a loose strand of hair behind her ear, and her cheeks turn the sweetest shade of pink.

"Yes. I've been working with King Asher for many years. I don't often discuss my job in bed," I tease. She wraps her arms around me in a tight hug, and I hold her close. We may have only seen each other once a year, but it doesn't change the depth of our friendship.

I release her and hold her hands in mine. She looks up at me with concern darkening her eyes. "Is he as bad as they say he is?" her voice wavers.

I shake my head, rubbing the back of her hand with my thumb. "He's not. Do you even want to marry King Asher?" I ask.

"No, but I don't really have a choice. It's what my father wants and what's best for Terra," she says, breaking eye contact. I lift her chin softly and see all the pain her father has caused her over the years. *I'll make him pay for that later.*

"You have a choice with us. King Asher won't make you do anything you don't want. Besides, you don't like men, Violet." I pop her on the nose, causing her to swat me away.

"I've been with men before. I can do it again if I must," she says with fragile confidence.

"You've been with two men, and you hated it." She pokes me in the chest.

"I'll have you know that—" I cut her off because I already know her answer. "Threesomes don't count if you don't let the man ever touch you." Her words get caught in her throat and she laughs.

"Plus, you'll be there, so I know I'll be fine," she says, looking at me with so much trust it breaks my heart.

"Why is your father pushing so hard for you to marry King Asher?" I ask, completely confused by the sudden offer of Violet to me. She looks around before leaning in close.

"There's a lot of unrest in Lux. My father said the viators are not returning to their jobs. They're disappearing. We've had a few who've left and not returned. No one knows where they are going," she whispers.

My shadows whirl inside their well at my core. I hadn't heard about anyone vanishing and wonder what is happening to them. "V, I can't explain it, but something is coming. I can feel it in my soul," she says, pain lacing her words.

"I know. I can feel it too. My mother always told me that's the gods talking directly to you. They're warning us, and I think we better start listening," I say, trying to hide any unease from my voice. She nods at me and takes a deep breath.

The sun beams through the high window, and I know I need to head to meet Junie.

"I need to be leaving. You're welcome anytime in Umbra, Violet. Just ask for the liaison at the gate, and they will come find me. I would love to show you what the kingdom is really like," I say, meaning it. I'm ready to show all of Omnia what Umbra truly is. No more hiding in the shadows.

I give her a soft kiss on the cheek, and she squeezes my arm in response. She smiles brightly up at me, and memories of our time together burst in my mind. I give the princess a proper bow before spinning on my heels and leaving the room.

I return to King Royce and tell him that King Asher will be in touch regarding his proposal and hurry off the castle grounds toward the white stone village of Terra.

Oakwell sits atop one of the vast rolling hills, providing a stunning view of the kingdom. Wildflowers in vibrant colors so bright they look more like a painting than real-life. The floral scent is sweet in the air as it mixes with the woodsy smell of the moss roofs.

I secure my hood over my head as I trek through the village heading to the tavern. I watch my surroundings as I go, looking for my princess. Ducking into the alley beside the tavern, I lean against the wall, half-bathed in darkness.

I take the antidote vial out of my pocket and roll it in my palms as I wait for Junie. My heart and mind race as I try to figure out what to say to her.

Light wisps of blonde hair dance in the corner of my vision as Junie steps into the square. She dismisses a dark-haired guard, who watches her as she stomps toward the tavern. Her long hair floats behind her like the seeds of a dandelion caught in the wind. She fists her skirt, bringing it up for an easier time walking.

Placing the vial back in my pocket, I push off the wall and drop my hood. I take a deep breath to calm my racing heart. Junie scowls hard at me as she enters the alley.

She steps into the darkness with me and smacks me across the face. I place my hand on my cheek and stare at her, utterly shocked. "How dare you use my dead friend to manipulate me! You're a vile person," she yells at me. I drop my hand from my face.

"A weak hit, but we can work on it. What are you talking about, Junie? Theo isn't dead." She raises her hand, and I snatch her wrist before it can reach my face.

"It's Princess Juniper!" she roars. "Why are you claiming you have Theo, and that my father is lying to me? Who do you think you are spreading such lies?" Lightning dances along her fingers as her anger rises. My shadows respond, swirling up her arm and twisting with the small sparks. I expect burning heat but find a friendly warmth welcoming the touch.

Junie stares, horrified, and jerks her wrist from my grasp. My shadows stretch with her before recoiling back. "Who are you?" she asks, voice trembling.

"A shadow looking for the light," I answer. I step toward her, making her flinch, and I bite back the pain it causes me. "You came here because a part of you wonders if I'm telling the truth. If you're willing to find out, let's have a drink, princess."

I gesture to the tavern and pray to the gods she takes me up on my offer. She chews her bottom lip as she stares at the ground. Without looking up, she leaves our shadowed spot. I expect her to keep walking, heading back to Lux, but she walks to the front door of the tavern.

Junie yanks it open, and I hurry after her into the overly warm space. Noise fills the packed tavern. The perfect scenario I was hoping for. Villagers fill almost every seat except for one corner table at the very back.

I grab Junie's arm to get her attention, and she pulls out of my touch. I resign to pointing at the open spot and striding toward it. Junie follows close behind. She pulls her cloak tight around her as her eyes dart around the tavern.

I wave at a few familiar villagers as I make my way to the back table and slide into the seat. Junie hesitantly sits next to me. "You're safe, princess. No one will harm you here," I say, trying to comfort her. By the glare she gives me, it doesn't work.

"Vivienne, long time no see," Ruth, the barmaid, says stepping to our table. She's worked here for most of her life and knows everything there is to know about everyone. A valuable resource for someone like me.

"I've been busy," I say with a shrug, leaning back in my seat. Her eyes drag to Junie, who fidgets nervously.

"I can see that. You definitely have a type, V," she says, smirking. "Some wine, like always?" I give her a nod and she leaves.

"So, Vivienne, what truth do you want to tell me?" Junie asks, frustration clear in her tone. I hate the sound of my alias on her tongue.

"Don't you call me that," I grimace. Junie stares at me wide-eyed.

"But that's what the barmaid called you," she stammers.

"That's not my name," I say, watching as her eyebrows pinch in confusion. "I'm a girl with no name trying to get it back. That's why you're here, princess."

"I don't know you. How am I supposed to help you with that?" she says with a huff. I take a moment, debating on where to start. Thankfully, Ruth returns with our wine, and I take a few long pulls, delaying further.

When I put down the mug, Junie is studying me. Her eyes fixate on my hair as her brows pinch tight together. I want to reach out and tell her everything, but I know that will only cause her to run away.

"I think we can help each other. But first we need to ensure there are no lies between us," I say, pulling the vial out of my pocket and setting it on the table. The black liquid swirls in similar agitated spirals as my shadows.

Junie scrunches her nose, as if catching a whiff of something unpleasant from the vial. "What is that?"

"It's a truth elixir. To move forward, we must unravel the lies. This is how we do that," I say, opening the vial. "The only side effect is a mild headache which should pass quickly." I place a few drops of the thick black liquid on the tip of my finger. It's oddly warm against my skin.

I show Junie the dots before sticking out my tongue and wiping my finger across it. I shudder as the rough metallic tone of the elixir bites at my taste buds. Picking up my mug of wine, I down the rest of it to get rid of the feel in my mouth.

Sliding the vial over to Junie, I wait anxiously to see if she's going to go through with it or if her courage has run dry. She closes her eyes, taking a deep breath. "For Theo," she whispers to herself.

I can barely breathe as she matches my movement and smears the black liquid on her tongue. The taste gets her too, and she drinks her wine, trying to douse it.

She sets her mug down and wipes her hands on her thighs under the table. I stare at her, frozen by my nerves and her bravery. She doesn't know who I am, yet she's willing to take a chance to get answers about her friend.

Gods, I hope this works.

Junie puts her elbows on the table, rubbing at her head. She winces in pain as the elixir clears the veil placed over her memories. I touch her arm and she jerks away, offended by my attempt to comfort her. I try not to let it sting, but it does. As far as she knows, we're strangers. Not long-lost best friends.

"How are you doing this?" She stares at me with a pained expression.

"Doing what, Junie?" I ask as her nostrils flare.

"Who told you about her?" She hisses at me. I narrow my eyes at her, trying to figure out what she's talking about.

Loma missed something. This isn't working.

Junie breathes raggedly as her face reddens with anger.

"Juju," I say hesitantly.

"Who told you about her?" She yells, slamming her hands on the table as she stands. I've never seen Junie this mad before, and my heart breaks because I did this to her. But icy rage freezes that emotion. *They did this to us.*

Looking around the tavern, several people have stopped their conversations to gawk at the princess having an outburst. "I'd suggest you sit down, Juniper. Unless you want this little chat to get back to your father because you're making a scene, and people around here like to talk."

Her gaze rises to see villagers staring, and she reluctantly sits. Her jaw flexes as she clenches her teeth.

"What hallucination elixir did you give me?" she asks. Her anger is palpable, and faint sparks of lightning dance along her fingertips. My shadows coil in response but want to soothe instead of harm.

"I gave you a truth elixir, Juniper. All the lies you've been told for the last decade are now gone. Your father stole your memories, and I gave them back so you could finally see me," I say, locking eyes with her as she glares right back.

"It's really me, Junie. It's Lily. I didn't die," I whisper, trying to break through her anger.

"You're a vile mortal. Lily's dead. There's no amount of elixir that's going to convince me you are her. You can wear her face, but you're not her," she says, pushing away from the table to stand. I need her to stay, but how?

"Do you remember the night before I died? We were in your quarters, and you asked me what I wanted for my birthday. I gave you the usual answer of wanting to spend time with my two best friends." I smile up at her as the memories spread warmth through me. It feels like a different life, that version of me. And in so many ways, it is.

"You didn't take that as an answer, though. I then told you that what I really wanted was to see if Theo felt the same way I did. If he could feel the constant pulling toward one another. Which is why you embarrassed me by the river the next day by asking him. Subtlety has never been your strong suit," I laugh as she lowers back to her seat. Her face pales as she breathes heavily.

"But then Theo kissed me for the first time, and it was one of the best moments of my life. I never got the chance to thank you for that," I say, fighting the urge to grab her hand and squeeze it. Her bright-blue eyes shine with unshed tears.

"How do you know that? I never told anyone about ..." her voice trails off as she stares at me.

"Because it's really me, Junie. Are you ready to hear the truth about what happened?" I ask, hoping she is. She gives me the slightest nod, and I take a deep breath.

I tell Junie everything from the past ten years but spare her some of the gruesome details. From her shifting expression, she understands without me needing to expand further. Which is what's best for both of us. She doesn't need to know all the horrors I went through, and I don't need to retell them. We have time now, though. We lost so much time because two power-hungry kings stole it from us.

"You've been alive this whole time," Junie says, anger coursing through her tone. "You let us suffer and grieve for you while you watched from the shadows. Theo punished himself every day because he thought he failed you." Words laced with venom spew from her, causing my frustration to grow with their bite.

"You don't think I wanted to tell you? I wanted my life back. I wanted to be free from the shackles that I wore every day—to step out of the shadows and be me again. But you barely believe me now with the antidote, imagine what would have happened if I told you without it," I sneer, clenching my fist hard enough for my nails to nip my palm.

She leans back in her chair, shoulders sagging with my harsh words. "Why now then? Why even tell us at all?"

"I've been searching for an antidote since Oren died three years ago. Since I became queen and death liberated me from his control. But I couldn't find it on my own," I answer, letting my sorrow rise to the surface. Junie closes her eyes as if it's all too much to bear.

"And this," I say, pulling my necklace out of my shirt. Junie opens her eyes, and they immediately widen in surprise. She reaches forward, trying to grab it.

"That was supposed to be buried with Eleanor," she snaps with a furrowed brow. Her eyes slowly raise to mine. "She ..."

"I know, Junie. I was there. But so was your father," I say, causing her to flinch.

"No," she answers, shaking her head. "He wouldn't."

"He did. Leopold helped Oren orchestrate everything. From me being kidnapped to them murdering my mother in front of me. That's why I know finding this is a message, a threat, to me and my kingdom." I fight to keep my tone down, but a few patrons still glance my way.

"How do you know that? He could be trying to get it back to you," she says, arching an eyebrow.

"Then why did he hide it in a trove safe inside Lux and tell everyone in the realm we took it?" I retort, narrowing my eyes at her.

"That's the amulet?" she asks. I give her a curt nod. "And you found it in our trade post." Another nod from me. Her breath quickens, and she swallows hard. "Did you kill that man? The shopkeeper?"

"Yes," I reply through gritted teeth. Her breath hitches as she stares at me, appalled by my actions.

"You murdered him. Why?" she retorts.

"Because he sat by and watched his king send guard after guard to my land to die. He allowed innocent people to lose their lives because he refused to ask questions. He chose money and power over the lives of his people." I pause to compose myself.

"If he spoke up, I wouldn't have needed to bury your men in my soil. He had their blood on his hands and deserved punishment for it." My shadows vibrate beneath my skin at the need for revenge. *Make them pay.*

"Thank you." Junie's soft voice breaks my downward spiral. "Since you know our traditions, I assume you gave them a proper burial?" She says with a soft knowing smile. A simple gesture of her gratitude that cracks something inside me.

"One Astra could be proud of," I answer, and she gives me a nod.

We sit in awkward silence for a moment, neither of us knowing what to say next. Too many years have passed between us. I had hoped we could start anew, but my heart breaks thinking we may never get that chance.

"Theo's alive and safe, though? He's happy?" she asks. Her features soften as she brings her gaze back to me. I can't stop the smile that curls my lips remembering the past month spent with Theo in my kingdom.

"Then who did we bury?" She asks softly, and my eyebrows raise. "My father told me King Asher killed him and left his mutilated body at his door. He didn't want me to see what was done to Theo, so I never got to say goodbye. But he's not dead?"

Tears stream down her face as she looks at me for confirmation. "He's not, Junie. He's with me, enjoying days of endless reading." I give her a smile as her bottom lip trembles. "I'd never let anything happen to him. I'd destroy this realm for Theo, Juju. And for you," I answer, meaning every word. She closes her eyes, taking in everything.

"I don't know how to feel. This is all so confusing. I'm not mad at you. I'm hurt. And scared." She looks how I feel, broken and raw.

"All I know is that I'm so angry with my father. He's hurt so many people I love for his own sick games." Her anger returns, but thankfully, this time she doesn't direct it at me. "He needs to be stopped. I'll help you. I'll figure out whatever he's planning so we can end this."

"Figuring things out together, just like when we were children," I smirk at how normal it all feels.

"Lils and Juju against the realm, right?" she says with her own smile. Air lodges in my throat and my heart stops at the use of my nickname. I freeze, my mind unable to process the words.

"Lily, are you ok? I'm sorry. Did I say something wrong?" Junie touches my arm, lightly. My shadows rush under my skin to her, seeming to remember her fondly.

I gasp as the sound of my real name echoes in my ears. "I'm not used to hearing my name." Her eyebrows pinch together in confusion. "Oren took away my name when he stole me. I rarely hear it. Honestly, I never thought I'd hear you say it again in this lifetime."

Junie gives my arm a gentle squeeze. I place my hand atop hers, expecting her to pull away, but she doesn't. Small tendrils of shadows leak from my hand as flashes of lightning spark from Junie's. Our powers mix and twirl together. The black of mine looks like specks of dust floating among the bright light of hers.

"It really is you," Junie's voice cracks as I drag my gaze from our hands. Tears roll down her cheeks as she stares at me. My heart shatters as she chokes back a sob.

"I'm sorry, Junie," I say, but she shakes her head.

"You're alive," she says, placing her hand on my cheek. I lean into her touch. Little taps of lightning pepper my face as if her power is showering me with kisses.

Junie grabs my shoulder and pulls me hard into a hug. Her delicate frame feels fragile in my arms, and I fear I might break her. Small sobs shudder through her body as we hold each other.

When we release one another, we sit and talk like two old friends for several long moments. Enjoying the time we've got back and not speaking more about what is coming.

By the time we exit the tavern, the crowd has thinned, and the sun tracks closer to the horizon. The white stone of the buildings reflects the golden light in mesmerizing waves. The village seems to glow as the afternoon fades into evening.

I pull my hood over my hair out of habit. Junie waves at the dark-haired guard from earlier, stopping his approach. A faint, deep hum sounds in my ear as if someone has plucked the lowest cord on an instrument. As quickly as it's come, it's gone.

"Theo never stopped loving you, Lily." Junie faces me. Her lips pinched tight together, but tears fill her eyes again. "Even believing you were dead didn't stop him. I think a part of him must have known you weren't really gone, and that's why he never moved on. He was waiting for you.

The threads finally led him home. Back to his Amari." A tear slides down Junie's cheek, and I wipe it away with my thumb.

"We're all together again, Juju. No matter what, we'll find one another," I say, pulling her into one last hug.

"If I find out anything, I'll send word to Umbra," Junie whispers in my ear before releasing me.

She walks to her waiting guard and disappears. I make my way over the rolling hills and wildflowers to find a secluded spot. Time to return home and figure out how to tell Theo everything.

While opening a portal, I ask the fates and the gods again to let this be my forever. To please let my punishment end and allow me this happily ever after. As if in answer, the end bringer story floods my mind. Dread washes over me as I step through the opening. If I lose Theo again, I fear I may become the thing the gods foretold.

CHAPTER 41

Nyx paces nervously in my chambers as I finish getting ready for the evening. He might wear a hole in my floor if he doesn't stop soon. I've delayed meeting with Theo all day. I selfishly want to believe if I don't tell him the truth, we can go about our lives in blissful happiness. But I know that isn't fair.

"Do you want me to come with you? We can explain it together. If needed, I can hold him down, and we can force the elixir down his throat," Nyx says, leaning on the door frame of my bathing chamber.

I laugh, turning my chair to face him. His hands run through his thick black hair, disheveling it. The anxiety seems to get the better of both of us tonight.

"While I love the show of support, I think it will be best if I talk to him alone. Just wait for me inside in case things don't go as planned." He pushes off the door, striding over to me. Kneeling, he cups my face as his familiar leather scent calms my racing heart.

"He has to believe you. If you have the connection you say you do, he'll know," Nyx whispers while gently running a thumb along my cheek. I stare into his soft, gray eyes and give a small nod. I have no words as knots twist my stomach.

He stands, releasing my face and offering me a hand to rise. I take one more look at myself before leaving my chambers with Nyx by my side. He slides his hand into mine as we walk down the quiet hallway to Theo's cell. My heart thunders in my chest with each step closer.

Down the hall from the cell, Nyx pulls me into a hug, and I take a deep breath, trying to ease my anxiety. It doesn't help. Waves of panic crash through my body, causing my shadows to swirl. My mind plays the worst-case outcomes in a loop.

Nyx kisses my forehead before releasing me, and I walk the remaining distance to Theo alone. He sits in his chair, hunched forward with his elbows braced on his knees, clearly waiting for my arrival. As soon as I cross the iron bars, Theo stands, taking long strides to meet me at the door.

He scans my face, eyebrows drawn tight together. "What's wrong?" he asks, grabbing my hip and pulling me close. I rise onto my toes and cup his face, kissing him softly. His body pulsates with tension under my touch. For a fleeting moment, I contemplate not telling him again. I break the kiss, reminding myself he should be able to choose what happens next.

"Walk with me," I say with a forced smile. I turn to head out the front entrance, but his grip tightens around my waist. His honey eyes pierce through me when I look back.

"I'm ok. New information that changes things has come to light," I say, rubbing a hand over his arm. Taking every opportunity to touch him as if it's my last. "Let's go talk."

Theo gives a small nod before loosening his grip. His hand finds mine as we walk to the bridge over the pool in silence and take a seat.

"What's going on? I'm worried," Theo rubs his chest, "I think I've been feeling you all day. Here." He takes my hand and puts it to his heart. My shadows caress his chest and my own heart flutters.

"What's got you so on edge?" His voice is soft and pleading.

I close my eyes and take a deep breath. *He's my Amari. If Junie believed me, he surely will.* The pep talk doesn't stop the little voice in my head, reminding me that the beast never gets the prince.

"We've known for a while that Leopold has been planning some sort of attack on Umbra. It's why he claimed we stole an amulet," I start, confirming what he already knows. He nods, giving my hand a small squeeze of encouragement. But no amount will quell the dread of having to tell him what Junie told me at the tavern.

"He sent all his men to a sure death and blamed Umbra for their demise. It seems that he went a step further and accused Asher of torturing and murdering you before dumping your body at the king's doorstep," I reveal.

"What? Obviously, I'm not dead. That's an easy fix, my queen. We can go to Lux, prove he lied, and put an end to all of this once and for all," he says, kissing my knuckles. The gesture nearly rips me in two.

"Theo, you can't go back to Lux. There was a kingdom-wide funeral to honor your sacrifice. He's using you as a martyr to come after us. Everyone thinks you're dead. If you step foot in Lux, you will be a threat to Leopold's honor and he will execute you for it," I say, my panic increasing. The thought of Leopold getting his hands on Theo makes my shadows claw against my skin.

Theo's eyes race back and forth, a clear sign his beautiful mind is working through different strategies. "What if we prove two lies at once? Then it may be too big of a mess for the king to deny. What if we found the amulet and used that as barter? Return something lost for my life to be restored in Lux. I think that could work," he says with a hopeful spark in his eyes.

"We already found the amulet, Theo." A sly smile spreads across his face as if his plan is all coming together.

"Where was it?"

"Hidden inside a trove safe in the trade post of Lux," I answer as my stomach twists into a tight knot. Theo's head falls, and he rubs his temples.

"Of course it was. Safely tucked away from sight. It's some worthless gemstone, isn't it?" He huffs a laugh as his eyes lift back to me. I run a finger along the smooth edge of my necklace, willing it to calm my racing heart. Theo's gaze narrows on it instantly.

"Where did you get that?" his voice and fingers tremble as he reaches for my neck. He strokes the multi-colored gemstone delicately with his thumb. "This was Lily's. It was buried with her mother."

"This is the amulet Leopold said we stole. It's a message to me. A reminder that he knows who and what I am," I say, grabbing Theo's hand and holding it in my lap. His lips part in a shaky breath.

"How does he know about you? I thought no one knew you existed," he asks, uncertainty in his voice.

"He was Oren's partner in everything. He helped to get me here and break me. Part of my deal is with him."

He looks like he is trying to process the new information, but it isn't quite reaching him.

"Even if that's the case, what does Lily's necklace have to do with you? I don't understand."

"Do you ever wonder why you and Junie have a hard time remembering details about Lily?" I ask as gently as I can.

"Grief. It's why my memories of my mother are so faded, too. The pain is so great my mind refuses to allow those thoughts to be clear," he answers matter-of-factly. *His mother?*

I shake my head gently.

"No, Theo. It's not grief. Leopold gave you both an elixir to make you forget. He stole your memories because he couldn't risk you knowing me," I say, my voice cracking. Theo slides his hand from mine, shaking his head.

He will feel the threads. He trusts me.

"You know how you said you've felt me? Here?" I touch his chest and feel his heart skip a beat as the threads tighten, "That's because the threads to your Amari never break. They grow tight, but they never break."

He pulls back and looks at me. Stunned into silence.

"The fates didn't give you a new Amari. They gave you back the one you thought you had lost. The same threads that linked us then are the ones you feel now." I continue cautiously, waiting for the look of realization to enter his eyes, but it doesn't.

I take a deep breath. *It's time. Please gods.*

"It's me, Theo. I'm Lily. I didn't die. What you saw was Oren stabbing me with a trove blade to make it look like he killed me. But he took me and made me into his monster." My chest tightens as he moves further away from me.

I watch him intently. *Say something.*

"No. Lily is dead. Why are you doing this?" He groans and leans forward to brace his elbows on his knees and rubs small circles on his temples.

"I'm not dead. Oren and Leopold needed you to believe I was, so no one would come looking for me. But it's me. I'm alive, Theo." I reach toward his chest again, and he jerks to a stand.

"No! Stop this right now. You're not her. Lily is dead. I felt her die. A part of me went with her that day," he yells at me, fist clenched tight at his side.

I reach out to take his hand, but he grabs my wrist, stopping me. His rough hands nip at my skin as he shoves me away, and I grit my teeth at the bite of pain.

"How did you do this? Why did you make me fall in love with you? Did you do it to somehow use Lily against me? I'm so stupid! First, you're a secret queen with no name, then you're King Asher, and now you're Lily? Who are you, really?" He snarls, lip curling up to show a hint of teeth. "Was this the plan the whole time? Play games with my mind until I bent to your will?" He shouts.

"No! The only plan is to get you back. I wanted to open your eyes, and it worked. Now I need that damned veil that blocks your memories of me to be gone too. I was waiting until I could make it happen, and now I can." I pull out the vial of black liquid from my pocket, showing it to him. "This antidote will help restore your memories. It worked for Junie, and it will work for you. Take it so you can see me, Theo. You'll see I'm not lying to you."

He shakes his head adamantly, stepping further away. "None of this was real. I told myself not to fall for it, but I did anyway. You tricked me! What other elixirs have you been giving me to make me like clay in your hands? Easier to manipulate and deceive?" His lips pinch tight as his nostrils flare in anger.

"I don't lie to the ones I love. I protect them. Even if that means hiding in the shadows for ten years and watching from afar. I have done everything in my power to keep you safe until we can be together again. Just take the antidote. Please," I beg him to listen to me.

"I don't even know you!" He shouts back, body shaking with fury. Each of his denials fractures pieces of my heart, one by one.

"I'm the girl you kissed by the river and made believe that fairytales were real. The girl you tried sacrificing yourself for, so she didn't have to die when the nobu attacked. But my shadows wouldn't let that happen." As if summoned, darkness swirls around us just like the day at the river, shielding us from everything.

Theo's gaze tracks the black vortex of shadows. His breath hitches at the sight. I keep going, "Then three months ago, you saved me from Jonathan when he thought he could put his hands on me at The Blue Stag. Those threads pulling you toward a barmaid who needed a knight in shining armor."

"How do you know about the barmaid? I never told you about that," he asks, his voice unsteady as fury flares through him.

"Because it was me. The veil kept you from recognizing me, but your heart and soul knew who I was. That I was yours," I answer. My voice is a plea for him to listen. He shakes his head and tries to step around me, but I cut him off.

Cupping his face, I force him to look at me. His honey eyes are cold, all warmth stolen from them. "I need you to see me, Theo. We don't have time for you to fight this. Our people need us. War is coming and we must protect them. Take the damn antidote, please."

Theo grabs my arms and shoves me away. I stumble back a few steps before gaining my footing.

"Don't touch me. This isn't my kingdom or my people. I have no duty to protect any of it," he yells, as I step back toward him. He bumps into the wall of shadows, causing a harsh jolt to rush down my spine. I grimace as the fiery pain shoots through me. I take a deep breath to calm my racing heart.

"You know that's not true. Why else would you have survived the haunted forest? The hare bowed to you because she knows you're destined to be king of Umbra. Ruling the kingdom beside me," I retort, tilting my head to the side. My heart is on the verge of complete undoing from his blatant denial of the life we are supposed to have.

He takes a step toward me, fury a blaze ripping through him. "I'm not tied to this gods-forsaken kingdom or to you. I'll never be king," he hisses as he storms past me toward the wall of shadows.

An icy numbness washes over me as Theo drives the last nail through my splintered heart. This is it. Nothing I say or do is going to get him to believe me. Breath lodges in my throat as I force down the sobs threatening to tear from me.

"I sacrificed my life for you, Theo. I survived starvation and torture in the hopes that one day we could be together again," I say weakly, turning to face him. My body doesn't feel like my own. Loose limbs move of their own accord. "I allowed them to turn me into a monster because it meant they couldn't hurt you. My scars are a testament to all the things I've done to keep you safe. And you won't even listen to me."

"I'm through falling for your lies. You did nothing for me. I don't know who you are, but I know you're not my Lily. You can't sweet-talk your way into my memories." He doesn't bother turning around to speak to me.

A deep growl comes from Theo as he glares at the shadows blocking his path. "I'm getting out of here. Move those damn shadows or they'll have to kill me!" He shouts, and they answer, recoiling back to me. His shoulders rise and fall with rapid breaths as he storms forward.

I chase after him into the tunnel walkway, back into The Keep. "If you return to Lux, Leopold will kill you," I yell at his back, and he pauses his retreat. "If you leave my kingdom, I can't protect you anymore. No matter how much I love you, I don't think we will get another chance," my voice cracks as the control of my emotions breaks.

"I'll take my chances. I think my odds in Lux are better than if I stay here." He resumes stomping toward the front door.

"At least sleep on it, Theo. If you want to know the truth in the morning, the antidote will be with Loma in the apothecary. If you decide to leave, I won't stop you, and I won't come after you. You'll be on your own." He halts, grasping the door handle.

Devastation consumes me, as I know he won't believe me. I've lost him, and I have no way of ever getting him back. "I should have let Oren kill me all those years ago. At least death would have been more merciful and painless than this right now. Your denial of what we are hurts more than anything Oren ever did to me." I can't hold back the tears anymore. They fall like rain down my cheeks.

A breath later, the door of The Keep opens and slams shut. Theo's gone, likely forever. My heart shatters into a million pieces as I try to will myself to walk back inside. I'm a shell of a mortal as parts of my soul chip away with each step. A deep heaviness settles in my stomach knowing I'll never be whole again.

As the door clicks, light footsteps scramble behind me as Kira pops out from an alcove in the hallway, tears stream down her face.

"Oh, my gods. I'm so sorry. I didn't know he was your Amari. I can't take it back. I'm so sorry," her words are broken and make no sense. They barely register as my realm crumbles.

"Not now, Kira," is all I can say as I choke back sobs.

"I thought he stole you from me. I never thought he could be your Amari. I can't stop it now. It's too late," she wails as she steps toward me.

"Not now, Kira! Go away!" I scream as the dam inside me breaks. My shadows burst from me like large black raven wings stretching from my sides, waving as if in mid-flight. Ash consumes my mouth as my emotions and power become untethered.

My knees and hands slam into the floor. The ground shakes with the impact. The well at my core transforms into a bottomless pit of darkness. Black seeps into my vision, stealing all color and light. And I welcome it. The thunderous beating of my heart echoes in my ears as I allow the dark to pull me down with it.

The warm scent of leather invades my senses as large hands pull at me, lifting me to sit back. "What's going on?" Nyx's voice cuts through the pounding in my ears. I can't see him through the dark haze clouding my eyes. A ragged gasp comes from Nyx as his fingers dig into my arms.

"Lily?" His voice wavers. The darkness invading my mind pulsates, flashing in harsh hues, too quick for me to see clearly. Nyx cups my face, hands trembling.

"Whatever happened, we can fix it. I need you to come back to me. Please, Lily." His voice cracks as he presses his forehead to mine. I fight the hold my power has on me, but the talons dig deeper.

I grapple at Nyx's chest, trying to anchor myself to the present. I yank him hard into me, burying my face in the crook of his neck. His muscular arms wrap tightly around me, and I inhale his musky smoke scent.

With all my mental strength, I push back against my power trying to take full control and drag me into the darkness, never to be seen again. I force the lid over my well. A faint hiss, as if water douses the embers of a fire, echoes in my mind as the seal falls into place.

I sag in Nyx's arms as sobs rip through me. He squeezes me hard, his breathing as ragged as mine. He shifts me, sliding an arm under my legs and lifts me into the air.

Nyx walks me back to my chambers, tucked firmly against his chest. He sets me down on the edge of my bed. He tilts my face up toward him, but I can barely see him through my tears.

He seems to sigh in relief when he looks at me. "What happened?" Nyx asks, his voice gentle.

"He refused to believe me. He won't take the antidote." A choked sob escapes as I try to speak. Nyx closes his eyes, taking a deep breath.

"In the hallway, Lily. Your eyes were black. It felt like you were being pulled away from me. The cord was tight. Is that what you meant by your power feeling different lately?" He asks as his eyes scan me, looking for anything out of place.

"Maybe. I'm not sure. My power was pulling me in, wanting full control. It was different, like something ancient was crawling out of my well. Clawing its way through my mind and not letting go," I answer, confused by all of it myself.

Nyx's hand falls from my chin, and he abruptly turns away. I snatch his wrist, pulling him back. "Where are you going?"

"Everything starts and stops with Theo. I think it's time the captain and I have a talk," he says with a huff.

"No. Please stay. I need you. I don't want to be alone right now, Nyx," I plead, tugging him back to me. He huffs before taking a seat beside me and drawing me close to his side. Tension ripples through him, causing his muscles to twitch.

"What do you want to do now?" he asks, looking down at me. Reaching into my pocket, I pull out the antidote and hand it over to him.

"There's nothing we can do. He's made his choice. Please take this to Loma in the morning. I don't think I can face her right now." He nods in agreement.

I pull out from his side and crawl up my bed, tucking under the covers. Theo's cedar scent welcomes me as I lie down and soak it in one last time. I pat the bed behind me for Nyx to come lie with me.

He joins me, wrapping an arm around me. He places a soft kiss on the back of my head. "I'll fix this, Lily. I'll figure this out. I promise." The only response I can give is a small nod, as sobs overtake me, and I cry myself to sleep.

CHAPTER 42

THEO

*S*oft, *gentle arms wrap around me as the scent of lilacs warms my heart. I pull back from our embrace and stare down at my mother. Her dark-hazel eyes filled with all the love and warmth I remember.*

"Mother?" My voice is childlike as I scan her face.

"My sweet Theodore. Look at how handsome you are," she says, cupping my cheeks. She smiles brightly up at me, reminding me of how much I have missed her.

As her hands fall from my face, I take in the empty room around us. There's a faint hue of purple floating in the air, dancing on an absent breeze. The ground is firm beneath my feet, but when I glance down, there's nothing below me.

"You need to remember who you are, Theodore. It's always been your destiny. The realm is depending on you." Her lilting voice brings my attention back to her.

"What do you mean? What destiny?" She pats my cheek, and I lean into her touch, soaking it in. I could stay here like this—with

her. I've missed the way she calms all my fears and her sweet humming that always brightened my days.

"You need to remember the stories I told you. She can't save the realm without you. She needs you just as much as you need her." My mother places a kiss on my cheek before releasing me and stepping back. I reach for her, not wanting our moment to end.

"Please stay. Don't leave me again. I need you, mother. Please," I say, pleading like a child as my heart aches with the loss of her.

"You must remember who you are, my sweet boy." The mist next to her thickens and a shapeless figure steps from it. My mother looks at the veiled being and smiles. The mist thins slightly, and my mother walks into it. A hint of red hair gleams from the top of the figure before the mist disappears entirely.

My eyes snap open, and I'm back in my cell. The scent of lilacs clings to my skin. I scan the cell, expecting to see my mother, but I'm alone.

I rub my face, trying to wrap my head around the bizarre dream. It felt so real. I swear my mother was truly speaking to me. There's a faint dampness on my cheek where she kissed me before leaving.

I should have left last night, maybe then the strange dream wouldn't have plagued me. The logical part of my mind told me to run, see how far I can make it before the queen has her Cypres rip apart my mind. But a soft voice urged me to stay. I took it as a warning from Astra that worse would happen if I fled in the night, opting to hide away in the cell one last time.

Crawling out of bed, I try to shake off the strange feeling and get ready for the day. After a quick shower and shave, I slide into the same outfit I arrived in. The once familiar clothes feel odd against my skin, as if they never belonged to me. *Just the queen's words messing with your head again.*

I take a deep breath, collecting myself. The threads around my heart hum, and I try to remember the last time they felt taut. I've grown so used to them being stretched since losing Lily. Only in the past few years have they relaxed and warmed, but within a day or two, the tightness would return.

My breath quickens, and my heart races as I realize that, since arriving in the shadow kingdom, the threads have seemed to rejoice. Especially after meeting the queen. My body responding to her presence as if she were the other half of my soul finally found. *That's not possible. She's not Lily.*

My mother's words ring in my ears. What do I need to remember, though? My mind has been so twisted by the games and emotions of the past month that I don't know if anything in my life is real anymore.

I groan, dragging my hands down my face, knowing I need answers to make sense out of all of this. The dream about my mother has shaken my once-firm hold on what is the truth and what is the lie. Her words, dark and ominous, are a stark contrast to her sunshine personality.

Swinging open the cell door, I head to the dining hall to ask Pyke where the apothecary is. He graciously points me in the direction, and I push through the crowd to make my way there.

The door chimes as I enter the shop. The herbal scents overwhelm my senses, and I wrinkle my nose. Loma stands at the counter, her eyes locked on me. "Theodore," she flatly states.

"You can call me Theo," I say, stepping up to the counter with an uneasy smile.

"No. Your name is Theodore. Your mother named you that for a reason," Loma answers with a scowl. My eyebrows draw together, confused by her statement. Her hazel eyes scan me, seeming to assess my worth.

"You're a gift from the gods for her." She slams the vial of black liquid on the counter. "You'll be the reason this realm is built anew or bathed in darkness for all eternity." She narrows her eyes at me, lips pinched tight.

Pushing the vial toward me, she taps it on the counter. The clink of the glass on wood echoes through the shop. I pick it up hesitantly, unsure of what to do. "For the sake of all the mortals in Omnia, I hope you make the right choice, my king."

My breath lodges in my throat at the title. I back up slowly, forcing my body to move. I exit the apothecary, my eyes never leaving Loma's.

My feet feel heavy as I drag myself back to the dining hall for breakfast. The vial is too warm in my hands, and I place it in my pocket. I go through the motions of gathering food on my plate. My mind lost in Loma's words, shaking me to my core.

Taking a seat at the table I usually share with the queen, I pull out the vial, setting it atop. I stare at it, debating if I should take it or not. My stomach turns as anxiety builds. Pain flares across my mind, and I rub my temples, trying to force it away.

"Please tell me you've come to your senses and have taken the antidote," Nyx says, dropping into the chair in front of me. I don't look up from my plate. "Well, hurry up. Loma said it's fast-acting. Then you can go apologize to Lily for all the horrible things you said to her last night."

My grip tightens on my fork, the metal bending with the force. "Don't say that name," I scream at him. He narrows his eyes at me.

"Why? That's her name. She lost it trying to protect you," he sneers at me, showing his teeth. I shake my head and glare at him, matching his anger.

"It's not. She's not Lily. I'm so sick of the lies you all want me to believe." I try to focus on my food and ignore his eyes burning into me.

"Take the antidote, Theo. Your mind will clear, and you'll see we are not the ones lying to you." Nyx pushes the vial toward me. My eyes snap up to him.

"What's in this for you? Why are you so determined to get me to drink that?" I shove the vial away. His jaw flexes as I take an aggressive bite of bacon.

"I'm sick of putting her back together because of you. I've been doing it for the past seven years, and after last night, I can't anymore. You're breaking her to a point I can't bring her back from. Drink it before it's too late, and we both lose her to the darkness."

I drop my fork, letting it clang against my plate. Sitting back in my chair, I cross my arms. "And why should any of that matter to me?"

Nyx groans loudly.

"Because you love her, and she's your Amari. Just as she is mine." His voice is a harsh whisper. I pick up the mug of coffee and take a sip before setting it back on the table.

"A mortal can't have two Amari, General. It must only be you then." My heart pings as if warning me about lying.

His hands drag over his face in frustration. "You know that's not true, Theo. You're tied to her heart, and I'm bound to her soul. Two Amari tethered to one."

The wooden chair scrapes loudly across the floor as I shove it back. It slams into the floor with a violent *crack*. I lean on the table, towering over Nyx in his seat. "Your king murdered my Amari," I scream at him.

Nyx stands to match my temper. "No, he didn't, and you know that. Your mind may want you to believe the lies Leopold has fed you, but your heart knows better. She's here, begging for you to see her," he yells, echoing through the hall. Everything falls silent as we stare at each other. Our breaths are rapid from anger.

Rushed footsteps click beside me as Hiram grabs my shoulder, forcing me to face him. "What's going on over here? Why are you so mad, Theo?" He looks me over as I clench my jaw hard enough to hurt. I push at him, trying to get him off. He slaps my shoulder, and I grimace from the sting of pain.

"Do we need to go for a run? Or maybe a sparring session with the queen will help? I am sure she can knock some sense into you," he smiles at me. I knock his hand from my shoulder and shove him hard away from me. He stumbles backward. His eyes go wide as he stares at me.

"If you die, I won't be able to put her back together, Theo. She'll never recover from that. Losing you for good will destroy her," Nyx speaks softly from the table.

I snatch the other chair from beside me and take a seat. Grabbing my coffee, I sit back, staring at him. "That's not my problem. Now, leave me alone." Hiram grabs Nyx's arm, pulling him from the table and out of my sight. I close my eyes, trying to calm the rage surging through me.

Taking a sip of coffee, the taste of iron blooms in my mouth, and I wonder if I cut it from clenching so hard. I run my tongue along my teeth, looking for the source but come up empty.

I take another sip, swirling it around my mouth to rinse away any lingering hint of blood. The metallic taste coats my tongue, and I take another bite of bacon to get rid of it, but it doesn't help.

Pushing away from the table, I stride back to the front in search of water for some relief from the awful taste. Out of the corner of my eye, I catch Nyx leaving Hiram to chase after me. I take long strides, hurrying to the kitchen to put distance between us.

Abrupt pain shoots through my mind, and I stumble forward, slamming into the serving table. Dishes and mugs clink as they shake with the impact. Nyx grips my arms as my legs threaten to give out with another fiery burst of pain.

"What's wrong?" Nyx's deep voice rings in my ears.

"My head. It hurts," I answer, my words uneven. Nyx helps me stand as the wave of pain subsides and I can finally take in a breath.

Nyx releases me and backs up a few steps, shaking his head. "Loma said it would be a headache. It's not supposed to be painful like that. Something's not right. We need to go see her right now," he says, reaching for me.

I jerk out of his reach. "Did you put the elixir in my coffee? I said I didn't want to take it. What happened to having a choice?" I shout at him as the pressure builds in my head.

He steps into my space, nose-to-nose. "You get a choice if it doesn't harm the woman we love. She's my priority, not you. I did what I had to do to save Lily."

I throw my arm out to punch him, but the pain overtakes me, and I lean on the table. Fire and lightning streak across my mind, ripping it apart. Images flash behind my closed eyes—all of them of Lily.

As if in bursts of light, each memory flares and fades away. Pictures of us playing as children with our mothers watching, beaming smiles on their faces. The first time she let me hold her hand. The first time I kissed her by the river. Her blood-soaked body, limp in my arms. Her lifeless jade-green eyes staring at the sky above. *Oh gods, I can see her face.*

My breath lodges in my throat as tears threaten to fall. She's no longer a distant memory veiled in haze. The vibrant color of her red hair doesn't hide her face anymore.

Nausea turns my stomach, and I can't get enough air. The pain fades again, and I shove off the table, scrambling out the door of the dining hall. Using the stone wall, I follow it out the front entrance of the Keep.

As I push through the doors, another blast of pain overtakes me and I fall, crashing into the wall. My mind is being torn to shreds, as simple as if it were paper being ripped into a million pieces.

The image of a red-rimmed mist near the end of my bed. A thin red-haired girl chained to a wall as a dark-haired man places a hand on the surface. Her broken and bruised face set in a scream, but there's no sound. She pulls against the iron with all her strength, trying to get to me. *Lily tied to the wall of my cell. No. It can't be.*

I can't catch my breath. I vomit as image after image rushes through my mind as if flipping through the pages of a book. When the pain eases for a moment, I drag myself out of the walkway into the field. My breaths are ragged as I rush across the grass.

A hand grabs my shoulder, pulling me back to spin me around. I lunge, my mind not entirely my own, landing a punch to Nyx's jaw. He staggers back a few steps, rubbing his face.

Searing pain burns through my mind, and I grab my head, groaning as the waves crash into me. Memories flash in broken segments of a night out at The Blue Stag. Lily standing behind the counter, smirking at me. Jonathan putting his hands on what's mine. The animalistic rage that consumed me before my fist met his face. Lily asking me to touch her in the alley. The sparks that ignited my body the moment my lips slammed into hers.

I choke on a sob as the pain eases, and I fight to stay on my feet. My sense of reality is quickly being unraveled. Nyx grips my arms, helping me to stand.

"Theo! Look at me!" Nyx yells as I try to catch my breath.

"I remember, Nyx. Oh gods, everything she said was true. But it hurts so much." I dig my nails into his arms as tears streak my face. He stares at me, fear darkening his eyes. My head throbs as if I've taken too many hits to it.

"It should be over soon, but we need to get you to Loma and Lily. They will know what to do," he says with hesitation.

My stomach rolls as bile climbs my throat, and I swallow hard to force it down. "She's alive. My flower is alive," I say, my voice trembling. Nyx nods as he holds me upright.

I gasp as my words and actions from last night replay in my mind. "I shoved her away like she was nothing. She's the only woman I've ever loved, and I hurt her, Nyx. Help me fix this, please. Tell her I'm so sorry. I didn't know." I fist Nyx's shirt, begging him to save me from my mistakes.

Fiery agony rips through my mind again, worse than the rest. I scream as my head feels as if it's being cleaved into tiny, fragmented pieces. Nyx holds on to me as my body shakes under the force of the elixir tearing at the veil.

My mother's sweet voice rings in my ears as a flashback plays crystal clear in my mind. She rubs gentle fingers through my hair as she tells me stories about the gods and their final decree.

I gasp for air as the last sliver of haze fades away. My memories return unhindered mixing with the ones over the past month in Umbra. All the broken parts sliding into place and becoming whole again.

"Oh no," I whisper as words click everything together. Nyx stares at me with pinched eyebrows.

"Please don't kill each other. The queen will kill me if you do, and I rather enjoy living," Hiram shouts as he races across the field, stopping beside us. "Gods, Nyx, what did you do to him?"

"I know why they made me forget," I say, tightening my grip on Nyx's shirt. "The story is wrong. There's a second half that's missing."

"What's he rambling about?" Hiram asks Nyx, who responds with a shrug and shake of his head.

"With gift of heart and soul of night, powers grow to the gods' delight," I stammer, earning confused looks from both men. "Roots stretch as they descend, bringing forth the very end." I release my hold on Nyx. Numbness floods my body as I remember what my mother once told me. "*Your destiny doesn't lie in this kingdom, my sweet boy." She knew.*

"Let's get you back inside. I think the elixir broke something not even Loma can fix. Hiram, help me with him," Nyx says as both men take an arm. But, like a tree, I'm rooted to the ground and don't budge.

I stare at Nyx as words get jumbled in my mind. "Loma was trying to warn me. Only her Amari can save the realm. Without tethers, darkness will descend, vast and unyielding. All light stomped out, never to be seen again." Tears well in my eyes as my destiny becomes clearer.

"What are you talking about, Theo? You're not making any sense. We need Loma, now," Nyx says, tugging at me to move.

"Everyone will die. She will die," I say, forcing the words out.

"Who?" Nyx stares at me, eyebrows cinched together.

"The end bringer." A single tear slides down my cheek, knowing how terrible of a mistake I've made. This could have ended, all because I refused to see what was right in front of me.

Nyx narrows his eyes, lips pinched into a thin line. His gaze darts to the side as if trying to figure out my senseless ramblings. His lips part as his face relaxes and his eyes go wide.

"Wait. No." Nyx shouts, grabbing my arms. His nails nip at my flesh. "No." He shakes with rage as he slots all the pieces together.

Abrupt agitated bellows rise from the nobu. The pool ripples as white, pupil-less eyes break the surface of the water. Enormous jaws of jagged teeth stretch wide as the roars grow louder.

Nyx's hands fall from me as the three of us turn to look at the beasts. One by one, they step onto the shore. Their scales shimmer in the sunlight. Eyes wide with panic, we glance at each other as more nobu leave the water.

Blood-curdling screams come from the haunted forest behind me. The air vibrates as the sound charges it. "What was that?" I shout at Nyx and Hiram. Nyx's face pales as he stares at the trees.

"The Cypres. I've never heard them make that sound. We need to get inside, now!" Nyx yells. Shadows dance across the field as small fractures split the ground. A boom cleaves the air as blue lightning crackles through the sky.

Hiram screams as an arrow lodges deep in his chest with a cracking thud. It plunges into his skin with remarkable ease, blood spraying from the fresh wound.

"Hiram!" I yell as Nyx lunges for him, taking them both to the ground. Another arrow whirls past our heads, narrowly missing us. The screams of the Cypres become louder as the nobu thunder toward us. The land beneath our feet shakes with the pounding of their feet.

I step toward Nyx with an outstretched hand. We all need to get inside if we want to survive this attack. Hiram holds pressure on his wound with one hand while Nyx wraps an arm around his waist, taking his weight. Nyx reaches up for me, our hands locking on each other's forearms.

A large hand clamps onto my throat, yanking me backward. The force rips Nyx's grasp from mine, hurling him and Hiram back to the ground. Hiram screams in pain as Nyx scrambles to get back to his feet.

A damp cloth presses tightly to my mouth, making it hard to breathe. The sickeningly sweet smell causes my stomach to turn, bile rising. I claw at the hand against my mouth, but my head becomes fuzzy. The grip around my throat tightens, cutting off my air.

"Theo!" Nyx bellows as he pulls a dagger from his hip and races after me. The realm stands still as I'm dragged away from my kingdom. The nobu charge across the field, barely missing Hiram kneeling in the grass.

The edges of my vision darken as my body goes limp against the hard chest at my back. Nothingness welcomes me in like a warm hug, and I can't refuse its embrace, no matter how much I try. Nyx's pained screaming of my name echoes in my ears as everything goes black.

About the Author

BIO

As a late-in-life reader, L.B. discovered a love of books in 2022 and quickly devoured book after book across multiple genres. However, she found herself desperately wanting to read more empowered female characters, so she set off to write her own. Encouraged by her best friend, she wrote her debut novel, In The Shadows. Now she can be found downing copious amounts of black coffee and pretending to be a corporate professional, all while crafting intricate, rich stories with captivating characters that she hopes will pass on her newfound passion for reading.

CONNECT WITH THE AUTHOR

Facebook: lbaugustauthor

Instagram: lbaugustauthor

TikTok: lbaugustauthor

Author's Website: www.lbaugustauthor.com

Also on Amazon, TOME, & Goodreads!

Acknowledgements

Theo's Flowers—Prim means first, so I dedicate this character to you. The ones who helped me from the beginning. The ones who took a chance on a friend and helped me learn how to be a better author. I don't have words to express how much I appreciate every single one of you. Thank you for loving ITS from the very first draft and helping to make this dream a reality. The original Theo's flowers: Ariana, Ariel, Briana, Cassie, Dani, McKensie, Meagan, and Karrie.

Ariel—Thank you for pressuring me to write this. You always had the confidence in my abilities even when I didn't. There's no one else I'd rather text at all hours of the day with the most unhinged questions. Thanks for always being the wall I can bounce ideas off even if they don't make sense. I never would have started this journey without your encouragement. You're now my forever emotional support person and stuck with me.

Karrie—Thank you for always being willing to talk me off the ledge and not letting me delete ITS. No matter how many times I wanted to. Thanks for always being available to work through dialogue with me when it wasn't sounding right to me. As well as spicy scenes when the angles and movements needed to be double-checked.

Dani—Thank you for being my Photoshop pro because gods know I don't have the patience to figure it out anymore. Thanks for helping guide me through this mess of self-publishing and trying to ease my mind when I thought I was failing.

Tali—I couldn't have done this without you. As I've told you before, you were the key to open the door to my writing. With your guidance, I found my voice. I think the fates and the gods were on my side for this one, leading me straight to where I needed to be. Thank you will never be enough and I hope you know that. Thank you for believing in ITS and loving it as much as I do.

Sloth Fam—Ladies, you are the best. I wouldn't have made it without your extra hype and overwhelming love. Whenever I was down, I knew I could lean on you all for support when I needed it most. Thank you, my sloth loves.

All my bookstagram and booktok friends—Thank you for all your support. I've met some of the most amazing people over the past year. I have been so fortunate to find some truly inspiring, caring, and wonderful people who have cheered on ITS at all stages. I appreciate every single one of you more than you know.